W9-CKR-638

	DATE DUE		

what they did for weeks to come. Each chapter is full of people you would just swear you know from your own hometown!"

DON REID, THE STATLER BROTHERS

Under a Cloudless Sky

"Fabry captures the political and social climate of an Appalachian mining community in this evocative novel set between 1933 and 2004. . . . Fabry weaves the events of the past and present into a finely layered story exploring the relationships of faith, forgiveness, and family in the midst of healing from pain buried deep in the past."

PUBLISHERS WEEKLY

"Fabry's latest is a multilayered, engaging story with rich details and interesting characters. Thanks to the historical coal mining backstory, *Under a Cloudless Sky* should appeal to both readers of Southern historical fiction and inspirational fiction."

RT BOOK REVIEWS

"A poignant story of innocence, good people in hard circumstances, misunderstood family relationships, deeply buried wounds, and the healing of God's grace. A definite must-read!"

MIDWEST BOOK REVIEW

"*Under a Cloudless Sky* captivated me from page one. I cared immediately what happened to Ruby and Bean, and the stakes kept rising as tidbits of history were revealed, unraveling the mystery that held Ruby captive. A terrific reading experience!"

FRANCINE RIVERS, *NEW YORK TIMES* BESTSELLING AUTHOR

The Promise of Jesse Woods

"[In this] soul-searching novel of faith, friendship, and promises, Chris Fabry invigorates the small-town lives of three teens in 1970s West

Praise for Chris Fabry

A Piece of the Moon

"*A Piece of the Moon* has it all. Quirky, endearing characters. A rich story arc full of surprises. Lines so funny you'll want to read them aloud to anybody within earshot. And a tender thread of redemption that runs from first page to last. Spending time with Waite and TD and Clay and Pidge and all the other folks in Emmaus was pure joy. The best novel I've read in ages."

LIZ CURTIS HIGGS, *NEW YORK TIMES* BESTSELLING AUTHOR OF *MINE IS THE NIGHT*

"Few earthlings spin a more endearing, heartwarming yarn than Chris Fabry. The guy is a national treasure. *A Piece of the Moon* is an instant classic because it takes you someplace new, a place filled with off-kilter characters who make you laugh and tear up, a place you don't want to leave. This book brought joy, lack of sleep, and a pain in my right arm. I sprained my wrist turning pages."

PHIL CALLAWAY, HOST OF *LAUGH AGAIN* RADIO, AUTHOR OF *LAUGH LIKE A KID AGAIN*

"*A Piece of the Moon* represents what I love most about fiction: the ability a novel has to transport you to another place in time. Fabry's voice as a writer is engaging and dripping with charm and nostalgia. It took me back to the years of small radio stations and the earthy music of the old days. The fact that it comes with its own playlist is a brilliant way to reintroduce some of the great music of the past to new audience. A fantastic story written by an absolute treasure of a human being. I highly recommend *A Piece of the Moon* (and by the way, isn't that a great title!)."

CINDY MORGAN, AUTHOR AND GRAMMY NOMINEE

"Chris Fabry has done it again! If you're looking to have fun and you like country, this is the story for you. The characters jump off the pages and into your heart and you'll be smiling at what they said and

Virginia with his exquisite, lyrical writing. . . . A literary delight . . . this novel is worthy of a standing ovation."

SHELF AWARENESS

"This riveting, no-punches-pulled coming-of-age tale is reminiscent of Richard Bachman's (Stephen King) short story, 'The Body,' which was made into the movie *Stand by Me*."

BOOKLIST

Dogwood

"[*Dogwood*] is difficult to put down, what with Fabry's surprising plot resolution and themes of forgiveness, sacrificial love, and suffering."

PUBLISHERS WEEKLY

"Solidly literary fiction with deep, flawed characters and beautiful prose, *Dogwood* also contains a mystery within the story that adds tension and a deepening plot."

NOVEL REVIEWS

June Bug

"[*June Bug*] is a stunning success, and readers will find themselves responding with enthusiastic inner applause."

PUBLISHERS WEEKLY

"I haven't read anything so riveting and unforgettable since *Redeeming Love* by Francine Rivers. . . . A remarkable love story, one that's filled with sacrifice, hope, and forgiveness!"

NOVEL REVIEWS

"Precise details of places and experiences immediately set you in the story, and the complex, likable characters give *June Bug* the enduring quality of a classic."

TITLETRAKK.COM

Almost Heaven

A Piece of the Moon

OTHER NOVELS BY CHRIS FABRY

CHRIS FABRY

A
PIECE
of the
MOON

Tyndale House Publishers
Carol Stream, Illinois

Visit Tyndale online at tyndale.com.

Visit Chris Fabry's website at chrisfabry.com.

TYNDALE and Tyndale's quill logo are registered trademarks of Tyndale House Ministries.

A Piece of the Moon

Designed by Julie Chen

Edited by Sarah Mason Rische

Scripture quotations are taken from the *Holy Bible*, King James Version.

Judges 6:11 in chapter 8 is taken from *The Living Bible*, copyright © 1971 by Tyndale House Foundation. Used by permission of Tyndale House Publishers, Carol Stream, Illinois 60188. All rights reserved.

Some Scripture referenced by characters has been paraphrased by the author.

A Piece of the Moon is a work of fiction. Where real people, events, establishments, organizations, or locales appear, they are used fictitiously. All other elements of the novel are drawn from the author's imagination.

For information about special discounts for bulk purchases, please contact Tyndale House Publishers at csresponse@tyndale.com, or call 1-800-323-9400.

Library of Congress Cataloging-in-Publication Data
Names: Fabry, Chris, date- author.
Title: A piece of the moon / Chris Fabry.
Description: Carol Stream, Illinois : Tyndale House Publishers, [2021]
Identifiers: LCCN 2020036664 (print) | LCCN 2020036665 (ebook) | ISBN 9781496443441 (hardcover) | ISBN 9781496443458 (trade paperback) | ISBN 9781496443465 (kindle edition) | ISBN 9781496443472 (epub) | ISBN 9781496443489 (epub)
Subjects: GSAFD: Christian fiction.
Classification: LCC PS3556.A26 P54 2021 (print) | LCC PS3556.A26 (ebook) | DDC 813/.54--dc23
LC record available at https://lccn.loc.gov/2020036664
LC ebook record available at https://lccn.loc.gov/2020036665

Printed in the United States of America

27	26	25	24	23	22	21
7	6	5	4	3	2	1

For Seeb

Better is little with the fear of the Lord than
great treasure and trouble therewith.

PROVERBS 15:16

Everyone is a moon, and has a dark side
which he never shows to anybody.

MARK TWAIN

All good songs leak from a broken heart.

MACK STRUM

PROLOGUE

Love, like treasure, stays buried until somebody decides to dig. That's what this story is about, along with life and death and a stammering tongue and a little radio station. It's also about the power of an old country song. Mostly it's about events that occurred in the summer of 1981, set in motion by a fellow named Gideon Quidley, who was, in my opinion at the time, several bales short of a full loft.

The whole thing started a few years earlier, the year his wife, Opal, died, which was the same year the Nixon administration came apart at the seams and Sam Ervin talked about being an "old country lawyer" in the Senate Caucus Room. That was the year Gideon said he heard the Lord speak.

"Get thee up and gather thy fortune and fashion an ark. Hide thou the treasure in the hills where thou art from and fashion thee a map using my Word as a compass. I will use thee to turn many toward truth."

1

The Almighty spoke in King James, Gideon said, and though Gideon didn't understand all he heard, he was the type to fling himself full bore at life, as he had done when he was involved with the space program. So he gathered his gold and silver and withdrew stacks of hundred-dollar bills he secured with rubber bands, and using specifications from the book of Exodus, he drew a schematic of the Ark of the Covenant. But since he was an engineer and not a carpenter, he spent considerable time creating something only a craftsman should attempt. And by the time that truth dawned on him, there was a peanut farmer in the White House.

Gideon eventually contracted with a company in Gallipolis, Ohio, that specialized in "unique, handcrafted furniture," and drew up a legal document that forced the company's silence in perpetuity. Then he got busy with the Almighty's second directive.

The map conundrum—"fashion thee a map using my Word as a compass"—vexed Gideon, but the upside was he was able to focus on something other than Opal's death. And that was a grace to him. He thought of Opal every day, of course, and felt an ache at night as he stared at her empty pillow. The truth was, Gideon not only heard the Lord, he also heard Opal say, *"Gid, you have lost your marbles."* That made him smile and he fell asleep with tears and dreams so real he was sad to wake from them.

One summer night, as the moon rose high and bright and peeked into his bedroom window like a star of wonder, Gideon sat straight up in bed.

"That's it!"

His voice startled his dog, Jubal, who barked outside as Gideon raced to his desk where he kept his Strong's Exhaustive Concordance and his Bible dictionary, as well as his underlined and dog-eared red-letter edition of the KJV. In a frenzy, he wrote chapter and verse, Scriptures flowing like the river Jordan. His theme was true treasure, and he presented biblical clues for eternal life.

"For what shall it profit a man, if he shall gain the whole world, and lose his own soul?"

When he'd transcribed the eternal-treasure clues, he then searched for verses that might pinpoint coordinates of a specific hiding place in the hills. But that's when he came up empty. Being a man of faith who was content with all he knew and didn't know, Gideon gave thanks for the moonlight flash of inspiration and went outside to feed Jubal. And as he poured the Alpo, he glanced at the sky and saw the fading orb that had awakened him, and in that moment he decided to place his most valuable possession in the ark, a priceless treasure only Gideon and Opal and one other man on the planet knew he owned.

In celebration, he dressed and drove into town to his favorite diner and sat with his Bible in front of him. When the waitress brought eggs and hash browns and toast, no butter, he folded his hands and thanked the Lord for his kindness and beseeched him again for wisdom.

"Show it to me, Lord. I've put the map to eternal life together. Now I need your help to know where to hide the treasure."

After the prayer, he poured a copious amount of ketchup, salt, and pepper on his eggs and hash browns, took a bite, then flipped open the Bible as if it were a wet fleece. And it came to pass that verily the pages fell open to the Acts of the Apostles, chapter 2, and there it was, staring at him. The word jumped off the page twice in the same chapter, telling him exactly what to do. He'd found the oxcart, as it were, that would transport his ark.

"Thank you, Lord," Gideon whispered. "I'll put the ark inside. But where do I hide it? What spot are you calling me to?"

He pinched the pages, like you would pick up a Communion

wafer, closed his eyes, and flipped again and the pages fell open to Luke 24. His eyes tracked down the page until he stopped, unable to breathe. The location could not have been any clearer if the Almighty had spoken aloud.

After breakfast, he left a modest tip for Wilma, the waitress who always took his order, and he got in his half-ton Chevy C10 and drove directly to a car dealer in town and set his plan in motion.

In the end, that plan would lead to division and death, as well as riches untold and a search for love and forgiveness. Whether he actually heard from the Lord, I'll let you decide.

PART 1

CHAPTER 1

Robby Gardner let the rope slide through his gloved hands as he descended a rock wall near Ephra, West Virginia. He paused a moment to catch his breath and still his racing heart, glancing at the vista he would never forget. Stretching out as far as he could see was God's green earth, trees and hills and lichen-covered rocks, gorgeous and untouched as Eden.

Fifty feet below was a ledge he had spied a week earlier from the other side of the ravine. Sunlight peeking through the clouds had glinted in the recesses of the rock, and with binoculars he spotted a sparkle of gold.

Every day since then he had thought of that sight, and the world seemed a little brighter and more colorful. And something close to hope rose inside. On this Monday morning, he had told

7

no one where he was headed, not even his wife, and as he paused, the rope tight and his feet firmly planted against this rock wall, he thought of her and how they had begun their morning by quietly making love while their children slept.

When Sharon rose from the bed, he watched her, then turned toward the light peeking through the window and thought that outside of salvation, Monday sex was God's best gift. He'd written that in his journal a few times, and he wondered if, in the future, his wife or his children would find his intimate scribblings and blush or just shake their heads and smile. *That Robby. What a rascal.*

This is the last time she'll have sex with a poor pastor, Robby had thought. *After today, everything changes.*

He had dressed and gathered his things and waited in the kitchen. Sharon came out with raised eyebrows. "What got into you, tiger?"

"You," he said. He gave her a hug, her hair smelling like a field of ripe strawberries. He kissed her neck and pulled back and looked into her eyes.

"I thought you'd sleep in today," she said. "Where are you off to so early?"

He didn't answer. He just studied her like a spy on the border of a land flowing with milk and honey.

She cocked her head to one side. "Please tell me you're not still looking."

"I'm not still looking."

"Then where are you going?"

"I'm not still looking because I've found what I was looking for."

"Aww," she said, smiling. She thought he meant her. Then her face turned blank when she realized he didn't. "Robby, don't do this. Let it go."

"You're going to be singing a different tune when I get back."

"You said you were done with this."

"I was. And then I saw something. It was between the lines."

"Between what lines?"

He put his hands on her shoulders and leaned toward her. "Think of the things we could do. We could finally go on a honeymoon. We never had one."

"I don't need a honeymoon."

"We could give enough to build that orphanage your parents have talked about down in Mexico. Send it to the mission board so they can build ten orphanages."

She crossed her arms and looked away. "I got a bad feeling about this."

"And I got the best feeling in the world. All the struggle we've been through. All the praying and hoping for things to get better. The Lord knew we needed this. And he's let me figure out what nobody else has."

"Robby, you know deep down there's nothing out there. People say the only ones crazier than Quidley are those who believe he actually hid a treasure."

"I'm glad they feel that way. It's not as crowded. And it's right there in my grasp. I've seen it, Sharon."

She pulled away. "What do you mean?"

"I've seen the gold. I've seen the seraphim."

Her face grew tight. "I don't want you to go."

"And you know I have to."

"You don't have to. Stay. We could take the kids to the lake and have a picnic. You can fish. Relax."

"Everything changes after today."

She sighed, her shoulders slumping. Then she grabbed a Bible beside the telephone and pulled his hand on top. "Promise."

"Promise what?"

"Promise if you don't find it this time, that'll be it. You'll stop."

He thought a moment. Then with one hand on the Bible, he raised the other and stood tall. "I solemnly swear that if I don't find the treasure of Gideon Quidley today, I will stop looking and henceforth abandon the search forevermore, amen."

"So help you God?"

"So help me God."

He laughed and tried to tickle her, but she squirmed away and opened the refrigerator, looking inside. "Want me to fix us something?"

"I'm too keyed up to eat. I'll get coffee at the gas station. Then I'm on the road to riches. I can't wait. Now I probably won't bring the whole thing back—it'll be too heavy. But I've got a backpack I'll fill with gold and silver to show you I was right."

She shook her head. "Where are you looking?"

"First clue. Psalm 121. 'I lift my eyes to the hills.' The treasure's in West Virginia. No doubt about it."

"Why wouldn't he hide it closer to where he lives? Pennsylvania has hills."

"He was born and bred here. Trust me. I've done my homework."

"What town?"

He kissed her forehead. "I'll tell you when I get back."

"Robby, how far away are you going? At least tell me that."

He looked at his watch. "I'll be home this afternoon."

As he backed down the gravel driveway, she was standing at the front window, her arms crossed over her breasts, looking plaintive, like it might be the last time she ever saw him. He couldn't wait to see her face when she saw what he brought back.

After the gas station, he popped in a cassette of his favorite pastor from Memphis, taking mental notes for his own sermon the following Sunday. Two hours later he drove off the road and up a hill as far he could, then hid his truck in a grove of willow trees. He grabbed his gear and climbed to the top of the hill, using saplings to pull himself up the steep slope. At the edge of the rock face, he looked over the ravine. What a sight.

Robby had been a fair athlete in his younger days. Good enough to play high school ball. Now he'd put on a few pounds and after the climb he felt the old knee injury. This wasn't like walking hospital corridors or playing church softball.

He tied the rope tightly and took a breath, then gingerly descended. He was so close to the treasure of Gideon Quidley he could taste it.

What would people think when they heard? What would his tiny congregation do when they discovered their pastor had put the clues together? He could see himself on TV, Phil Donahue asking him questions. He'd explain how it finally dawned on him as he studied the life of the biblical Gideon.

"And why are you still at that little church when you're richer than rich?" Phil would ask.

Robby smiled at the thought. He wouldn't have to work another day in his life, but he would be in that pulpit every Sunday. Maybe that was why God had allowed him to figure it out. The treasure wouldn't sway his heart toward temporal things.

"Blessed are the pure in heart."

He was about ten feet above the ledge now, craning his neck for a glimpse of what he knew was below. He heard a noise above and looked up and thought he saw movement. Was it an animal next to the tree? Was there a person near the rope?

"Hello?" he called, his voice echoing.

Convinced it was nothing but the wind, he leaned back to get a better look at what he'd only seen through binoculars. What appeared from a distance to be simply a crack in the rock wall looked more like a recessed cave from this vantage point. And that sent his heart racing faster.

The rope dangled beneath him. He had plenty to get to the ledge. But looking down had caused fear to creep in, and immediately he thought of the verse in Romans about doubt, the one that said what wasn't done in faith was sin. Robby smiled. He was just like old man Quidley. He had a verse for everything.

It was at this moment that another thought swept over him. If the treasure was here—and he fully believed that—how had a crotchety old guy made this climb? No way he could've done that alone. Who had helped him? Who had he trusted with that knowledge?

Robby pushed away the questions as he pushed his feet from the wall to make his final descent. However, when he did that, the rock he'd planted his feet on dislodged and Robby pitched forward. Instinctively he reached out a hand to steady himself on the smooth surface, forgetting in that moment that he wasn't strong enough to hold on to the rope with only one hand.

And as instinctively as he reached out a hand, Robby yelped a prayer before he fell.

CHAPTER 2

At 4:30 a.m., the streets of Emmaus, West Virginia, were empty and the only stoplight gave a ghostly glow as Waite Evers held his foot on the brake. He had no earthly reason to stop at the red light, but something inside told him if he started picking and choosing which laws to obey, he'd find a reason to go around all of them. If you followed rules when nobody was looking, you didn't have to guess which ones applied.

Staring sixty in the face, Waite was a barrel-chested man who believed in a clean shave and the power of routine. Window down, he felt the warm, heavy air and heard the soundtrack of crickets and katydids along with his truck's idle. Fog hung low like a blanket. When the light turned green, Waite rumbled through in his F-150 and smiled when he saw lights on inside Mel's Donuts. He parked and let the engine idle as Vivian, Mel's wife, unlocked the door and handed him a white paper bag. She took his thermos and filled it from a steaming pot.

"Morning, Waite."

The aroma of dough and sugar and coffee was like sniffing a little bit of heaven, the sweet smell of hope to every bitter morning. He could taste the bite of the black coffee even before he took a sip.

"Don't know what I'd do if you two weren't here. There'd be no reason to get up and go."

She screwed on the lid. "Feel the same about you. Play me some Conway today?"

"A little Twitty for your Tuesday?"

She smiled. "If you ever get Conway to come to that station of yours or the Opry, you tell me."

"You'll be the first to know, Viv. Listen right after the Farm Report, okay?"

She nodded.

"You sure I can't pay you for this?"

"Get out of here," she said, rolling her eyes as she locked the door. He got in his truck and backed out, hitting the radio's FM preset.

". . . and then Waite and TD will be along here on Country 16. The Farm Report and all the news you need and some you might not. Their jokes are corny and their breath is stale, but we know why you're here, and that's for the best country in the country."

The DJ's real name was Edgar William Wilson but everybody called him Possum. That was partly because he only came out at night but also because he ate everything he could get his hands on. When the FM had been approved at 120 watts, Waite had gone looking for someone to host overnights, and Possum had just been let go from a station in Beckley. In fact, just about everybody who worked at Country 16 had been let go from somewhere. They were a revolving door of misfits and castoffs, a radio Goodwill, and Waite liked that because he thought everybody deserved a second chance.

"Let me take one more call before we wrap up," Possum said. He had a high-pitched, squeaky voice. Definitely not the deep golden pipes you were supposed to have to succeed in radio. But Waite knew there was more to a man. A voice was like a good song. One could take you far, but it couldn't keep you there. Possum had personality. He had a peculiar view of life and there was a bit of the philosopher in him even if he did sound like a clucking chicken when he laughed.

Waite rolled his eyes when he heard the caller, Sally from Lick Creek. Everybody at the station referred to her as Psycho Sally because she talked fast and her words were always two turns ahead of her brain catching up.

"I just got up from a dream I had about Gideon Quidley's treasure. And I wonder if anybody has thought about the possibility it could have been abducted by aliens. Did you hear the report of those strange lights over the high-tension wires near the interstate?"

She talked like a machine gun with endless rounds of ammo.

"She'll keep going till the sun comes up," Waite muttered.

Somehow Possum wedged himself into the salvo. "Well, I don't believe I've heard that theory floated yet. In fact, I haven't heard many people who are still talking about the treasure other than Waite, so we'll get him to address it for you, Sally."

Waite quickly flipped to the AM band and hit the button for 780. WBBM out of Chicago was all news and he could hear it at this time of the morning and catch up with national and world events. He'd once had designs on working in a big city, but life had a way of changing desires.

Headlights swung away from Country 16 and he recognized the rumble of the newspaper delivery guy. You could hear Kelvin Purdy's muffler two counties away. Waite waved as he passed, then again hit the button for Country 16 and nearly drove into the ditch. He heard the familiar finger pick of the six string, the plaintive sound of steel guitar and mandolin chuck. A simple tune with simple words that stuck to the wall of his heart.

All my life I've waited for you.
All my dreams are yours.

The chorus always got him. Funny how grooves in an old record could bring back the pain. Words and chords and memories.

He parked in the upper lot beside the metal building. A red light blinked on top of the tower in a field nearby, and a yellow glow peeked over the edge of the hills behind him, but there were dark clouds above the yellow. It felt like rain or something close to it. The sun was trying to chase the night away, but in Emmaus, it seemed to struggle like everyone else in town, straining to get over the ridge or working hard to get where it was going until night came. The moon never seemed to have that problem, perhaps because its appearance changed so often. The moon moved on a whim and chose between full or half or quarter whenever it felt like it, or so it seemed.

Unlocking the front door and kicking the newspaper inside without picking it up, he spied Possum in the control room rocking back and forth. The man had grown to such a size that he could only fit into a wooden chair with no armrests. TD called it *the throne.* Possum's inertia shifted to his knees and he grabbed the edge of the console and pulled himself upright. Waite prayed he'd make it without the whole thing tumbling.

"Let me get that chair," Waite said, handing Possum the paper bag. "Vivian says hey."

Possum gave a crooked smile and for a moment showed his bad teeth. "I've got the AM warming up for you."

Waite put the chair in the corner and stood out of the way as Possum ambled toward the door. The spinning 45 undulated on the turntable, a slight imperfection in the pressing making the record rise and fall with each orbit like it was a wave on an ocean.

"That one's not on the playlist, Possum."

"Had a request. Listener always comes first, right?"

"Hmm. And what about the station manager? Where does his opinion fall?"

Possum turned. "What's the deal with that song, Waite? Why don't you want us to play it?"

Waite had grabbed the log and stacked carts for his first stopset, avoiding the question.

"He grew up here," Possum continued, lobbying now. "He listened to the station when he was a kid. He told me that in the interview. Seems like you'd want to play it every day."

"Nope."

The front door opened and TD Lovett entered with his headphones in one hand and his thermos and lunch box in the other. He bent down and picked up the newspaper, then dropped his headphones and cursed.

"I need to sign on the AM," Waite said.

He studied the clock like he'd studied the traffic light. Nobody would know if he hit the Power button a minute or two early, but that wasn't the point. He'd know. As the second hand swept past the six, he heard the familiar rip of paper from the UPI machine, and TD yelled something at Possum about not changing the ribbon. Possum and the bear claws had left the building.

When the second hand hit the twelve, Waite stepped into the sound lock and hit the red button and the transmitter surged with a hum. He closed the door and worked his way around the console and played the simulcast ID, then went straight into Waylon and Willie.

He picked another green-sleeved 45 out of the first bin mounted in front of the turntables as TD trailed a twelve-foot line of yellow paper behind him, all the news that had come over the wire since Possum had last checked.

TD grabbed the wooden chair and dragged it to the lobby to spray Lysol. "You can't get the fat man smell off that chair."

Waite stifled a smile. "Late night?"

"Two-car wreck out near Billups Gap. One rolled over the hill."

"Anybody hurt?"

TD shook his head. "Both walked away." He rolled a different chair into position, but he hit the table so hard the needle on the record flew. Waite stared in disbelief as TD caught the turntable arm in midair and tried to figure out where to drop it.

Waite waved a hand and keyed his microphone. "And with that abrupt ending to Waylon, Willie, and the boys, we begin another broadcast morning here on Country 16. How you doin', Emmaus? Time to rise and shine. Grab your coffee and maybe one of Mel's donuts—I hear the bear claws are fresh today." He hit a sound effect of a bear growling. "Top of the morning to truckers listening from the interstate—" sound effects of a semitruck's horn—"and hey to you, TD. You doin' all right?"

"Upright and ambulatory, Waite."

"That'll do. You got the Farm Report?"

"Ready when you are."

"Okay, we'll get to that after we hear from Tom T. Hall, assuming he doesn't get derailed like Waylon and Willie." He chuckled and pushed the switch above the round knob on the Gates board and said, "'What Have You Got to Lose,' on Country 16, the best country in the country."

He turned off the microphones as Tom began his belly-to-the-bar drinking song.

"Sorry about that, Waite."

"I'm gonna have to put you back in the production room."

TD scowled and Waite knew the mistake pained the man.

TD was tall and on the thin side, almost thirty. He had work-worn hands from cars and trucks he'd fixed or towed or both. TD was a man of motion, meaning he couldn't sit still. He fidgeted. He was the kind of person who seemed like he was two exits short of where he wanted to be and had his thumb out hoping life would pull over and open the passenger door. His real name was Titus Daniel Lovett, but he went by TD and it fit.

"If anybody calls me for a reference, I'm going to tell them you get too close to turntables." Waite smiled. "Hear anything back about those air checks?"

TD circled stories with a Bic pen and shook his head. "Nothing yet. But I heard about an audition for a radio spot. I think I got the right voice for it."

"Well, good luck with that."

Waite riffled through the solid gold bin. He found what he wanted and cued the next song, moving the 45 back and forth until it was a half-turn from the first note of the intro. Two minutes later, as Tom T.'s song faded, he hit the Farm Report theme, complete with chickens clucking, cows mooing, and a rooster crowing.

"This is Country 16, Emmaus, West Virginia, the best country in the country. And it's that time, friends. Here's TD with the Farm Report."

After the report, which included prices of livestock and a reading from the Farmers' Almanac, Waite played the same sounder that began the segment, then gave the time and temperature over the :09 intro to "Fifteen Years Ago" and said, "This is for you, Vivian."

TD leaned forward when he heard the plaintive voice of the singer. "You thinking about making it a two-Twitty Tuesday?"

Waite smirked and cued up "To See My Angel Cry."

As the music played, Waite studied the misspelled words on the daily log. A public service announcement from the US Forest Service voiced by an owl named "Woodsy" was listed as "Wodoy Owl." Spelling wasn't Ardelle Bellweather's strength. In fact, he wasn't sure what the station's secretary's strength was, but she showed up each day and that was enough.

TD clipped local stories from the newspaper.

"Don't get discouraged that you haven't heard back on those air checks," Waite said.

"I thought for sure the station in Bluefield would bite. I'm making a new tape to send out this week."

"Last one sounded good. I would have hired you."

"You'd hire anybody breathing, Waite. That's the trouble."

Waite wanted to mention something about the irony of that statement but he held his tongue. Sometimes love is less about what you say and more about what you don't. He'd learned that lesson the hard way.

"I'm working on the full-time thing for you with Boyd," Waite said. "But we're not there yet. Don't move to Bluefield. Just hang on—"

"I'm tired of being half-in and half-out. And to be honest, some of the people you hire . . . Wally mumbles so much you can't understand anything but the time and temperature. And DeeJay,

God bless her, she's got a good voice but she runs a board loose as a goose. You could drive a truck through the dead air between songs. And Possum . . ."

"I won't argue with you." Waite stifled a smile and said, "I offered Sunday mornings and you wouldn't take it."

TD glared. "You know I could never do Sunday mornings."

Waite nodded. "I want to give you more hours and bring you on full-time. But you have to be patient."

"And you have to do something about our air sound, Waite. There's a reason we don't show up in the Arbitron."

"TD, they have the Arbitron to let stations like ours know there's nobody listening."

"Right there. That negativity will keep us small. It's that kind of thinking that makes me want to get out of here."

"Yeah, but getting out means consequences."

"Like what?"

"Your love life for one."

TD shook his head. "There's no life to it. Just when I think I'm making progress, she closes up like a morning glory at midnight. Like she's scared or something."

"Maybe she's scared you'll try to move her to Bluefield."

TD said something under his breath, then added, "I don't think I'll ever understand women."

Waite chuckled.

"What are you laughing about?"

"Every song we play agrees with you." Waite put on his headphones and gave the time and temperature, then played spots listed on the log. He lifted one earphone as he grabbed a cart with a purple sticker. "You got anything for the feature this morning?"

"Come on, Waite, you're not doing that today, are you? You're beating a dead horse. Nobody's thinking about that anymore."

After Woodsy Owl sang "Give a hoot! Don't pollute," Waite played the theme from *Raiders of the Lost Ark*. The film had released a month earlier and people were flocking to theaters.

"That song means it's time for a Tuesday Treasure Update. When we hear fresh news about the location of the hidden ark, or when someone discovers a crumb on the treasure trail, we bring it to you first. And today's clue comes from Sally over on Lick Creek."

"Oh, for crying out loud," TD said, off-mic.

Waite brought the theme down so it didn't overwhelm the conversation. "That's right. I heard Sally talking with Possum this morning. She knows why the treasure hasn't been found."

"You mean other than it doesn't exist?"

"Now, if you're tuning in for the first time, TD is the resident Quidley skeptic, but as I've said before, he'd figure out this mystery if he ever put his mind to it."

"I like solving real mysteries, not imagined ones."

Waite forged ahead. "Well, a week ago there was a report of some strange lights near the high-tension wires that run by the interstate. And Sally put that together with the treasure hunt . . ."

Waite paused and played the sound effect of a timpani drumroll.

"I can't wait to hear this," TD muttered.

"Sally believes the treasure . . ."

The drumroll ended.

". . . may have been abducted by aliens."

TD put a palm to his forehead. "And I'll bet Bigfoot helped them load it into their flying saucer."

Waite pushed the music hotter. "Folks, TD may be coming around."

"What in the world would aliens do with gold, silver, and cash? Answer me that."

"Now that's where you get off track. Don't criticize a theory, listen to it. Sally wasn't analyzing—she was brainstorming. Which makes me think we ought to try to talk to old Gideon, though I've heard he's not doing interviews anymore."

"Why not interview the aliens who beamed it up to their starship?"

"If you get their number, I'll put them on. I'm glad you're jumping into the hunt, TD."

"I'm not jumping in. This whole thing turns my stomach. You know I don't truck in religion. I won't stop you, but don't expect me to sign on."

"Then that's one less person crowding the trail. But for the life of me I don't understand why you wouldn't want to find that fortune."

"How can you trust a fellow who made it plain his motivation is to get people to read the Bible? That's the reason he put the clues out there. If you can't see through that bait and switch, I can't help you."

"Well, it's been quite a while since we've heard anything new from old Gideon, but the clue of the day comes from the list in his original press release. Psalm 137:2 says, 'We hanged our harps upon the willows in the midst thereof.'"

Waite noticed a phone line blinking and wondered if it might be Psycho Sally.

"That'll pinpoint it for you," TD said, deadpan. "Look for willows with harps hanging on them."

Feeling adventurous, Waite took the call and dipped the theme music even more. "You're on Country 16. Who is this?"

A shaky female voice. "I don't think you all should be joking about this."

Waite gave TD a look. Most listeners loved the banter about Gideon Quidley. They saw it for what it was.

"And why is that, ma'am?" Waite said.

"Because it's not funny. It's serious."

Waite regretted his impulse to pick up the phone. "Well, that kinda throws a wet blanket on our fun. Who am I talking to?"

"My name's Sharon."

"All right, Sharon. Explain yourself."

"I heard you joking . . . Some people take this serious." The woman sounded like she'd been crying.

"Well, I suppose some people are serious about it, but you have to admit there's a bit of humor in it, too."

"Especially when aliens get involved," TD said.

"You don't understand."

"Tell us about it, Sharon."

She choked something back. "My husband left yesterday morning. Said he'd be back in the afternoon, but he never came home. He said he knew where it was."

"The treasure?"

"Yeah. I tried to stop him, but I couldn't."

"I'm sure he's going to be all right," Waite said.

"No, he won't. You don't know Robby. He never does this type of thing."

"Robby Gardner?" TD said.

"Yes."

Waite glanced at TD, whose face had paled. "You know him?"

TD nodded.

"When I heard you all laughing, it struck a nerve." Then the dam broke and the woman sobbed.

Waite grabbed the volume control for the phone line and turned it down. "Sharon, you hang on." He took a breath. "Folks, you're listening to Country 16 as we get up and go on a Tuesday morning, and what I thought would be one thing has turned into something else. That's the way life goes. We're going to sort this out with Sharon off the air and while we do, here's Barbara Mandrell on the best country in the country."

Waite took off his headphones.

"I went to school with him," TD said.

"Why don't you go back in the production room? Talk to her from in there and find out what's going on."

TD nodded and Waite picked up the phone. The woman was in full panic mode, crying and sniffling.

"I told the sheriff all I knew," she said. "This is not like Robby."

"Sharon, I'm going to get TD on the line. He knows your husband. We're going to help any way we can."

"There's nothing you can do."

"Well, maybe one of our listeners has seen him."

She didn't respond. Waite saw TD through the window waiting to pick up the phone.

"I'm sorry about your husband, ma'am. I'll be praying for him."

"I got three little kids over here waiting on their daddy. And you two were yukkin' it up."

"I hear you. I'm sorry."

Her voice broke again. "I felt like this treasure deal was a hoax from the get-go. But Robby didn't."

Waite nodded and TD picked up the line. "I apologize again, ma'am. Here's TD."

A few minutes later, Ardelle Bellweather burst into the station and snuffed out a Pall Mall in the glass ashtray on her desk before making a beeline to the control room. Ardelle had short red hair and walked like she was on her way to cash a winning lottery ticket. She wore tight polyester that swished with every step, and TD cautioned that one day she would start a fire. Waite had hired her on the day she applied because the last secretary had left without a word. Ardelle seemed like an answer to a prayer he hadn't had time to pray.

"I heard that Sharon lady. What happened to her husband?" Her voice always had an edge, like she knew information was being withheld.

Waite nodded toward the production room. TD had the phone to his ear, rubbing his forehead as he talked.

"I don't know any more than you," Waite said.

"Are you going to talk about it on the air? Because you got to tell people what's going on."

Another phone line blinked. "Would you mind taking that? I'll fill you in as soon as I know something."

Her brow furrowed. "You can't leave us hanging." She closed the door and Waite watched her retreat to her desk through the double-paned window. Her perfume, a sickly sweet honeysuckle fragrance, lingered.

Waite played another song, keeping one eye on TD, who still had the phone to his ear.

Ardelle trudged back and handed Waite a pink call slip. "It's Boyd. He wants you to call him. He sounds p—" She thought a moment. "He's concerned."

"About what?"

"He didn't say."

"All right. I'll call him."

She opened her mouth to say something, then moved out of the way for TD, who walked inside and attempted to close the door. Ardelle stuck out her foot and said, "I want to hear."

"This is private, Ardelle. Station business."

TD glanced at Waite. Waite frowned and dipped his head.

Ardelle removed her foot. "I work here too, you know." She glared at Waite and headed to the restroom.

"What did Sharon tell you?"

"It's not good. Robby left before breakfast and promised to be back with some of the treasure. Never made it home. Yesterday was his day off."

"The sheriff knows?"

"They're looking into it. She said they're asking all kinds of questions. Like they were suspicious."

"About what?"

"I don't know. Maybe that he ran off and used the treasure hunt as an excuse."

"Why would he run off?"

"Sounded like they thought that's the kind of thing pastors do."

"He's a pastor? Where?"

"A little church out in Alum Gap."

"The Evangelical Free Church?"

"I don't know what stripe it is."

Waite frowned. "But you went to school with him?"

TD bowed his head. "We used to run together until he got religion. Went off to study the Bible. I haven't talked to him in years."

Waite thought a minute. "Did Robby tell her where he was headed?"

"No. Just said he'd be back in the afternoon."

Waite scratched at his cheek as "The Midnight Oil" ended. Waite threw on his headphones and segued Ronnie Milsap, giving the time and temperature over the intro to "Smoky Mountain Rain." Ardelle stood outside the window peering in like she was looking into a fishbowl.

"Did she say he's been acting strange lately?"

"What are you getting at?"

"What if he did run off? What if he had this planned?"

TD grimaced. "I got more reasons than anybody not to trust

Bible-thumpers. Robby's different. I'm surprised you would think the worst."

"I don't know him from Adam, TD. I don't mean any harm. But this is probably how the sheriff is thinking."

TD leaned forward. "What if somebody followed him? Knew he was looking for the treasure and like that *Lost Ark* movie, he gets the gold idol and then it gets stolen?"

Waite shrugged. "I haven't seen the movie. But he could just as easily have gotten lost. Got bit by a copperhead. Or he might be stumbling into his house right now."

TD handed him a piece of paper. "He drives a red truck. License number's at the bottom. I told her you would mention it on the air."

"Seems like the least we could do."

"I might go over to their house after the show."

Waite saw something in TD's eyes. Something he wasn't saying. But he decided not to ask.

CHAPTER 3

THE UNNAMED GRAVEL ROAD that led to the parking lot of Country 16 turned to dirt a few yards later and continued downhill, winding like a dusty brown snake toward the floodplain of the Mud River. The rutted road ended at an inward-leaning chainlink fence that surrounded Emmaus Salvage. The Bledsoes preferred *salvage* to *junkyard*, but you can call a wet dog anything you want—it smells the same.

Inside the office, Pidge Bledsoe sat in a constant state of trying to align herself to the height of a wooden counter too high for a regular chair and too low for a barstool. The building was not much more than a shed attached to the double-wide trailer she lived in. The office walls were not plumb, light peeked through, and there was a three-inch plywood gap between the top of the rattling air conditioner and the window jamb. The room stayed hot in the summer and cold in the winter.

On the counter by the wall sat a pink transistor AM radio tuned to Country 16. It was the only station Pidge could get, or better put, the only one she was able to clearly hear during the daytime. No matter how far up or down the dial she went, the nearby radio tower splattered its signal, so she let the classic country play. She liked those songs because many of them touched nerves of longing and regret. The station and the people there had become her friends at a distance.

A gray-and-white pigeon perched on the radio. The bird had hit a guy wire to the station's tower years earlier and Pidge had watched helplessly as it swirled to the ground. She found it flopping in a circle in the tall grass by the chain-link fence, as if praying for help or pleading for a merciful end. Pidge had seen herself that day, a metaphor if you will, and she'd gently gathered the injured bird and taken it inside, much to the chagrin of her father.

"You ought to stomp that thing on the head and put it out of its misery. Bird like that don't deserve to live."

"You don't stomp something just because it's wounded, Daddy."

He stared at the bird with disgust. "I don't want a flying rat in here. It's probably got lice."

"Well, so do you."

He'd shifted his gaze from the pigeon to her and stood with a face filled with lines and creases, partly from age but mostly from wear and worry, along with the furrows tobacco and empty bottles will plow. She'd stared back and recalled what he had said about the castaway cars and furniture and appliances that surrounded them.

"Every piece of junk has a story. And every man's trash is another man's treasure."

The bird became a symbol, a reminder that Pidge was here on her own terms, in this junkyard but not of it. That day an uncommon friendship was born, not to mention a nickname for her that stuck like mud. Her real name was Pamela, but nobody who cared about her called her that.

Flap, her name for the bird, had outlived his life expectancy and become the mascot of Emmaus Salvage. He walked the wooden counter Pidge's father had cobbled from broken furniture and warped boards from a barn collapse. When the old man walked inside, Flap retreated to the air conditioner or to the green military filing cabinets that stood at attention like retired soldiers, as if they held up the back wall by their weight and girth, which was close to true.

The old man would never say it, but he grew to love that bird. He'd swat and curse, but there were times when Pidge climbed the hill to the mailbox beside County Line Road and when she returned, she'd pause at the door and see him holding out seed. She supposed there was something gentle in every man, even the mean ones.

Scrap Bledsoe, whose real name was Thomas Blevins Bledsoe, was born in a hollow on the back side of Wolf Pen Ridge. If you picked up a walnut from the front porch of his childhood home and flung it as far as you could, walked to it and picked it up and threw it five more times, you would have hit the tin roof of the home of Pidge's mother, Esther Small. The two were born in a hollow, grew up in a hollow, went to church in a hollow, and got married in a hollow. So it was no surprise they settled in a hollow by the Mud River.

It was Pidge's observation that toleration rather than love was what kept her parents together. They were yoked like horses to a plow and they moved through life pulling something neither could see that kept them a safe distance from each other. There was something both admirable and sad in their marital work ethic, and Pidge promised herself she wouldn't settle like they had. It was a promise she broke.

To understand why Emmaus Salvage bloomed where it was planted, you must understand that Scrap Bledsoe, before he was known as Scrap, had an unparalleled passion for cars. People drove limping Mustangs and Impalas down the rutted dirt road and left them. More often than not, they drove them out of there after Scrap worked his magic.

Even though he would arrive home dog-tired from work at the plant, cars kept coming and he'd tinker all hours of the day and night. He didn't charge, which was a hardship to his family, but there is no gift to the world like a man doing what he enjoys. Scrap was said to smell like engine oil, ether, and grease cleaner, and Esther joked that every night it felt like she was sleeping next to a dirty carburetor with elbows. Sharp ones.

Pidge caught the bug and crawled beneath cars propped on cinder blocks and studied the craftsmanship of people in Detroit. She never felt closer to her father than when they were under the belly of a Buick. He would narrate the play-by-play of what he thought might be wrong, what the sputtering engine meant and clues from fluid leaks. Pidge sometimes fell asleep down there.

After the accident at the plant, once his disability was approved, many thought Scrap would give up. Instead, Emmaus Salvage was born.

Pidge's older brother, Samuel John Bledsoe, caught the same bug for cars and barely finished high school because he didn't see the point. There was talk of him going to a trade school for auto body repair but that was before the jack failed—which isn't fair to say, since a jack was never designed to hold up a car at such an angle. Scrap found Samuel pinned underneath and never let himself off the hook for going inside for a pack of smokes and sweet tea. He dropped the glass that day and Pidge heard her father's cry and came running. She called for an ambulance, but there was nothing the paramedics could do.

They buried Samuel in the cemetery by the river and a year later Scrap buried Esther beside him. She had finally agreed to go to the hospital for her pleurisy and she picked up an infection. That was life. You try to help and you make things worse. Scrap and Pidge were left alone with these regrets and a few more that would soon arrive.

Like Dudley.

Pidge called him Dud and he fit the name. A lot of her problems and wrong thinking could be laid at the feet of Dudley Saunders, but Pidge dutifully picked those up and carried them like they were her own. *Divorce* was a word Pidge swore she'd never use, but Dud expanded her vocabulary. Dud called her names and left in a cloud of dust and that was that.

At the counter, Pidge bobbed her head as the Gatlin Brothers sang "Broken Lady" on Country 16. Waite Evers, the morning DJ, said he believed everybody was broken on the inside and that most people tried to hide the cracks and move on like nothing happened.

"You got that right," Pidge said out loud.

She talked to the radio. At times, she talked to herself. She talked to Flap. She even spoke to flies that wandered through the office and out the opening above the air conditioner. When TD gave the Farm Report or the weather forecast, she talked to him and wondered if she could risk her heart to someone again. But mostly she talked to Waite. He had a kind voice, even when he joked with TD, and there was something that made her feel she could trust him. He'd been kind when her daddy died. The station sent flowers. She'd kept them on the table until they wilted and the petals fell, just hung on to them until they were so dry they crumbled in her hands. For some reason she couldn't toss them.

The phone rang that Tuesday morning and Flap flew to a filing cabinet. Pidge turned the radio down, closed her eyes, and as if staring at a crystal ball said, "Muffler and tailpipe."

Then she answered, "Emmaus Salvage."

"Yes, I'm trying to reach Pamela Bledsoe, please."

The voice was official, curt, without feeling. Office noise in the background. Pidge pictured a woman in a pantsuit from the Sears catalog and her mouth went dry. "Can I tell her who's calling?"

"This is Jennifer in the business office at Clarkston Medical Center. I need to tell Pamela about action that's being taken. We've sent several letters."

"What action is that?"

"Is this Pamela?"

Pidge didn't want to lie but didn't want to admit the truth, so she didn't answer.

A sigh on the other end. "It concerns Clayton's bills. Pamela is responsible for those, right?"

"I believe so."

"The account is being forwarded to collections because of lack of payment."

"That doesn't sound good."

"It's not. But since we've received no response from *Pamela*—" she said the name like it had four letters—"we have no other option. This is *Pamela's* last chance to avoid collections."

"And what would *Pamela* have to do to avoid that?"

"She could set up a payment plan, but I would need to speak with her."

"Okay, give me your number."

Pidge wrote the number down on the back of an unopened gas bill and felt a pang in her stomach, like every day was bad news and worse than the one before it, and that was all you could expect from life. Before she hung up, she asked how much the bill was just to see if the number had gone down. It hadn't. But it was more than she could imagine ever paying. And then she thought of Clayton and that home he had come from. If he stayed there, he wouldn't have a chance in the world.

"What are we going to do, Flap?"

The bird stared at her.

"Maybe if you flew outta here and found that treasure, we could pay the bills. But there you sit."

Like others, Pidge had heard of Gideon Quidley's treasure and wondered for years if there was anything to it. The fellow had a verse for everything and believed all the good and bad in life was a gift because God was working out his plan in his own way in his own time. She wanted to believe that too. A hymn she had sung in church came to her. It said, *"Though the wrong seems oft so strong, God is the Ruler yet."* But there was part of Pidge that wondered what "ruler" meant when cars fell on brothers and mothers got infections and teenagers harmed themselves and caused insurmountable bills.

One of the clues Gideon had parceled out was a verse from the Gospel of Matthew: *"For where your treasure is, there will your heart be also."* She had relatives who lived in the town of Harts, West Virginia, down in Lincoln County. Was it there? Better minds than hers had studied the clues. Who was she to think she could solve such a riddle?

She stared at the phone and the stack of unopened hospital bills. And then she thought of Clayton. Sitting there waiting for another phone call wasn't going to help him. She needed to do something.

Faron Young was singing "Hello Walls" on the radio when she walked out the door and up the hill in the late-morning heat.

CHAPTER 4

After the morning show, TD checked with his dispatch and responded to a stalled car at the A-Z market. He could tell it was a bad battery when he popped the hood. The question was how the older woman had gotten the car started in the first place. She wrung her wrinkled hands and seemed confused and told TD she had lost her husband six months earlier. He saw this a lot. Men who never let their wives take care of cars. TD vowed if he ever married, he'd love the woman enough to teach her to change her own oil and fill a battery with water.

He carried two batteries on his tow truck, but they weren't the right size, so he drove the woman to the auto parts store and showed her which one she needed. She paid for it and he drove her back and tried to clean the corrosion on her terminals.

"You're going to need to replace these. I'll get it started, but you need to have a shop change the connectors."

"Can't you do it?"

"I could but I don't have the tools, ma'am. This should get you by, though." The car started and he gave her the number to an auto shop.

"How much do I owe you?" the woman said.

He waved a hand. "No charge. Just get it into the shop."

She rummaged through her purse. "Are you that fellow on the radio? I think I recognize your voice."

"I do the news for Waite every morning."

"I thought so. Now listen, I don't approve of the music you all play, but I laugh at you two. You're something else." She handed him a five-dollar bill.

"Ma'am, you keep that. I'm glad to know you're listening."

She pulled her mouth tight. "I want you to take it. Don't argue with me."

TD took the bill and shoved it in his pocket and waited until she drove away. He checked his watch, used the CB to radio dispatch, and told them where he was headed.

TD slowed as he passed the empty parking lot of Alum Gap Community Church. Under the sign it said, *Evangelical Free*. Farther down the hill were a few houses and he noticed cars parked by the road in front of a little brick one.

He rang the doorbell and tipped his hat back so whoever answered could see his face. A doe-eyed boy holding a chocolate-covered donut appeared. The kid had more on him than in him, and TD smiled. A woman appeared behind the kid and whispered something, then wiped at the chocolate on the doorknob.

"Can I help you?" She pushed the screen door open and stepped onto the porch barefoot, wiping icing on her shirt.

He stepped back and took off his hat. "I'm TD Lovett, ma'am. We talked this morning on the phone."

Sharon nodded. "Robby's talked about you. I didn't tell you that."

He glanced at his truck, then shoved his hands into his pockets. "Have you heard anything more?"

She shook her head.

"Waite gave the information on the air. I don't know if anybody's called about seeing him."

She crossed her arms and when she looked down, TD studied her. She was short, not more than five feet tall, and probably weighed less than a sack of feed. She had dark hair that fell on her shoulders. Puffy eyes. He noticed her fingernails. Shiny. Perfectly groomed. Why he noticed a thing like that he couldn't say. But he knew then that Robby had married up. There was no question.

"What does the sheriff say?" TD said.

Her face grew hard. "They won't say it, but from the questions they ask, it's like they think he had this planned."

"Had what planned?"

"Ask them. Maybe they've seen so much bad in people it makes them distrust everybody."

"That's not what you need."

"No, it's not."

"They don't know him like you do. But listen, we'll find him. You can bet on that."

She looked toward the church and when she turned back, there was water in her eyes. "I don't doubt it. But I got a real bad feeling. From the time he drove away, it felt like it was the last time I'd see him alive."

"You need to care for your children. Stay strong." He glanced at the cars parked by the road. "Looks like you have help."

"My mother's here. Our church family has come alongside."

"Good." He put his hat on and straightened it. "And it's only been a day. He might just be lost."

"Robby don't get lost. If you know him, you know that."

TD cleared his throat. "The reason I drove out was to see if you could tell me more. About where he was headed."

Sharon retreated into the house and he thought he had said something wrong, but then she returned wearing flip-flops and carrying a set of keys. "Come on. I need to show you."

She walked toward the church and he almost offered to drive her, but it looked like she needed to move. He shortened his stride to match hers.

She crossed her arms and stared at the pavement as they walked. "Something happened between you two."

He studied the electric wires overhead that ran from the road to the church. "I reckon. Did Robby talk about it?"

"He said you two were tight when you were younger. I know you're on his prayer list. Keeps it in his Bible. I always figured he'd tell me about it when he was ready."

"Well, when he gets back, you have him do that."

"Did he do something bad to you?"

"He got religion. I'll leave it at that."

She climbed the steps and opened the door of the church. It was dark in the narthex and he picked up the old church aroma, a mixture of aging wood, thin carpet, and dusty hymnals. It was the smell of TD's childhood.

Sharon led him through the swinging doors into the sanctuary. To their right were pews and beyond sat a piano on one side and an organ on the other. A pulpit with a cross on the front of it stood on a raised platform.

To their left was an open room with round tables and chairs on a tile floor. Potlucks and Bible studies, he guessed. In the corner was a door with a sign that said, *Pastor Gardner*. Sharon unlocked it and TD followed her inside.

She pointed to a closet. "It's in there."

TD found a large cardboard box full to the brim. He picked it up and placed it on the desk. His mouth dropped open when he saw the mound of newspaper clippings and onionskin pages with yellow highlights. Spiral-bound notebooks with index cards falling out. A folded and marked-up map of West Virginia torn from the Rand McNally Road Atlas with pinholes. In the corner of the box was a stack of cassette tapes held together by a rubber band and on the first one was written, *GQ-C16 #9*.

"He recorded you and Waite," Sharon said. "Every time you opened your mouth about that treasure, he taped it."

TD swallowed hard and felt sick to his stomach. "Did you tell the sheriff about this?"

"I tried. All of that was in Robby's shop in our garage. He had a pegboard with pins in the map and sticky notes. I asked him to stop. He said he would. But he squirreled it all here. I swear, I wish he'd never heard about it."

"Don't jump ahead. You and Robby are probably going to have a good laugh about this down the road."

She shook her head. "I don't think we're going to laugh now or later."

"Can you think of anything he said? To know where he was headed?"

She pulled a receipt from her pocket. "I found this in his shorts pocket when I was doing laundry yesterday. He bought an extra-long rope at the hardware store Saturday."

"Does the sheriff know that?"

"Yeah. And I saw the wheels spinning when I showed it to them. They think he either ran away or used the rope to . . ." She bit her lip. "He's the least likely person on the face of the earth to take his life."

TD nodded, unable to look at Sharon. He had a cousin who talked about conspiracies 24-7. The Trilateral Commission. The Mark of the Beast. He picked dates for the Rapture and thought the current president was the Antichrist because there were six letters in his first, middle, and last names. This box reminded him of that, a man whose mind focused on one thing that took over his life.

"Before Robby left, I made him promise if he didn't find it this time, he'd stop. I even had him put his hand on the Bible and swear."

"Well, that's good."

"No, it's not. The only reason he swore was because he was sure he'd find it. I keep thinking maybe he took some kind of chance he shouldn't have because I made him promise."

TD fished a page out of the box and held it up. It was a typed, systematized collection of clues from Gideon Quidley. Most of them sounded like central passages in an Evangelism 101 class. *"Salvation in no other name but Jesus." "Come to me all ye who are weary and heavy laden."*

"Can I take this with me?"

Sharon thought a minute. Then she looked up and he could see where that little boy with the donut got his doe eyes. There was all the hurt in the world there.

"Why are you doing this?" she said.

"I want to help."

"But why come back now?"

"I was thinking that instead of us wandering all over creation, you could give a clue as to where—"

"You're not listening. Why are you taking an interest in Robby now, after all these years?"

He stared into the box like it was a bottomless pit and tried to come up with something that sounded close to the truth. "I feel bad for you. For your family. And after seeing these tapes, kind of responsible. It's got my brain spinning, trying to figure it out."

"You're not trying to find the treasure?"

TD scoffed. "I feel the same way as you. It's not about the treasure now. It's about Robby."

He picked up the box. He wanted to just look at her and spill out the truth about the past, but truth could open wounds. Instead he said, "When I heard your voice this morning, I knew it was something I had to do."

CHAPTER 5

Waite's conversation with Boyd Cluff, the owner of Country 16, was uncharacteristically tense. The man was usually easygoing and affable with an aw-shucks approach to life. However, Boyd tersely informed Waite that Gideon Quidley's son, Milton, had called, fuming about what had happened on the air that morning. How he'd heard about it all the way over in Clarkston, the biggest city close to Emmaus, Boyd didn't divulge and Waite didn't ask, but there was talk of "legal action" and those words sent a penny-pincher like Boyd over the edge.

"Do you know how much lawyers cost an hour, Waite?"

"Have him call me. I'll smooth things over."

"No, you call him!"

"All right. I can do that. It'll be fine. You'll see."

"Milton Quidley is the most powerful man in the county.

Probably the state. He's bought up land and businesses and now he owns—"

"Boyd, I know about Junior. He's a big fish and thrashes like one. But there's nothing to sue about. We're not doing anything wrong."

"I don't stick my nose into how you run the station. I've been hands-off."

"And I appreciate that."

"But I told you to pull back on this treasure deal, didn't I?"

"You did."

"There's no reason to even mention it anymore. But this is going to come back to bite us. Mark my words."

"I've marked them. And my hope is, the next call you get from Milton Quidley will be all cotton candy and bonbons. I'm going to turn on the charm."

"You'd better turn on something because that man can make trouble wherever he wants. Expensive trouble."

Waite paused. "Boyd, while I have you, I'm wondering if we could talk about a personnel matter?"

"We can't afford another full-timer, if that's what this is about."

"TD is sending out air checks. I'm afraid somebody's going to snag him."

"We hardly make payroll, Waite. You know that. Let him be snagged."

"He's dedicated. Works hard. I'd like to hire him."

"I can't talk about this now. You get with Quidley and patch things up."

"And then you'll consider TD?"

"Just call Quidley."

The line went dead. He should have put off talking about TD until Boyd was in a better mood. He got out his phone book and looked up the number for Quidley Enterprises in Clarkston and wrote it on the bottom of his desk calendar, tapping his pen and glancing at a picture on his desk. Something inside churned.

He turned up the monitor to the station and listened to *Middays with Wally Wallace*. Wally's real name was Darvis Walter Reynolds but he had changed it when he arrived. He was always prompt for his air shifts, showing up at least thirty minutes before, carrying a personal pair of Sennheiser headphones with yellow foam earpieces that were falling apart. He had a bushy mustache and wild eyebrows and a skin condition that made what looked like snow cover his thick eyeglasses.

At his last station his marriage trouble had spilled over into his work. His wife had interrupted him reading a public service announcement about blood donation. In her defense, the bulb in the on-air light outside the door had burned out. She'd walked in accusing him of being lazy and a poor provider and a terrible lover. The way she said these things in the doorway, the words she used and the descriptions and accounts of the aforementioned, included things the FCC ruled should not be broadcast. Wally, flummoxed by the intrusion, didn't turn off the microphone or play a song. He just sat there stupefied. Those who tuned into the altercation said it was the most entertaining thing they'd ever heard. They also said they could understand his wife better from ten feet away than Wally right next to the microphone. Everybody laments a train wreck after the fact, but while it's happening, it's hard not to watch.

Not long after that, Wally walked through the door of Country 16 and like most who landed there, he found a place where he could get his feet under him. Waite knew pity-hiring was dangerous, but there was something about Wally.

Other than his hygiene and marital struggles, Wally's

enunciation was his biggest drawback. He had a resonant, pleasing baritone voice, but he spoke with his jaw locked and his teeth about a millimeter apart.

Though Waite tried to spread the commercial load to different voices, local businesses had requested "anybody but Wally." So he was given public service announcements to record and community calendar events and his voice was heard on the EBS test.

"This is a test of the Emergency Broadcast System. The broadcasters of your area, in voluntary cooperation with the FCC and other authorities, have developed this system to keep you informed in the event of an emergency."

Before and after the message came a series of screeching tones. The system was for national emergencies, but the tones just sent dogs in Emmaus into a tizzy.

Waite made a note on the calendar to have another conversation with Wally about his diction. As he wrote, he heard a swishing down the hallway.

"Somebody to see you," Ardelle said.

"Let me guess, Milton Quidley?"

She shook her head. "It's that junk lady over the hill."

"Pidge? Send her in."

Pidge walked into the office like a mouse in a trap factory. "If this is not a good time, I can come back."

Waite smiled and shook hands and her strength surprised him. Her calluses had calluses. "Get in here and sit down."

Pidge had mouse-brown hair she kept in a tight ponytail and a cute nose, blue eyes, and dimpled cheeks. She had fair skin and freckles on her face and arms. She wore work clothes, a cotton T-shirt and jeans that looked like they were a size too big, like they were inherited or maybe she'd shrunk since she'd bought them. She had a slight cleft in her chin that reminded him of someone.

"It's kind of funny listening to you in person rather than through the radio," she said. Her voice was smooth and husky. He could always tell a voice that was radio-worthy.

"Sometimes I hate to ruin the illusion. People get in their head what you look like and then they see the real thing. They always say, 'You don't look a thing like I thought you would.' And that's part of the magic. I'd rather people think I resemble Robert Redford."

She smiled and her dimples showed. She had stubby teeth and he got a vision of what she must have looked like as a child. Innocence with calluses.

"TD's told me what kind of man you are."

"Really? And what kind of man is that?"

"The kind that gives people a chance. You tell stories about the three-legged dog you had as a kid. That tells me you have a big heart. TD says it's too big."

"I don't think the worst thing you can do is give somebody a second chance."

Pidge looked at the floor. "No, sir."

"You didn't come here to compliment my aorta. What can I do for you?"

She rubbed her hands on her dirty jeans and sat straight, like she was getting up the nerve to head toward white water in a leaky canoe. "I got a situation."

"With TD?"

"No. Well, I got that situation, too, I guess."

"You got a lot of situations."

"I reckon. The one I'm here for is a relative who's living with me. He's fifteen. I agreed to take him in."

"That's kind of you. What's his name?"

"Clayton. Goes by Clay. He's not a bad kid, but he's made mistakes. I think he just needs direction."

Waite rubbed his chin. "And there's a reason you're telling me this, right?"

"About the only thing he brought with him was a radio. He's been complaining that he can't hear other stations because of where we live. I got to thinking, maybe if he got a glimpse of what goes on here, how it all works . . ."

"You mean a tour?"

"Sure. That would be nice."

"TD could do that."

Pidge shook her head. "That would complicate things." She thought a moment and leaned forward. "I don't want to ask too much. But I thought maybe there's something around the building he could do. Cut the grass. Take out the trash. Just a day or two a week?"

The phone buzzed. Waite held up a finger and picked up the handset.

"Milton Quidley's on the phone for you," Ardelle said.

"Tell him I'm in a meeting and I'll—"

"I told him that and he said he wants to talk now."

"I'd be better be going," Pidge said.

Waite shook his head. "No, sit down." To Ardelle he said, "Tell him to hang on. And if he can't, I'll call as soon as I'm done."

"Your funeral," Ardelle said.

"You're busy and I'm intruding," Pidge said when Waite hung up.

"I think your idea about Clay is good. I'll find something for him to do."

"Really?"

"Does he like country music?"

"He hates it."

"Let me guess, he's into Lynyrd Skynyrd? Foghat? Grand Funk?"

"Probably. I just know he hates country. That's not a problem if he's just cutting the grass, right?"

"It's probably better he hates it. If he loved it, he'd be distracted. This way, he'll learn the mechanics. How everything works. Kind of like a Mustang lover working on a Pinto."

Pidge gave a smirk.

Waite leaned back in his chair and glanced at the phone line still lit. "I made a promise to the Lord a while ago. I said whoever you bring through the front door of this station who's down-and-out or struggling with some big mistake, if you show them the way to Emmaus, I'll do all I can to help."

Pidge swallowed hard.

"Now, you showing up to tell me about Clay means God isn't through with me. I've walked that same road he has, Pidge. I've messed up six ways to Sunday and God never forgot me. I started in radio when I was twelve, believe it or not. And my experience is, find what a teenager's interested in and give a little push. Once he gets momentum, turn him loose. I assume he's going to Emmaus High in the fall?"

"Yes, sir. But there's something else you ought to know. A couple things, actually. First, he has a real bad stutter. And I don't know how to help him."

"I stuttered when I was younger."

"Really?"

"I'd go for breakfast at the diner and by the time I ordered, they were serving lunch."

She smiled.

The phone line went dark.

"Half the problem is he can't hear what he'd sound like if he spoke unbroken. I might be able to help. What else do I need to know?"

"He's got an injury. Got cut right here." She pointed to her wrist and stared at it. "And there's a bunch of hospital bills."

"The bills come with him as a package deal?"

She nodded.

"Maybe you ought to hunt for old Gideon's treasure."

"That would solve a few of my problems."

"Not according to Gideon. That's one of his clues. 'Riches make themselves wings and fly away like an eagle.' Maybe whoever finds it will get more trouble than they bargained for."

"I'd take some of that trouble." Pidge glanced out the window. "My biggest concern's not the money, though. The hospital bills and all."

"Then what is it?"

"I ain't never done this. Taken somebody in. I'm afraid I'm going to make things worse for him."

"How could you do that?"

She looked toward the hills. "I don't know that you can give something you don't have."

There it was. The hopes and fears of all the years in Pidge's heart.

"Well, if there's something you want to give that you don't have, maybe you'll find it." Waite put his elbows on the desk calendar and lowered his voice. "You have a good heart, Pidge. You're going to be okay with this boy."

She nodded like she'd heard the tune but didn't remember the words. Like she wanted to believe him but couldn't.

He wanted to ask about TD, if she thought there was any hope for the two of them, but Milton Quidley was on his mind. "Why don't you tell Clay to come by tomorrow morning. I'll show him the ropes and maybe bring him a donut from Mel's."

"He'd like that."

Pidge rose and shook Waite's hand again, and when she walked toward the hallway, he picked up the phone and dialed the number for Milton Quidley. He talked with two people before he got to an executive assistant who told him Mr. Quidley was unavailable. Waite took that as a bad sign.

CHAPTER 6

TD walked into Waite's office in the early afternoon and plopped Robby's box on the desk. "You know what this is?"

Waite looked up, startled. "Enlighten me."

"This is a peek inside a disturbed mind."

"Whose mind would that be?"

"Robby Gardner's." TD grabbed a stack of cassettes and held them so Waite could read the scribbling. "Country 16 is part of why he's missing."

"You mind backing up this truck and taking another run?"

TD told Waite what he'd learned from Sharon and what the box contained. "When we was coming up, Robby never did anything halfway. He was whole-hog. Same when he got religion. It fits that he would take this treasure deal seriously."

Waite looked through the box. "He does appear to have been a little obsessed."

TD placed a spiral notebook in front of Waite. "I found this. It's kind of his treasure journal. Robby was convinced the Quidley fortune was hidden in West Virginia."

"That's not a news flash, given what Gideon said. A lot of people have thought that for a few years."

"He also thought it was hidden near a town with a biblical name."

Waite pulled his head back. "How'd he come up with that?"

TD pulled out a yellowed clipping from a pocket inside the notebook. "Gideon did an interview with a newspaper in Pittsburgh two years ago. I have no idea how Robby tracked it down." He put his finger on the words and followed them across the page like a second grader in a reading circle. "The reporter says, 'Can the location of your treasure be found with these biblical clues, or are you trying to get people to read the Bible?' Gideon says, 'Well, I believe if you read the Bible, you will find a treasure infinitely greater than the one I've hidden. So we're talking about two treasures. And I hope people find the one that lasts for eternity. But if the temporal treasure is what you want, I'd look in a place where it all began.'"

Waite sat back and rolled the words over on his tongue. "*Where it all began*. What in the world is that supposed to mean? Is there an Eden, West Virginia?"

"There is," TD said, raising his voice. "It's in Upshur County. Robby went up there. It's in his journal. Didn't find a thing. But something came to me reading all this. I'm not trying to figure out what Gideon meant with his clues. I'm trying to figure out what Robby *thought* he meant. Do you catch my meaning?"

Waite computed that and nodded. "I'm tracking with you."

"Now look at this." He flipped the page on the spiral notebook. "This is from June 29, Monday a week ago. Robby says, 'Got another idea about *where it all began*. Can't believe I didn't think of it sooner. I'm headed there to scout today.'"

Waite's phone buzzed. He picked up the intercom line and TD heard a commotion behind him, like a strong wind was blowing toward them.

"Move the box," Waite said to TD.

TD grabbed it as Milton Quidley strode into the room. The man stared at the box as TD placed it on the sofa. Waite stood and came around the desk and reached out a hand. "I've been trying to get in touch with you, Mr. Quidley. Thanks for stopping by."

TD had heard stories of why Milton had settled in West Virginia, but he wasn't sure any of them were true. The most plausible was that Milton saw an opportunity to buy land and build a business empire more easily here than in some other state.

Milton stood six feet tall and wore a coat and tie with shiny tan shoes. TD could have shaved in their reflection. Quidley looked dressed more for a state dinner than a visit to Country 16. He had a hangdog face with sad eyes and sagging cheeks, reminding TD of the cartoon dog Droopy. His hair was short, balding on top. There was a vertical crease in the space between the man's eyes, and TD kept waiting for it to disappear but it stayed, as if the man lived in a constant state of concern. The one thing TD didn't notice was a resemblance to Gideon Quidley, but he was sure it was there somewhere—in his intelligence and financial acumen, perhaps.

Milton ignored Waite's hand and glanced at TD.

"This is my cohost on the morning show, TD Lovett," Waite said.

TD reached out a hand. "Nice to meet you, Mr. Quidley. I've heard a lot about you."

Milton looked at Waite, ignoring TD's hand too.

"Why don't you sit down?" Waite said.

Quidley didn't move. He spoke in measured tones as if prophe-sying pestilence. "This is not a social call. I spoke with your owner this morning. I assume he shared my concerns."

"Boyd and I talked. He explained what you said and I told him—"

"Save the prepared speech," Quidley said, cutting Waite off. "I thought this nonsense had died out. But you've fanned the flame. The call you took this morning confirms that."

TD wondered how Quidley had heard about Sharon's call.

Milton was just getting started. "I begged him to stop. He's obstinate. Believes he's following God's will. How do you argue with that?" Quidley ran a hand over his bald spot. "And even if I convince him to abandon the fantasy, people like you exploit him."

"Exploit?" TD said, unable to hold back.

Waite gave him a look that said he should leave, but TD didn't budge.

"Waite talks about things on people's minds. He's not exploiting anybody. I've never believed this treasure business, Mr. Quidley. But to accuse Waite, that's crazy talk."

"You're the tow truck driver, right?" Quidley said.

"Yeah, what about it?"

Quidley paused as if waiting for the right moment. With gravel in his voice he said, "This is all you'll ever do. Do you know that? This is all you'll ever be."

Waite stepped between them. "Hold on a minute." He glanced at TD and lowered his voice. "Why don't you let us talk?"

TD fought the rising bile inside. "I'd rather be a tow truck driver than a—"

"TD!" Waite shouted.

"I'm done here," Quidley said.

"Please," Waite said. "Don't leave. The situation the woman called about today—we think your father might be able to help."

"You will have no contact with my father. Understand?"

"Well, we were thinking if we could show your father what we've found, he might give us an idea of where we might look for this woman's husband."

Milton Quidley set his jaw. "Are you hard of hearing?"

TD felt his hands ball into fists. "Mister, there's a fellow missing and his family's scared to death. Your daddy could help."

Quidley closed his eyes and took a deep breath. "Do you know what a restraining order is?" He looked at Waite. "If you speak more of this on your station—"

"I understand," Waite said, holding up a hand.

"No. You don't. I'm protecting my father from himself. I'm protecting him from miscreants who believe him. People who could force him to give a location of something that doesn't exist. I'm protecting him from being held responsible for some idiot . . ." He didn't finish the sentence. He turned to leave.

"I got a question," TD said.

The man stopped in the doorway, his neck and the top of his head flushing red.

"Where's your family from originally?"

The man scowled at TD like he was something to step over in the barnyard. As quickly as he had entered, he strode out of the room and down the hall.

TD cursed under his breath as a swishing sound approached.

"Wanted to make sure you two were still alive," Ardelle said.

"Would you call Boyd and tell him we had a good chat with Junior?" Waite said. "Set his heart at ease."

"What do I tell him?"

"Just that everything's okay. We had us a productive talk."

"Didn't sound like it from where I was sitting," Ardelle said. She turned and swished away.

TD moved to the couch and sat next to the box. "I don't get it. One little station in a town that don't count for a hill of beans to Milton Quidley. He's acting like what you say on the radio is the most important thing in the world."

Waite chewed on the inside of his cheek. "He's just scared."

"How do you get that?"

"Fear works itself out. When people spout, it's usually more about the spouter than those in the room."

"You're just a DJ and I'm just a tow truck driver. What do we know?"

Waite smiled. "No, we're miscreants." He shook his head. "The power of life and death is in the tongue. What he said to you, don't let that bother you."

TD shifted on the couch. "And why would I care about his opinion?"

"Some people only see the outside of a man."

"Some people need a punch in their piehole."

"Maybe if you'd kept your piehole shut, things would have gone better."

"I thought you said we weren't the problem."

Waite chuckled.

Ardelle stuck her head around the corner of the hall. "TD, your dispatch just called about a tow job."

"I'll see you in the morning," Waite said.

TD picked up the box and hurried to his truck.

CHAPTER 7

Waite stood outside Mel's Donuts until Vivian unlocked the door and filled his thermos and handed him a white bag. He asked for an extra donut for a new hire and she obliged.

"What would you do with a million dollars, Waite?"

"Maybe pay you back for all the coffee and donuts you've donated?"

She scowled. "If I found that Quidley fortune, you wouldn't see me up this early. I'd buy a beach house on Sanibel Island and sink my toes in the sand."

"You'd move to Florida?"

"I don't know. Maybe Myrtle Beach. Virginia Beach."

"You'll never move from these hills, Viv, you know that. They're in your blood. And besides, I've read the fortune's a lot more than a million. Might be as much as five million."

Viv thought a moment. "Maybe I wouldn't move. Maybe I'd get tired of the ocean. I tell you what I would do. I wouldn't rent this building. We'd buy it outright."

Waite turned to leave but she lingered in the doorway.

"You record your Sunday show yet?"

"Gonna do that today."

"Play me some Oak Ridge Boys. The *real* Oak Ridge Boys."

He nodded and lifted the thermos in a toast. "To you and Mel. And to staying put."

Waite drove to the station. When he entered, Possum had already moved his chair to the back of the control room and gathered his things.

"Did you hear it?" Possum said.

"Hear what?"

"Mack Strum. I played the interview last night."

"Is that so?"

"And I pitched the *Dispatch* about an article. They might be interested. He's a legend."

"Maybe you should write a regular column. 'Possum's View.' That kind of thing."

His eyes sparkled. "I never thought of that. That would be great promo for the show, the station. Do you think they'd pay me?"

"No harm in asking."

Possum ambled out the door as TD barreled through carrying Robby's box. Waite had cleared the wire and left it by the turntable.

"Any news on Robby?" Waite said.

TD shook his head. "I talked with Sharon last night. It's not looking good."

"Any more ideas from the box?"

"I got a couple of leads. I'll explain in a bit."

After the Farm Report, Waite played Jimmy Dean's "Big Bad John," and it was in the middle of the song that he remembered Viv's question.

"That's Jimmy Dean here on Country 16, the best country in the country. Good morning, it's twenty past six. We have seventy-eight degrees collected for you and about a dozen more for our high today. Add a 50 percent chance of rain, and you have enough humidity to last the summer. Dress accordingly. TD, this morning, Viv over at Mel's Donuts asked me something that got me to thinking."

"Well, that doesn't happen often."

Waite chuckled. "She asked what I'd do with a million dollars. And I turned that back on her. Her answer makes me think I don't want her to find a million dollars."

"Why's that?" TD said.

"Because she and Mel might retire and stop making the best coffee and donuts in the county. Move to a beach somewhere."

"That would be the end of the bear claws, wouldn't it?"

Waite hit the bear sound effect. "Exactly. And we need bear claws and cinnamon rolls to start the day. But that got me to thinking about you, TD. How would you answer that question?"

"What would I do with a million? I'd fund the search for Robby Gardner. Buy a helicopter, maybe."

TD gave the description of Robby's truck and the license number and asked anybody who had information to call the sheriff. He gave that number as well.

"That answer is a lot better than you buying a bass boat," Waite said.

"Well, that ran through my mind, to be honest."

Waite gave the phone number to the station and asked listeners to respond, then played a stopset with four spots. The station's two lines blinked and he got names and cued up Donna Fargo's "The Happiest Girl in the Whole USA."

"What would you do with a million bucks? First up is Cindy."

"Hey, Waite and TD. First thing that came to mind was to build a resort and invite Vietnam veterans. They came back without any thanks and fell through the cracks. I think they deserve a break, you know?"

"Sounds like you're speaking from experience," Waite said.

"You bet your rice paddy. My little brother, Jimmy, ain't been the same since he got back. Breaks my heart." Her voice trembled. "I'd like to do something for him and others like him."

Waite let her words sink in. "Well, Cindy, I agree with you, and if I could give you a million to build that resort, I'd do it. At the same time, you might have something better—you've got a tender heart. Your brother's lucky to have you in his life."

"I thank you, Waite."

He punched the phone button and stifled a smile. "Next up is Sally from Lick Creek. What would you do with a million dollars, Sally?"

What happened next was two minutes of rambling about UFOs and the government's use of chlorine to sterilize the population and make them vote for a Communist. Then she mentioned she would buy back the land the Harper family had sold to the coal company. "I'd kick them out of there and dismantle those dams. That was a beautiful area just a few years ago and now it's under muck and sludge."

Waite jumped in when he could and thanked her, then ping-ponged to line one without knowing who it was or what they might say.

"Am I on?" a man said.

"It's your turn," Waite said.

"All righty. If somebody plopped a million dollars in my lap, I'd do the same thing old Gideon Quidley's done, and that's to challenge people to read the Bible."

Waite frowned, lamenting that the station had no delay. He forged ahead. "And why is that?"

"When news came out about his treasure, I started digging into the Bible—for selfish reasons. God got hold of my heart again, and I'm back in church. I'm feeding on the Word. And I don't care that people think he's a loon. I think old Gideon has the right idea."

Waite jumped in and turned down the pot. "There you have it—what three people would do with a cool million. But you know what? It wouldn't take a million to make Donna Fargo happy. She's got a different reason to go skippity-do-dah."

"Shine on me sunshine, walk with me world . . ."

After the news at seven, TD asked Waite to play Bill Anderson's "Double S," a B side song used by DJs to take bathroom breaks because it lasted five minutes. Everybody had their favorite long tune, but Waite knew something was up.

"I stayed up till dark thirty last night combing through Robby's box."

"Come up with something?"

"Here's what I'm thinking. Robby went somewhere last week. Sharon said he told her he was going back to the same spot."

"But we don't know where that is."

"Right. But I've been thinking about *where it all began*, and I wondered if Robby might have thought it had something to do with Gideon's own kin."

"You mean instead of talking about something in the Bible."

"Right."

"Is that why you went fishing with Junior yesterday, asking where his family came from?"

TD nodded. "Robby found every biblical town name all over the state. He'd crossed off Eden. Even towns that hinted of the Bible like Beulah Mountain and Cross Lanes."

"What about Emmaus?"

"Crossed that off, too. He evidently searched high and low around here. Then I got to thinking, maybe he traced his lineage back to some ancestor, like a great-grandfather who's buried in a graveyard in some forgotten town. And maybe that has something to do with the hiding place."

"You think he dug up his grandpa and buried the treasure?"

"I don't know. Seems like a stretch that an old guy could dig a hole big enough to bury an ark replica. But Gideon seems capable."

Waite stared at the wall. There was something here he couldn't put his finger on. The song was nearing the :30 fade at the end and he cued up Roy Clark's "Yesterday, When I Was Young."

"Keep thinking," he said.

"It's all I've been doing," TD said. "And Robby's still out there somewhere."

"Unless he ran away."

Toward the end of the shift, Ardelle stuck her head into the control room and gave Waite a sly grin. "Know what I'd do with a million dollars? They've got this machine now that sucks all the fat off your belly and hips. I'd get that done and buy a new wardrobe. Then maybe TD would notice me."

"Don't go changing, Ardelle. You're good the way you are."

She rolled her eyes. "Easy for you to say."

"TD's heart is stuck on somebody else," Waite said.

"Story of my life. Is it the junk lady?"

He ignored the question. "If you have to get things sucked out of you in order to get men to notice, they're probably not the ones you want to spend your life with."

He saw the smile again before she closed the door.

Wally took over when the morning show was done and Waite took a coffee break, then got his Bible and went to the production room to record his Sunday morning program, *Waite, on the Lord*. Most people didn't hear the comma and Ardelle listed it on the log as *Wait on the Lord*. He didn't have the heart to correct her.

He chose a few albums from the "gospel" shelf, then threaded tape on the reel-to-reel Scully and studied the clock as he cued up the Oak Ridge Boys. He didn't know the exact talk-over time to "He Never Said a Word," but he had an idea. He'd heard of stations that had countdown timers for song intros and that seemed like cheating. A timer could help you get out of the way of the first vocal, but it couldn't bring the magic. And it seemed like the world was becoming less about magic and more about timers every day.

Before he hit the Record button, he bowed his head. He prayed for Robby, that he'd be found and his family comforted. He prayed for TD, for Pidge and Clay. And he prayed for one other person on his heart.

Lord, you know who's going to be listening Sunday morning and what they need. I don't. Use me in some way to draw hearts to you. Amen.

"Welcome to *Waite, on the Lord*. And a good Sunday morning to you and yours. Stay with us for the best gospel in the country for the next sixty minutes here on Country 16. We're going to set our minds on things above, where moth and rust don't corrupt. And let's start with this thought—if you're running from God, listen to this by the Oak Ridge Boys."

He felt the music and stopped talking just as Richard Sterban began the first verse. They called it "hitting the post," and there was no feeling better than ending right at some musical hit or when the vocal began.

There was a crossover controversy with the Oak Ridge Boys. They'd gone from gospel to country and paid a price with some. Waite had received the same criticism with his drive-time program. One letter, written in scrawled pencil, said, *How can you play all those drinking and cheating songs and think a few gospel tunes on Sunday will wash away your sin? You're a plastic Christian, Waite.*

The writer had signed her name and given a return address but he didn't answer. All who wrestled in the mud got dirty. He'd learned that the hard way. He'd also learned that some people had the spiritual gift of discouragement. Wisdom said it was best not to indulge them.

Next, he played Grandpa Jones singing "I'll Meet You in the Morning," and he thought of his wife. One day he would meet Connie again. The thought brightened his heart and clouded it at the same time.

He was about twenty minutes into the recording when the air pressure changed, which meant the door had opened. He glanced back, past the series of tiles with shag carpet mounted to deaden the sound. Album covers were placed like picture frames between the shag. A yellow light swirled outside the door when the mic went on like there had been an accident.

"There's somebody to see you," Ardelle said, whispering.

Waite looked at the record spinning beside him. He liked to record the whole show instead of splicing the new tape. But he had forty minutes left. "Who is it?"

"Some teenager. He stutters."

"His name's Clay. Have him wait till I get to the next song."

He cued Tennessee Ernie Ford's "Just a Little Talk with Jesus." Being familiar with the beginning and ending of just about every tune in the stack, he knew it ended cold instead of fading. He played it, let it end, then hit the Stop button on the Scully, noting how much time was left in the hour and writing it on his Eddie's Tire Farm notepad. He made a white mark on the underside of the tape with a grease pencil so he'd know where to edit.

As soon as he saw him, Waite thought, *The Kid.* That's what he would call him. The Kid sat with his head down, silky hair covering his eyes. The boy looked up and Waite saw peach fuzz on his lip and the look in his eyes that a mistreated dog will give a stranger when he isn't quite sure if he'll get a kick or a treat.

"You must be Clay." He reached out a hand and the boy looked at it like it was a three-bean salad at a church picnic that had turned, but finally he grabbed it limply. Waite saw a flash of blue eyes and wanted to tell The Kid how to shake hands. He showed the boy to his office and had him sit opposite his desk. He turned down the volume on Wally, who had begun an hour of *Swap Shop*, and handed The Kid the white bag from Mel's. The Kid put it on the floor beside him.

The Kid was thin and gangly, elbows and kneecaps and long legs under jeans that looked a size too big and two inches short. He had on a long-sleeved shirt and Waite thought that strange because of the heat and humidity. Then he remembered what Pidge told him about the hospital bills. What in the world was he getting himself into?

"Pidge tells me you just moved here."

The Kid nodded, putting his left foot on his right knee and fiddling with the fraying laces.

"She says you're interested in radio."

The Kid shrugged. Anything to keep from talking, probably. Waite felt the ache from across the desk.

"Ever been in a station before?"

The Kid shook his head.

Waite cleared his throat and leaned back in his chair, which squealed like a wounded duck. He had to find some WD-40. "When I was a little younger than you, there was a man in our church who was an engineer at a radio station. They broadcast the local Lutheran church services live. We'd sit in a booth in the balcony and I'd wear headphones and adjust a knob, like a pilot will let somebody hold the steering wheel of a plane. It was magic watching that preacher talk into a microphone, knowing there was somebody in a car somewhere listening. I couldn't figure it out.

"Afterward, he'd return the equipment and I'd go into the station. I'll never forget seeing all the buttons and switches. His shop was by the transmitter room. I can still smell that room and feel the heat of those tubes. Engineers are the kindest people on the planet."

Waite wondered if anything was getting through. It felt like he was talking to a wall with hair hanging like curtains.

"You want to take a tour?"

The nod was less than enthusiastic but Waite accepted it. The Kid put both feet on the floor and Waite put up a hand.

"Before we go, I need to hear you. Tell me your name."

The Kid stared at him, slack-jawed.

"It's all right. It's just you and me."

He shook his head.

"Pidge told me you had a stammer. It's okay. Just say your name."

The Kid looked up at Waite, then at the floor. Finally he said, "C-C-C-Clayton." He looked like he'd just passed a kidney stone the size of a basketball.

"*C*'s are hard, aren't they?"

"Y-y-yes, s-s-sir."

"Got any letters that work? Ones that roll easier?"

He shrugged. "N-n-not r-r-really."

"Okay. I'm going to call you The Kid. And when you do your reports, that's what you'll call yourself."

A look of terror struck him. Sheer panic.

"Don't get discombobulated. I'm not going to throw you on the air before you're ready."

"I-I-I'll n-n-never—"

Waite looked him straight in the eye. "I used to stammer. I couldn't imagine not stuttering. The thought of getting behind a microphone? I'd rather have an ice pick shoved in my ear. Is that how you feel?"

The Kid nodded.

"All right. Follow me and we'll take a look around. I promise it'll be painless."

As Waite reached the door, Ardelle met him. "You need to come up front quick."

He found the county sheriff's deputy in the waiting area and thought about Robby. The deputy held a piece of paper.

"It's about Wally," Ardelle whispered.

Waite glanced at the control room, then back to the man in uniform. "What's wrong, Art?"

Arthur Palermo was the son of Maxine and Marco. Maxine had met and fallen in love with Marco, whose family owned a blueprint business in Philadelphia. After several years and a few children, Marco gave in to Maxine's request to return to the hills and they settled in Clarkston, which had the only Catholic church for fifty miles. Marco's family had a history of both blueprinting and badge wearing, and Arthur gravitated toward law enforcement.

Arthur had a choirboy face, a pouty mouth, and he wore a St. Christopher medal. His Catholicism made people in Emmaus nervous.

"It's his wife, Waite." Arthur handed him the paper. "I'm here about the car."

Waite's mouth dropped open. "His car?" He took a step left, like he was line dancing, and peered through the trees to the lower parking lot. The deputy's cruiser was there and so was TD's tow truck. Beside both of them was Wally's beater, which seemed to be held together with nothing but hope and Ziebart. "That makes no sense, Art."

"It's a court order. Nothing I can do."

"That car's keeping him employed, Arthur. What's he supposed to do, walk? He lives twenty miles from here. You can't take his car."

Arthur didn't answer. Waite took the paper and stared at the on-air light.

Wally said, "Again, if you're interested in Carl's 1964 Chevrolet Impala with a V8 engine, no rust and no working transmission, call him now." He gave the phone number. "Let's take another call on the Country 16 *Swap Shop*." *Kathunk.* "You're on the air."

Waite was at an angle where he could see the meter on the console jump when Wally punched the phone line. He'd need to talk to Wally about keeping the pot down until after he punched the line. He turned back to the deputy. "I'll stop him after this call and get the keys."

Art nodded. "That'll work."

"This is Sally over in Lick Creek."

Waite shook his head and wondered what they were in for. He glanced behind him. The Kid stood in the hall observing.

"I've got something I need to do, kind of an emergency," Waite said to The Kid. "You okay waiting?"

The Kid nodded.

"I've come upon a Bible with all kinds of markings and underlines and notes," Sally said. "I'll sell it to the highest bidder."

"Is it a family heirloom?" Wally said.

"No, I can't say how I got it."

Wally tapped his Bic pen against his spiral-bound notebook. "Well, the rule is you have to declare a price, Sally. Or you can trade it for something of equal value. Is there anything you'd trade it for?"

"Sure is. The treasure the owner of this Bible says he hid."

Wally sat ramrod straight. "Are you saying you have Gideon Quidley's Bible?"

"That's exactly what I have. At least I think so."

The mention of Quidley sent Waite into action. He opened the door and Wally turned and saw him, then saw the deputy. His face went white. Waite closed the door. The speakers were off, so he only heard Sally through Wally's headphones, which he kept at jet-engine decibel levels.

Waite made a cutting motion with a hand to his neck and pointed at the cart machine. Wally pointed at the clock. Waite pulled Wally's chair away from the board and leaned down to the mic, punching the phone line and cutting off Sally's voice.

"We interrupt today's *Swap Shop* on Country 16 for a message from our sponsors."

He hit the green flashing button on the cart machine and a commercial for Eddie's Tire Farm played. Waite turned off the microphone and lowered the speaker volume.

"What in the world?" Wally said. "I still have ten minutes left for *Swap Shop*."

"No, you don't. The sheriff's deputy is here with a court order. Your wife wants your car."

"My car?"

73

"I don't get it either. Arthur will explain."

Wally took off his headphones and placed them on the console. He moved in slow motion, absently picking up the notebook and putting it under his arm.

When the commercial ended, Waite hit the sounder with jingle singers. "The best country in the country, Country 16!" Then he segued the song Wally had cued up on the turntable, "He Stopped Loving Her Today," which Waite thought was more than ironic, though the song was about a man whose love ran so deep it only ended when he died.

Wally walked out and Waite cued up Dolly Parton. Art said something to Wally. Ardelle sat at the desk, pretending not to listen. And The Kid stood with arms crossed by the paneled wood behind her.

Waite waved The Kid into the control room. "Baptism by fire. Stand here by these switches and when I tell you, flip that first one. Okay?"

"I-I-I—"

"Get over here. Switch won't bite you."

The Kid inched toward the board, clearly intimidated by the knobs, buttons, and lights. Waite saw how everything made sense and fit together, but he remembered how terrified he was when he sat down the first time and realized all he didn't know.

"This is a pot. It controls the volume of whatever's hooked to it. And this . . ."

The Kid held up a hand like he was in a classroom. "Wh-wh-why is it c-c-c-called . . . ?"

"Potentiometer. Try saying that and you'll realize why they abbreviated it. When this song is over, you're going to flip that switch and you'll see how I go from one song to another smooth as silk. Nothing to be scared of. You ready?"

George Jones was almost finished. To Waite, it was all a matter of feel, the eyes on the meters, ears on the song, hands on both pots, but the intangible was how it was supposed to sound, how moving from one song to the other was most pleasing to the ear. He wasn't sure it was something you could teach someone as much as awaken in them.

"Hit it," Waite said.

The Kid flipped the switch. The turntable clunked and reached playing speed within a half-turn and there was a tune from a guitar in A minor. Waite turned the pot down on the finished record and hit the voice-over that said, "The best country in the country, this is Country 16."

Dolly Parton sang, *"Jolene, Jolene, Jolene, Jolene . . ."*

The Kid's face said it all. It was like he had uncovered the secrets of the universe.

Waite lifted the needle from George Jones and put the 45 back in the sleeve. He pulled another record from a bin, placed it on the turntable, and dropped the needle, explaining the process.

"I've got this in cue while Dolly sings. Only you and I will hear it." He lifted a round knob to disengage the turntable and moved it by hand until he reached the drum hit. "You find the first sound and go back a half-turn so the song doesn't 'wow.' That's why it took a half second after you flipped the switch for 'Jolene' to start. Did you notice that?"

The Kid nodded, mesmerized.

"Look at the time. This song is going to end close to top of the hour. We don't have network news, we rip and read, so we don't have to hit it on the nose, but we try to get close. I'll grab head-lines from the UPI machine, play the legal ID, and hit the news sounder. This is all on the log, on the clipboard there. It tells you everything coming up."

Waite walked to the teletype room and returned. The Kid was glued to the same spot on the floor.

"Everything all right?" Waite said to Ardelle.

"As all right as it can be while you're watching a man's life get flushed down the toilet."

Waite closed the control room door. "Sit there and watch." He thought about telling The Kid to stay quiet, but there was no need.

The Kid sat, shaking the hair from his eyes, which Waite thought was a good sign. Focused now, Waite glanced at national stories, made a mark or two, then crossed out a story about the Palestinian Liberation Organization because he couldn't pronounce the names of those Middle Eastern leaders. The song ended and he played the legal ID, made a mark on the log of when it was played, then hit the news sounder and keyed his microphone.

Twenty minutes after the hour, Wally returned. Waite had The Kid cueing up the next record.

"I tried to get him to listen to reason, Waite."

"Court orders are hard of hearing."

Wally stared at The Kid, then looked at Waite. "I want to finish my shift and figure out what to do."

"I've got this if you want to gather yourself."

"It'll help me to finish, if you don't mind."

"All right. After you're through, come by the office. We'll work out a plan."

Waite led The Kid to the lobby and paused by the front door looking at the parking lot. The deputy stood by TD.

"What did you think?" Waite said to The Kid.

The Kid nodded. Then he glanced at Ardelle. He opened his mouth, then closed it.

"Why don't we call it a day? Come back tomorrow morning. Say, seven? Is that too early?"

The Kid shook his head.

"Don't forget your donut in my office."

Waite reached out a hand and The Kid took hold—limply at first, then he squeezed harder. Waite thought he saw the hint of a smile on the boy's face.

Waite descended the rickety stairs and caught Art as he was leaving. "Heard any more about Robby Gardner?"

"No. We're doing all we can."

"TD and I have some ideas about why he left."

Art frowned. "Why don't you do your job and let us do ours?"

Waite shook his head as he watched Art leave. He found TD muttering to himself.

"Pure spite is what it is," TD said. "This court order don't make a lick of sense. And I got to be part of it. Would you tell Wally this wasn't something I wanted to do?"

"He knows that. But I'll tell him."

TD finished securing the chain to Wally's car and tightened it with the motor. Waite watched him—the economy of movement, the worn gloves, the sweat-stained shirt. It was like poetry, he thought, the way TD did his job. He treated the junker the same as he would a Mercedes or a Cadillac.

When TD was through, he turned off the truck's engine and jumped down into the gravel. He handed Waite a green-and-white umbrella. "It was in the back seat. Wally might need this if he's going to hitchhike."

"I'll pass it on to him."

TD pushed back the bill of his hat, standing in the shade of a low-hanging maple. "It's killing me not to be out looking for Robby."

"You say the word and I'll head out with you."

"I don't know where to go. I keep thinking I should track old Gideon down and talk with him."

Waite leaned against the wrecker. "And you know what that would lead to."

"There's got to be a way to figure this out."

"Maybe somebody will see his truck and report it."

TD spat on the ground. "Who was that boy that walked out of the station?"

"Relative of Pidge. You don't know him?"

"I haven't talked with her in a while."

"He's staying with her now."

"Where's he from?"

Waite shrugged.

"What's he doing at the station?"

"He's interested in radio. Sharp kid. Has a bad stammer."

"And you're going to let him work here, aren't you? That's just what we need. I swear, Waite, if you owned a wallpaper store, you'd hire every one-armed man you could find."

"They said the same when I let you do the morning show with me."

"Who did?"

Waite smiled. "Nobody. I'm giving you a hard time. Where you headed?"

"Impound lot, then I might head over to Sally's place to look at that Bible she's selling."

Waite stifled a laugh. "I thought you said the *Swap Shop* made us sound like a hick town?"

TD rolled his eyes. "Maybe I'll walk down and see Pidge before I leave."

CHAPTER 8

PIDGE HEARD CLAY dragging his feet in the dirt outside the office and wondered how it had gone with Waite. She let him go. No sense jumping on him with questions. He'd clam up. Not that he was a river of information, but she tried to pull something from him each day. She'd discovered he liked the pizza sandwich they served at the Pizza Barn in town and vowed she'd try to get him there every couple of weeks, even though she couldn't afford eating out.

The door opened and Flap fluttered. It was TD with his baseball hat pushed back, smiling like he meant it. She felt something warm inside but looked at the desk as she spoke. "What brings you here?"

"I was up at the station hauling Wally's car away." He described the court order.

Pidge shook her head. "Probably the last thing he needed."

"Some people have more than their share of trouble. Wally's one of them." TD closed the door and studied Pidge's calendar. "I saw a boy walking down here. Waite said he's a relative?"

"Yeah." Pidge told him Clay was her nephew and would live with her for a while.

"Why didn't you tell me he was coming?"

She gave him a squint. "Didn't know I had to."

"You don't have to get testy." TD softened his voice. "It's nice of you to give him a place to stay. Waite said he stutters. It'd be just like him to . . . I mean, Waite said he's pretty sharp."

"Is that what he said?"

"Told me just now. How long's he staying?"

"You writing a book?"

"No, just curious. I thought maybe he got into some trouble. I want to make sure you're okay."

"I can take care of myself, TD."

TD sighed heavily. "I know that. Look, I'm out of sorts because of Wally and the whole Robby Gardner thing."

"Is there any news about him?"

"No. Waite and I are putting our heads together to figure out where he went."

"You think he'll turn up?"

"I hope so." He tapped the counter twice. "I came down to ask if we could get dinner. You and me?"

Pidge glanced at him and saw the look of hope in his eyes. It took nerve for him to ask. She compared TD to all the other men she'd known. TD hadn't pawed at her like Dudley and some of the others who had treated her like she was fresh pie at the dessert table. At the same time, though he wasn't forward, she could tell he was interested. Was it the look in his eyes? The way he hooked his thumbs through the belt loops on his jeans? She couldn't say—she just knew.

"I'm pretty much tied up with Clay."

"Bring him along."

"I wouldn't want him taking up too much of your time ordering." She said it with more than a pinch of sarcasm.

"Pidge, I try to be nice and show concern, and you push me away."

She stared at the calendar and clenched her jaw. She thought she heard movement in the back of the house and imagined Clay with his ear to the Sheetrock.

"Keep your voice down," she said.

TD turned and walked out, slamming the door behind him.

Waite gently closed the door to his office and Wally dropped into a chair. His shoulders slumped, he took off his glasses and a cascade of dandruff fell like snow.

"I don't know what to do, Waite."

"Take it a step at a time. Beginning with you working here. You want to stay, right?"

"Country 16 is the only station that'll have me. You know that."

"Well, you've got a job as long as you want it. Okay?"

Wally nodded. "My wife gets half of everything I earn. We sold the house. I'm renting a room from a widow who took pity. I'm two months behind."

"You got a lease?"

"It's just a handshake. An arthritic one."

Waite smiled. Anybody who could retain a semblance of humor in Wally's shoes was going to make it. "Why don't we figure out how to get your stuff and bring it here?"

"To the station?"

"Sure. You could sleep in the storage room. But my back bedroom is crying out for somebody."

"I couldn't do that, Waite."

"It's just till you get your feet under you."

"I don't understand . . ." His face contorted, eyebrows converging, lines in his forehead.

"There's no understanding this. You got somebody making life hard. That's all you need to know."

"I was the one who made it hard."

"You probably added to the pile. It's good to look at your part. But her problems are hers. Just move forward, okay?"

Wally looked up with red eyes. He didn't speak.

Waite leaned forward, his voice softer now. "You've had a bad streak."

"It's more than a streak," Wally whispered. "Do you think it's true that whatever doesn't kill you will make you stronger?"

"From my experience, whatever doesn't kill you will back up and try again."

Wally nodded and there was a hint of a smile.

"Losing the car feels like the last straw. But what if saying goodbye to that clunker is the best thing that could happen?"

"I don't see how that's possible."

"Streak ends today, Wally. Life's taking a U-turn."

"How do you know?"

Waite handed him the green-and-white umbrella. "Your wife didn't get this. That's a start."

Wally put his glasses on and studied the umbrella, turning it in his hands. "Why are you treating me this way?"

"I used to want to go out and save the world. God cured me of that."

"How?"

"He showed me he could bring everybody I needed to help right here. And today that's you."

"I don't deserve to be helped."

"Well, we're going to have to disagree about that." Waite leaned forward and pulled out his billfold.

"No, you're not doing that," Wally said.

"Hear me out." Waite pulled out a crisp twenty-dollar bill. "See this? How much is it worth?"

"You know how much it's worth."

Waite crumpled it in his hands into a quarter-size wad. Then he unfolded and flattened it. "It's all wrinkled, though. What's it worth?"

"Twenty dollars."

Waite put the bill on the floor, stood, and stomped on it a few times and rubbed it back and forth along the thin carpet. He picked it up. "How about now?"

"The same," Wally said.

"What if I washed it by mistake at the Laundromat?"

"The same."

"Dipped it in the Mud River? Or the septic tank out back?"

"The same."

"That's right. We've all been baptized in something we didn't want to be baptized in. Doesn't mean you've lost your value."

Wally stared at him.

"You need new vision. You need to see what I see. You've got a lot going for you."

"Me?"

"Yeah. A man with a working umbrella can go through a big storm and come out the other side. Open it up and start walking, Wally."

"What happens if I get struck by lightning?"

"Call it a power surge." Waite raised his eyebrows and saw something cross Wally's face. "You don't have hope right now. Hang on to some of mine, okay?" He stood. "Let's get your stuff. But for crying out loud, don't open that umbrella in here."

TD dropped Wally's car at the impound, his stomach churning over the argument with Pidge. He regretted slamming the door. With Pidge, he expected one thing and always seemed to get another. How would he ever break through the hard shell of that tortoise? Not that she looked like a tortoise. She looked like summer squash or a flowering rhododendron. She had a quiet beauty he couldn't explain, something that drew him like the scent of horehound candy and sweet oats at the feed store. She was a mystery and at the same time something he felt he'd always known. She would always be part of him, part of the longing of his life. The question was how to get her to let him inside that shell.

He drove to County Line Road listening to DeeJay Bailey's show on Country 16. From the moment he saw her, TD had thought DeeJay looked like Dottie West. Her hair billowed around her like cotton candy and framed her face in a puffy red cloud. She always had a smile that seemed a little too big, too bright, and too happy. She wore long eyelashes, which TD assumed she paid handsomely for, and too much makeup on her eyelids and cheekbones. TD guessed that somewhere underneath all the glitter was a woman in her forties who longed for her twenties. Her smoky voice didn't belong in Emmaus but somehow it's where she had landed. Something had happened that only she and Waite knew. Neither would talk about it and nobody asked.

TD had once heard her singing along to Henson Cargill's "Skip a Rope" when he walked into the studio. She was enveloped in a cloud of smoke from her Camels. He apologized and closed the door.

Another day he ripped news for her as the clock neared the top of the hour. He rolled the yellow paper into a scroll and presented it to her as a goodwill offering. She smiled and thanked him as she looked over the headlines.

"Does any of this ever get to you, TD?"

"What do you mean?"

"All the suffering and pain we tell people about. And we're supposed to be positive and talk with a smile. I read these stories and wonder how long I can keep it up."

"You do a good job of it."

"I've had lots of practice."

He'd worried about her after that. And the worry led him to pull over one night when he saw her car parked crooked along the road about a hundred yards from the Dew Drop Inn. He went inside and found her at the bar, staring into a drink.

"I broke down, TD," she said.

He took her by the arm and escorted her out and towed the car to the shop. He left it there with the keys under the mat and a note under the windshield wiper saying it was DeeJay's, then drove her home. She smelled of stale beer and perfume. She kept repeating how sorry she was and tearfully asked him not to tell Waite.

"I promised I was going to stop," she said. "And the car gave out right at the bend. Started coughing and sputtering. I saw the Dew Drop and it felt like a sign."

"Sounds more like a fuel pump."

"I wish I could change parts like you can a car." She cursed and a tear ran through her makeup. "I've made such a mess of my life. Things were supposed to turn out different."

TD felt an urge to say something profound, but he figured he'd be talking more to the Budweiser than DeeJay. The most he could muster as his brakes squealed to a halt in front of her house was "Get some sleep, DeeJay."

She looked at him with the cotton candy hair wilted and drooping down past her sad eyes. "I'll pay you back for this."

He was going to say something about her doing no such thing, but as soon as she got the door open, everything she'd had to drink gushed onto the gravel driveway. He got out and came around the tow truck, the diesel engine rumbling and chugging, and a light came on next door.

"I'm okay now," she said, gasping.

He helped her up the walk to the front step but instead of opening the door, she turned. "Go on. I'll sit here a minute."

He stood with her for a while, then got in his truck. That image of her sitting on the darkened step, DeeJay at her worst, was what TD thought about as he listened to her talk over the segue from Johnny Cash's "Man in Black" to a song by Jimmie Davis. Over the transition, which was loose but tolerable, she said, "The best country in the country, this is Country 16. I'm DeeJay Bailey—it's eighty-nine and muggy in Emmaus. Stay cool this evening. Have a glass of tea on me. Here's an oldie—'Nobody's Darlin' But Mine,' on Country 16."

She finished just as Jimmie sang, *"Come sit by my side, little darlin'."* The music rose and he wondered what DeeJay was thinking as the song rolled along like a lonely train into the countryside.

TD turned onto Lick Creek Road, a familiar destination for him and Robby when they were younger, and images flooded his mind. High schoolers liked to park at the end of the road. TD wished he could keep driving to their familiar drinking spot and find Robby.

Sally Childers's house sat on a knoll above the road and was surrounded by yellow-and-green euonymus that had decided they were taking over like Hitler took France. TD didn't want to mess up the woman's gravel driveway with his heavy wrecker, so he parked at the edge of the road.

He'd never met her face-to-face, but he had a concept of what she would look like. Older. Wearing a shawl in the dead of summer. Varicose veins. But when she came to the screen door, he wanted to say, *You don't look a thing like I thought you would.* She was younger than he'd imagined. She had oil on her face that glistened in the sunlight. He assumed it was to keep her skin young-looking, but it might have been a UFO deterrent. She was thin as a wisp with curly blonde hair that looked recently trimmed. She wore a satin kimono-like robe that reached the floor.

He took off his ball cap and held it in front of him. "Miss Sally, I'm TD Lovett from Country 16."

"I know who you are," she said in rapid fire. "Get on in here. You want to take a look at that Bible, right? That *Swap Shop* guy cut me off. There was a lot I didn't get to tell him. I swear I can't understand half of what that man says."

TD followed her inside and stood by the door, partly out of respect and partly because the front room was filled with stacks of newspapers and magazines. Sally continued her verbal torrent as she made her way through the maze. He wanted to explain why *Swap Shop* was interrupted and agree about Wally's voice, but he never got the chance.

"You take a look and tell me this is not a Bible from Gideon Quidley," she said when she made it back. "Leaf through it. Go on."

TD took the hardbound book and studied it as she continued her play-by-play of where she'd found the Bible and what she encountered inside. The cover had a greenish hue and when he opened it, he saw what Sally was talking about. Underlining in black and red ink. Note cards with verses copied. References to Gideon Quidley.

"Miss Sally, I don't think this is Gideon's."

She pulled her head back. "What makes you say that?"

"I'm no expert, mind you. I have my doubts about the treasure, but every verse and clue comes from the King James Bible. *Thee*s and *thou*s and *verily, verily*. This here is one of those Living Bibles that came out a few years ago."

"You're saying this is fake?"

"No, ma'am. It's a real Bible, I just don't think it's Gideon's."

"Maybe it was one of his relatives? It's clear somebody is trying to figure out where that treasure is. And there's clues all over the place in there." She took the Bible back. "Look here. In the book of Judges, this whole section about the fleece is underlined. This is the part where an angel sits down by an oak tree and tells Gideon what he needs to do."

"Can I see that?" TD said.

He took the Bible and read until he came to verse 11. *"But one day the Angel of the Lord came and sat beneath the oak tree at Ophrah, on the farm of Joash the Abiezrite."*

A strange feeling came over him, like something had just changed. He handed the Bible back to her and turned to the front door.

"You don't want to buy it?"

"No, ma'am. But I thank you for showing it to me."

Sally stood on her porch and spoke to TD's back, explaining many of the mysteries of the universe she had solved. TD waved and hurried to his truck. He had to get to Waite.

CHAPTER 9

WAITE WAS ON THE PHONE with the owner of Elaine's, a women's apparel boutique on Main Street, getting information about an upcoming sale when TD ran into the office out of breath. When Waite hung up, TD said, "I think I got something on Robby."

"I'm all ears."

"Ever heard of an Ophrah, West Virginia?"

Waite shook his head.

"I got to thinking, what if *where it all began* wasn't about Gideon's family, but Gideon in the Bible?"

Waite cocked his head. "Keep going."

"Maybe Robby was looking for a place on the map that related to the fellow with the fleece. And if so, *where it all began* could mean something about that fellow's life."

Waite reached for his Bible.

"Judges 6 is where it's at," TD said.

"For somebody who doesn't truck in religion, that came pretty fast."

"Some things don't wash out."

"Okay, I see it," Waite said, skimming the passage. "Looks like Gideon was born in the town of Ophrah." He reached for his West Virginia Road Atlas and looked at the O's. "Oak Hill. Oceana." He scanned the rest. "No Ophrah."

TD cursed. "I was sure it had something to do—"

"Hang on a minute," Waite said. His chair squeaked as he turned to his shelf and pulled down a Bible dictionary he sometimes used for his Sunday show. "Here we go. Ophrah means 'a fawn' in Hebrew. It's a town of the tribe of Benjamin. Probably the same as Ephron in 2 Chronicles and Ephraim in John chapter 11." Then his mouth went dry and he could feel his heart beating loudly.

"What is it?" TD said.

Waite looked at TD. "The other name of that town is Ephra."

TD looked out the window, whispering the name, deep in thought. "I've been through Ephra. It's not much but a bend in the road."

"How far of a drive would you say it is?"

"I don't know. Maybe a couple of hours." TD's eyes widened. "That fits, doesn't it?"

"Like a glove."

"That could be what Robby was thinking. Should we tell the sheriff?"

"He'll call it a wild-goose chase. Tell us to let the professionals handle it. Us miscreants."

"Then we ought to head up ourselves, don't you think?"

"If we leave now, there would still be daylight left to hunt for him."

TD glanced at the clock. "I'll call dispatch."

"We'll take my truck. I already dropped Wally off at my house for the night."

TD gave directions and by 7 p.m. they were on the state route that wound its way up to Ephra. The landscape changed from rolling hills to dramatic vistas. They spotted rocky crags from the roadway and TD recalled being carsick as a child driving such roads.

"Think we should have told Sharon about this?" TD said.

"If we find him, she won't give a hoot that we didn't call first. And if we come up empty, she didn't need to know."

"We're not going to come up empty."

"I hope you're right."

TD scanned the side roads and countryside for Robby's red truck. When they passed the *Ephra, Unincorporated* sign, Waite slowed. There were houses and trailers scattered like dry leaves along the hillside.

"I'll holler if I see any willow trees with harps on them," TD said.

Five miles later, Waite pulled off the road and turned around, muttering as he did. They drove slowly back over the same route, pulling over to let cars pass that stacked behind them on the two-lane road.

"There's an awful lot of country around here," TD said.

Waite pulled into a gas station and went inside and spoke to the cashier. When he got back in the truck, he sat, staring out the windshield.

"No luck?"

"Kid said he's seen lots of red trucks. All from around here."

"We could head down some side roads," TD said. "Or start knocking on doors."

"Sun will be gone in an hour."

"And the alarm clock goes off early in the morning."

Waite dipped his head and closed his eyes. At first TD thought he was resting. Then he saw his lips moving. It looked like he was praying, so TD kept quiet. No reason to disturb the conversation, even if it was one-sided.

Waite finally looked up. "We need us an abundance of counselors."

"Excuse me?"

"Proverbs. 'Plans fail when you get no advice. But they succeed with an abundance of counselors.'"

"Lead on, Solomon."

They drove to the outskirts of town and pulled up to a trailer.

"Probably best to split up, don't you think?" TD said.

"You take that side of the road. I'll take this one."

TD knocked on doors and asked if anyone had seen a red truck or a man in his late twenties wandering about. He mostly got blank stares. One husband and wife on a porch invited him to sit on the swing and have lemonade. He politely declined.

He and Waite met at the truck and drove to the next gravel road leading uphill. They split the houses between them and came up with more of the same and continued as the sun shone bloodred over the horizon, fading fast.

TD knocked on a screen door that was all door and no screen. A girl in cutoff jeans who looked to be fifteen or sixteen stepped onto the porch. When TD mentioned a red truck, she looked up, surprised.

"I did see one."

"When?"

She glanced behind her and lowered her voice. "I was with a friend over near Rocky Top earlier. A red truck came racing down the hill lickety-split. Kicking up dust."

"Did you see the driver?"

"No, it was too far away."

"Did you see where it went?"

"Yeah, it went to the main road and a few minutes later I saw dust kicking up over on Grissom Creek. It's a dirt road. I can't say for sure it was the truck, but that's my guess."

"Could you show me where that is? We're looking for a fellow who went missing."

She pointed to a curve and gave directions. TD hurried back to the truck and whistled for Waite. He came running and TD explained what he'd discovered. Waite spun gravel.

They passed Grissom Creek Road because the sign had been knocked down. Waite turned around and drove the wooded lane, evening shadows falling and the sound of crickets and whip-poor-wills rising.

Waite slowed at the first house, which had a fenced yard and two Beware of Dog signs. When they drove past, it was clear the signs were there for about ten good reasons, which ran back and forth near the fence.

"She said the dust kicked up a ways down the road," TD said.

They kept going, the road dipping by the creek in areas that were washed out from summer rains. There were craters here, not just dips in the road, and TD wondered how anybody could get up enough speed to kick up significant dust.

They had driven nearly a half mile when Waite pointed at a house and a barn in a low-lying plain. There was no red truck in sight, but there was a station wagon parked in front of the house. Waite backed up and drove past a mailbox with the name *Wheeler* painted on it at an angle.

In the yard were several chickens that scattered when they rumbled to a stop. The house had peeling paint and a roof with blackened shingles. Behind it was the barn, which was a generous way to describe the structure.

Nobody came to the door and after a moment, Waite got out and moved toward the house while TD moved toward the barn. There was just enough light to see inside and TD noticed a full hay wagon. Tire tracks in the dirt led to the door and a few more steps let him see the side of what looked to be a Ford.

"Waite, I see something."

Out of his peripheral vision, TD saw a black streak. A dog stopped a few feet from him, the hair on his back standing up and his teeth showing. TD tried to calm the dog with his voice but that only made him more upset.

"Can I help you?" someone called from the house.

TD saw a grizzled man in coveralls carrying a shotgun. The man stepped toward the cinder block stairs leading from the porch. A curtain fluttered at a window.

Waite raised both hands. "We don't mean any harm. We're looking for somebody."

"Can you call off your dog, mister?" TD yelled.

"He won't hurt you. As long as you don't move."

"I'm not moving," TD said, the dog still growling.

The man took the steps gingerly, wincing with what looked like hip pain. He looked to be in his fifties to TD. He called the dog and it backed away slightly. TD gingerly moved backward, keeping his eyes on the dog.

"You two need to get back in your truck. You won't find any-body around here."

"Is it Robby's truck?" Waite whispered when TD drew close.

"I don't know. I couldn't see the license plate."

Waite smiled at the man by the porch. "I'm assuming you're Mr. Wheeler."

The man didn't respond.

"We're looking for somebody who came up here in a red Ford. And we noticed the truck in your barn there. Do you mind if we check it and see if it's his?"

"There ain't no truck in my barn. Only vehicle in there is a Massey Ferguson that hasn't started since Eisenhower was in office."

"Mr. Wheeler, I can see it from here," TD said.

"Don't go nosing around in my barn. I don't know you two from Adam."

Waite scratched his head. "Let me introduce myself, then. My name's Waite Evers. From down in Emmaus. TD's my partner. We do a radio show together."

"Radio show?"

"Country 16. Best country in the country."

"Never heard of it."

"We got a phone call from a lady whose husband is missing. He's a pastor down there."

"I got nothing to do with it."

"They have three little kids. We think he might have come up this way."

"For what?"

Waite shook his head. "That's a long story. But it would help if we could just make sure that's not his truck. If it's not, we'll get out of here."

The man stared at them like they were space aliens. "I done told you—there's no truck in my barn. So turn around and get out of here."

"We should call the sheriff," TD said to Waite.

"Sheriff?" Wheeler said. "Now hang on." The man spat in the dirt.

A PIECE OF THE MOON

Waite turned to TD and lowered his voice. "Get in the truck. Let me talk with him."

"Waite . . ."

"Get in the truck."

TD shook his head and walked to the truck and climbed inside, his window down. The black dog panted heavily and glared at TD.

Waite took a step toward the man, rubbing the back of his neck. "It won't take long for the sheriff to get here. They're out looking for him. If you help us, there might be a reward."

The man looked at his gun. "You said he's a pastor?"

"That's right."

"Oh, for crying out loud, come on. I'll prove it to you."

TD got out and followed, and the black dog darted toward them until the man yelled and kicked dirt at him. The dog scampered underneath the house.

Wheeler led them inside the darkened barn and stopped, his mouth dropping open. "Where in the world did that come from?"

TD spoke the license number out loud.

"That's it," Waite said. "That's Robby's truck."

CHAPTER 10

TD's HEART BEAT WILDLY as he opened the door to Robby's truck. Empty. In the truck bed was a toolbox with a rolled-up tarp stuffed behind it. He couldn't help thinking the worst and he looked for evidence of a struggle or maybe blood. He didn't see any.

"Appears I owe you two an apology," Wheeler said. "I was gone all day. I have no idea how that got here."

"Gary found it."

TD turned to see a towheaded girl in the barn doorway, silhouetted by fading light. She was maybe six with a dirty face and a bad haircut. TD thought she looked like one of the *Whos* in *Who*-ville. She pronounced the name "Gurry" in her squeaky, high-pitched voice.

"Who's Gary?" TD said.

"That's my son," Wheeler said, stepping toward the girl and

propping his gun against a hay bale. He leaned forward, hands on knees, and looked into her eyes. She folded her hands and stared at the barn floor.

"Where's Gary at, Maggie?"

She shrugged.

"How do you know he found it?" Wheeler said.

"I seen him drive it into the barn."

Wheeler sighed heavily. "Maggie, look at me. Did he tell you where it came from?"

Brown eyes as big as the world. "He told me finders are keepers. I told him you'd be mad, but he said you always say finders keepers, losers are sweepers."

Wheeler didn't correct her. He stood as straight as his injured hip would let him.

TD looked at the truck's cab again. There were no keys in the ignition and wires dangled from the steering column.

Wheeler came up behind TD. "You got to understand about Gary. If he finds something in the woods, he thinks it's his. Don't matter what it is. Deer antlers. Lost dogs. He brings it all home."

"We should get the sheriff," TD said to Waite.

"Now hold up," Wheeler said. "There's no need." He went to the front of the barn and yelled, "Gary, wherever you are, get out here! Now! And I mean it."

"I don't like this," TD said to Waite. "It's getting dark. If something happened to Robby and this Gary had something to do with it . . ."

Waite squinted at something behind TD. Then his jaw dropped. "Would you look at that?"

TD turned and saw a boy in a ratty T-shirt with his head down, his hands shoved into his pockets. He walked toward Wheeler. He looked no more than twelve. When he got in range, Wheeler cuffed him on the back of the head and Gary yelped. TD guessed that wasn't the first time it had happened.

"Why'd you steal that truck? What were you thinking?"

"I didn't steal it, Daddy. I just brought it here to take care of it. It was 'bandoned."

Wheeler shook his head and cursed. "They're going to lock you up one day and throw away the key. There's a fellow missing out there in the woods. They think you did it."

"Did what? I didn't do nothing. I swear."

Waite joined the two and knelt on one knee in front of the boy. "You drove that truck here by yourself?"

Gary wiped something from his face. "I can drive as good as anybody."

"He hot-wired it," TD said.

Waite waved a hand behind him and TD rolled his eyes.

"Gary, did you see the man who owns the truck?" Waite said.

"No, sir. I didn't see nobody."

"You sure?"

"Did I stutter?"

"Watch your tone, boy," Wheeler said, pulling back a hand.

Gary pursed his lips. "I didn't see nobody."

"When did you find it?" Waite said.

"Yesterday. I saw it in a grove of willows on the other side of Rocky Top."

Waite glanced back at TD.

"It was still there this morning, so I figured it was up for grabs. I don't know how long it's been there. Started right up."

"Could you show us where you found it?" Waite said.

"I reckon. Get in. I'll drive you up there."

"Let's take my truck," Waite said, smiling and putting a hand on the boy's shoulder.

TD got in and closed the door. Waite drove and Gary sat between them with Wheeler following in his station wagon. Gary pointed out the turn that forked off the main road and snaked up a hill, and TD thought they would never have taken this path. Waite pulled to the side of the road when they came to the willow grove. Fireflies rose as Gary got out and walked to the area where he said he'd found Robby's truck.

TD pointed to the mountain. "He probably went up there, don't you think, Waite? Remember the rope?"

"Robby!" Waite yelled. He waited. No answer came. After a moment he said, "Lead the way, TD."

They had two flashlights and TD took one and ran point. He pulled himself up tree by tree with Gary right behind him in the bramble. He yelled for Robby as he climbed but heard nothing but the wind through the branches and his own breathing. He finally made it past the trees into a rocky area and slowed. Gary passed him and hustled to the edge of the cliff.

"We call it Rocky Top 'cause it feels like you can see all the way to Tennessee," Gary said, hardly out of breath. Oh, to be twelve again, or however old he was.

TD shone the flashlight across the rocks and gingerly walked to the edge and looked into the darkness.

"There!" Gary said. "Shine it a little right of that—right there! See it?"

A rope dangled and TD trained the beam of light up to the top where the rope was tied to a pine growing between two boulders. He tracked the rope down with the light and noticed it dangled in front of a hole in the rock wall about two-thirds down the rope's length. He shone the light to the floor of the canyon, but the wall jutted and blocked his view, so he moved up toward the pine.

"Find anything?" Waite said when he and Wheeler arrived, huffing and puffing.

"Found a rope," Gary said.

Waite's flashlight was brighter and he trained it on the ground below the rope. The sight took TD's breath away. If Robby had fallen, he could not have survived. The height and the jagged rocks below made death a certainty.

TD glanced at Waite. The look on his face said he agreed.

"You think he could be in that cave?" Gary said, pointing. "I can climb down and check."

"You'll do no such thing," Wheeler said. "That's all we need is you splattered on those rocks down there."

TD moved his light further out. "Waite, shine your flashlight over there. No, to the right a skosh."

Waite moved it.

"Does that look like somebody's leg by that rock down there?" TD said, leaning over the edge.

"Could be a tree trunk," Waite said, handing the flashlight to TD. He put his hands around his mouth. "Robby! Hey, Robby!"

His voice echoed and TD thought it was the most lonesome sound in the world, calling somebody and only hearing your own voice return. And then he thought of Sharon and those kids, especially the one with chocolate on his face. What would they do when they were told? Maybe the sheriff would do that. Maybe it was better to leave the whole mess to the sheriff.

No, TD couldn't leave without resolution. He had to find Robby's body.

The thought sent a shiver because TD had always been skittish about death and what lay on the other side, as well as what happened just before you got there. As a kid he'd been scared to death of hellfire. He was taught hell was a place where the *"worm dieth not, and the fire is not quenched,"* and he could never figure out why a worm would stay in such a place.

"It is appointed unto men once to die, but after this the judgment." That was another truth he'd heard as a child. One day everybody would stand before the Judge. Looking over this precipice brought back the fear and dread.

"Whoever's down there ain't moving," Wheeler said. "If it's a person, that is."

"What's the best way to get down there?" TD said.

"Safest way is back down the way we came and then around," Gary said. "Quickest is that way." He pointed toward a peak above them.

"I wouldn't suggest it," Wheeler said.

"What if he's still alive?" TD said. He looked at Waite. "What do you think?"

Waite sighed. "No sense taking more risk. Let's climb back down and send somebody to call the sheriff."

They had gone a few steps when Gary yelled, "Hey! Did you hear that?"

They rejoined him at the edge of the rocks.

"I don't hear anything," Wheeler said.

"It was a voice. Coming from somewhere down there."

The wind picked up and the men strained to hear. Then TD heard a soft sound, almost a whisper.

"Help me."

"Robby?" TD yelled. "Is that you?"

Silence. Wind in the trees. Wings flapping. Then, faintly, they heard the voice. "Yeah. I'm in bad shape."

"He's alive," Waite said.

TD tried to figure the location of the voice. It sounded like it came from the other side of the ravine.

"Where are you, Robby? Did you fall to the bottom?"

Robby gave a sickening, wet cough. "I'm in the cave. Side of the rock wall."

"Told you," Gary said.

"What in the world happened?" Wheeler muttered.

"Hang on, Robby, we're coming!" TD yelled.

Waite turned to Wheeler. "We need the sheriff. And an ambulance. Might need a rescue team, too. Where's the nearest fire department?"

Wheeler told him and grabbed his flashlight. "The gas station is the closest phone. I'll make the call."

"I'm going down to him," TD said.

Waite tried to stop him but finally gave in as Wheeler scampered down the hill. TD gathered the dangling rope and tied it tightly around his waist while Waite and Gary slowly let it slip through their hands. TD used the tension to walk backward down the rock face like he was stepping on the surface of the moon.

He stumbled at the edge of the cave but kept his balance and crawled inside, pulling the flashlight from his back pocket and untying the rope. What he saw took his breath away. Blood all over Robby's face. He'd lost teeth and his nose was swollen and crooked. His right leg, which should have looked like a small case l, looked like a capital L, bent at a ninety-degree angle at the shin. There was a lot of blood.

"TD?" Robby said as if he were dreaming.

"I'm probably the last person you expected to see."

"You got that right. What in the world are you doing here?"

"You want me to leave?"

Robby gave a bloody smile. "No. How'd you find me?"

"Just relax and stay quiet. We're going to get you to a hospital."

"I been praying God would send an angel. Never thought he'd send you."

"I ain't no angel. Just lay still."

"My leg's busted."

"I can see that." TD pointed the light at his leg.

"How's it look?"

"I've seen worse," TD said, lying. "What happened?"

"Stupid. That's what happened. Lost my balance. When I fell, the rope wrapped around my leg and I smacked into the rock with my face. Knocked me out, I guess. I don't how long I dangled. I should've died, TD."

"Well, you didn't."

"You mean, not yet."

"Don't talk that way."

Robby put his hand to his mouth. "How's my face look?"

"Like you went three rounds longer with Muhammad Ali than you should have."

"Sharon's going to kill me."

"I doubt that. She won't recognize you."

"She told me she had a bad feeling. I should have listened to her."

Waite yelled down to them. "You got him, TD?"

"Yeah. His leg's broken. Probably a concussion. No way I can carry him out. We need one of those basket deals."

"All right. Hang tight. Help's on the way."

Robby spat blood and TD wondered if that came from his lungs.

"I could use a drink of something."

TD yelled to Waite to pull the rope up. He asked them to get Robby something to drink.

"I kept thinking of Psalm 91. I'm in the secret place of the

Most High right here. I'm in the shadow of the Almighty. I kept saying that over and over. He is my refuge and my fortress."

"Mm-hmm," TD said.

"I need you to tell Sharon and the kids I love them."

"You tell them yourself, Robby."

"You got to promise, TD."

"I'll tell them. But you hang on."

"I think I've lost too much blood. I tied a tourniquet. Is it still bleeding?"

"You did a good job."

"I haven't seen you in a coon's age. Can't get you to call me back."

"Well, here I am. Better than a phone call."

"Tell me how you found me."

"We got lucky."

"Luck had nothing to do with it. It's a miracle, TD. I didn't have the strength to crawl in here. It's just a plain miracle. Will of God."

"Maybe it was your will to live. To get back to your family."

Robby shook his head. "There's something bigger going on."

TD shrugged. "If you say so."

"Seriously, how did you know to come up here?"

TD swept the light to the edge of the cave. It was no more than a ten-foot hole in the rock, sloped up. All he saw was lichen and the detritus of a hawk's nest. No treasure chest.

He told Robby the story of Sharon calling the station and how he'd gone to the church with her and found the box in his office.

Robby closed his eyes tightly. "I swear, she's gonna kill me for not letting it go."

"Stop saying that."

"What day is it?"

"Wednesday."

Robby relaxed a little and put his head back. "Feels like I've been here a month. And it's only been two days."

"You probably went in and out of consciousness."

"I didn't tell anybody where I was going."

TD pointed the light at Robby's leg for another look. "I read your chicken scratching about the treasure. Me and Waite put two and two together."

"Waite Evers?"

"Yeah, he's up top with the kid who hot-wired your truck. He's the one you ought to thank."

Robby let out a wet sigh. "I'm glad I didn't throw away those notes. No telling how long it would have been till somebody . . ."

TD couldn't see Robby's face but he heard whimpering. He was probably thinking he'd come close to dying alone. And about what it would be like for somebody to find his bones years from now.

Robby grew quiet and reached out a hand. "I can't feel nothing in my legs."

"Maybe that's not such a bad thing right now."

"Bottle coming down," Waite yelled.

The dangling rope swung back and forth until TD grabbed the warm, half-finished bottle of Mountain Dew. Robby drank the whole thing in one gulp.

"So you didn't find the treasure?" TD said.

"I was sure it was here. Saw gold sparkle last week. Guess it was my imagination."

TD took the bottle from him and tossed it aside. When Robby spoke next, there was a tremble to his voice.

"We went through a lot together, TD."

"Save your strength. You're going to need it when the rescue team gets here."

"I called you."

"I've been busy."

"Nobody's that busy."

"Maybe I kinda knew what you were going to say."

Robby's breathing was more like gurgling now and TD wondered if there was something he should do. Prop him up or push on his chest or try to clean the blood off his face.

"I gotta ask you something."

"No, you don't," TD said.

"Yes, I do. If I don't make it—"

"You're going to be fine. Now hush."

"The Lord brought you here."

"Right."

"And maybe it wasn't just to find me."

"This is the reason I never called you back. I knew you'd play the God card like it was the Rook."

"This ain't a card game, TD. I was this close to checking out. And I've been laying here preparing my heart for eternity. But I'm worried about you."

"Worry about yourself. That's your job."

"We never talked. After what I said that hurt you. You know what I mean."

TD turned his head and tried to quell the storm inside. The moon was up. He could see shadows on the other side of the ravine. "I heard you went off to study the Bible. And you got married. Cute kids. I'm happy for you."

Robby tried to push himself up onto an elbow, but the effort made his head loll and he winced. He closed his eyes and his head fell hard onto rock.

It took two hours for the rescue team to get everything in position to lower the basket with a paramedic inside. He crawled into the cave and treated Robby as best he could, then secured him in the basket. They hauled him out and carried him down the mountain through the willows to the waiting ambulance.

TD waited with the paramedic in the cave. "You think he'll make it?"

"He's lost a lot of blood. I don't like the look of that leg."

"But if he makes it to the hospital . . ."

"He's got a better chance now. We just have to wait and see."

TD sat with his thoughts and the questions of his life and the longing inside. Then he thought of Pidge. If he was to find the key to her heart, he felt he'd find the key to his own.

The team returned and lowered the basket and brought TD up, then the paramedic. TD told Waite on the drive back that seeing a man that close to death made an impression and Waite agreed. And it was on the drive back with the radio on low and the wind whipping through the cab of the truck that another thought began to grow white-hot inside of TD.

PART 2

CHAPTER 11

The word of the Lord again came to Gideon Quidley, this time as he was eating breakfast and reading the morning newspaper.

The chatter in the diner faded as he read the story about the pastor who had searched for treasure and wound up losing a leg. If it hadn't been for some Good Samaritans, the man would have died.

Gideon had made a promise. His yes was yes and his no was no. But he wondered, at that vulnerable moment, if he'd been off-kilter about hiding his treasure. Could he have misheard the Almighty? Doubt began to grow.

He had wrestled with doubt, particularly with the proverb about bringing up a child in the way he should go. When his son, Milton, had grown older, he had departed. But Gideon had come to believe that the proverb wasn't as much a promise as an observation from somebody who had walked away and returned himself. It was designed to give hope and guidance for any parent tempted to give up walking the narrow way. He and Opal had comforted themselves with this interpretation. They believed that, by the grace of God, Milton would eventually come to his spiritual senses. And as he stared at the newspaper, Gideon was honest enough with himself to admit that he had hoped hiding the treasure would be a jolt to his son. He wanted to force Milton to realize his temporal inheritance was gone and that he needed to focus on a lasting one.

Gideon went back to the top of the news story and read again about the pastor who had climbed down a rock wall in Ephra, West Virginia. He shook his head. "Why in the world did he think it was there?"

He studied the picture of the man in a hospital bed, his wife and children next to him, grateful but wounded. They had no insurance and the hospital bills were mounting. His poor congregation was trying to help. What would the future bring?

And just like that, with half-finished hash browns, Gideon heard the whisper. He believed that, like the old hymn said, "God moves in a mysterious way, His wonders to perform." Maybe God knew all this would happen and was working out his plan through it. Maybe he was moving people's hearts and minds in a way Gideon hadn't considered, like Joseph saving his family by being sold into slavery.

"God's ways are not our ways," he whispered as he sipped black coffee. And he was comforted by realizing God's ways were not something he had to figure out in order to obey. Maybe instead of a mistake, this man's "accident" was part of the plan. If so, Gideon hadn't misheard.

He drove home and found Jubal waiting, his tail wagging and his nose pressed through the chain-link fence. What a gift of God to have something waiting, shaking its hips with excitement as he pulled into the driveway.

Inside, he picked up the phone in the kitchen and used the rotary dial to make two calls. When he was done with the first one, he made the second and talked with two gatekeepers before his son came on the line.

The more important you are, the more people you have to go through.

"Did you hear about the pastor who got hurt looking for the treasure?"

"That was last week," Milton said. "You're just hearing about it?"

"Saw it in my paper today."

"Well, I heard. And I told you this was going to happen."

Gideon had prepared himself for this. Milton thought he knew everything.

"It's not over," Milton added. "People are talking again. There will be more of this. Someone's going to get killed."

"So you're a prophet now?"

"I've been concerned about this from day one."

"Really, Son? Are you concerned about people getting hurt or is it something else you're concerned about?"

"Dad, why did you call?"

"As a courtesy. To let you know I've made up my mind there's not going to be a next time."

"What do you mean?"

"Nobody else will get hurt. I've heard from the Lord."

Milton said something inaudible. "Every time you say that, something bad happens."

"Well, we'll have to disagree about that. The Lord's told me to give the treasure to that pastor. That's what I aim to do."

Silence on the phone line.

"Did you hear me?"

A heavy sigh.

"I wanted you to know I'll be heading out. I'll be gone a day or two."

"Please, for once in your life, listen to me. You're in no condition to go traipsing around the countryside."

"I can traipse anywhere I want. And I don't need your permission. Never have."

Another sigh. "If the box is as big as they say, how are you going to lift it? How will you transport it?"

"As big as who says?"

Milton didn't answer.

"Who have you talked to, Son?"

"You haven't thought this through."

Gideon felt a twinge in his gut. "Did you call that outfit in Gallipolis?"

"Dad, let me drive up there and pick you up. Are you at home?"

"I had a contract with them. They can't tell anybody about the ark."

"I'll cancel my meetings for the rest of the day."

Gideon took a deep breath. "Well, good for you. Enjoy the downtime. I'm going hunting for treasure. And for your information, I won't have to lift it. I'm going to take a few coins as a down payment for that pastor and there's something else in there I need to retrieve. I got to make things right with it. But I'll leave the rest."

Silence on the line again. Gideon nearly hung up.

"Who else knows about your trip?" Milton said.

"Not that it's any of your business, but it's just the Lord and me. And now you."

A pause. Gideon heard papers shuffling through the phone line.

"Hold up a minute," Milton said. "Don't you have a doctor's appointment tomorrow?"

Gideon glanced at the calendar on the refrigerator. Sure enough he'd written the appointment down.

"How in the world did you know that? I haven't told you anything about my appointments."

"I'll come that way tomorrow, Dad."

Gideon laughed. "You'll do no such thing. And if you come, you'll go home alone."

"At least tell me where you're headed."

"No can do. But I'll tell you what—I'll give you a hint. Only seems fair, don't it?"

"Dad, don't do this."

"How long's it been since you cracked a Bible?"

"Dad, please."

"Here's my last clue. Two words. You ready?"

Milton didn't answer.

Gideon smiled and slowly said, "Acid reflux." Then he hung up and laughed again. Served his son right for sticking his nose into his doctor's visits.

Tomorrow he'd gather what he would need for the trip and take Jubal to a neighbor's house on the way to his doctor's appointment. Then he thought better of leaving the dog. Maybe it would be good to have a companion on the journey. Especially with how Jubal fit into all this.

CHAPTER 12

TD SAT IN A SOUND BOOTH at the recording studio in Clarkston with walls treated with what looked like egg cartons. He snapped his fingers in front of the long silver microphone with the word *Neumann* on it. The room was so dead TD could hear his heartbeat. And that microphone looked like it cost more than his tow truck.

In front of him sat a clear acrylic stand holding ad copy and he read it through silently. Butch Williams had car dealerships in three states and ran spots on stations in all of those markets. They were looking for an "authentic" voice that stood out. This was TD's chance.

A bearded man in the control room pushed a talkback button and spoke into TD's headphones. "It's Titus, right?"

"I go by TD."

"All right, TD. Whenever you're ready. I'm rolling."

TD rubbed his hands on his jeans. His tongue felt thick, his mouth full of cotton. The door opened in the control room and someone stepped in and stood in the dark corner.

"If you're looking for a deal on a new or used car, come see Butch. We've got dependable, affordable used cars that won't break your budget. And Butch has a full line of '82 . . ."

TD stopped. He tried to lick his lips.

"And Butch has a full line of the new '82 models red—ready . . ."

He looked up and saw the engineer's disembodied face through the glass. "You think I could get a drink of water? My mouth's kindly dry."

"Sure. No problem. Fountain's down the hall."

"A'ight. I'll be right back."

TD removed the headphones and stepped into the hall. He spotted the fountain but stopped at the control room door because he heard laughter. He listened, unable to move, as the voices leaked through.

"Where'd you get this guy? Sounds like he just walked off the set of *Hee Haw*."

"They said they wanted authentic."

"Hand that guy a banjo and he could make it on *Deliverance*."

"Stop it. You're awful."

The bearded one tried to hold back, but they both laughed and TD walked to the fountain and stared at it. Then he walked through the office area and out the front door and drove back to Emmaus, a burning sensation inside. He couldn't get the laughter or the words of Milton Quidley out of his head. He was just a tow truck driver and that was all he'd ever be. He realized he was gripping the steering wheel a little tight when he glanced down at the speedometer. Then he saw swirling lights in his rearview.

"What's the hurry, TD?" Deputy Palermo said when he walked up to the open window. "You on a call?"

TD shook his head. "I'm headed back to Emmaus for a date."

"License and registration."

TD's jaw dropped. "You giving me a ticket, Art?"

"Afraid so."

"I was only going about ten over."

"Fifteen. I got you on radar."

"When's the last time you had that calibrated?"

"License and registration, TD."

TD leaned over and opened the glove box. "This got anything to do with me and Waite finding that fellow before you did?"

"This has everything to do with your lead foot."

TD saw Pidge's truck in the parking lot of the Pizza Barn and he gave a deep sigh. He'd finally gotten her to say yes to dinner and when he parked and hurried inside, he found her and Clay sitting at a booth in the dark restaurant. A line of people stood in the back moving with bovine speed toward the all-you-can-eat buffet.

"How'd the audition go?" Pidge said as he sat.

TD smoothed a hand over the red- and white-checked table. "I don't think I'm what they're looking for."

"Why not?" Pidge said.

"Just a feeling."

Clay studied the menu and the waitress came and brought large glasses of ice water. "You all ready, or you want a few minutes?"

"We're ready," Pidge said. "Clay will have the pizza sandwich, pepperoni. I'll take the salad and spaghetti."

"And for you, sir?"

"I'll try the sandwich. Same as Clay." TD handed her his menu. "One check. Bring it to me."

"I'll get this started," she said, disappearing into the kitchen.

Clay looked at his hands.

"Waite says you're making a lot of progress at the station," TD said.

"He don't want to be on the air," Pidge said.

"I understand."

Clay motioned toward the arcade in the back of the restaurant and Pidge handed him a dollar. He scurried off into the dark.

"He likes playing Skee-Ball," she said.

TD leaned forward and tried to be heard over the jukebox playing "In the Air Tonight."

"Thanks for coming, Pidge."

"You don't have to pay for us."

"I want to. I feel bad about . . ."

"Slamming the door the last time you came around?"

"Yeah."

"You ought to feel bad. You scared Flap half to death."

He saw a hint of a smile. "I was upset. Mad that I'd messed things up again. And I didn't know what I did wrong."

The waitress brought Pidge's salad and TD leaned back. She picked cherry tomatoes off one by one and put them on a napkin. "You want my tomatoes?"

He thought about asking if she was speaking in code. Waite would think that was funny, but he didn't want to offend her. When he hesitated, she shook her head and dug into the salad. He reached over and pulled the napkin toward him and ate a tomato.

"I wish I hadn't slammed the door. Sometimes I feel like I got all this stuff bubbling inside, and it leaks out."

"What's inside always leaks out eventually, don't it?"

"I reckon so."

"Tell me about the audition. You were excited about it."

TD stared at the table.

"What happened?"

"Nothing."

"Something must have happened. Have they already picked somebody?"

TD set his jaw. "They laughed at me."

She put her fork on the table. "What do you mean?"

He told her what he'd heard through the closed door. He thought he saw something glisten in Pidge's eyes in the dimly lit room.

She picked up her fork. "They'll regret it."

"Why's that?"

"When you go off and become famous, they'll wish they'd said yes."

He stared at the top of her head and kept quiet until she looked up. Phil Collins banged on his drums as TD looked into those blue pools. She didn't smile often, but when she did, her dimples showed, little crinkles around her mouth, and the closest he could come to a comparison was a cute cartoon character he'd seen on TV as a kid. He loved that face.

"What?" she said.

Her eyebrows. He'd never studied that striking part of her face, how her eyebrows set off the milky-white skin above. It was like looking at an art gallery painting. Not that he'd ever been to a gallery, but he'd imagined that you walked in and found a painting that grabbed you and stood there and thought about what had gone through the painter's mind as the brush touched the canvas. And the more you looked, the deeper you went into the painter's soul.

TD thought all of that while he noticed the painting in front of him had changed. Her eyebrows were in a position below wrinkles and there was an edge to her voice when she spoke.

"I'm not letting you pay for this. I don't want to be beholden."

"I asked you to come—and you said yes, so I'm paying."

"No, you're not."

"Pidge, what's wrong? What did I say?"

"I don't want to feel obligated."

"Obligated?" TD pushed the napkin back toward her. "You mean you don't want to date me?"

She looked up, her eyes hard as marble. "It's not personal. Why is everything personal to you?"

"How could it not be personal?"

The waitress came with the food. Pidge got up and walked to the arcade.

"No matter what she says, you give me the check, understand?"

"Yes, sir."

Pidge returned with Clay, who had won a Pizza Barn key chain. They ate their food without speaking. The noise of the jukebox drowned out the conversations around them. TD kept looking at Pidge, hoping she'd see that he couldn't keep his eyes off her. Then he heard the strains of Mack Strum, the familiar fingerpick of the six string and the plaintive voice singing "A Piece of the Moon."

Pidge twirled her spaghetti and wiped her mouth with a napkin. There was something about the song that seemed to capture her, and she stared out the window until it finished.

When Pidge excused herself and went to the restroom, TD signaled the waitress and she brought the bill and he handed her cash. Clay studied him silently.

TD handed him two dollars. "You can go back to the arcade if you want."

Clay disappeared into the dark and Pidge returned, fishing in her purse and looking for the waitress.

"The bill's paid. The manager picked up the check."

"He did not."

"Yeah, he said it was on account of your beauty."

She cocked her head. "I told you I pay my own way."

"Come on, Pidge."

She shook her head and got up from the table.

TD stopped her. "Let me bring him home. You go on. He's having fun."

Pidge slung her purse over her shoulder and her face seemed to soften. "All right." She turned to leave but stopped and looked him in the face. "I'm sorry they laughed at you."

TD came to a stop at the end of Pidge's driveway. Clay got out and went in the house without a word. TD sat there, wondering if he should just leave or knock on the door. He wanted to talk with her again. He saw a light on in the office and got out, cutting off his engine.

The office door opened and light spilled out and there she was, a silhouette. Flap walked along the desk behind her, pecking at seeds.

"Thanks for bringing him home," Pidge said.

"Glad to do it. Glad to have company at supper, too."

"How's that pastor friend of yours?"

"Robby? From what I hear, he's getting better. Looks like it's going to be a long road."

"I'll bet his wife was grateful to you."

"She was. It's going to be a long road for her, too." He shoved his hands in his pockets. "Driving back after we found him, I had the thought that if Waite and I could figure out where Robby went, maybe we could figure out where old Gideon hid his treasure."

"I thought you didn't believe there was one."

"Yeah, but what if there is? It would pay Robby's hospital bill and then some."

"If you put your mind to it, you can do anything you want, TD."

"You think so?"

Pidge nodded and closed the door behind her and leaned against it.

"Then why can't I get through to you? I've been putting my mind to it. And I don't feel any closer today than I've ever been."

"I went to the Pizza Barn with you, didn't I?"

"You did."

TD studied her in the darkness. Pidge was like a question on *Jeopardy!* you knew from the moment Art Fleming opened his mouth, but you came up empty after saying, "What is . . . ?"

"Thank you for saying what you did about those guys laughing. It helped."

"Good."

He heard something and turned toward the trailer and saw a window curtain flutter. Pidge must have heard it too, a muffled chuckle, like somebody had banged their funny bone on a table edge. She took a few steps away from the office door.

"Clayton, it's a sin to poke your nose into other people's business." Her voice ran to the river and echoed off the hills.

She walked past TD without looking back, as if she knew he would follow her like an old dog. Truth was, he'd follow her to hell and hitchhike back if she wanted. But maybe she wanted to go alone. Or she wanted something else.

The red light of the station blinked above them, and over that were clouds that looked like they were on their way to somewhere else but for the moment had decided to watch their conversation. Their edges rimmed with shimmery moonlight.

Pidge stopped and turned to him. "I don't think we'd be good for each other, TD. Both of us are towing a load of hurt bigger than we can pull. And we're both going uphill."

"Maybe we could pull it together. Or I'll get out and push."

"I've thought a lot about it. I do care about you. And I know you care about me."

"Then what's holding you back? Are you waiting on somebody taller or shorter? Somebody with more muscles or less dirt under his fingernails?"

"It's not any of that. I don't want to make another mistake. And I don't want to be a mistake you'll regret."

"Pidge, you would—"

"Stop for a minute and listen. I swear, radio people sure like to run their mouths."

"All right. I'm listening."

"It won't work. You're running from something you'll never get away from. And it's not my place to help you figure it out. I got enough to figure out on my own."

"Are you talking about God now? You sound like Waite."

She lifted her hands like she was surrendering to somebody and took a step back.

"Pidge, I just want to see you be happy."

That sent her over the edge. She tilted her head back like it was the last thing she wanted to hear. "Is that what you want me to believe? That you want me to be happy?"

"I don't want you to believe anything you don't want to believe, but I'm telling the truth. I want to make you happy. And I don't want to see you alone."

"TD, you can't make me happy. Don't you understand?"

Her words stung, but he shook it off like a charging bull will ignore a bee sting. "And how do you know if you don't let me try?"

Pidge ran a hand through her hair and TD thought he'd like to be that hand. He wanted to move toward her, reach out and touch her shoulder, rub her back, just make contact. Grab her in his arms and kiss her. But he didn't.

"It's not your job to make me happy. I got to be happy with my own life before I let somebody else back in."

"I could help. I could be part of the process."

"If I have to have you or anybody else in order to be happy, I'll never be happy. And if you have to have me, you'll never be happy. Love don't work that way."

"How does it work? Tell me."

"I can't do this, TD." She turned toward the door.

"You don't choose who you love, Pidge. It just happens."

She stopped. The moon peeked out from behind a cloud for a moment and he saw her profile as she turned and his heart melted. He was on a sandbar in the river of her heart now with no way to get to the shore except stepping into the water. And he had no idea how deep it was or where the current was running.

"What would it take, Pidge?"

"What do you mean?"

"What would it take for you to give me a chance at your heart?"

He let the words float there between them and made a promise that he wouldn't say another thing until she spoke. He'd let what he said be the last thing he said to her in his life until she answered.

Pidge looked at the sky as if she were making an inventory of the stars. Finally she spoke.

"How about you bring me a piece of the moon?"

He remembered the song from the jukebox and all the times he'd heard it. He stared at her in the soft light, the crickets and frogs in symphony. Lightning bugs rose like a conductor's baton around them and the world felt alive. He didn't understand all she meant by the words, but they were enough to give him hope.

"A'ight, Pidge. I'll figure it out. I'll get you a piece of the moon."

CHAPTER 13

Waite awoke to a jangling by his bedside. The room was pitch-black except for the glowing hands on the Big Ben alarm clock, both pointed straight at the three. His internal timepiece was precise and he had awakened before the alarm just about every day since he started the morning show at Country 16. He picked up the phone.

"Waite, have you heard what's on your radio station?"

Waite cleared his throat. "Who in the world is this?"

"Art Palermo."

"Hey, Deputy. No, tell me."

"Nothing. Dead air. We got a call about it."

"All right, let me call over there."

"I've dialed the number. It just rings. I can drive out there but thought I'd call you first."

"I can be there in fifteen. Possum might have nodded off."

"Has that happened before?"

"Yeah, if he ran out of coffee."

"Let me know what you find out."

Waite had his pants and shirt laid out on the reading chair in the corner. At the foot of the chair were his shoes, with rolled-up socks stuck inside one of them. He'd begun the ritual to avoid waking his wife. After she died, he didn't see a reason to change. It gave him a measure of comfort to keep the light off and avoid looking at the empty side of the bed.

He walked out of the room fully dressed, except for his shoes and socks, which he carried. A door opened and the hall light went on and there was Wally in his boxers. How pasty white could a man get?

"Is something wrong?" Wally said, mumbling.

"Station's off the air. I'm guessing Possum fell asleep."

"You want me to go with you?"

"No, go back to sleep. I'll see you later."

Waite turned on the front porch light and walked barefoot around Wally's bicycle to the truck and wiped tiny gravel from his feet when he got in. He bounced down the rutted driveway and flipped on the radio. The FM had a clear signal. The transmitter was working, but there was no music. He turned the volume up, with the knowledge that if a song started, it would blow his speakers. There was a faint ticking sound, the UPI machine clacking in the distance. Possum must have left the control room door open.

He mashed the accelerator and didn't slow when he reached the light, which stayed green. He pulled in at 3:25, feeling justified for speeding because the deputy had awakened him. He hoped Possum would jolt awake and get to work so Waite could get donuts and coffee.

The station's front door was locked tight, as it should have been. He banged on the glass. A light blinked on the phone at Ardelle's desk. The control room door was open about a foot. No sign of Possum. The on-air light was lit above the open door.

"Possum, if you're asleep in there . . . ," Waite muttered, pulling out his keys and unlocking the door.

The next few moments were surreal. For reasons Waite couldn't explain to the deputy later, the first thing he did was answer the phone at the front desk. On the other end was Psycho Sally talking fast and asking what had happened.

"One minute he was talking and the next he just stopped," Sally said. "And then I heard gasping. And then a crash."

"Sally, call back later." Waite hung up.

"Possum?" he called from across the room, knowing his voice would be heard through the open microphone.

He hurried to the control room, pushed back the door, and all the air left his lungs.

"Lord, help us," Waite said.

Possum lay sprawled on his back with bits and pieces of wooden chair underneath him. His face ashen, his mouth gaped, and when Waite saw him, adrenaline kicked in. He felt Possum's neck and knew by the warmth there was hope.

He had brought a local paramedic onto the morning show the summer before who gave lessons in the Heimlich as well as CPR. TD said it was for TV, not radio. Waite began chest compressions and remembered the microphone was on.

"Sally, if you can hear me—or anybody—call the sheriff. We need an ambulance right now at Country 16 on County Line Road."

He pinched Possum's nose and blew hard into his mouth, then moved back to pumping his chest. He caught sight of the record cued up on the turntable. *Possum's last song.* He flipped off the microphone and hit the switch for the record. An acoustic guitar strum shattered the silence and Waite kept time to Eddie Rabbit's "Drivin' My Life Away."

"Come on, Possum," Waite said. "Hang on."

He was nearly out of steam when the paramedics arrived. They took over and got a pulse and it took the two paramedics, four firefighters, and Waite to roll Possum onto the gurney.

"Is there anybody we should contact?" Deputy Palermo said when he arrived.

Waite bit his lip. "He's got a sister in Tennessee, I believe. I don't know how to get hold of her. Maybe he'll come to."

"It doesn't look good, Waite."

Waite stared at broken bits of chair on the floor. "I tried to encourage him to take better care of himself. But at the same time I brought him crullers and éclairs from Mel's."

"I'm sure he doesn't blame you."

Dog-tired from finishing Possum's shift and doing the morning show, Waite drove to Clarkston Medical Center in the late morning. A doctor came to the waiting area and told him Possum's condition was critical.

"He's had a massive heart attack. Probably shouldn't have made it. But we're trying to get him stable enough for surgery. I'd prepare for the worst."

Waite thanked the man as TD stepped off the elevator. Waite brought him up to speed.

"What are you going to do about overnights?"

"I'll find somebody. In the interim I was thinking maybe you'd be available."

"And give up the morning show?"

"You'd get more hours. Might pave the way to full-time."

"Midnight to six pretty much wipes you out."

"If The Kid were further along, I'd have him do it," Waite said.

"Waite, he can't talk. How's he going to do an air shift?"

"He's been at the station every day. Fastest learner I've ever seen, except for one."

"Who's that?"

"I'll give you a hint. Wally's sleeping in her room."

TD nodded.

"Just plan on doing overnight the rest of the week, okay?"

After TD left, Pastor Billy Gentry walked out of a room down the hall and sat by Waite. Reverend Gentry had a live Sunday morning preaching program on Country 16. He was a tall, stocky man who leaned forward like a downhill skier. He had a neatly trimmed beard and thick eyebrows that looked like fast-growing ivy. His cheeks and double chin fluttered when he talked, and he worked the microphone too closely and popped his *p*'s. He wore a navy blazer when he preached and stood with a Bible in front of him, his rich, baritone voice booming on the radio.

His wife, Betty, accompanied him to the station each Sunday and stood behind him strumming her six-string Silvertone, which she carried like a cross. Pastor Gentry invited listeners to attend Sunday services while Betty strummed three chords in no particular order. Her closer was always "Leaning on the Everlasting Arms," which she sang in a high-pitched twang that sounded a little like Tammy Wynette and a lot like George Jones.

Waite knew from experience that the man had a good heart. He'd observed it in the man's sermons through the years, but it wasn't until the pastor had come alongside him during a personal storm and had given comfort that Waite realized the man's depth. He liked to think that experience had enabled him to do the same for others. It almost made the storm worth it, but not quite.

The big man put a meaty hand on Waite's shoulder. "I'm sorry to hear about Possum and I want you to know we've got our prayer team working overtime."

"I appreciate it, Pastor. I know Possum does, too."

"Do you know if he's a believer?"

"I asked about that when I hired him. He wasn't ashamed to say he knew Jesus. Because of his weight, he stopped going to church. He broke a pew once and offered to pay for it as his tithe, but the church said they'd use insurance. He never went back."

"A lot of people feel self-conscious about one thing or another."

Waite nodded. "I think his weight has kept him from other people. But on the radio he can be himself. The station is kind of his church."

"Well, I'm praying we celebrate his recovery instead of conducting a funeral."

"You and me both. Did you come to see Possum?"

"Him and Pastor Gardner, just down the hall." He looked at his watch. "Before I go, I've always wondered about something."

"What's that?"

"I appreciate your Sunday program. But the rest of the week you play drinking and cheating songs. Isn't that kind of like dancing with the devil?"

Years earlier, Waite would have argued with the man and mentioned the fact that preaching on the Sunday program was a bit of a dance, as well. Now, in a fog of fatigue, he paused in thought. Finally he said, "Pastor, you're called to shepherd your sheep. I'm called to a different flock. These are people who get up and put one foot in front of the other and try to make sense of all the bad in their lives. I'm just blooming where I'm planted."

"I hear you." The pastor smiled. "I apologize if I came on too strong. I wonder what would happen if you did *Waite, on the Lord* full-time?"

"Wall-to-wall gospel? My wife and I had long conversations about that."

"Maybe the Lord will turn the honky-tonk into a beacon of hope."

"And maybe he already has."

The man put his hand on Waite's shoulder again. "I'm praying for you and for Possum."

When Pastor Gentry left, Waite walked toward Robby Gardner's room and peeked around the corner. He'd been moved from intensive care since Waite had last seen him. Robby's face was still bandaged and he looked like a mummy.

"You up for company?" Waite said softly from the door.

Robby spoke through missing teeth. "Sure thing, Mr. Evers. What brings you here?"

Waite told him about Possum.

"I'm sorry to hear about that. I'll be praying for him."

"Thank you. How's your family?"

Robby looked away. "It's hard on Sharon. This whole thing is hard."

"It looks like you're on the mend," Waite said cheerfully.

"Is that what it looks like?"

"You've got a bunch of good people behind you. There are better days ahead."

"I hope you're right. Thank you for what you and TD did. I couldn't believe it when I saw him in that cave."

"He told me the two of you drifted apart a while ago."

"It wasn't a drift—it was a clean break."

"If you don't mind me asking, what happened?"

"He didn't tell you?"

"No. He just said things went south when you came to faith."

"Yeah, that's true. Maybe it's better if he told you. I been praying for that old boy for a long time. Ever since . . . well, for a while."

The phone rang. Waite grabbed it and handed it to Robby, who answered. Then he paused. "Who did you say this is?"

Waite waved and stepped out, wandering toward the waiting room. He poured himself a cup of coffee and returned as Robby finished the call.

"That's about the strangest conversation I've ever had," Robby said.

"Who was it?"

"Milton Quidley."

Waite raised his eyebrows. "What did he want?"

"He said he wanted to check on how I was doing. But I don't think that's why he called."

"Why not?"

"He asked about my condition and said he was glad I was alive and asked about Sharon and the kids and blah, blah, blah. Before he hung up, he acted like something had slipped his mind. That's when he said he had a Bible question. Now why would Milton Quidley call me about a Bible question while I'm in the hospital?"

"Maybe he doesn't want to ask his daddy. From what I can tell, the two of them are like oil and water."

"That sounds about right."

"If you don't mind me asking, what question did he have?"

"Acid reflux."

"Excuse me?"

"He wanted to know if there was anything in the Bible about acid reflux."

"Where in the world did that come from?"

"Beats me. And why would he ask . . . ?" Robby glanced up at Waite.

"What is it?"

"You won't tell my wife about this, right?"

"I don't have a reason to, do I?"

"It's just that I got the feeling this might have something to do with Gideon."

"You mean the treasure?"

"Yeah. And when I couldn't come up with an answer, Milton kind of laughed and said he was sorry to bother me. Then he hung up."

"Curious," Waite said.

"Acid reflux," Robby said. "What in the world?"

Late in the afternoon, TD drove by Country 16 and sat in the upper parking lot until Waite and Wally came out.

Waite noticed TD and came to his truck. "I thought you'd be home sawing logs."

"I tried to take a nap," TD said. "Decided to get on the road and see if I could get a tow or two."

"Wally and I are going to grab a burger. You want to join us?"

"I already ate, but thanks. Any word on Possum?"

"Talked with a nurse. There's no change. I guess that's good news."

"I hope he pulls through."

"I have news about Robby Gardner. I saw him at the hospital in Clarkston."

"How's he doing?"

"Better than Possum. He's still wrapped up like a mummy, though." Waite told TD about the phone call from Milton Quidley.

TD thought a minute. "Junior asked that? I thought he wanted to stop talking about treasure clues. What was it again?"

"Acid reflux. It's where the stomach acid comes back up the pipe."

"Yeah, my uncle had that. They gave him medication that made it worse."

"I've been thinking about it since Robby told me. First thing that came to me was the fish that spit Jonah up on dry land."

TD laughed. "God's acid reflux. Is there a Nineveh, West Virginia?"

Waite shook his head. "Then I thought about Paul saying to Timothy to take a little wine for his stomach. I don't know. It's all conjecture."

"Waite, why would Milton Quidley call up a fellow as bad off as Robby and ask that? There's got to be a reason."

"Well, we might never know."

CHAPTER 14

THOUGH HE TRIED, TD couldn't get the words *acid reflux* out of his mind the whole evening. He tried to recall any notes Robby had penned about gastric distress, to no avail.

A summer drizzle saturated the hills and a heavy creosote smell hung in the air. TD rolled down his window and let the wet air blow through the cab of his truck as he pulled his wrecker onto the state route and flipped the radio on.

As Hank Williams finished "I'm So Lonesome I Could Cry," DeeJay Bailey said, "Sometimes lonesome is all you have to keep you company. Hank Williams on Country 16. Good evening, drive carefully on the wet roads tonight. And here's Tammy Wynette on the best country in the country."

Tammy sang, *"Sometimes it's hard to be a woman."*

"Yes, it is," TD said out loud to the radio. "And it's hard to be a man who loves a woman, too."

The beating of the windshield wipers lulled him and Tammy Wynette's slow ballad didn't help. How would he stay awake all night? Maybe drive to the truck stop for a gallon of coffee.

Yellow lights lit the wet pavement as TD rounded a curve. A car had pulled off the road on the opposite side with its flashers on. TD slowed and saw a burly man with a flashlight by the road.

"Need some help?" TD said. He didn't recognize the man.

"The old guy drove into the woods," Burly said. "Looks bad."

TD saw lights angled toward the treetop and steam rising, but he couldn't see the vehicle because of the brush.

"What in the world happened?" he muttered. He parked nose to nose with the man's car and turned on his wrecker lights. TD flipped his CB to channel 19. There was no one at dispatch this time of night, but somebody at the truck stop would be listening. Two truckers were going back and forth about road conditions. He waited for static, then clicked the mic.

"Break 1-9."

"Go ahead break."

He reached the truck stop, told them his location and to call the sheriff. He wasn't sure whether they needed an ambulance, but better safe than sorry.

When he finished, Burly approached, waving his flashlight as he walked the uneven ground. "I couldn't get back in there."

"You think he's drunk?"

"Don't know. I came around the curve and saw his truck accelerate into the brush and it slammed into that tree."

"Is he alive?"

The man shrugged.

"I got hold of the truck stop. They're calling the sheriff."

"That's quick thinking."

TD got his flashlight. "I'll see if I can make it through."

"I don't think you will, but good luck."

"You leaving?"

"Yeah. You look like you have this under control."

"Suit yourself," TD said. Some people.

He walked straight into the tangle of briars and vines that had been crushed by the vehicle. When he stepped on top, his feet sank and it was easier to move through the untouched areas. He heard groaning and whimpering.

"I'm coming, mister! Hang on."

From an early age, TD had been scared of snakes. His father had told him that if he didn't bother them, they wouldn't bother him. But stepping on the middle of a copperhead when you couldn't see it was a thought that came to him now and he wouldn't have blamed a snake for raring up and biting him in the leg. Despite this, he willed himself forward through the brush. It was like wading into the ocean against tall waves.

The overgrowth thinned a little, and TD spotted the truck's taillights. He pointed his flashlight and saw *CHE* and knew it was a Chevrolet. Now it was step by step, just trying to free himself from the briars so he could move farther. He wished he'd put on his gloves but there was no turning back now.

"Can't breathe!" the man yelled from the truck.

"Almost there, mister!" TD yelled.

"Help me!"

How would paramedics get back here? And why had the man gone so far into the brush? He had to have sped up once he got off the road. Mashed his foot onto the accelerator rather than the brake, probably.

TD heard the engine hiss, the radiator no doubt mangled by the impact. He pointed the flashlight to the rear of the truck and saw it was a C10. Pretty thing, but old. Pennsylvania license plate.

That made sense. The fellow wasn't familiar with the winding roads around here.

Seeing movement in the undergrowth, TD felt something wet on his arm and he jumped. A dog, licking at his hand, nervous. Where had he come from?

He pointed the flashlight at the back window of the truck and saw a sight he would never forget. Man and nature in perfect disharmony.

A deer was sprawled on the hood of the vehicle, its head through the windshield. One antler was outside the truck and stretched across the roof, almost to the back window. Huge buck. He'd never seen one that big. His body had bowed the hood. When he reached the driver's-side window, he saw where the other antler was. It had gone around and through the steering wheel and several points were lodged deep in the driver's chest. He'd seen a lot of things in his day but never anything like this.

The dog whimpered beside TD, putting his paws up on him like he was praying. The deer didn't move. The impact had probably broken its neck.

The driver panted, his tongue out, gasping. Blood from the deer on his chest. Or maybe it was his own blood. TD couldn't tell.

"You're going to be all right," TD said, trying to calm the man. "We got you now. Help's on the way."

The man's eyes darted. He tried to say something but couldn't.

"Don't talk, just relax."

TD studied his face. Pale as a ghost. A day's growth of beard. There was something familiar about him.

TD tried to ignore his revulsion at the sight, just put it in some back drawer of his mind. He gently put a hand on the man's shoulder. "Mister, there's an ambulance on the way. You hang in there. Just stay still."

More panting. A trickle of blood ran down the man's chin and dripped. "He jumped out at me."

"Yes, sir. There was nothing you could do."

"Jubal."

"What's that?"

The dog put his paws on the door and whimpered. TD looked at the name tag.

"He's right here, mister. He's doing all right."

"I came here . . . to help that pastor. Pay his hospital bills."

"What? You talking about Robby Gardner?"

The man swallowed hard. "Yes. He was looking for my treasure."

It clicked with TD. Like a flash of lightning.

"Mr. Quidley?"

"I need you to tell my son . . ." He gasped.

"Tell him what?" TD said.

The man grabbed TD's arm tight, pulling so hard it surprised him. TD leaned in and so close he could smell the man's breath. He could see the deer's antler disappear where the fellow's left lung probably was, from what he knew about human anatomy.

A gurgle now. A rattle. He was no doctor, but blood in the mouth and that sound coming from the man's chest made TD think this was it. And it made him think of another time when he'd heard something similar.

TD shook the memory away. "What do you want to tell your son?"

The man's breathing became shallow. More blood from his mouth. TD wiped it with a hand. Quidley's eyes were fully open, a blank stare. TD bowed his head and closed his eyes.

A hand on his arm. He nearly jumped into the tree. He looked into the man's eyes, now full of life.

141

"I need to ask you something," Quidley said.

"Sure, Mr. Quidley."

"Do you know the Lord, son?"

"Mr. Quidley, hang on. We can talk about that later."

"No. I need to know."

TD didn't know what to say or do. Where was the ambulance? How long would it take?

The man opened his mouth again but before he could speak, hooves and antlers and glass flew everywhere. TD fell back as the dog barked and the deer pulled free from the truck and rolled off the crumpled hood, scampering into the briars and bramble, the dog chasing it, barking.

TD recovered and opened the door. Gideon Quidley was held tight by the seat belt, but his head lolled forward and the trickle of blood had become a gush. TD put his hand over the man's chest and pushed as hard as he could.

"Hang in there, Mr. Quidley."

CHAPTER 15

Waite took a deep breath as the song faded about God, green apples, and Indianapolis. He turned his head. "You ready?"

TD nodded.

"Eddy Arnold on Country 16, the best country in the country. If you're just waking up and you haven't heard the big news, boy, we have some. Last night there was an auto accident near Emmaus. Our own TD Lovett was on the scene and he's here to give us a report. TD, you've had a long night."

"That's true, Waite. And I could use some sleep, but I'm so keyed up right now I doubt I'd be able to."

"Because of Possum's illness, I asked TD to do the overnight. But the accident threw a wrench into that."

"And a few briars and poison ivy too."

143

"There are lots of accidents. You tow lots of cars. This one was different."

"Yes, sir. That's because the Chevy truck I pulled out of the bramble last night belonged to Gideon Quidley. And he was in it."

"Tell us what happened. It was a deer vs. truck accident, right?"

"That's right. My guess is that Mr. Quidley tried to avoid the deer when it jumped out but instead of hitting the brake, he hit the accelerator and that took him off the road quite a ways."

"I contacted the hospital a half hour ago, but we don't have word on his condition. As far as you could tell, he was alive when the ambulance left?"

"He was talking to me throughout the whole ordeal, at least he was trying to. He was having trouble breathing because of his injuries."

"How did you get hold of the sheriff and the ambulance?"

"Same way I alerted you, Waite. I used the CB and got hold of Mountain Mama's Gas 'n' Go. And I want to thank them for their help. They called for the ambulance. So a big shout-out to them this morning."

"They're one of our sponsors, of course, so thank you, Barbara and Karl, the owners there, and you folks be sure and thank the whole crew when you fuel up next time. So Gideon ran off the road and into a tree. I don't want to be too graphic, but the deer came through the windshield as I understand it, and one of the antlers . . ."

"*Impaled* is the word, Waite."

"Well, I was trying not to say that."

"Sorry."

"Let's say it this way: The deer antlers were holding him in place. Is that fair?"

"Yes, sir. One of them was. And the way it was sticking him

made me think he needed to stay put until the paramedics got there. I responded to an accident once where a piece of metal came off a truck on the interstate and came through a windshield and went right through—"

"Hold up there, TD. I think we get the picture."

"Well, what I was going to say was, they had to cut the piece of steel off in the front and back of the driver and take him to the hospital that way. They couldn't pull it out or he might have bled to death. That was all I was going to say."

"All right. So the deer wasn't moving."

"No, sir. Lifeless. Just glassy-eyed. But it turns out he was just stunned. That was some animal, Waite. I didn't count the points, but he was majestic."

"So when the deer woke up . . ."

"He jerked awake and pulled his head out of that windshield and glass went all over creation. You know how it crackles into little pieces. I fell back as it thrashed around and the dog started barking."

"What dog is that?"

"I believe Gideon brought him along. He's here at the station laying down by Ardelle's feet right now."

Waite saw the phone light but he ignored it. The interview was a no-brainer. He didn't care what Boyd or Milton Quidley thought. And he didn't care if it got him fired. This was something God had dropped into their laps.

"What happened next, TD?"

"Well, I had a buddy who fought in Vietnam and he told me a story about treating a friend with a sucking chest wound. I hope that's not too graphic."

"If it is, it's too late. Go ahead."

"I thought of that story, so I took off my T-shirt and made a compress and put pressure on the wound. And then I figured I ought to get Gideon to the road for the ambulance, but the bleeding was so bad I knew I had to stay."

"Your heart must have been beating out of your chest."

"You got that right, Waite. I was concerned, but we got through it."

"Now tell us what Gideon said to you."

"Well, he tried talking, but it was a struggle. And I don't think I ought to share too much. He was gurgling a lot. Is that too graphic?"

"You're fine, TD. Did he say why he was in this area?"

"Well, I wasn't conducting an interview. I was trying to keep him alive. Except he did say one thing that I'm not sure I should divulge."

Waite saw movement in the window outside the control room. At first he thought Ardelle was pointing to the phone. Then in front of the window came a man with a camera on his shoulder and a bright light that made TD put up a hand to shield his eyes.

"It looks like we have company at the station. I'm going to let TD catch his breath. You're listening to the best country in the country. I'm Waite Evers and this is Country 16."

He hit the stopset and a commercial for Mountain Mama's Gas 'n' Go played. As soon as the on-air light went off, the door opened and a reporter clambered in holding a microphone with the Channel 8 logo. The station was a CBS affiliate, an hour's drive from Emmaus.

"Kathryn Stringfellow, TV-8 news," the woman said in an official-sounding voice.

"Hold up," Waite said. "If you want to record from out there, that's okay. You can't be in here."

Kathryn gave a quizzical stare. "This will be great publicity for your station. This is going to be national news."

"Maybe so, but this is not a press conference. I'm talking to a friend of mine. Just stay out there, if you don't mind."

Kathryn didn't back down. "I have to get this story. My news director woke me out of a sound sleep and told me to get over here."

"Well, I'm sorry you didn't get the sleep you wanted, but you can stay out there."

"We can't hear you clearly."

"I'll get Ardelle to turn up the speaker."

Waite rose and moved to the door, but the woman stood her ground. She was wearing a pleated pantsuit and silk blouse along with enough lipstick to paint double lines on the county road. The ozone layer had taken a hit from her hair spray, it looked like.

"My spots are ending, ma'am. I need to close the door."

"This is not fair. You can't keep this information from the public."

"I'm not trying to. TD will talk with you after the interview. Right, TD?"

TD looked shell-shocked. His face had gone white. "Sure. I guess so."

The commercial ended and there was dead air. Waite glared at her and Kathryn stepped back. He closed the door and locked it as Ardelle turned up the speaker on the lobby wall.

Waite sat and keyed his mic, quickly giving the weather, which was hot and muggy with a chance of showers. Reading words on the page settled him. He turned to TD and noticed several new faces in the lobby. The Kid was by Ardelle's desk, smiling, the dog pawing at his chest.

"Let's get back now to TD Lovett and his encounter with Gideon Quidley at the accident last night near Emmaus. TD, did the paramedics say anything about him?"

"They told me I did a good job keeping pressure on the wound. They were pretty focused trying to get him through the brush and off to the hospital. They had an oxygen mask on him when they drove away."

Waite took a breath, following his radio dictum "Think like a listener." What did the listener want to know at that moment? The biggest question didn't concern Gideon's health.

"There's no doubt Gideon's presence here brings up questions. You've believed from the beginning the treasure was a hoax. Did he say anything to make you change your mind?"

TD paused and Waite sensed listeners leaning in to hear the answer. That's what people did on the other side of the double-paned glass. From the corner of his eye he saw The Kid moving toward the production room, the dog following closely. Waite winked at him and nodded.

"I'm not going to get into everything he said, but . . ."

There were times when Waite could feel something happening on the air. There was a special magic to a conversation or a song. This was one of those times.

"But what?"

"He was able to say that he wanted to take care of Robby Gardner's bills. He evidently heard about his accident. And I got one more thing to say. I know there are people who will hear this and think about nothing but the treasure. I want to say that right now this is not about a treasure. It's about a man's life."

"Well said, TD. I want to encourage everybody listening right now to lift up Gideon and pray for his recovery." Waite flipped the switch to the first turntable. "Time for a little music. Here's Tom T. Hall and 'Sneaky Snake' on the best country in the country, Country 16."

Waite took off his headphones and turned to look at the gaggle of people in the next room. It was starting to look like a convention. TD looked to be in a daze.

"You okay?" Waite said.

"I'm thinking about the trouble I've just caused."

"You mean with Milton and Boyd?"

TD nodded.

"I don't see how they can fault us. It's like having the *Hindenburg* crash in your backyard and being criticized for screaming, 'Oh, the humanity.'"

Someone knocked hard on the control room door and Waite heard the reporter's authoritative voice.

"You want me to unlock it?" TD said.

"No, let 'em simmer," Waite said, cueing up the next song.

TD looked at the bloodstains on his shirt and pants. "Do you think everything happens for a reason? A deer jumping in front of Quidley—is that part of the plan? Or is it coincidence?"

"That's a theology question. You sure you want an answer?"

"I asked, didn't I?"

Waite thought a minute. "You're really asking if there's a God. And if there is, is he in control? Does he make things happen or just wind the world up and let it go?"

"I reckon that's what I want to know. Does he make a deer jump in front of a moving vehicle or was that chance?"

"And was it chance that you showed up?"

"Right."

Another knock at the door. A deeper voice than the reporter this time, telling them to open up.

"You don't have to talk to these people if you don't want to," Waite said.

"I'll have to wade through them to tow Quidley's truck to the impound."

TD opened the door and the TV reporter shoved the microphone in front of him. The person with the deep voice was actually Art Palermo and he took TD by the arm.

"He said he would answer our questions," the reporter said.

Across the lobby, the front door opened and a tall man with a thumb-like head entered.

"Oh, for crying out loud," Waite muttered under his breath.

"I want that man arrested," Milton Quidley shouted.

The cameraman got the whole thing.

CHAPTER 16

TD SAT ALONE IN A SMALL ROOM at the sheriff's office drinking tepid black coffee from a Styrofoam cup. He wasn't in handcuffs, but the feeling was the same. He'd thought Art Palermo needed Gideon Quidley's truck towed pronto, but he'd been shown directly to the cruiser and put in the back.

TD thought of Waite. Milton Quidley would come down hard on him. He regretted going on the air to tell the story. It had seemed like a good idea.

Art Palermo had been quiet on the drive, almost sullen. TD asked about Gideon's condition but Palermo just looked in the rearview. Did they think TD had something to do with the accident?

Now Palermo entered the conference room and leaned against the wall. Another tall man in uniform entered. TD had seen his face on signs at election time. *Frank Franklin for Sheriff.* He was older, with touches of gray. He walked like he was trying to put pressure on the floor, to teach it who was boss, and he wore a grim, pensive look. He held a manila folder in front of him and sat across from TD and plopped it on the table.

"It's Titus, right?"

"Yes, sir. People call me TD."

A slight nod. "Art tells me you were the first on the scene, Titus. Why don't we back up? Tell us the whole thing."

"What whole thing?"

"What happened out there last night?"

"Well, I sure don't have anything to hide."

"Evidenced by the fact you went on the radio this morning."

TD swallowed hard. "Is that a problem?"

"It might be, depending on how this shakes out."

TD furrowed his brow. "Waite and I are friends. We talk about everything whether the mic is on or off. And nobody said I couldn't talk about the accident." He looked at Palermo and back to the bigger man. He'd always had a good relationship with law enforcement. Always respected them. "Am I under arrest for something?"

"We're asking questions, Titus. Trying to figure out what happened. Let's start at the beginning."

That sounded plausible, so TD relaxed a little. "All right. I was getting ready to do the overnight at Country 16, taking Possum's shift—"

"No," Franklin said, interrupting. "Why don't we go back even further."

"What do you mean? Earlier in the day?"

"Go back to the box of stuff you took from the church office." Franklin stared a hole through him.

CHRIS FABRY

"What's that got to do with the accident?"

"You tell us, Titus. You seem awful hot to trot about that treasure."

TD frowned. "You don't know me very well, then. Only reason I took the box was to find Robby. Which we did." He glanced at Palermo. "And I didn't take the box—Robby's wife gave it to me. She said you all weren't interested."

"Where is it now?"

TD cocked his head. "I don't understand. Are you accusing me of something?"

"Answer the question, TD," Palermo said.

"I'm keeping it till Robby gets out of the hospital. If he wants it, I'll give it back. He and his wife are at odds over all of this."

"So you're keeping it at your house?" Franklin said.

"That's none of your business."

Franklin nodded at Palermo and Art left the room.

"I am being arrested," TD said.

Franklin glanced at the window, then back at TD. "Titus, why don't you want to cooperate with us?"

"Who is *us*?"

"Art and me. We're trying to figure out what really happened last night."

"You know what happened. The paramedics can tell you. Gideon will tell you. Ask him."

"The paramedics told us they found you with blood all over you and a man with chest wounds."

"I was helping. He would have bled to death if I hadn't."

"Did you have a little conversation with him before he got those chest wounds?"

"What? He hit a deer and its antlers stuck in his chest."

"Yeah, see, the problem with that is, we didn't find any dead

153

deer. Or deer blood. Or deer tracks. Or antlers. Or anything like that. No skid marks on the pavement."

"The deer ran away. He was stunned, I guess, and then woke up and took off. Take a look at his windshield and there will be deer hide and blood in there. I guarantee it."

"That kind of thing can be planted, Titus. Come on. What really happened?"

"I told you."

"You've been studying the clues. You were following old man Quidley. And you ran him off the road."

"What? That's crazy. I didn't even know it was him out there."

"It's pretty convenient that only you saw the accident. Is there anything else you want to say about that?"

"I wasn't there when it happened. I came upon it."

"And what about the other vehicle? We know you weren't working alone. Tell me about the other car."

TD looked at his hands, picking at the Styrofoam cup. "There was a fellow with his flashers on by the side of the road. I stopped and he told me he saw the truck shoot over into the brush."

"That's not what you said on the radio."

"I left that part out. The fellow took off."

"Mm-hmm."

"That's the truth."

"And you didn't get his name. License plate. Just a stranger who happened by? Is that what you want us to believe?"

TD put the cup down. His stomach knotted. "I was focused on whoever was in the truck. Look, ask Gideon. He'll tell you." TD was ready to stand up and leave. Or call Waite to get him a lawyer.

"There's a lot of inconsistency in your story, Titus. But let's do this. Why don't we focus on what Gideon said to you. How about that?"

"I'll tell you the same thing I told Waite. He said he wanted to help out Robby and his family. To take care of his bills."

"Mmmm."

"Gideon was having a hard time breathing."

"I'll bet he was after you got through with him."

"What's that supposed to mean?"

"Keep going."

"I tried to get him to settle down, relax, and breathe normal."

"You were just helping him out."

"Exactly. Told him to hang in there, the ambulance was on the way. See, that's the other thing about what you're saying—if I had run him off the road, why would I call an ambulance? Why would I try to save his life? That makes no sense. I would have just left him there."

"Maybe you knew he wouldn't make it," Franklin said. "Maybe you were surprised he was still breathing when the paramedics got there and that's when he got the chest wounds. Pretending you were helping would cover your tracks, wouldn't it?"

"I didn't cover any tracks."

Franklin nodded. "I guess it could be like you've said. Maybe you're the Good Samaritan. Just being neighborly."

"That's exactly what I was being."

"All right. What else did Mr. Quidley say?"

TD thought a moment. "He wanted to know about his dog. I guess he brought it with him. And he mentioned his son."

"All right, what about his son?"

"He wanted me to tell him something. Seemed important to him."

"And what was that?"

"He never got to it. The deer jumped. From there on I was pressing down on his wounds to keep him from bleeding out."

Sheriff Franklin stared at the table.

"Can I go now? I need to bring his truck over here and then get some rest. I've been up all night."

Franklin took off his glasses and cleaned them with his handkerchief, then put them back on. "You know what I think, Titus? I think you planned this. And I got to hand it to you. The whole thing was pretty ingenious. You and the pastor—who's a friend of yours, right? You grew up together? The two of you come up with a scheme all these years later?"

"I haven't spoken with Robby since high school."

"Really? So a pastor goes off on a treasure hunt and gets hurt. You show up and sift through a box of notes to solve some Bible mystery. Come on, Titus. You're not *that* smart. You knew where that old boy was. So after a couple of days, to make things look good, you go up there and make a miraculous rescue. Knowing all the while that a pastor getting hurt would play on the heartstrings of somebody like Gideon Quidley, who's not all there, let's be honest. Now, of course your pastor friend didn't plan on being injured that bad, but boy, that made it look good, didn't it? Him being laid up in the hospital. Losing a leg."

"There's not a bit of what you just said that's true. You can ask Gideon Quidley and all of this will be cleared up."

"Did you go fifty-fifty? Was that the deal you worked out?"

"Sheriff, you're barking up the wrong tree."

"And then you waited. You knew old Gideon would hear about that pastor, didn't you? You waited and hired somebody to follow him, that mysterious person along the road with the flashers on. The two of you were going to work on him until you got the information you needed. Run him off the road, rough him up. And when he wouldn't talk, things took a turn. That sounds plausible to me."

"Mister, listen. You're as far from plausible as a body could get."

"Five million is a powerful motivator, Titus. You want that treasure. It's the break you need. You deserve it. You didn't mean to hurt that old man. That wasn't the plan. But accidents happen, right?"

TD stared at him. "You're not looking for the truth. You've made up your mind and you're twisting things. And when you talk with Gideon, you're going to be sorry about all this."

Franklin leaned forward and lowered his voice. "Admit it, Titus. When he wouldn't tell you where the treasure was, you got mad. All he had to do was tell you where it was. And then things escalated. You threatened him. He wouldn't talk. Then you did something you regret. Is that how it happened?"

"I'm going now," TD said, standing.

"Sit down." The man stood and shoved TD into the chair. "Maybe it was this other fellow who attacked him? The one you hired to follow him."

TD thought of the burly man. He'd seemed a little off. And he'd known the person in the truck was an old man. He'd said that to TD. Had he been following Gideon? "I didn't hire nobody."

Franklin crossed his arms. "Does it make you mad the treasure might already be located?"

"It don't make me mad at all."

Franklin lowered his voice almost to a whisper. "When you got mad, did you stab him?"

"I didn't stab nobody. I took my shirt off to make a compress. I was trying to save him."

"So if we go to your house, are we going to find anything you wouldn't want us to see?"

"I got a full laundry hamper. That's about it." TD stood again. "The best way to settle this is talk to Gideon. Just ask him. He'll tell you."

"I doubt that's going to happen, Titus. Gideon's in a coma. They don't think he'll ever regain consciousness."

TD sat hard in the chair.

Someone knocked on the door and Franklin left the room. When he returned, he sat on the table and pushed a yellow legal pad and pen in front of TD.

"You're in a pickle, Titus. Art's over talking with that pastor friend of yours."

"Good. He'll tell you the truth. You're wrong about me."

"I hope so. Here's what I need you to do: Write out your statement. Tell everything that happened. And if you get the notion to tell the truth, write it down."

TD stared at the legal pad.

"One more question," Franklin said. "Does the term *acid reflux* mean anything to you in regard to all of this?"

TD stared at the man, recalling the conversation with Waite. He shook his head. The man left and TD scribbled his story the best he could, thinking of the old man, the fear in his face, and how TD might have been the last person he'd spoken with. He hoped Gideon would recover. But what if he didn't?

As his story leaked onto the page, TD's mind spun. It was in the process of focusing on one thing that another bobbed to the surface. And he realized what Gideon meant with his final clue.

CHAPTER 17

WAITE WATCHED FOR ARDELLE'S SIGNAL, then walked through the crowd in the lobby, straight to the front door, and exited. Wally was advancing up the rickety steps, about to be engulfed in the firestorm that had become Country 16. Wally seemed dumbfounded by the TV truck at the side of the building and the cars parked in both lots.

"I need you to take over for me on the board."

"What's going on, Waite?"

"TD found Quidley earlier this morning."

"Old man Quidley? Are you serious? Where?"

The front door opened and the fellow with the camera rushed out recording. They called it B-roll. Just random shots of movement and action they could cut to in their report. Waite grabbed Wally by the arm and walked around the side of the station through the weeds. Some creature had burrowed into the ground by the concrete slab and left a residue of soil and a hole Waite wanted to crawl into and hide. He knew he couldn't.

Waite hurried to the back entrance, but for once someone had obeyed the sign taped to the other side of the door that said, *Keep locked at all times. No exceptions.* He cursed under his breath, the stress and fear getting the best of him. He apologized to Wally.

"Tough morning, huh?" Wally said.

"The sheriff took TD, so I need to get in touch with him. Milton Quidley came and left. Boyd's been calling. So if you could finish my show, I'll try to get the circus out of here."

"Whatever you need, Waite."

Miraculously, the door opened and Ardelle was there, as if she were telepathic. "Feleena's about to kiss the cowboy. You'd better get in here."

It took him a second to understand what she meant. Ardelle knew the playlist backward and forward, having heard the tunes from childhood. He made it to the board in time to segue from Marty Robbins to Roger Miller. He keyed the mic and said, "Country 16, the best country in the country. Now, from that tragic story in Texas, we hop a train with the 'King of the Road,' on Country 16."

Wally opened the control room door and stashed his brown-bag lunch deep inside the soda machine and closed the door before the group could get to him. Waite slipped through the transmitter room into the hallway and made his way to the lobby. Another TV truck had pulled up and a reporter scribbled notes, leaning as close to Ardelle as he could so he could hear her over the din. He demanded a recording of that morning's program. That was something they never did, but Waite remembered The Kid had rolled tape from the production room.

When they saw him, the group swarmed Waite like piranhas on a warthog that had lost its balance by the river.

"Why was your employee arrested?"

Waite's brow furrowed. "He wasn't arrested."

"Are you sure? The sheriff took him away in his cruiser."

"Do you have an update on Gideon Quidley?"

Waite pushed his way through without saying more. The group followed, his frame casting a hulking shadow on the walls made by the camera light. He closed his office door and pulled the black-and-white TV from the floor, moving the rabbit ears to get a signal. He had brought it to the station during the Watergate hearings and had never taken the TV home. Waite grabbed the channel knob and pushed it in and to the left and suddenly the picture showed a five-day forecast with the low-pressure symbols across the map of West Virginia.

The scene switched to a reporter in front of a hospital. He turned up the volume.

". . . and the doctors haven't released information. All we know is that Gideon Quidley was transported here late last night. He spoke with a tow truck driver who found him at the accident site near Emmaus. And now that driver has been taken into custody. Melanie Waters, TV-8 News. Charlie, back to you."

"Melanie," the news anchor said, "is there any indication what Gideon Quidley might have said before he was taken to the hospital?"

"We're working on getting an answer to that, Charlie. Kathryn Stringfellow is following that angle. We do know from the discussion on Country 16 in Emmaus this morning that the tow truck driver said Gideon Quidley was severely injured but conscious and able to speak."

"All right, Melanie. Stay tuned to TV-8 news for more on this breaking story."

Waite put his elbows on the desk and prayed for wisdom. Maybe he'd been wrong to put TD on the air. Nothing he could do about that now. Then he prayed for Gideon. He was a tough old bird. Surely he'd pull through.

The noise in the other room grew and Waite's phone buzzed. It was Ardelle.

"These reporters won't take no for an answer, Waite. I had to go the production room to get a minute's peace. And the phone won't stop ringing. They want to talk to you."

Waite sighed. "I don't have anything to say."

"Maybe if you told them to set up their cameras in the lower parking lot, I could lock the door after they leave."

"That's not a bad idea, Ardelle. But it wouldn't be right. Just stay in the production room until I figure something out. Where's Quidley's dog?"

"The Kid has him in the storage room. Seems like he's found a friend."

Waite looked out the window at Emmaus Salvage. There was something to be said for the simple life. Caring for other people's junk. He'd felt like he'd put one foot in front of the other after he moved here and took over for Boyd. He felt like the Lord had called him here. Now, with all the losses, he wasn't sure.

Dust rose from the valley and Pidge rolled to a stop in her truck outside. She rolled down her window and waved and Waite hurried out the back door.

"TD called," Pidge said. "He asked me to pick him up at the sheriff's office. Said he called you but there's no answer."

Waite looked at the TV truck. "Mind if I go with you?"

"Hop in."

Waite spotted TD sitting on a stump at the far end of the parking lot at the county courthouse. Pidge gunned the engine and drove to the end of the lot and Waite scooted to the middle.

"Get me out of here," TD said as he climbed in. "I think I'm losing my mind."

"What happened?" Waite said.

TD told them in an avalanche of information what the sheriff accused him of doing, and then he dropped the bomb that Gideon was in a coma and wasn't expected to survive.

Waite sat, slack-jawed, taking in the news. Pidge muttered something under her breath.

After a moment Waite said, "They think you got a deer to jump through his windshield? That makes no sense."

"Something weird's going on, Waite. After I wrote my statement, I called you and couldn't get through—" He leaned forward. "Thank you for coming, Pidge. Anyway, I found a place to wait outside, and guess who walked out of the station and got in his Cadillac and drove away?"

"No," Waite said.

"Yeah, Milton Quidley, in the flesh. He'd been in there, probably behind the glass listening to them accuse me."

"That's creepy," Pidge said.

"Why wasn't he at the hospital with Gideon?" Waite said.

"And another thing. I figured out why Gideon drove down here. I can't believe we missed it."

"What are you talking about?" Waite said.

"Sheriff Franklin went on and on about me planning this and following Gideon. I thought they were going to put me in a jail cell. He went out of the room and when he came back, he told me to write a statement."

"Did you do it?" Waite said.

"Yeah. I told the truth. But here's the squirrely part. Franklin asked if Gideon said anything to me about acid reflux."

"Same as he asked Robby."

"Exactly. So you know where the question came from."

"What are you two talking about?" Pidge said.

"Milton called Robby and asked if there's anywhere in the Bible that talks about acid reflux," TD said. "So as I'm writing, I can't stop thinking about it. And finally it came to me. What happens when you get acid reflux?"

"You get sick to your stomach," Waite said.

"Right, but what do people complain about?"

"Heartburn," Pidge said.

"Bingo. Now where in the Bible does it talk about that? And remember the clue *where it all began*."

"I don't know where you're going with this, TD," Waite said.

"You're the *Waite, on the Lord* guy and you don't know this?"

"Heartburn," Waite said, mulling the word. He said it slower, separating the words. Then he said, "'Didn't our hearts burn within us?'"

"There you go."

"I don't understand a thing you're saying," Pidge said.

"After the resurrection," TD said, "there were two disciples on the road. Jesus comes up and walks beside them, but they don't know who he is. And he acts like he doesn't know what just happened. The crucifixion and everything. By the time they recognize him, he disappears. Poof, just like that."

"How do you know all that?" Pidge said.

"Learned it as a kid."

"And what does that have to do with Gideon Quidley?" Pidge said.

"The disciples looked at each other and said, 'Didn't our hearts burn within us?' Heartburn. And they took off lickety-split to tell the others."

Silence in the truck. Then Pidge said, "Where were the disciples headed?"

Waite looked at TD and nodded.

"The town of Emmaus," TD said.

PART 3

CHAPTER 18

From his perch at Country 16, Waite observed how the news about Gideon Quidley's presence in Emmaus sent residents into a tizzy. Waite and TD didn't reveal what they believed about the treasure on the morning show, but there was electricity to each day following Gideon's hospitalization. Phone lines lit with people who wanted to talk about him, the treasure, and the clues. And there was consternation that if Gideon slipped the surly bonds, the man's will would lead his son, Milton, to the location.

In response, the town turned to divine help. As Waite drove to work, he saw lit signs in front of every church he passed that said, *Pray for Gideon.*

On the Sunday morning broadcast, Pastor Gentry encouraged listeners to "lift up our brother's situation to the Great Physician."

A prayer vigil was held at the United Methodist Church, which had the largest seating capacity and the most comfortable cushioned pews in town. The meeting brought together all theological stripes. Baptists sat beside Nazarenes and Pentecostals. Staid Presbyterians who prayed with heads bowed and eyes closed in a posture of reverent entreaty prayed next to members of the Holiness persuasion who lifted hands and pointed faces upward in rapturous, noisy intercession. These seemed moved by an unseen force, swaying and filling the aisles, as if it might give them a better angle for answers. Others seemed planted, a bit nervous about the emotion and commotion of the gathering. That which is foreign is often feared, especially when it comes to prayer.

Waite also noted the fervent prayer for Gideon was matched by a general disregard for biblical clues and more of a frantic search-and-destroy effort. Residents dug in backyards and combed through barn lofts and cornfields with abandon. Farmers put up No Trespassing signs along fence lines. Late one night, someone took a backhoe to the home end zone of the Emmaus High football field and damaged the turf.

Waite did his best to keep putting one foot in front of the other. And with all the confusion and furor in the town, he focused his energy on The Kid. Waite lived by the dictum that all most people needed was a little encouragement and about half as much criticism in order to succeed. He heaped encouragement on The Kid like it was fertilizer, but at times gave gentle correction. He noticed that even though The Kid was slow of speech, he liked words. This came from observations he made when The Kid would jot things down in a ratty spiral notebook he carried.

Waite gave him the assignment of writing a thirty-second announcement for Elaine's on Main Street. Elaine had advertised for years and Waite was confident The Kid could write the live spots they needed. He'd fully intended to edit The Kid's work, but he'd forgotten.

After the morning show, Waite called The Kid into the production room. "You wrote this copy, right?"

The Kid stuttered, "Y-y-yes, sir."

"And you used the previous copy I gave you as a template."

"Is s-s-something wrong?" The Kid looked over Waite's shoulder.

"At 6:15 this morning, during the Farm Report, I read this live. I made the mistake of reading it cold. That's on me. I should have checked it. I didn't stop laughing till about 8:30. Did you mean to make me laugh? Make me turn blue?"

"No, sir."

"Elaine called me in tears. She said she'd never advertise with us again."

"Why n-n-not?"

Waite handed him the page. "See any reason somebody would hear that and think it's funny?"

The Kid read it and looked up, his brow furrowed. At least, it looked like his brow might be furrowed under all that hair. "N-n-no, sir."

Waite dipped his head, locking eyes. Firm, not mean. "The sale is 50 percent off, one day only. Today. In the past they've had a buy-one-get-one free sale. But this is buy something that costs ten dollars, and you get it for five."

"H-h-half off."

Waite sighed. "Right, but when you say it out loud, it has a different meaning for a women's clothing store. Right here it says, 'All dresses are half off. All bras and panties are half off.'"

"But th-th-that's what they are. H-h-half off."

Waite stared at him. Didn't say a word. Then The Kid's eyes got big and he put a hand over his mouth.

"Yeah," Waite said. "Now what you mean is, come in today and take 50 percent off of your total purchase. Right?"

The Kid nodded.

Waite pointed at the last sentences and read them aloud. "'Elaine has everything half off. Come in and see her today.'"

The Kid looked at the floor, as if the next words would be *"You're fired."* Waite handed him a second page. "This is what I changed it to after I read it once. Saying 50 percent off throughout the copy takes away the double meaning. Study that and see if you can see what I did. The trick is seeing it. And reading it out loud will help."

The Kid held both pages in front of him, going back and forth. Then a smile crept across his lips as if he'd solved a mystery.

"Truth is," Waite said, "I think Elaine will be all right. People like to laugh. I spent three minutes on a thirty-second spot because I couldn't catch my breath. She got more than she paid for."

"I'm s-s-sorry," The Kid said, handing the pages back.

Every heart's a treasure, Waite thought. A line from the Mack Strum song.

"You're here to learn. Everybody makes mistakes. Don't let mistakes hold you back. Learn from them. You hear me?"

The Kid nodded like he understood. Waite's words hung between them and he wondered if they applied more to The Kid or himself.

"Once you get into radio, it gets in your blood. You carry it with you wherever you go. But there's something I've noticed about this business—you can come back in twenty years and tell me if I'm right."

The Kid stared at him through the silky hair.

"I've never met a fellow in radio who had a good relationship with his father. They're always trying to impress somebody. To get their daddy to pay attention. Some had abusive fathers. Some had dads who abandoned them. Some fathers they could never please.

And a lot of men who get into radio are looking for a surrogate. Do you know what that is?"

The Kid shook his head.

"Somebody to take their father's place."

The Kid pointed at Waite and raised his eyebrows a centimeter.

"Yeah, I fit the bill for some. But I don't think most men connect their emptiness with how they live. They don't know what they're looking for."

"Wh-wh-what ab-b-bout you?"

"Guilty as charged. My daddy wasn't a drunk or mean, he just worked all the time. Tried to provide. I think he was scared he couldn't. So he basically worked himself to death." He pointed at his chest. "Every man has a hole right here because of something. And for some reason, fellows who take up radio have a father hole they're trying to fill."

The Kid stared at the floor.

"Well, enough of that sermon." Waite laughed. "I'm giving you a new assignment today." He pointed to a rectangular metal object attached to the reel-to-reel machine. "This is a splicing block. And this is a grease pencil. Today your life changes, Kid."

Waite pulled a small, rectangular box from a drawer and slid it open. "These are razor blades. Take one."

The Kid looked at him like he was crazy. Then he reached in and picked out a blade and held it like it was dynamite.

"Keep the cardboard cover on it until you're ready."

He saw fear and a little shame in The Kid's eyes.

"Watch this," Waite said. He hit the Play and Record buttons on the Scully and it *kathunked* to life, rolling like two wagon wheels. The tape passed over the heads of the machine and he flipped on the microphone and read the weather forecast, making two intentional mistakes. When he was finished, he hit the Stop button and rewound the tape, using the Rewind and Fast-Forward buttons to manage the rewind speed.

"Wh-wh-why did you d-d-d-do that?"

"You don't want to just hit Rewind and stop. It's kind of like rushing up to a red light and mashing on the brake pedal."

The Kid nodded.

"Now this is the record head here and this is the play head. Got it?"

The Kid nodded again.

"When you find your edit point, you mark the back of the tape with a grease pencil. But you don't want to get grease on the heads, so you mark it over here." He made a white mark on the back of the tape several inches to the right of the play head. "Then you go forward and find the place where the good take starts." He found the next edit point, marked it, then unspooled the tape and fit it onto the groove in the block. "Best place to edit is after the natural breath. Right before you talk. Line up the first white mark you made to this mark on the splicing block, then cut it." He made a diagonal cut with the blade. "Then you do the same with the second edit."

Waite removed the edited tape and dropped it in the trash. He pointed to a spool of blue tape in a dispenser. "This is splicing tape." He cut off a piece about an inch long and placed it over the splice and rubbed his finger back and forth. Then he removed the tape from the block, tightened it on the Scully, rewound it a few turns and pushed Play.

The look on The Kid's face was priceless. It was as if he'd discovered the secrets of the universe. Gravity and motion and "every action has an equal and opposite reaction." Waite knew The Kid had the power to cut the bad and find the good. He stood and had The Kid sit in the chair, placing the weather forecast in front of him. Then he turned on the microphone.

"Read it."

The Kid looked up as if he'd been asked to jump the Grand Canyon on a tricycle. Blindfolded. Waite hit Play and Record on the Scully and pointed at him.

The Kid shook his head.

"You can do it. Just start talking. Trust me."

The call Waite had dreaded came late that morning. He'd felt it coming ever since the sheriff had taken TD into the station for questioning. He'd tried to sweet-talk Boyd, to make promises he couldn't keep, but in the end, he couldn't change the man's mind.

By his desk was a cardboard box filled with air checks and résumés. He called it the "Box of Hope" because he knew there were people behind every tape with the hope that Country 16 would say yes to them. He made a couple of phone calls and set his plan in motion.

Ardelle swished to the office and stood in the doorway with a cup of coffee and a Pall Mall with ashes about to fall. "I got a friend at the hospital." She raised her eyebrows.

"You've got friends everywhere, Ardelle. You know anybody in the White House?"

Ardelle ignored him. "She says old man Quidley's still alive, but not by much."

"It's hard to kill a Quidley, or anybody from the hills for that matter. TD is hoping he'll wake up long enough to tell everybody where the treasure is and that it ought to go to Pastor Robby."

"My friend doesn't think that'll happen."

"Well, there sure are a lot of people praying for him to pull through."

"What do you think'll happen to the treasure if he doesn't make it, Waite? Do you think he'll give it away in his will?"

"He might. I just hope we locate it before somebody digs to China."

Late in the afternoon, Waite called Elaine at her store and the woman could hardly speak to him because of all the commotion. She'd brought in two part-timers to help with the sale and all three of them were busy.

"I swear, Waite, you've made me a believer in the power of radio. Everybody who comes in here heard you laughing this morning."

"So you forgive us?"

"I don't have time to forgive you—business is too good. Oh, and run that spot again tomorrow. We're extending the sale. And make sure you read it the way it was originally written."

Waite smiled when he hung up. He'd have to tell The Kid what Elaine said.

A knock on his door. Pidge stood there with a hollow look on her face.

"Pidge, come in. I was going to call you. I need to talk about something."

She crossed her arms. "I guess we both do."

He motioned for her to sit in a chair opposite his desk, but she shook her head.

"I don't need to sit."

"All right. Well, a couple of things. I was going to ask about Quidley's dog. I didn't expect you to take him in. I wanted you to know that."

"Clay and that dog are inseparable now. I hear Clay talking to him. Practicing doing the weather."

"Is that so?"

"Which makes what I got to say even harder for me."

"What's wrong?"

"I came to say today was his last day. I don't want Clay working here no more."

She turned and walked out of the office as if she'd washed her hands of Country 16 and was leaving Waite with Barabbas. He caught up with her as she was pushing the front door open.

"Pidge, wait. What's this about?"

"I've made my decision and I'm not going back on it."

Waite chewed the inside of his cheek, trying to decipher what she was saying. He glanced at Ardelle, who was typing the logs.

"Come back in. I want you to hear something in the production room."

Pidge shook her head and pursed her lips.

"Come on. It'll only take a minute."

She sighed and followed him, and he closed the door behind her and scratched his cheek. "Is this about what I had him do today?"

"You had no right, Waite." Her eyes watered. "I thought I could trust you. I explained the problems that boy's had and what do you do? You hand him a box of razor blades."

"Okay, I admit it seems a little risky, but—"

"A little risky?" A vein stood out in her forehead. "Have you seen his scars? Do you have any idea what he's been through?"

Waite put up a hand. "Let me show you something, okay?" He grabbed a box in a cubbyhole by the gospel records that had *The Kid* written on it. He took the tape out of the box and threaded it on the reel-to-reel machine.

"There's nothing you can play that will get me over this," Pidge said.

"A lot of people with scars have been through these doors. Some you could see and some you couldn't. Remember the promise I made to the Lord? He brought that boy here and I see something in him. I know it's there."

"You don't understand."

"No, I think it's you who doesn't understand. Listen to this."

Waite turned up the pot on the board and hit the green Play button. The machine *kathunked* and the room filled with a baritone voice that shook the sound tiles on the walls. The delivery was stiff and unpolished, but it flowed.

"Here's today's weather for Emmaus. Partly cloudy with a high of ninety-three. Chance of showers is 40 percent. Tonight, partly cloudy and breezy with a low of seventy-eight. Relative humidity is 57 percent. Current temperature is eighty-six degrees at Country 16. This is The Kid reporting."

Pidge stared at the speaker, her mouth agape. She glanced at the control board as if there were someone inside who needed out. Then she looked at Waite. "Was that really him?"

"That's what he sounds like without the fits and starts. Fifteen seconds is all it is."

"How did you . . . ?"

"It's the miracle of the splicing block. Took him ten minutes to record it. I showed him how to edit and he went to town. I'm keeping this in a safe place so I can bring it out down the road. Show him how far he's come."

"That's amazing."

"It takes a sharp blade to get that sound. I thought hard about giving it to him, with his past."

Pidge studied the carpet.

"A blade can be used for good or evil, just like everything else. I needed him to hear what I hear. I needed him to see the possibility. And you should have seen the look on his face. It kind of looked like yours right now."

"What are you going to do with that? You're not thinking of putting him on the air, are you?"

Waite chuckled. "You think I'd miss the chance to put somebody famous on the radio for the first time? You bet I'm going to put him on the air. He's going far, Pidge. And I don't mean he's going to become somebody someday. He is somebody right now. It's my job to help him see who he is."

Pidge's chin trembled and she wiped the side of her face. "It still scares me, the razor. I took all the sharp things out of the house I could find."

"Trust me. He's going to be all right. You did a good thing bringing him here."

"All right then. I guess he can stay." She grabbed the doorknob, then turned. "What was it you wanted to see me about?"

"Let's go to my office and talk."

CHAPTER 19

Thirty minutes before TD wrapped up the overnight show, Waite walked in and sat behind him. He handed TD a cup of black coffee from Mel's.

"Any news on Possum?"

"It's touch and go still, but I think he'll be back eventually."

"Well, I'm getting kind of used to the new routine. I can help out for as long as you need."

"Yeah, about that. I came a little early to tell you something. . . . There's no easy way to say this. Boyd called. I don't know if he's getting pressure or he's just skittish, but he wants me to hire somebody else for overnights."

"What did you tell him? You didn't just roll over, did you?"

"I pushed back as hard as I could. This is not the time to fight. I promise this is just a bump in the road."

"I thought this was my chance for full-time. At least I can go back to doing news on the morning show."

"About that . . . Boyd doesn't think that's a good idea. I guess because of the sheriff."

"That's not fair, Waite. You know I didn't have a thing to do with old man Quidley's accident."

"I agree. This is not how I'd handle it if I had a choice."

TD stared at the undulating 45 on the turntable. "You're always talking about giving people second chances."

"I know. Believe me—this is going to work out. Give it time."

"If I can't make it at Country 16, where can I, Waite?"

"Look, I told Wally that losing his car felt like the end of the world. On the *Swap Shop* yesterday, he found a Buick in good condition. Better than the one he had."

"Excuse me if I don't do a backflip over Wally finding a running Buick."

Waite smiled. "From the time I met you, I've known what's inside. Show everybody what you're made of by how you handle this. Okay?"

TD started the next record without doing a talkover. "So is this my last shift?"

"I found a fellow who's coming by tonight. I'd like you to train him, show him around the station. He's got experience, so it should be easy."

"You hired somebody already?"

"I had to, TD. And I want to bring you back. Show Boyd what's inside. Be a team player."

"Team player, my foot."

"Maybe this will let you go full-time on Quidley. Find that treasure and you can help Robby and buy a hundred stations."

The sun yellowed the horizon as TD trudged toward the parking lot. He was dog-tired but wired with the news from Waite. He'd thought about the treasure a lot and had gone through more of Robby's box and decided he wouldn't head out haphazardly with hope and a shovel like others. He would be more methodical in his efforts. Smart. The prospect of focusing fully on the treasure now might have made another man smile, but TD couldn't get past the deep feeling of failure inside at ending his stint at Country 16.

He heard movement in the gravel around the corner and was surprised to see Pidge's truck. She leaned against it and pushed the toe of her boot through the gravel. She looked like a picture with the sunrise and the tear in her jeans above the knee.

"What are you doing here?" TD said.

"Want to get some breakfast? It'll be on me."

TD studied her. Of course he wanted to get breakfast with her. He'd drain a septic tank with a spoon if he could be next to her while he did it. But why had she shown up today?

"Hop in, I'll drive," Pidge said.

They listened to the Farm Report as she drove to the Village Grill, one of a handful of restaurants in Emmaus. They sat across from each other in a corner booth and looked over the menu. TD ordered the cheapest special, biscuits and gravy, and they drank black coffee from heavy white mugs.

Over the clinking of plates and silverware, TD said, "Looks busier than normal."

"Everything's busier since Gideon came to town."

TD was glad Pidge had reached out to him, but he couldn't get the news Waite had given him out of his head. He looked up and caught her staring at him.

"What?" he said, bewildered.

"Waite told me what he was fixing to tell you this morning."

"So that's what this is about. You two were afraid I'd climb the tower and jump off?"

"I showed up because I care. Waite does, too."

"Not enough to stick up for me."

"He didn't have a choice, TD."

"I swear, Pidge, if I can't even make it at a bottom-of-the-barrel station like Country 16, where am I going to go?"

Somebody dropped a plate and it shattered and there was silence, then laughter and clapping from the kitchen.

"That's what I feel like, right there. Dropped on the floor. Shattered dreams."

Pidge tipped her mug back and drained her coffee. She turned the mug around on the table between them. "You need to decide who you're going to believe."

"What's that mean?"

"Waite told me about what Milton Quidley said. That all you'll ever be is a tow truck driver. Is that what you believe?"

"Ain't nothing wrong with being a tow truck driver."

"Except that's not what you want to do the rest of your life, right?"

"I reckon not." He saw his reflection in the black coffee. "I don't want to believe it, but I'm scared he might be right."

"Waite don't believe that. And I don't believe it."

"What do you believe, Pidge?"

The waitress brought their plates. Pancakes and eggs and bacon for her. Biscuits drowned in sausage gravy for him. Then she brought the pot and refilled their mugs.

"I believe there's more ahead for you than you know." Pidge poured syrup on top of the pat of melting butter and studied it as it spread over the warm pancakes. "I think I figured out why I've been holding back with you."

TD kept his lips tight, not wanting to interrupt any of the flow, as if she were finally opening the top of her heart and tipping it over to let it drain.

"I've been caring for people all my life. Though he was older, I was supposed to keep an eye out on my brother. I kicked myself when I wasn't there for him. I still do. I took care of Mama when she got sick. Sat with her at the hospital. Same for my daddy. And now Clay. And in between there was Dudley."

She shook her head and took a bite of pancake and a drink of coffee. It looked like she needed the pause to break up the pain of mentioning the man's name.

"I haven't heard much about him," TD said.

"I don't know what I was thinking. I thought I was getting somebody who loved me. Instead, I got somebody who loved himself and wanted me to join the party. I wound up doing what came natural. I took care of him."

"You don't have to talk about it if you don't want."

"I know that."

"What made you stop taking care of him?"

"It got bad. He got violent."

"You deserve better than Dudley."

"Took me a while to believe that. Every now and then I think I see him in the window. Or I dream about him walking into the house, knocking things over. I've had a hard time forgiving myself for that mistake. And I promised I would never make it again."

"You won't."

She stared at him. "Then here you come. And I see a hard worker and somebody with dreams. A good heart. I also see somebody who wants me to take care of him."

TD put his fork down.

"Don't jump in just yet," she said. "Hear me out. You got to hear the verse and the chorus, not just the intro."

TD raised his eyebrows and picked up his fork again.

"I don't need a weak man. And don't say I'm looking for perfection. That ain't it. I need somebody strong enough to look at himself and be honest. Somebody who ain't afraid to see who he is and why he's that way."

"And be willing to change?" TD said. "I got to become somebody else for you to love me?"

She pushed her plate away. "I'm talking about finding somebody willing to own who he is, not become somebody else. Somebody willing to stand straight and not run from something or chase something else. Or think that finding a treasure is going to make everything all right."

"You don't think finding that treasure would change things?"

"All the money in the world's not worth a hill of beans if you're not willing to see the truth about yourself. Treasure just takes the problems you've got and makes them bigger."

"You know this from experience?"

"It's common sense. Name me one rich person who's satisfied."

TD thought a moment. "What about Gideon?"

"All right. But look what he did. He gave it away. Or at least he's trying to."

"What are you saying, Pidge? What's the truth about me?"

"I'm not the one to figure that out. But I'll tell you this. There's something I can see that you can't."

"What's that?"

"Something's holding you back. I don't know what it is. I think it might have something to do with Robby and what happened a long time ago. Or it's something else. I see it, buried deep."

TD gulped. It was like she was reading the fine print of his life without a magnifying glass. "Is that the piece of the moon? If I figure this out, you'll move ahead?"

She pulled her plate back toward her and ate a few bites of bacon. "I'm being honest. Something is hanging over you and I don't know what it is. And there's something else bothering me."

"I'm listening."

"I can't be with somebody who don't believe in God. I can't live double-minded."

"I never said I didn't believe in God."

"You said it to Waite one morning on the radio. I heard you."

"I said I don't truck in religion. That's different. That just means I've seen the bad side of religion. I wouldn't let that hold you back."

The waitress brought the check and TD reached for it.

"You take that after I said I was paying and you can walk back to the station."

TD raised both hands in surrender and smiled. "It's all yours, Pidge."

Out of the corner of his eye he saw a black sedan pull into the parking lot. Two men in suits got out. They looked like government men. Why in the world were they in Emmaus?

CHAPTER 20

PIDGE DROPPED TD OFF AT THE STATION. He pointed at the lower lot, where a Cadillac was parked.

"That's not good," he said.

Waite came out rubbing the back of his neck and stood by Pidge's open window. "Milton Quidley wants his father's dog."

All the air went out of Pidge's lungs.

"Did Gideon wake from his coma?" TD said.

Waite shook his head. "I told him we were glad to take care of it as long as he needs. Then I told him about The Kid and how attached the two of them have become."

"He sleeps at the foot of Clay's bed," Pidge said. "Won't leave it."

"Milton won't take no for an answer."

TD opened his door and spoke through gritted teeth. "I'll talk with him."

"Hold up," Pidge said.

"I'll tell him the dog ran away," TD said.

Pidge frowned. "Is he in your office?"

Waite nodded.

Pidge walked into the station and heard Willie Nelson singing, *"All of me, why not take all of me?"* She said hello to Ardelle.

"Waite ain't back there."

"I know. I'm here to see somebody else."

"Good luck. You're going to need it."

She'd only seen Milton's face in the newspaper in black and white and when she saw him standing by Waite's desk, looking at the pictures on it, she nearly turned away. Something about him brought back the look on Dudley's face when he was in bad shape.

"Did you bring the dog?"

No hello. No introduction. No kindness of any sort. He looked at her like he might look at a possum that didn't make it across the road before a semitruck arrived.

She held out a hand. "I'm Pidge Bledsoe. I run the salvage yard yonder. I'm sorry about your daddy. We're praying for him."

He shook her hand reluctantly and she saw a leash in his hand that still had the price tag on it.

"I understand your son has my father's animal. I want it back."

"He's not my . . . ," Pidge started to explain, then held up. There was no need. "Sir, Clayton has had a rough patch. And even though that dog has only been here a short time—"

"I understand." He reached in his back pocket and pulled out his wallet. "I'll pay you for your trouble. You probably had to buy food."

"No, sir, that's not what I mean. You don't owe us. I was just wondering if maybe you could see fit to let him stay until your daddy gets better. It would mean a lot to the boy. And to me, sir."

Creases in the man's forehead seemed to disappear. He pulled a ten-dollar bill out and handed it to her. "I need you to get the dog."

She'd been in situations, particularly dickering about a junker, when she wanted to say something but knew there was more to lose by talking than keeping quiet. Knowing what she could sell the engine for and resisting the urge to laugh or walk away or tell the seller he was crazy. She steeled herself and gave it one more try.

"A dog like that needs to be outside, sir. Not be cooped up or put in a kennel."

The man put his hands together in front of him and cocked his head to one side. "What part of *I need you to go get the dog* don't you understand?"

Pidge turned without taking the money and walked outside to her truck.

"Any luck?" Waite said.

She shook her head and slammed the door and barreled down the long driveway, a plume of exhaust and dust behind her. Clay stood outside the office, tossing a stick toward the river and watching Jubal run, grab it, and return, his tail wagging. Scrap would have said, "Happier than a coon in a cornfield."

She got out and walked to Clay and bit her cheek. "Fellow who owns the dog wants him back. He's up at the station." She hooked her thumb behind her and turned away from him because she couldn't bear looking into his eyes. Waite and TD were in the parking lot looking down and that was almost a worse sight.

"I th-th-thought . . . ," Clay stammered, looking at Jubal.

"The old man's son is up there. I asked if he would let us keep Jubal until his daddy got better. He's set on taking him. I don't know why."

The look on Clay's face was something Pidge would never forget. It was like watching a pigeon hit a guy wire. He looked out at the river, then back at the dog, then bent down and scratched Jubal underneath his heavy collar. It broke her heart to watch.

Then something changed. His eyes flashed, and it scared her at first. Clayton stood and turned to her, shaking hair from his eyes. At times, she could see her brother in him clear as day. His quiet way. Figuring things out in his head because it was the only space he could call his own. She'd given Clayton the choice of bedrooms and he'd taken her brother's room—his father's—which was pretty much the same as Sammy had left it. Fading posters on the wall. A corkboard with ticket stubs to Cincinnati Reds games. Issues of *Popular Mechanics* and a Warshawsky catalog of auto parts from Chicago.

Clayton hurried into the house and she thought he was probably too emotional to say goodbye to Jubal. Would this push him over the edge? Was he in there finding something sharp to hurt himself again?

She'd couldn't live that way. She couldn't worry all the time. So she got Jubal in the truck and was about to pull out when Clay appeared carrying a Ball jar. He jumped in the passenger seat. The jar was half-filled with white powder of some sort.

"What's that?"

"Y-y-you'll see."

Jubal licked Clay's face and he pushed the dog to the floor, where he sat between Clay's feet, ears bouncing as they drove up the hill.

"We can get another dog," she said. "I'll take you to the pound."

Clay stared straight ahead.

When they pulled up, Milton Quidley stood beside TD. Pidge figured Waite had to tend to the music.

From the looks of things, TD and Quidley hadn't exchanged a lot of words. They stood at a distance from each other, TD ramrod straight. She knew he'd objected to Waite bringing Clay on at the station, but now she could tell he was as upset about the dog as she was. Maybe more. And somehow, in the midst of the billowing dust and exhaust that wafted over them when she stopped, and the feelings stirring inside about Clay and all he'd been through, she knew she loved TD. She wouldn't have been able to explain ten reasons why, she just felt it at that moment, a fire burning inside, and she knew the heart was not something to explain but listen to.

Clay got out and Jubal followed. Milton had stepped back to avoid the dust plume and clapped his hands and called the dog. Jubal stood at Clay's side, tongue lolling, panting, staring at the man in the suit holding the leash down like it was something that would catch the dog's interest.

"Jubal, come over here," Milton said, his voice higher pitched and sweet.

The dog didn't move from Clay's side.

"T-t-toss it h-h-here," Clay said.

Milton folded the leash up and tossed it underhand to Clayton. It landed three feet short and Pidge glanced at TD, who rolled his eyes.

Clay picked up the leash and knelt before Jubal. He hooked the latch onto the dog's collar and led him toward Milton. The man took the leash and Clay took three steps backward and Jubal followed, straining at the leash.

"Come on, Jubal," Milton said, turning and heading toward the wooden steps.

Jubal threw gravel, trying to gain purchase. He pulled, his legs scratching ground under the gravel.

"Come on," Milton said, jerking the leash. The dog's head flew back, front legs in the air. Pidge put a hand to her mouth.

"That ain't no way to treat a dog," TD said, his teeth clenched.

"H-h-here. L-l-l-let me." Clayton held a hand out and reached for the leash.

Milton hesitated, then gave it to him and the dog relaxed. Milton walked toward the wooden steps but Clayton didn't move. The man stopped and turned, lifting his hands as if to say, *What's the holdup?*

"I-I-I'll p-p-pay you f-f-f-for him."

It was a pitiful sound because Pidge knew Clay had no money. And neither did she. Everything she had was going to pay off the monthly hospital bills she'd finally agreed to before going to collections. She'd had to scrape the cashbox for the breakfast she and TD ate, but she felt it was worth it. He'd listened to her and seemed different. Maybe it was the fatigue or the loss of the morning show, but he had seemed more open.

"Yeah, how much you want for him?" TD said.

"He's not for sale," Milton said. "Now get him in my car."

"P-p-p-please, m-m-mister?"

Milton dipped his head. "It must be something in the water around here. You people really can't hear, can you?"

Waite walked out the door and Pidge heard a gravelly voice singing about The Gambler. Waite must have heard some of the conversation through the door because he said, "I can advance The Kid some of his first paycheck, Mr. Quidley. How much you want for Jubal?"

Milton laughed and shook his head. He reached for the leash. "Give him to me."

Clay walked the dog toward him and Jubal obeyed, then growled when Milton reached for the leash. Milton looked down and slowly took the leash.

"W-w-w-wait h-h-h-here, then."

Clay turned, ran to the truck, and retrieved the Ball jar. He handed it to Milton, who stared at it.

"J-j-j-just sp-sp-sprinkle it on h-h-h-im f-f-f-for a c-c-couple days. That-that-that'll k-k-k-kill 'em."

"What are you talking about?" Milton said.

Pidge crossed her arms and forced a pained look. "The bottom down there is full of fleas. Sevin will do the trick. Right, TD?"

"That's what we use," TD said, picking up without missing a beat. "Couple days and they'll be dead. But you probably want to treat him before you get him in your car."

"Yeah," Waite said. "Last thing you want in a Cadillac is an infestation."

Milton took a visible step back from the dog.

"They'll jump on you if you don't watch out," TD said.

Milton's eyes darted, as if he was computing a cost-benefit analysis. He looked at Clayton. "I'll take a hundred dollars. Cash. You got it?"

Clay looked at Pidge. TD pulled out his billfold. She would have married him right there if he'd asked her.

"I told you I'd advance him his first paycheck," Waite said. "Stay right here."

Waite slipped inside the station. Pidge glanced at TD, who gave her a smirk he tried to hide, turning and looking into the sun. Waite returned and handed several bills to the man.

"If your daddy pulls out of this and wants the dog back, you let The Kid know," Waite said. "The two of them can dicker on the resale."

Milton Quidley stuffed the bills in his pocket, hurried down the rickety steps, and drove away.

"That was quick thinking, Kid," TD said.

"Is that really Sevin?" Pidge said.

Clayton smiled. "G-g-g-gold M-m-medal f-f-flour."

Waite laughed. "Can you imagine that dog running around with Gold Medal in his fur? If that don't beat all."

Clay looked up at Waite. "I-I-I d-d-don't have a h-h-hundred dollars."

"Which is why you need to get in here and go to work, Kid. And bring Jubal with you. He's our new mascot."

CHAPTER 21

AFTER A FEW HOURS' SLEEP, TD drove to the hospital. First he went to Possum's room and found the man hooked up to more wires and machines than he knew existed. He was asleep and TD didn't want to wake him. A nurse approached and TD asked her to tell Possum he'd had a visitor and she said she would.

On the floor below he found Robby Gardner's room. Ball cap in his hand, he walked in and nodded at the fellow in the first bed and went around the curtain. Robby sat trying to read a book over the sound of the *Nightly News* from the man next to him. It looked like he was fighting a losing battle.

Robby appeared somewhat better than the last time TD had seen him. He was sitting upright in his bed and there was color to his face, although his nose was still heavily bandaged. TD couldn't look down at his leg.

"Came by to see how you were doing."

Robby nodded. When he spoke, his voice was soft and he kept his jaw set, only moving his lips. "The Lord's been good to me, TD. Doctors say I might go home next week."

"That's great. I'll bet Sharon and the kids are glad. You going to get back in the pulpit?"

"I want to. I sure have a lot to say. A lot I've been thinking about. We'll have to figure out a way to get the wheelchair up the steps."

"Somebody will figure that out, I'll bet."

TD pulled a chair close to the bed so he wouldn't have to talk over John Chancellor. Before he could speak, Robby touched his shoulder.

"I had a dream last night."

"Is that so?"

"You were in it."

TD shook his head. "Couldn't have been me. I was at work."

Robby chuckled, then closed his eyes. "Don't make me laugh. It hurts."

"Sorry. I hope it wasn't a dream about you in a cave."

"No, but it was about the treasure. I dreamed you found it, TD. You were the one who figured it out. It was so real I could see the gold."

"Where was I in this dream of yours? Got a location for me?"

"I don't know. But you were celebrating."

"You heard about me finding Gideon."

"I read it in the paper. He's here in ICU, evidently. I've been praying for him every day."

"The whole town is going crazy. I've seen teenagers with shovels roaming the countryside."

"It'll probably get worse before it gets better."

TD nodded. "You heard he wanted you to find it. To get help with the hospital bills."

"Yeah. That buck came between me and prosperity. But I read a proverb today. 'Don't wear yourself out to get rich.' That's the New Robby Version. It's a reminder to me that silver and gold won't solve our problems." Robby bit his lip. "TD, I got something to ask you."

"I got a lot to ask you, too. Go ahead."

"I've been thinking about what I said to you a long time ago."

"We don't have to go into that."

"No, I want to. Sometimes people like me can come on too strong. I wanted to say something that would help. But I wound up saying a hurtful thing. That what happened to your family was God's will. I think that was what drove you away."

"It didn't make me want to follow you to Bible school."

Robby nodded. "Bottom of my heart, I'm sorry. I wish I could go back and have a do-over."

"I didn't handle it very well myself."

"Can you find it in your heart to forgive me for how insensitive I was?"

"I hurt myself by staying away. I should have pushed back and hashed it out with you. But I couldn't at the time. Instead I turned tail."

"I can't tell you how glad I am to hear that."

TD leaned close. "Now that we got that out of the way, I've been looking through your box. Gideon wasn't just passing through Emmaus. He came here on purpose. And I'm trying to figure out where he was headed."

"Are you sure he was here for the treasure?"

TD glanced at the curtain. "Trust me on this. Can you think of any clue that would help? He was headed north on County Line when he hit the deer."

Robby scratched at his neck. "I've been going over it in my head. Lick Creek's up that way. Harper Creek is above that, but they flooded that whole area. I wouldn't have risked climbing down that rock in Ephra if I thought the treasure was in Emmaus."

TD nodded. "Why don't I bring you some of your notes? Maybe it would help jog your memory."

Robby's face paled and his eyes tracked away. TD sensed a presence behind him.

"Hi, honey," Robby said sweetly.

TD turned. Sharon stood behind him with a hand on her hip. TD stood and pulled the chair back.

"Don't let me interrupt anything," Sharon said with an edge to her voice.

"I just came by to see how he was doing," TD said.

"Is that so?" Sharon grabbed the curtain and yanked it back. "Mister, would you mind turning that down?"

The volume decreased and TD touched Robby's shoulder. "I'll be going. We're pulling for you. If you need help building the ramp at the church, holler."

"I appreciate it, TD."

Sharon followed him into the hallway and stopped him by the elevator. "Don't do this, TD. Haven't we been through enough?"

"What are you talking about?"

"I know why you're here. I can't take any more. You burn that box. Or give it to me and I'll burn it."

"That box led me to Robby."

"That box nearly left my kids without a father. And it took his leg. Don't use him. Don't come around here with your treasure questions."

He wanted to say he was looking for the treasure so he could help pay their bills. Instead he just said, "All right."

TD couldn't get Sharon's hard stare or the venom in her voice out of his mind. He drove to the station and took over for DeeJay, watching for the headlights of the man who would replace him on his last few hours of work at Country 16.

After midnight, lights shone through the tree limbs. He was playing "Amos Moses" when the man walked through the door and shook himself like a wet dog. He wore a Kansas City Royals baseball cap and a green military flight jacket with the name tag torn off that he hung on a hanger by the front desk.

"Hey, sorry I'm late," he said in a deep, crusty voice. He reached out a hand and shook firmly. "You TD?"

"That's me. You must be Ronald."

"Don't call me by my real name. I don't go by that on the air." He opened his wallet and unfolded a piece of paper he had stuffed inside. "Where do I put the license?"

TD pointed to the wall by Ardelle's desk and the man pulled Scotch tape from the dispenser and taped the paper to the frame that held all their licenses.

"You play ball in high school? Is TD for *touchdown*?"

"No, just my initials."

"It fits. Good air name. Strong. I like it."

"What do I call you if you don't want to use your name?"

"I've been thinking about that. It's best to use my radio name from the start." The man scratched at his thinning hair. "I want to use something that goes with Country 16. The *K* sound. Kurt. Kent. Kenny."

"You choose your name after you get hired?"

"I change it to keep it fresh. Different formats, different regions, a different name. I've worked at Top 40, album rock, oldies, you name it. I've been Jim O'Toole, Burt O'Shea, Dan Music Murphy."

"How many stations have you worked at?"

He laughed. "Tough to count. I've had this voice since I was thirteen. I'm like Johnny Cash—I've been everywhere, man."

He coughed and gave a big smile and there was a twinkle in his bloodshot eyes. They called it charisma but it looked like a guy who was aging too fast. He had bad breath and TD wondered when he'd last showered.

"Where are you coming from?"

"Lexington. I was there about a year." He looked at the console behind TD. "Morning drive for a Top 40 country station. It was a dream as far as equipment goes. Huge monitors. Sennheiser mics processed so you boomed like a blowtorch. It was a great sound."

"Why'd you leave?"

"Life happens, you know?" He moved closer to the board. "Is that a 44-BX? I haven't worked an RCA like that since Roanoke."

TD nodded and glanced at the microphone. He didn't know much about microphones and the man's knowledge intimidated him. "Lexington is almost a top 100 market, isn't it?"

"Close. Louisville's bigger. That's where I was hoping to land next."

"So why are you here?"

"Isn't your record ending?"

TD fired the cart playing the station's jingle with singers harmonizing, "The best country in the country, Country 16." He hit the switch and Charlie Pride's "Kiss an Angel Good Mornin'" began.

"Nice segue," the man said. "Tight."

"Thanks."

The man sat heavily in a chair. "What do you think of Kurt Stevens? Like the Country 16 K and S. Does that work?"

"Sounds fine. But how do you remember who you are from one station to the next?"

"Wait. Cody. Country Cody Stevens," he said. He grabbed some discarded news copy and flipped it over and wrote, *Cody Stevens, the best country in the country, Country 16.* He scribbled the call letters in the corner and wrote, *Emmaus, West Virginia.*

"That's how I remember. My cheat sheet. It'll take me a couple of days, then I won't have to have it in front of me."

TD reached out a hand. "I've never met anybody who just figured out their name. Nice to meet you, Cody."

TD cued up the next record and explained the music rotation. Cody nodded but seemed like he already had a better idea.

"When I was in Eau Claire, the station had a list you played in a specific order. The music director figured out how to play each song so that nobody would hear the same one in that hour for a whole month."

"But what if there's a song you want to hear again?"

"Exactly what I said. You have a good head on your shoulders, TD. If I like a certain song and have to wait a whole month to hear it again, I'm going somewhere else, right?"

"Where's Eau Claire?"

"Wisconsin. I didn't last the winter up there. It's like Antarctica. Like I said, I've been all over. Topeka. Mobile. Savannah."

"What's the longest you ever stayed in one place?"

"I did two years in Little Rock. Sounds like I went to prison, doesn't it? I was married at the time. The marriage lasted until Toledo."

Cody said he'd been as far west as Nevada and as far south as Key West, Florida. "Bugs down there are big enough to barbecue. Spiders as big as my hand." He shook his shoulders. "I hate spiders."

"If you don't mind me asking, what happened in Lexington?"

"That is a sad tale, TD. They hired me to cohost a morning show with a fellow named Darrel Dandy. I came up with the name Jimmy Fine."

"Fine and Dandy," TD said.

"Yep. They had billboards that said, 'Wake up to Fine and Dandy.' And Darrel was good. A born salesman—he sold commercials."

"What happened?"

"He was selling more than time, if you know what I mean. And now he's doing it. I had no idea until the police showed up one morning with a drug-sniffing dog that went crazy in his office and at his car. I learned a hard lesson that day."

"You weren't involved, though?"

Cody shook his head. "No, but the two of us were so inter-twined, the station said they had to make a clean break. They threw out the Fine with the Dandy."

"That is a sad tale."

"You're only as innocent as your cohost. Remember that."

"Where are you staying?"

"Until I find a place, I've got a camper cover on my truck and a mattress back there. Is there a shower here?"

TD shook his head and segued "(I Never Promised You a) Rose Garden," then showed Cody the supply room. When they returned to the control room, Cody said, "Hey, since I'm here, why don't I climb in the cockpit and give it a whirl?"

"Well, I was going to finish my shift . . ."

Cody slapped on the headphones and turned up the volume to a deafening level. He bounced in the chair as if gaining momen-tum for takeoff. "Lynn Anderson, on Country 16, the best country in the country! Cody Stevens with you, and here's the smooth sound of Don Williams, on Country 16!"

He clipped off the mic as Don Williams sang, *"Sometimes you may think I take you for granted."* He turned, smiling. "What did you think?"

"Impressive," TD said. "But you haven't done a lot of overnights, have you?"

"Why do you say that?"

A phone line blinked. "We try to tone things down a little after dark."

TD picked up the phone and listened to the voice on the other end. "All right, I'll tell him, Sally."

"Who was that?"

"Psycho Sally from Lick Creek. She calls a lot."

"There's seriously a place called Lick Creek?"

TD ignored the question. "She said she keeps the radio on all night and when you talked just now, her cat jumped and knocked over a lamp."

Cody snickered. "I'll pull back on my intensity."

"Well, go ahead and run the board. I need to get something from my truck. I'll be in the production room if you have questions."

TD riffled through Robby's box as he listened to Cody spin records, read news and weather, and bring a professional sound to the station. He had a presence to him and even though he was new, TD figured Cody would be given the weekly gig as MC at the Mountaineer Opry House, something TD had never been asked to do.

When morning came, TD would be back to his tow truck. The words of Milton Quidley whispered to him again. Maybe the man was right.

He stared at the sheet of verses Robby had copied. John 3:16

and the Romans Road and *"I can do all things through Christ"* and *"Behold, I stand at the door, and knock."* There was a verse from Ezekiel that said, *"A new heart also will I give you, and a new spirit will I put within you: and I will take away the stony heart out of your flesh, and I will give you an heart of flesh."* All of those and a few more were on a sheet marked *Eternal Treasure.*

The next page was marked *Temporal Treasure*, and TD agreed with Robby that these were the clues that pointed to Gideon's ark, to a fortune in cash and gold and silver and who knew what else. Everything from *"I will lift up mine eyes unto the hills"* to *"We hanged our harps upon the willows in the midst thereof."* He scanned the verses and put them through the grid of Emmaus and felt as lost as a sock.

Maybe Gideon had gotten lost or disoriented when he drove to Emmaus. Maybe he had taken the wrong exit off the interstate and was driving the back roads by the rivers of his memory. TD and everybody in town could be exhausting themselves for nothing. If only the old guy would wake up and just tell them.

All TD had was a box full of clues. There were verses on pages and articles with crumbs and scraps of conversations. TD went back to the *Eternal Treasure* page and scanned the list. He turned the page over and noticed something scribbled at the bottom.

Wilma at diner.

"Who in the world is Wilma?" he said aloud. Maybe he could call Robby and ask. Then he thought of Sharon's face and pushed the idea aside.

Fatigue and frustration set in and TD rubbed his eyes with the heels of his hands. Through the glass he heard Crystal Gayle singing about her brown eyes being blue.

At that moment, TD allowed a thought to slip through the cracks of his soul and settle like gold dust. He knew there was someone else on the planet who had an encyclopedic knowledge of the Bible just like Gideon. And that man was the last person on earth TD would ask for help. Not a chance in Charleston he would ever go to him.

The phone line blinked and Cody turned and pointed to it. TD nodded and picked up the receiver. "Country 16."

"TD, is that you?" Somebody with a raspy voice barely whispering.

"Yeah, who's this?"

"It's Possum. The nurse said you were over here. Sorry I missed you."

"I was just checking on you. You ought to be sleeping."

"Old habits die hard, TD. You know I'm a night owl."

TD heard beeping in the background. "I hope you're feeling better."

"Well, depending on how you look at it, I'm doing a lot better than Gideon Quidley."

"What do you mean?"

"There was a hullabaloo over here. The nurse said she couldn't tell me what was going on, but she gave enough info to piece it together."

"What happened?"

"The nurses tried to stop it. They were all out of sorts. Milton Quidley pulled the plug on his daddy. Gideon died an hour ago."

CHAPTER 22

Two days after Gideon's death, Waite walked into a special meeting held at the First Baptist Church. He brought The Kid, who had asked if he would have to talk. Waite said no, he wouldn't.

The past two days had been nothing short of a free-for-all in Emmaus. With the news of Gideon's death, more news trucks rolled in and, close behind, treasure hunters. John Chancellor had introduced a report about the life and death of Gideon Quidley on the *Nightly News* that was only fifty-three seconds long, but that was enough to remind people of the kooky old guy with the Bible treasure hidden in the hills. That sent a horde of seekers scouring under interstate bridges and in vacant lots. TD told Waite the tow business was booming because stores were calling to tow out-of-state vehicles from their parking lots.

Someone had climbed into the airplane that was affixed in the center of town as a WWII memorial and had left a hole in the fuselage on their exit. The conjecture was that it had to be someone from out of town because nobody from Emmaus would have been so unpatriotic.

They sat near the front of the church, catching Pastor Gentry's attention. Waite introduced The Kid, a hand on his shoulder.

"It's great to have you with us, son," Pastor Gentry said to The Kid. "I heard you do a weather forecast. It was good."

"He's a natural, isn't he?" Waite said, winking at The Kid.

Pastor Gentry walked to the microphone and got things started. "We're here tonight because several churches and concerned citizens want to propose a plan involving the treasure of Gideon Quidley."

A hush fell over the room. Men in work shirts leaned forward in their pews. Women fanned themselves with week-old bulletins they'd found stuck in hymnals.

"I can't tell you how I came by this information, but I have it on good authority that Gideon did not divulge the location of the treasure in his will."

A murmur ran through the congregation. Waite looked at The Kid and raised his eyebrows as a door opened in the back and a camera crew walked through. Waite shook his head.

"However," Pastor Gentry continued, "I also know there's an envelope that will be opened thirty days after the reading of the will. Nobody knows the contents of that envelope, but I believe old Gideon will probably tell the location."

"Who gets to open that envelope?" someone shouted.

"Hold on, let me finish. Those who agreed to call this meeting believe that if Gideon's treasure is here, we ought to share it with our neighbors."

"And not all these out-of-towners that are flocking here," a woman shouted.

Some people applauded and some in the back turned around and glared at the TV camera. There was a general distrust of the media growing with every news report.

The pastor of the Holiness church raised a hand. "I believe we asked for this to be a closed meeting. I don't think we ought to have the media present."

Applause and a few *amens*. Pastor Gentry nodded and looked at Waite. "Would you mind helping usher our friends out? They can be on the property, just not in the sanctuary."

Waite told The Kid to stay put. Pastor Gentry spoke up and informed the reporter and camera operator the meeting was closed and politely asked them to leave. There was a brief, combative conversation with Waite, but the two finally moved outside.

When Waite returned, the owner of the Village Grill, Nye Evans, walked toward the pulpit, ambling with a limp he had sustained after a bad fall near the restaurant's grease trap. He hadn't walked straight since.

"We've all been thinking about the treasure for a long time. And so far, nothing has come of it. I think it's time we pool our resources. Instead of competing with each other, why don't we hunt together?"

Pews creaked from the collective shifting weight.

"What's that mean, Nye?"

"It means we sign a contract. I talked with Wendell over at his law office today. I wrote something and he made a couple of changes and thinks it works."

"What kind of contract?" someone said from the back row.

"It says that no matter who finds the treasure, we'll share it equally among the churches and businesses and families of

Emmaus. If what Quidley said about the contents is true, everybody would get a sizable payment. And this way we don't fight over it. We come together like good Christian people. Share and share alike. It'd be just like the church in Acts—they had all things in common."

Someone behind Waite muttered something about "socialism." A few asked to see the contract but no one seemed ready to sign it.

Pastor Gentry returned to the pulpit. "I think this could be a testimony to the world that God's people can work together. And wouldn't old Gideon be happy to know that! Let's remember why he hid the treasure in the first place. He wanted people to read and understand God's Word. Amen?"

There rose an unenthusiastic *amen* from a few. Some were reading the *therefore*s and *party of the first part* in the contract. Most were in an agitated state of suspicion.

"Gideon wasn't just offering money. He wanted people to find eternal life through Jesus. That's why he did this."

Waite turned and noticed several people slipping into the back pews.

"Here's what we have going for us," Pastor Gentry continued. "Billy Ed Crowley has a high-powered metal detector he's going to donate to the cause. Plus, Nye is offering to cater as people do sweeps of fields and woods and barns."

A hand shot up. "What if Gideon hid the treasure on public land? Would we still get to keep it?"

Elton Conner, a plumber and pipe fitter, stood, his workworn hands steadying himself on a back pew. "I think it's back on Barker's Ridge. There's a big willow up there, but it's in some pretty thick brush. I'd bet my last dollar it's there."

Another person mentioned a suspicious grave that had no marker at the Mount Olive Cemetery. Another suggested they drain the reservoir. Waite watched The Kid sitting mesmerized at the rapid-fire conjecture.

A piercing female voice rattled the congregation. "Remember back when the mining company came in and started digging and putting in the dam? There's talk that they've brought more than coal out of that mountain the last few years."

Waite leaned down and whispered, "That's Sally from Lick Creek. Once you get a shift at the station, you'll be talking to her regularly."

When Sally switched from the mining company to the government's poisoning of the populace using chlorine, people shifted in their seats and whispered to each other.

Finally a man raised a hand and stood. "I don't mean to cut you off, Sally, but I've been hearing all this talk about the ark and I don't even know what we're looking for. Can you describe it and tell us how big it is, Pastor?"

"I can do better than that," Pastor Gentry said. "Someone hit the lights." He pulled down a screen in front of the baptistery and stepped down to the main floor and flipped on an overhead projector. He placed a drawing of the ark on the screen with dimensions and comparisons to other items.

"How would Gideon Quidley hide something like that?" a woman said. "He couldn't have lifted it on his own, could he?"

Clifton Elkins, an engineer at the mine, stood. "Probably not. Unless he rigged some kind of pulley, which is always possible. Gideon had a sharp mind. For those who don't know, he worked in the aerospace industry. And he was instrumental in getting us to the moon."

"I've got something to say."

The voice came from the back pew and carried all the way to the front. At first, Waite thought it sounded like TD. He turned and saw a tall man striding forward. He wore a white-collared shirt and a thin black tie.

"Reverend Lovett, it's good to see you," Pastor Gentry said.

Waite whispered to The Kid, "That's TD's daddy."

Reverend Lovett stopped at about the middle of the congregation and those in front of him turned. Because of the strength and deep resonance of his voice, everyone heard him without a microphone.

"I've tried to stay out of this since I first heard of it. But I can no longer remain silent. 'No man can serve two masters: for either he will hate the one, and love the other; or else he will hold to the one, and despise the other. Ye cannot serve God and mammon.' And that's exactly what's happening.

"Friends, we are dealing with God's Holy Word. To use it as a hidden code is not right. And you're talking as if the answer to all our problems is finding gold and silver."

"It would sure help out the building program," someone muttered behind Waite.

Gladys Vernill raised her voice. She attended the nondenominational Emmaus Bible Church. "Why would you be against a man using his possessions to get others interested in the Bible? Seems to me, Gideon brought revival. And God's going to get the glory if we can stand together instead of tearing each other apart. I'm disappointed in you, Reverend. Why can't you be like that fellow who said, 'If this is of God, don't fight it'?"

"You're speaking of Gamaliel in Acts chapter 5."

"Exactly. If this is man-centered, it'll die. If God told Gideon to do this, you don't want to be against it."

Reverend Lovett paused and measured his words. "You mentioned revival. You cannot revive that which isn't alive. And the spirit I see here is not revival. It's a spirit of the lottery."

"You're just upset you haven't found it yourself, Lovett," someone said and others clapped.

"If you don't want to be part of the search, good," Gladys said. "That's more for the rest of us."

Some clapped again, while others stood and walked out. Across the sanctuary a melee ensued with someone grabbing a contract from someone else and ripping it up. Another man tackled the contract ripper and a pew tipped and feet flew in the air.

Waite stood and pushed The Kid toward the back of the church. "I'm sorry you had to see that."

CHAPTER 23

OVER THE NEXT WEEK, TD watched the slow unraveling of civility in Emmaus from his perch in the tow truck. He heard chatter over the CB from people hot on the treasure trail. They used handles like "Golddigger" and "Ark Hunter." There was a buzz on all the channels and anxious anticipation that at any moment someone might scream, "We found it!"

From what he gathered over Country 16, prayer services at local churches had morphed into Bible studies with the intent of finding the treasure. People brought verses printed on three-by-five cards, but they held them close, as a poker player might clutch a winning hand.

TD went on a call one morning and found Fred Hickman's Chevelle rolled sideways into the rosebushes lining Turkey Creek Road. The elderly man had become distracted and the car left the pavement and came to rest on its side. Fred was all right but concerned about something he had in the car, and TD discovered it was his research about the treasure, which he'd been taking to show a pastor in town.

In the course of the discussion, Fred told TD that he'd taken a correspondence course in Greek from a seminary. And while looking at the clues Gideon gave, he'd gone back to the original language and come up with an algorithm whereby he wrote down every fifth letter of the words in the verses and used them as a jumble that he said showed the treasure's location. Why he chose every fifth letter and not every third or seventh, TD didn't know and didn't ask.

At the gas station, TD saw more evidence of the toll the treasure hunt was taking. Locals gassing up questioned those with out-of-state license plates.

"What brings you to these parts? You here visiting family?"

There was also denominational suspicion and whispers that "The Methodists just want to build a new gymnasium." Or "Those Baptists are talking about buying a fleet of buses if they find the treasure. You know how Baptists love bus ministries."

On Wednesday morning, TD came upon a sight he would never forget. Near the elementary school was a rickety, single-lane covered bridge that everyone in Emmaus agreed needed to be replaced, no matter the historic value. Most people avoided going over it, especially with heavier vehicles.

Lester Jenkins, who loaded hay and sacks of oats at Johnny's Feed and Seed, believed he had seen the ark through the wooden slats of the bridge. And he convinced his cousin, Randy, to lower him down from the middle using a chain Lester had secured around his midsection. Lester had made the mistake, TD learned later, of not setting out the terms and conditions before Randy began the lowering. When Randy called out that he wanted half of the treasure if it was down there, Lester protested. Randy threatened letting go of the chain, and it was during this stalemate that TD rolled up. Randy wouldn't allow Lester to descend farther until they agreed on a percentage and Lester wouldn't back down from his position that, as TD heard him shout, "You don't deserve a percentage. All you're doing is holding a chain."

Randy again threatened to let go and climb down himself. Lester responded it would be the last chain Randy would ever let go of, to which Randy said, "Well, let's see about that," and he let go. Into the muddy water went Lester and the weight of the chain nearly took him to the bottom.

Randy made it to the underside of the bridge and was suspended with his feet wedged between two pieces of rotting wood when Lester came scurrying out of the water like a wet muskrat. He ran toward the bridge swinging the chain like it was a lasso and screaming at Randy. By this time several cars had pulled over, and when the word *treasure* was heard, a mob descended on the bridge. Both Lester and Randy wound up in the water, punching each other as they floated downstream.

TD thought it was both the funniest and saddest thing he'd seen, and he wished he was still on the morning show to relate the story. That thought sent him in a downward spiral.

Clay did everything Waite asked him to do around the station and even volunteered to mow the grass at the side of the building. Nobody wanted to push the mower out there because Ardelle had seen a snake, which was why she wouldn't even walk on that side of the building. The story didn't deter Clay.

He was in the production room when he overheard Ardelle asking Waite why anybody in their right mind would volunteer for that job.

"Maybe he's not in his right mind," Waite said. "Or maybe he's had experience with snakes where he came from."

Clay smiled at that.

Waite called him into his office and Jubal followed and settled at Clay's feet. Waite asked if he liked working for Country 16 and other questions, including how he felt about starting school in September. When Clay shrugged, Waite said, "You've got to be a little bit nervous going to a new place and not knowing anybody."

"I reckon," Clay said fast. He'd practiced the words so he didn't stammer.

"I believe if you make one good friend, you can get through just about anything."

Clay looked at his hands.

"I know the shop teacher at the high school. I can introduce you. And there's kids in your grade that go to my church. You might come with me one Sunday and meet a few. There's some pretty girls there."

Clay looked up and saw that Waite had his eyebrows raised, his eyes twinkling in the fluorescent light.

"You're probably one of the few students with a steady job. And nobody works at a radio station. That'll bring the girls flocking."

The mention of a flock of girls made Clay's stomach hurt. And going to church was a foreign idea. He'd rather drive a nail into his eyeball than sit in some room in the back of a church among girls with talcum-sweet skin and perfect, silky hair that smelled of Johnson's baby shampoo. It wasn't that he didn't like girls. He just felt uncomfortable around them. And if he was asked a question or told he needed to read something out loud, well, it was all over. Better to just give up on the whole thing than try because his cheeks flushed red thinking about it.

"Let me know if you want to go. Afterward, I like to get a bucket of chicken and go over to the lake. You like fishing?"

Clay nodded but said he didn't have a pole.

"I'll fix you up. I used to take . . ." Waite stopped, then tried again. "I have an extra rod and reel and all kinds of tackle. At the lake, this time of year, the bass bite on spinning lures. Some Sundays I have to throw so many back, it's almost like they want to jump in the boat with me."

"A b-b-boat?"

"It's nothing fancy. It'll float. I keep it at the lake and people use it and put it back."

Clay thought a moment, then said, "D-d-do I have t-t-to . . . ?"

Waite put his elbows on the desk. "We could go to the lake on a Saturday if you'd rather. Has Pidge ever taken you to Hamm's? It's a family restaurant. The people who own it, their last name is Hamm. Sweetest root beer you ever tasted and they serve it in a frosted glass mug. They pile ham about a mile high on toasted buns and melt cheese all through it. They cut sweet potatoes up and fry them. And the onion rings are about as big as a Frisbee."

"I like h-ham," Clay said.

"Me too. They're part of the Gospel Hamms. We have some of their records in the production room. *Hamm'n Up the Hymns* is one. They used to be the Hamm Family Trio and then it was the Hamm Quartet, and then there was a divorce and they settled on the Gospel Hamms."

"D-d-do they have a f-f-family arou-around here named Eggs?"

Waite chuckled. "That's good. Hamm and Eggs. With a name like that you have to have fun with it. You'll probably meet some of the Hamms in school. Their oldest boy is a senior this year, Sam."

Clay stifled a smile.

"I hear he's dating one of the Burgher girls. It'll be a Hamm-Burgher wedding."

If Clay had been drinking pop, it would have spurted out his nose.

"All right, we'll go fishing and get over to Hamm's."

"I'll t-t-try ch-church once."

Waite raised his eyebrows. "We'll go on Sunday, then. Now the real reason I called you in here is because I have an opportunity. DeeJay is . . . uh, how do I put this. DeeJay is having a procedure." His eyes darted like he was trying to figure out how to get from Emmaus to Tupelo in a rowboat. "She needs to be gone for a while and I'm trying to fill the on-air slot. I've worked it out so that the only time not covered is between eight and eleven in the evening, so three hours a day. And I was thinking, since you live over the hill and school hasn't started, you could cover that."

"H-h-h-how do I . . . ?"

"I'll record some drop-ins and we've got the music imagers. You can edit the weather like you do in the mornings and play it. People will be glad to hear more music, to be honest, and not so much gab. We'll skip the news at the top of the hour."

"Wh-what about m-m-my l-l-license?"

Waite handed him an envelope. "Came yesterday. I applied for you. Tape it to the frame by Ardelle's desk and you're good to go."

Clay opened it and stared at his name on the paper.

"What do you think? You want to do it?"

Clay did the math in his head. More than twenty hours. He'd get paid and get to do something he liked. "S-s-sure. But I should ask P-P-Pidge."

"I talked to her. She said for you to bring a flashlight and Jubal."

"R-r-really?"

"You'll meet Cody, the fellow who took Possum's place. He should be here on time except for Saturday. They asked him to MC over at the Mountaineer Opry, so he might be a little late."

Clay made it through the first night without many mistakes except for "wowing" "Wichita Lineman." He'd just cued it up too close to the guitar intro and it sounded like a cat meowing. He kicked himself for it and stared at the phone but it didn't ring.

He was almost more scared of the request line than he was of opening a microphone. When it rang, he just watched the light blink. Finally, toward the end of his first shift, the main phone rang and he picked up.

"You're doing great, Kid," Waite said. "How you feeling?"

"O-o-okay."

"I've been listening. Remember, this is not about being perfect. You'll make a mistake or two. The key is to learn. And have fun. If you have fun, people listening will enjoy it, too. Got it?"

"Y-y-yes, sir."

The call made him feel warm inside. Growing up, all he'd heard was how bad and stupid he was. And that was from someone supposed to love him. Waite lived differently.

Clay kept an eye on the clock and left the control room door open so he could see when Cody arrived. Lights flickered outside and at 10:57, Cody unlocked the door and sauntered in, putting a brown bag in the soda machine and his headphones on the chair just inside the control room door.

Jubal growled.

"You must be The Kid," Cody said, stretching out a hand. His voice was crusty and loud, as if he had a hard time hearing himself. He had a shadow of a beard and his breath smelled funny.

Clay unplugged his headphones.

"No, stay there. Play the next song. I have to hit the head."

Cody closed the bathroom door loudly. When Bill Anderson finished "Five Little Fingers," Clay hit the legal ID, then played the next song in the queue, Tanya Tucker's "What's Your Mama's Name."

Cody returned, buckling his belt as he walked, and as Buford Wilson was being laid to rest by the county, he cursed. "Listen, don't play such depressing songs in a row. Women dying and men getting tossed in jail for solicitation of a minor. We need to lighten the mood, don't you think?"

Clay moved and watched Cody shuffle through the music stack looking for something. He tossed a 45 on the open turntable like it was pizza dough and cued it up with lightning speed, then plugged in his headphones and turned the volume up.

"Listen to this," Cody said.

At the end of the Tanya Tucker song, at just the right moment, he hit the switch for the turntable and lifted his hand in the air like a conductor. The music seamlessly transitioned and Cody flipped on the microphone, bouncing on his chair.

"Country 16, I'm Cody Stevens, it's just past eleven, and here's Glen Campbell, 'Rhinestone Cowboy,' on the best country in the country."

As Glen sang, Cody switched off the microphone and clapped his hands. "Did you hear that? Now that was a segue, wasn't it? Songs in the same key that fit like a hand in a glove."

Clay nodded.

"You should work on that. I was listening driving in. You want things tight, no space between. It ought to flow, you know? Like water in a river, always moving, no breaks. That's the sound you're going for. It ought to be a continuous river of music and voices so the listener has no chance to tune away. You catch them into the current of what you're doing and they get caught in the flow. Understand?"

"Y-y-yeah."

Cody sighed. "Not that it matters here. This town's like the back side of the moon. Of course with the treasure hunt, there's more activity. I'll bet you've been out looking, haven't you?"

Clay shrugged.

"I worked at a station in Kansas that tried to gain listeners with a cash stash. The owner gave one-word clues each day to the morning team and you had to listen at the same time in order to hear it. Problem was, he was the only one who knew where the cash was stashed and after two days, he keeled over in his office. Nobody ever found it."

He cued up another song and kept talking and Clay was captivated by his voice, his constant movement and demeanor.

"It doesn't matter how big the station is or how many people listen, you can work on your craft wherever you are. When I worked in Montgomery, we had a list of songs you could play back to back and it sounded so good, like butter melting on hot bread. I was Wayne Wilson at that station and my morning partner was Ollie Waxman, so it was Wax and Wayne in the morning. That was a fun show. But listen to this song coming up. I'll show you what I'm talking about."

He plugged a cart into the machine.

"I've been listening to the station imagers. They're a little dated, but they work. When you have a song that fades like 'Rhinestone Cowboy,' you have to catch it at the right moment, like a train leaving the station, and when the caboose passes, you hit the sounder, pull the pot fast, then start the next song up full. Listen."

Cody turned up the monitor so high the walls shook and when Glen Campbell's voice faded, he hit the green button on the cart machine, a drum hit interrupted the music, and then voices sang, "The best country in the country, Country 16!"

In one motion, the man turned down one pot, hit the switch for the turntable, turned up the other pot, and played Bobby Gentry's "Ode to Billie Joe." Clay stood mesmerized at how effortless it seemed. Cody was right. Though there was a lot going on behind the scenes, the sound was smooth and fluid.

"You don't learn this overnight, but you have to hear it first. And if you can hear it, you'll be moving to bigger pastures."

Clay nodded.

"Of course, you have to lose the stutter." He laughed, then coughed. "That's a bummer. I've known people who have kicked that, though. And since it looks like you're still in high school, man, the chicks will be all over you. They love a guy with a radio voice."

Clay watched how Cody cued records and prepared the cart machine and answered the phone. He soaked in the stories, some of them a little too adult. The man didn't notice Clay blushing when he talked about women. Cody seemed larger than life, and though he was consumed with himself, Clay felt drawn to him.

"New York City, man. The Big Apple is where I'm headed. And I'm not stopping until I make it—like Sinatra, if I can make it there, I can make it anywhere."

Clay thought it was an awful long way from Emmaus to New York City. And for the first time he wanted to defend Emmaus to somebody who was putting it down. That's how he knew it was more than just a place for him to stay. It was becoming his home.

CHAPTER 24

After midnight, Sunday morning, Clay sat at the control board keeping an eye on the front door. He knew Cody was at the Mountaineer Opry, but he hadn't expected him to be this late. At 12:45 lights shone in the trees. Clay unlocked the front door.

Cody stumbled inside with his arm around a woman with big hair and a low-cut blouse. They were laughing and smiling and using each other to stay upright.

Jubal stood and stretched.

"Mandy, meet The Kid. Kid, mark this on your calendar. You're going to remember this night." Cody was louder than usual and slurred some of his words. "This is a rising country star. Bigger than Loretta. Bigger than Tammy." He glanced at her. "Almost as big as Dolly."

Mandy laughed hard. "I think you're overestimating me." She held out a hand and Clay shook it.

"Too bad we don't have a camera to take a picture of you two. Kid, segue one more song for me while I get things set up."

Cody went to the production room and cued up a tape, which was strange. They played *Waite, on the Lord* and other recorded Sunday morning shows from there, but there was nothing on tape overnight.

It was after 1 a.m. when Clay and Jubal walked outside. Cody waved and winked, quickly locking the front door. Clay made it to the darkened upper parking lot on the east side of the building before he realized he had forgotten his flashlight. He went back to the front door and knocked, but Cody wasn't in the control room. Clay's flashlight hung on the coatrack where he'd left it. He knocked harder and waited but knowing Cody, the music was loud. Clay noticed the reel-to-reel machine going in the production room and through the door he heard a man singing, *"Make the world go away."* He knocked again, then gave up.

"C-c-come on, Jubal."

He was almost to the curve that wound down the hill when a light flashed behind him. The window in Waite's office lit in bright florescence. Strange. Waite always kept his office locked. Curiosity overwhelming him, Clay walked back to the building as someone closed the blinds. But one slat at eye level was askew.

Cody and Mandy slow danced by Waite's desk. Mandy giggled and put her arms around his neck. Cody moved her steadily toward the couch. The Kid felt bad looking through the window, but not bad enough to stop.

Mandy pushed Cody back and unbuttoned his shirt for him. He took it off, swinging it like an Elvis impersonator Clay had seen on TV. Mandy laughed like it was the funniest thing she'd ever seen. Then she stopped and pointed at a picture on Waite's desk and said something Clay couldn't hear.

Cody wasn't in a picture-looking mood because he turned Mandy around and they moved toward the corner and Clay couldn't see them.

Clay noticed another slat askew a little higher and put his foot on a rock to get a better look. The music pulsed. Who was running the station? As Barbara Mandrell sang "(If Loving You Is Wrong) I Don't Want to Be Right," Clay figured it out. Cody had planned this rendezvous. He'd recorded a tape of music. But how had he gotten Waite's office door open?

More giggling from inside and the two were on the couch and as he pushed himself higher, Clay lost his balance and fell hard against the window, twisting his ankle.

"What was that?" Mandy said breathlessly.

Jubal barked.

"Somebody's out there," Cody said. "Stay here."

Clay heard fumbling inside, but he pushed away from the window and tripped over Jubal, who yelped. He limped to the road and made it around the curve as footsteps crunched through the gravel. He kept hopping all the way down the hill toward the junkyard.

Pidge was awake and the sun was up when she heard pounding on the front door and wondered who could have gotten through the gate. Maybe Clay had forgotten to lock it the night before. She vaulted out of bed and ran barefoot across the linoleum and looked out the peephole.

A man with a receding hairline and sad face paced on the wooden porch. He looked like life had a sleeper hold on him and wasn't letting go. She opened the door a crack, stretching to the end of the chain on the lock.

"Can I help you?"

"I need to speak with . . . The Kid." He ran a hand across his forehead. "He lives here, right? I work up at the station."

She heard a door open behind her and footsteps in the hall. "He's not up yet," she said through the crack in the door. "But I'll tell him—"

"Could you get him?" His tone was insistent.

"It's early to be knocking on people's doors, mister."

He held up both hands. "Look, I understand. I apologize for disturbing you. I wouldn't be here if it wasn't important. Something happened last night."

Pidge turned and saw Clay wiping sleep from his eyes. She whispered, "What happened?"

He waved her into the hallway by the kitchen.

"You stay there, mister. I'll see if I can wake him."

She closed the door and followed Clay around the corner. He looked at the floor and rubbed his hands.

"What?" she said.

Stuttering and stammering, he explained that Cody had come in drunk with a woman. He told her about going back for his flashlight and what he saw through the window. He'd just wanted to know who was in Waite's office.

Pidge shook her head. So that was the kind of man Waite had hired. She put a hand on Clay's shoulder. "Go back to bed."

"Y-y-you'll t-t-t-talk with him?"

"I'll handle it. Don't worry."

Pidge wondered what he had seen, but if the man had come to their front door at this hour, she could imagine. She swallowed hard, then unlatched the front door and stepped outside, the morning dew thick on the wooden porch. Her feet got wet and chipped paint flecks stuck to them.

Cody turned, his hands in his back pockets. "Did you wake him up?"

"You got a lot of nerve."

"I've got nerve?"

"Clay saw a light in Waite's office and wondered who was in there. You must have a key to get in, right?"

"He was spying on me. A Peeping Tom. He waited around. There's laws against that."

"He forgot his flashlight and tried to get you to unlock the door, but it sounds like you were busy. You had company?"

"That's none of your . . ." He winced and closed his mouth to start again. "I need to talk to him."

"You ought to be talking to Waite, don't you think?"

"I just want to make sure he understands—"

"Oh, he understands. He's real sharp."

Cody gathered himself. "I need to know if this is going to be a problem. I need this job. And since Waite is kind of religious, I don't want him hearing about it."

She leaned against the loose railing that ran around the front porch and lifted her hands, ready for his explanation.

"I met someone last night. She's interested in radio and I invited her to the station. She's a singer. One thing led to another, you know? And The Kid skulked around outside the window like a—"

"He wasn't skulking and you know it," she said, interrupting.

"I just want to know if this is going to come back on me."

"Don't you think Waite will notice somebody was in his office?"

"We put everything back the way it was."

"That was real thoughtful of you."

"Can you just get him out here? Let me talk to him and clear this up."

She opened the door and slipped on her flip-flops and walked past Cody, and he followed her around the house. She stood outside the office, arms crossed in front of her.

"Mister, we got enough trouble around here without the likes of you."

He put out a hand. "The name's Cody."

She didn't shake it. "I was married to a dud like you. Last thing I need is you having influence on that boy."

Flap flew into the window and perched as if getting a better vantage.

Cody pulled his head back. "What in the world is that?"

She ignored him. "If Waite hired you, he probably wanted to help you. He's a good, decent man. You ought not pay him back like this."

"You're right. He is a good man. I'll give you that. And I'm trying to change. Turn over a new leaf. But it's hard."

"It ain't hard to be decent. To respect other people's locked doors. And to keep your nose clean for half a minute. What were you thinking coming in drunk? You need to leave."

"I didn't come here to make trouble. I wanted to explain. Help The Kid understand how hard it is to be alone sometimes."

"You came down here to make sure he wouldn't rat on you. I think he understands plenty. And so do I."

"I need to know he's not going to say anything. I'm at the end of my rope. Only reason I came here was . . ."

"Why don't you go find that woman you were with last night? I'm sure she'll help you out."

He rubbed the back of his neck and his face contorted. "The Kid's a pervert. That's what he is. A Peeping Tom."

"You've dug your own hole, Cody. Get out."

He didn't budge. Through gritted teeth he said, "He'd better not say anything to Waite. If he does, I'll call the police. File a report. People in town will know you're raising a pervert."

Pidge stared at him. "I'll call Art Palermo myself right now if you'd like. He knows us. He'll figure out who the pervert is."

Cody seemed at a loss for words. He looked around at the cars and appliances parked and stacked. "Emmaus trash. That's all you are."

He walked to his truck and drove away. Pidge turned and saw movement at Clay's window.

CHAPTER 25

AFTER HEARING WHAT CODY HAD SAID, Clay couldn't go back to sleep. He finally kicked the covers back and went to the kitchen and poured a bowl of cereal. Then he got dressed in his church clothes, a clean pair of jeans and a shirt that buttoned, and he sat on the porch and stroked Jubal's head.

"The best country in the country, Country 16," he whispered. He tried saying it without a stutter and almost made it. Jubal closed his eyes, enraptured by the physical touch.

Clay studied the dog's collar, which had Jubal's name and a square, boxlike contraption hooked to it. Clay figured it was a shock collar—he had seen those for a dog in his old neighborhood that always barked. But Gideon Quidley seemed too nice of a fellow to shock his dog for doing what comes naturally. He took the collar off and cleaned it with a rag. He couldn't find any metal to conduct electricity. Strange.

As he cleaned, he noticed an indentation on the underside of the plastic box and put his thumbnail in it and pulled. Nothing happened. He got a dime from his pocket and did the same. Nothing. He pushed it hard and heard a click. The plastic moved. He took the small panel away and looked inside, expecting to see leaking batteries. Instead, he found a car key. He took it out and studied it, noticing the *H* on the front, and he thought that was a weird but smart thing for Gideon Quidley to do, hide his extra car key in his dog's collar.

He shoved the key in his pocket, snapped the box shut, and put the collar on Jubal. He leaned down and kissed the dog on his head. "You stay here."

Clay closed the fence and walked up the hill to the station with Jubal barking his head off the whole way. He checked the clock inside the station when he reached the front, then sat at the top of the wooden steps. It would be another twenty minutes before Waite got there. Because the weather stripping was gone from the door, he could hear *Waite, on the Lord*. There was something about the songs and Waite's voice that made up for the twang and the lack of lead guitars. Clay had to admit there was a purity to the country and gospel sound. He still preferred Styx or Van Halen, sure. But there were a few songs he played that he actually liked and the rest of them didn't turn his stomach like they used to and he wasn't sure why.

Trucks and cars passed on the interstate and Clay noticed something through the trees. Across the road in front of the station was another road that dipped and went under the interstate. Under the bridge sat a truck with a camper on the back. It looked like Cody's.

What Cody had said to Pidge burned Clay. The part about being Emmaus trash and calling Clay a pervert. Cody was a smooth talker until he got cornered with the truth. Then, like a snake, the fangs and venom came out. But there was something Clay had seen and heard the night before that he couldn't shake.

He walked down the steps and crossed the road with his hands in his pockets, hearing 18-wheelers rumble overhead. He slowed when he came to the truck. Was it Cody's? He'd only seen it in the dark. He stood there for a moment, then walked to the front of the truck and looked inside and saw headphones on the passenger seat. Then he saw movement in the back.

"What are you doing here?" Cody said, his voice groggy. He rolled off the mattress and opened the back and crawled out of the truck in the same clothes he'd worn the night before.

Clay moved to the other side of the road.

"Get back over here." Cody blinked hard and wiped at his bloodshot eyes. "I met your mom this morning. She's a piece of work."

Clay didn't correct him. "I-I-I heard."

"I could cause you two a lot of trouble you don't want."

Clay nodded.

"Look, I'm not asking for the moon. I need this job. You understand? I've got tapes and résumés out, but in the meantime I need the paycheck. So . . ." He grabbed his head as if trying to stop something happening inside. "You're going to keep that stutterin' mouth of yours shut about what happened last night. You hear me?"

Clay stared at him. "I'll k-k-keep quiet if y-you t-tell me s-s-something."

Cody narrowed his eyes. "What?"

Clay stammered through the question. It was about Mandy and how she'd noticed the picture on Waite's desk. She'd said something about it.

Cody squinted as if Clay had spoken in Swahili. Then a look

of recognition. He leaned against his truck with something close to confidence. "Yeah, I remember now. You promise me you won't tell Waite what happened, and I'll tell you what she said."

Clay nodded.

"I need to hear it."

"I-I p-promise."

Cody lowered his voice. "You know what happens to people who go back on their word, don't you?"

"I s-said I-I p-promise."

Cody chewed on his lip, then said, "She told me she recognized the girl in that picture. She'd met her before. Now that's all I'm going to tell you."

"N-no. T-t-tell me wh-where."

"Where what?"

"Wh-where sh-she m-met her."

"You got a lot of nerve, Kid. You peep in the window and . . . How much of what happened in there did you see?"

"T-t-tell m-me."

Cody sighed. "She said it was a couple of years ago down in Florida. She was playing a show and the local radio station had somebody introduce the bands. The girl in the picture was one of the DJs."

Clay's mind spun. He'd seen Waite stare at the picture with a sadness in his eyes, but he'd never known why.

"What t-t-town?"

Cody shook his head. "I don't remember what town, for crying out loud. It was some island." He tried different consonants until he came to the *M*'s. He pinched the bridge of his nose. "Merritt. That was it. Merritt Island. That's all I got."

"Okay," Clay said.

"Who is she? Why does Waite have her picture?"

Clay shrugged. "B-but don't tell Waite this."

"Why not?"

"You t-tell Waite about the p-picture and I'll t-tell him about y-you and that woman."

Cody stepped close enough for Clay to smell his rancid breath. He poked a finger into Clay's chest hard. "You say anything to Waite about what happened, and I swear I'll kill your dog. Then I'll beat up your trashy mother. You got it?"

Clay clenched his teeth. He wanted to spit out words to put Cody in his place. He'd think of something an hour later. He turned and crossed the road and walked up the wooden steps and sat at the top to wait.

Waite found The Kid at the top of the stairs so he didn't have to drive to his house to pick him up. They drove toward the church with the radio on low, listening to the last few minutes of his program. Waite had ended with Dallas Holm's "Rise Again," one of his favorites.

"When did Cody get to the station last night?"

"After m-m-midnight."

"I was afraid of that. I'll talk with him. Maybe it's better to have Wally do the Opry."

The Kid didn't respond.

"Weather's supposed to be nice this afternoon. I thought we could go over to the reservoir and put a line in. Maybe get us a bucket of chicken from the Colonel? That sound good?"

The Kid nodded.

"I mentioned it to Pidge and she said she was fine with it."

When they made it to church, Waite opened the glove compartment and pulled out a box and handed it to The Kid. "Got you something."

The Kid lifted the top off and stared at the leather-covered Bible. He looked up at Waite and back down at the gift.

"I hope you don't mind I had them engrave it that way."

At the bottom right were words written in gold: *The Kid*.

Waite took it and pulled it out and showed him the tabs for different books of the Bible. "That's so you can cheat a little. When somebody says, 'Turn to the book of 1 Peter,' you can see it right there."

The Kid smiled and flipped to the front and saw what Waite had written. *To The Kid, from your friend, Waite Evers. God bless you.*

"Th-th-thank y-you."

The service was sparsely attended and Waite noticed several men from the congregation who had been at the meeting last week were missing. The Kid sat with Waite through the sermon, which was about bridling the tongue, from the book of James. When the pastor told them to turn there, The Kid read the tabs, found the book, and looked up at Waite, smiling.

After the worship service, Waite watched The Kid disappear downstairs to Sunday school behind a gaggle of teenage girls, carrying his new Bible like it was a prize he'd won at the county fair. Nobody said hello to The Kid or seemed to notice him and it pained Waite. That would come. In time he'd make a friend.

Afterward they drove into town and bought a bucket of chicken with biscuits, gravy, mashed potatoes, and coleslaw, and they ate at a picnic table by the reservoir. Waite had never seen anybody devour that many chicken legs in one sitting and he wondered how many Possum could polish off for Sunday dinner.

They got in the boat and Waite rowed them to a shady spot at the far end where it was quiet and there weren't as many families with children. He showed The Kid how to bait the line, but he already knew how. They sat with the water gently lapping the side and Waite leaned back and stretched.

"Now this is what a Sunday afternoon is supposed to feel like, don't you think?"

The Kid nodded and cast his line toward the shallows.

"All the treasure in the world won't give you this kind of peace. Best things in life are free."

The Kid reeled his Zebco until it clicked. "C-can I ask s-something?"

"Go right ahead."

"Who's th-that in the p-p-picture on your d-d-desk?"

The question surprised Waite. He didn't know The Kid had noticed. There were probably a lot of things Waite hadn't noticed.

"That's my daughter, Emily. I don't talk about her much, but I think about her a lot."

"Y-y-you l-l-look at her every d-d-day."

"I sure do."

A long, uncomfortable silence followed. Waite reeled in his line and cast it on the other side of the boat.

The Kid looked back at him. "Wh-where is sh-she?"

"You've got to learn something about people, Kid. There are times when they want to talk and times when they don't. Times when you ought to leave well enough alone."

The Kid looked at his bobber on the water and spoke with his head turned away. "Wh-what if . . . s-s-somebody n-n-needs to talk but w-won't?"

"That's when you give them time."

The Kid didn't speak and it unnerved Waite. He closed his eyes and saw the picture on his desk. Emily's sad smile. Every time he saw it, he shot up an arrow prayer for her. So far, no arrows had landed. At least as far as he could tell.

"All right, here's the story. I'm only going to tell this once, so pay attention. Got it?"

The Kid nodded.

"I brought Emily to the station when she was a little shaver. And she was just like you—she lapped everything up like a cat drinking a saucer of milk. You're holding her fishing pole. When she was sixteen or so, she got in with the wrong crowd. She'd talk to her mother but she wouldn't talk to me. I tried to get her to see what was happening. Tried hard. She was in love with this guy she knew in high school. And I got scared she was going to ruin her life, so I was mean to her. Yelled at her. My wife said to give her space, let her figure it out. Said I was going to push her away. I kept going because I thought that was the loving thing to do. But it wasn't. I can see that now.

"The boy got in an accident. Flipped his Jeep off the interstate. She was supposed to be with him, but I wouldn't let her go. I think she blamed me. She thought if she had gone, he would have driven more carefully. He wouldn't have died. After the funeral she stopped talking to me.

"The summer she graduated, a singer and his band came through town. Next thing I knew, she was gone. And that was the last I heard from her. I pray for her every day. Every time I see her picture."

"H-h-have you l-l-looked for her?"

"Of course. It's a big country, though."

"Who w-was the singer?"

"Fellow named Mack Strum. Used to live near here."

Waite's voice felt thick and heavy, like the words added weight to him. He pushed the emotion down and stared as if he could see her reflection in the water—like he used to on Sunday afternoons when she sat in the front of the boat.

"She called my wife a time or two. Only when Emily knew I wouldn't be there. Wouldn't say where she was. Just that she was okay. Then she stopped calling. And my wife got sick. And that brings you up to speed with the picture I keep on my desk."

Waite felt a burning in his chest as he spoke. "She might be with the angels, for all I know. I've been watching the road for a long time. And my prayer, my dream really, is that one day I'll look out and see her walking up those rickety stairs like she used to. Like the story of the prodigal, the father in that one was watching for a speck on the road so he could run out and hug his son's neck. I'd give a million dollars to see that speck. I'd give all of Gideon Quidley's treasure if she'd come back and let me tell her I love her."

The Kid listened from the front of the boat and didn't speak. And it struck Waite that the most powerful thing you could do was listen. It also struck him that all the things he said to others, the wisdom he tried to impart, were things he needed just as much as they did. He spoke about forgiveness on his Sunday program because he needed it. Maybe that's why people said he sounded real and why they felt they could trust him with their pain. He carried a load of his own without anybody knowing.

The Kid's rod bent nearly to the water and he looked back, wide-eyed and with all the hope in the world. Waite struggled to watch him reel the Zebco through blurry eyes as he recalled the squeaky-voiced girl who sat in the same seat with her life jacket on, squealing, "I got one, Daddy! I got a big one!"

He'd played out the dream a billion times in his mind. He went to sleep thinking of her and woke with the echoes of her calling him and realized she only said *Daddy* when he slept. If it ever happened, if she ever came back, he swore he would just run and grab her in his arms and not say a word. Just hang on. Listen. That's what he'd do.

CHAPTER 26

With twenty days left until the final envelope was opened, TD decided desperate times called for desperate measures. He took off from work one morning and woke at 3 a.m. to drive north. He listened to Cody as long as he could, then switched stations, hearing Larry King all over the dial. The man had a great voice and seemed pretty smart, especially when it came to baseball. TD smiled when people called in and tried to convert him to Christianity. Larry didn't seem interested and TD wondered why and if it was the same *why* as he had.

He pulled into the Sunrise, a diner Gideon had frequented, a little after 8 a.m., and he asked the young girl who got the menu for him to sit him at a table in Wilma's section. She nodded and he followed her to a section toward the back.

As he looked over the menu, a woman with graying hair brought a coffeepot and poured him a cup without asking.

"How'd you know I wanted coffee?"

"Nobody comes to the Sunrise and says no to the coffee. Fresh ground and brewed every morning. It's our Sunrise special blend."

"It's my first time here. What do you suggest?"

"Everybody likes the farmer special. You get a little bit of every-thing."

TD nodded and handed the menu back and told her how he wanted his eggs and what kind of bread for the toast.

"Where you from?" she said.

"West Virginia." He watched her face to see if she reacted. "I drove up from Emmaus."

She picked up the coffeepot she'd put down. "Long way to come for breakfast, isn't it?"

"I'm here for more than breakfast."

"Well, we'll get it out to you as quick as we can."

Wilma walked away and he thought she looked at him side-ways as she was putting in the order. When she returned to fill up his coffee and tell him his order would be right out, TD took the plunge.

"A friend of mine said you used to wait on Gideon Quidley. Is that true?"

"You could have saved yourself a trip if you'd just called."

"I did. My name's TD Lovett."

"Okay. I remember you."

"I remember you, too. And the sound of the phone hanging up."

"I don't have anything to say. I'm sorry."

He put his hand on hers. "Please."

She jerked away.

"I'm here because there's a pastor in the hospital. He's got three kids. I'm trying to help him."

She laughed. "Like I believe that. You're trying to help yourself, just like the rest."

"His name's Robby Gardner. He lost a leg and the hospital stay's costing a fortune. He thinks you might know something that could help us."

She rolled her eyes. "I had a woman come through last week whose whole family has cancer and she needed to find the treasure so they could get treatment. I don't believe a word anybody tells me anymore."

"His wife's name is Sharon. She didn't want him to go looking for the treasure. She had a bad feeling. You can call the hospital and talk with Robby. I'm not lying."

"Whether you are or you're not, I can't help you. I don't know anything about the treasure."

"But you talked to Robby. He wrote that down."

She put a hand on her hip. "Honey, you and Robby are a day late and a few million dollars short, okay?"

"Why do you say that?"

"I've had reporters in here. I've served people with maps asking me to show them where I think he hid his ark. I've had government people asking me questions. I've had—"

"Government people?"

"Yeah, black suits and skinny ties and government license plates on their cars. Some department of something or other. Like everybody, they want to know the same thing. And I keep telling them, your guess is as good as mine."

"Did the government people say why they were looking?"

She shook her head. "You got me. One of our cooks said they're after double eagles. Gold coins. Supposed to be worth a lot. Might be right, but I don't know."

"Gideon talked to you. He liked you. He must have said something. Didn't you see him write things down?"

Someone called Wilma's name and she returned to the kitchen, then brought a tray of food that TD thought even Possum couldn't finish in one sitting.

Wilma pulled out a chair and sat. "I remember Robby. He had a real sweet spirit. You say he got hurt?"

"Real bad. And Gideon found out and wanted to help him."

"And how would you know that?"

"I was the one who found Gideon. I drove up on the accident. He'd heard about Robby. He wanted to help him pay his bills."

Wilma ran her hand across the table in front of her. "Gideon and his wife, Opal, would come in for lunch every now and then. They weren't regular. Just the sweetest old people you've ever seen. He'd pay the bill and she'd come back in and add to the tip and wink at me. Then we didn't see them for a while and I heard Opal died. After that he'd come in for breakfast and we kind of adopted him. Knew all of us by name. And at some point, he said something about having big plans. Said I'd read about it in the paper one day. I thought, okay, that's just Gideon talking.

"Then one day, he was sitting right over at that table with his Bible next to him, which he liked to do, and I heard him say something out loud. He got real excited, like he'd discovered the cure for cancer or something. He just grinned through the whole meal. 'I figured it out.' That's what he said. And that's all I know. He handed me the tip that day and off he went."

"When was he last here?" TD said.

"The past few months he kind of pulled back. Brooding.

Everybody sensed it. Some thought it was just him getting old or missing Opal. I'm not sure. He never said. The only person he really talked to . . ."

"Who?" TD said.

Wilma looked at him. "Can I trust you? Are you like everybody else who's trying to solve his puzzle? Like the government people? They asked me ten ways to Sunday what he said to me and I kept telling them the same thing. They finally got fed up and left."

TD pushed his plate away. "Wilma, I don't know if I'm different. But the closer I get to him, to finding out what made him tick, the more I like the old fellow. I tried to save his life the night I found him. And in his last breath, I think he was trying to save mine."

"What do you mean?"

"He asked if I knew the Lord. A man about to head off into eternity was asking about somebody he'd never met before. That stuck with me."

She smiled. "I can see it has. You know, I thought there was something about you when you walked in here. I'm glad you got to meet him."

"I wish I could have done more for him."

Wilma pulled out a pad and wrote something down. She tore off the page and handed it to him. "Gideon had a friend. This was a man he'd been working on, praying for. He brought him in for a meal every now and then. He lives up the road a couple of miles—you'll pass Gideon's house on the way. You might talk to him. Tell him Wilma sent you, okay?"

TD followed the map out to a lonely road and as he passed Gideon's house, he slowed and pulled over. He expected it to be a mansion like the Beverly Hillbillies' or at least have a stone wall running around it for privacy. Instead, it looked like every other house by the road. There were mature trees on the property that gave it shade, but nothing said a rich man lived there.

In the driveway were several shiny vehicles and he wondered if they were Realtors looking at the house and getting it ready for sale. Then he noticed the government license plates and activity like a beehive.

The longer he looked at the house, the more questions came, and so did a man in a suit who carried a two-way radio.

"Can I help you?"

"I'm just wondering what's going on at Gideon's place."

"Are you a neighbor? A family member?"

"I know his son."

"Sir, I think you need to move along."

"I reckon you're right."

TD pulled away and in his side mirror he saw the man writing down his license plate number.

The paved road turned to gravel and then dirt. It wound through lush countryside and up a hill that TD thought would never end. On a little knoll looking down on the valley sat a ramshackle brown house that looked like a strong wind might flatten it. On the porch and around the house was a pack of dogs, some that ran barking to the driveway and others that stared. TD shut off his engine and watched the animals surround the truck, wagging their tails. They followed him to the house, jumping and sniffing. A couple of the dogs looked like Jubal.

A man with a scruffy beard and wispy hair that floated in the breeze stepped onto the porch. He had pasty-white skin except for his round, cherubic cheeks. His eyes were blue and inquisitive.

"Do I know you?" the man said.

"No, sir. But Wilma at the diner drew me a map and said I should come up here. Are you Corky?"

He glanced at TD's truck and back, wary. "Depends."

TD stood in the yard with the dogs circling him like he was a fire hydrant. He put down both hands and the dogs sniffed and licked at him, and evidently that was enough for the man.

"Yeah, I'm Corky, come on up."

TD sat in a wooden rocker that he wasn't sure would hold him, but it did. Corky collapsed into a swing that hung by metal chains, and when the man pushed back, it whined as if in pain.

"Did Gideon get Jubal from you?" TD said.

Corky nodded. "Right there's Jubal's brothers. They're getting old, like the rest of us. You knew him?"

TD explained how he'd met the man and Corky seemed to sit a little straighter with the story of the deer and the accident. TD told him everything and Corky stared at the trees and the valley below with a stoic face, as if hearing a familiar song.

"You must have come out here looking for the treasure, then."

"I know it ain't here. I'm not sure why I came, to be honest. I'm beginning to think there's more than the treasure I'm looking for."

"Did Gideon finish telling you what he wanted to say to his son?"

"No, sir. He never got the chance. At least with me. He might have said something to the paramedics, but I don't think so. And his son pulled the plug on him."

The man cursed, then made a humming noise deep in his throat that was close to a growl.

TD told Corky about Pastor Robby and finding him near dead in a cave in Ephra. Corky shook his head and said, "That's what sent Gideon over the edge. Not that he wasn't already there."

"What do you mean?"

"Gideon read the story in the paper. He called me that day and told me. Asked if I would watch Jubal. He needed to go somewhere. Then he called me again and said he was taking Jubal with him. Said the dog was part of it."

"What do you think he meant?"

"You could spend a lifetime trying to figure out what he meant by one thing or another. He was always talking about trusting the Lord for everything. A few years ago he called me from a truck stop about twenty-five miles from here and asked me to come pick him up. Said he'd been on an errand and that the Lord told him to get home hitchhiking. Driver of an 18-wheeler had pity on him and got him close. Gideon was like that. He'd just fling himself into things and then trust the Lord to get him out of trouble."

"I guess it didn't work on his last trip."

"No, it didn't. Poor thing. I keep thinking about that treasure. He had a proverb memorized . . . something about it being the glory of God to search for . . . No, it's the glory of God to conceal a matter. I think he felt like he was helping God out by hiding the treasure."

"Did you talk with him after he called about Jubal?"

"Nope. That's the last conversation we had."

TD stopped rocking. He had a million questions but decided to stay quiet.

"I was one of his projects. He tried to get me to come to Jesus. I don't know why I got on his radar. Maybe he liked the challenge. He bought Jubal from me before Opal died and I swear that dog was a bigger help than his religion. He would have disagreed about that, of course. I think it kept him going. That and the treasure nonsense.

"He used to come up of the evening and sit here on the porch and we'd watch the dogs play in the gloaming. Every dang time he'd work in a verse or two about the heavens declaring the glory of God or some such. I'd tell him to keep his religion to himself. But if you really believe you got an answer to life's problems and you don't tell nobody, what good is the answer? So I don't fault him.

Anyhow, Jubal and the ark occupied him after Opal died. But in the last year, he was more agitated."

"What about?"

"I think he might have questioned if he'd done the right thing. And he was worried somebody would find the treasure who didn't deserve it or would squander it. Or that his son would find it. I'm convinced that was part of why he hid it in the first place."

"He didn't trust Milton?"

"He lives down your way. You ever met him?"

"I have. Can't say I enjoyed it."

"Well, I rest my case. Gid thought Milton was trying to get him declared incompetent. Get him committed to a home. I don't know if that was true, but Gid believed it. Milton was his biggest disappointment. He tried to get him to see the light, just like me."

Corky pushed the swing back and forth and shook his head. "I miss him. I even miss fighting about the Bible. He sure knew it frontwards and backwards. 'We have this treasure in earthen vessels,' he used to say. Then he'd look at me say, 'Your vessel's a lot bigger than mine.'" Corky laughed.

TD watched the lightning bugs rise from the earth. "So you believe it's really out there somewhere."

"Oh, it's out there. He showed me a double eagle once. Gold coin out of circulation. He said people are going to be surprised when they open that ark. Said something priceless was inside."

"Didn't say what it was?"

"Not to me he didn't."

"Well, there's an envelope that will be opened in a couple of weeks. That'll probably solve it."

"And knowing Milton, he'll be first in line. You know, Gid talked about the clues. He was more than happy to quote verses. He told me he chose ones the Holy Spirit could use to convict people. Except the one about the willows and the harps. That was evidently important. And he mentioned something about Luke and two axes. And then . . ."

"Axes?"

"If I'd known he was going to die, I would have paid more attention. He said there was something people would discover once the ark was found that had to do with axes. You got any idea about that?"

TD thought a moment. "Maybe he marked the location with axes? Like crossed axes on a grave? Or a coat of arms, that kind of thing? Or there's a story in the Old Testament about an ax-head floating on the water."

"How do you know all that? You believe the same as Gid?"

"My father was a pastor. Made us go to every service. Memorize whole books of the Bible. Pray before meals, between meals. Never went to a movie theater. That kind of thing."

"Something bad happen?"

"I came up here to ask questions, not answer them."

"Suit yourself." Corky rubbed his hands on his jeans.

TD clenched his teeth together. He leaned forward with his elbows on his knees. "My brother got sick. Got the polio."

"I remember how scared people got. This was in the fifties?"

"Yeah. They put him in an iron lung. Kept me out until right near the end. Didn't want me to get it, I guess. It tore my mother up. And my brother seemed to be improving. I remember him looking up at me, touching the glass. I can still see him smiling."

"He didn't make it?"

"He might have if my dad hadn't decided to pull him out of there."

"Why did he do that?"

"He said God told him he was healed. He told us we needed to believe. Have faith."

"Poor kid."

"Yeah, he died not long after they removed him."

"No, I meant you."

TD paused. "I was a teenager before I thought much about it. I realized that I blamed myself. Thought it was my fault. I was scared he would die and I thought that meant I didn't have faith. And if I had, he would have lived."

"That's a big burden to carry, son."

"Yes, sir, it is. When I heard the talk about Gideon, it brought a lot of that back. And I didn't want anything to do with it."

"If Gideon was here, I bet he'd have a verse for you. Something to comfort you."

"He probably would."

"I'm real sorry that happened. Sorry about your brother. What was his name?"

TD felt short of breath all of a sudden, like the man's words had touched something inside he didn't know was there. "Timothy."

"You ever talk with your daddy about it?"

"I've avoided him for a long time."

"Mm-hmm."

"You mentioned the verse with the willows. Did Gideon say something about that?"

"He had mapped out the 'eternal treasure.' But he didn't get the one about the harps and willows until he found the place he hid his ark."

"Wait, you're saying he scouted out a place to hide it and found harps in willows?"

"Don't quote me, but that's what I presumed from what he said."

TD stood and reached out a hand. Corky stood stiffly and, instead of shaking his hand, embraced TD in a bear hug. "I'm glad to meet you, son. Good luck with everything."

CHAPTER 27

Clay had put together a working bicycle from spare parts he found at the salvage yard and he rode to the library one afternoon. He was sweating bullets when he finally got up the nerve to approach a librarian.

"May I help you?" The woman smiled and looked like she meant it.

"H-how c-c-could I f-f-find somebody in another s-s-state?"

"You mean an address? A phone number?"

"Either one. Or b-both."

"What information do you have?"

Clay handed her a piece of paper with everything he knew about Emily Evers. The librarian looked the page over and seemed to make computations. "If she works at a radio station, maybe we could get a list in that city and call and ask. Would that help?"

Clay nodded and followed the woman to another section. He wanted to do this without anybody knowing, certainly not Waite. The first hurdle would be to find his daughter, which meant he'd have to get up the nerve to talk on the phone. Then he'd have to figure out what to say to her after he found her. If he could get her address, that would be a start.

The librarian found a list of radio stations on Merritt Island and gave it to him complete with phone numbers and addresses. He rode away thinking libraries were filled with smart people who could find anything.

The next question was where to call from. If he did it from home, the long-distance charges would show up and Pidge would hit the roof and want to know what he was doing. If he called from the station, the same thing might happen with Ardelle. But if he did get hold of Emily, Waite likely wouldn't mind that he'd made a few long-distance calls.

He rode to the station and went to the production room with his sheet of paper and turned the microphone on and the light swirled outside the door. He recorded himself asking the question, made all the edits, and dialed the first number.

When the receptionist answered the phone, Clay flipped the switch that allowed him to play the audio from the Scully down the phone line.

"Hello, my name is Clayton and I'm trying to find Emily Evers. Do you know if she works at your station or another station in the area?"

Clay flipped the switch quickly so he could hear the answer on the other end. On the fourth call, he played the tape and heard a man cover the mouthpiece of the phone and say something.

"Doesn't Emily Evers work at the country station?"

There was a clamor in the background and the man, who sounded a lot like Cody, returned. "Yeah, you need to call Big Cat Country. Emily Travers does middays over there. That might be her."

Clay wrote down the call letters and matched them with the station on his list. There was a typewriter on the corner desk, and he retrieved an envelope and a blank sheet of paper with the station logo and rolled it around the spindle.

Dear Emily,

I hope I have the right person. If not, please let me know so that I can keep looking.

You don't know me. I would have called and told you this on the phone, but I've got a bad stutter. I figured it was better for me to write so I don't waste your time. Ha.

My name is Clay and I work at Country 16 in Emmaus, WV. People call me The Kid. If I'm right, your dad is Waite Evers. I won't go into how I heard about you, but someone said you might be in Florida and a lady at the library helped me. That's why I'm writing you.

Your daddy keeps a picture of you on his desk. And every time I see him look at it, there's pain on his face. I'm not telling you this to make you feel bad. In fact, I hope it does the opposite.

Waite brought me on at the station even though I'm only 15 and have a stutter. He gave me a chance. He showed me how to record myself and edit myself so that I can do the weather forecast and hear my voice the way it might sound if I didn't stutter. I don't like country music at all. But I love working here because he's been kind. He even took me to Hamm's. You might remember that restaurant.

He took me fishing one day and told me the rod and reel I was using was yours. And he told me a little about the

falling-out you two had. It took me a while to get it out of
him. I asked if he'd looked for you and he said he had but
hasn't found you.

He told me his dream is that one day you'll come walking
up the rickety steps of Country 16 like when you were little.
He said he'd give a million dollars to see you and hug your
neck and tell you he loves you.

I don't have a daddy. And my mother and her kin have
me living with my aunt Pidge. She's real nice. I don't have
any right to stick my nose in your business. But if there's any
part of you that's open to giving your daddy a second chance,
I know he'd take it. He's given a lot of people a second chance
here at Country 16. I can tell he's sorry about what happened
between you.

I'll stop. I'm putting my address and phone number
below. Please write because if you call, you'll have to bear
with my stutter. Or maybe you could just call your daddy
and tell him you're okay. Either way is fine with me.

Sincerely,
The Kid
(or Clay, whichever you prefer)

Clay folded the page and put it in an envelope. He walked
down the hill and asked Pidge for a stamp, then walked back up
the hill to the mailbox. He'd never really prayed before. But he did
that day as he lifted the mailbox flag.

CHAPTER 28

Without Possum to greet him and TD to banter with each morning, Waite felt untethered on his program. Vivian at Mel's mentioned the station felt a little lonesome. Waite had talked with Boyd about bringing TD back, but the man was adamant against it.

With The Kid's evening hours, Waite didn't see him as much, though he stopped by in the afternoon to write copy and do odd jobs and Waite saw him on Sundays. Maybe it was just Waite or wishful thinking, but he seemed to stutter less.

After the Farm Report, Waite played two Statler Brothers' songs back-to-back. That was another group that had started out gospel and veered toward mainstream country. Maybe it was the harmonies the men used that reminded Waite of four-part hymns. They counted flowers on the wall and watched *Captain Kangaroo*, then sang about the dreams and disappointments of the class of '57. The line that always got him was about Janet who taught grade school ". . . and probably always will." He thought about his life and his own "probably always will."

He found himself staring at Emily's picture more these days. He had regrets about his marriage, but he had overcome those mistakes and had loved Connie well to the end. When he visited her grave, the only lingering disappointment was that he felt responsible for Emily not being there when she'd passed. And he wouldn't just change one thing about his relationship with Emily, he'd do a slew of things differently. He could close his eyes at the control board and see her in the production room practicing on the microphone. Like it was yesterday. Where in the world had she gone? Would she ever find a place for him in her heart again?

"The best country in the country, this is Country 16. I'm Waite Evers, glad to have you along this morning. Hope we get you up and out with a smile and a song that helps you put one foot in front of the other. A little rain in the forecast, which should cool things off a bit this afternoon.

"Well, if you haven't found Gideon Quidley's treasure yet, and I think it's fair to say nobody has, today's the day they open the final envelope. Will it be one more clue? Did he give the exact location of the treasure? We'll have to wait till this afternoon to find out because only a few people will be in that room. I hope they let us know what's in that envelope. But while we wait, how about a story about a boy who stands up to a bully. Here's Kenny Rogers on Country 16."

While "Coward of the County" played, the request line rang. "Country 16."

"Waite, I love the station and your sense of humor. Could

you play some Mack Strum for me? I want to hear 'A Piece of the Moon.'"

Waite paused. "Do you have a second choice?"

"Maybe 'Wasted Days and Wasted Nights'?"

"I bet I could find that one for you. Thank you for calling."

There were songs that came close to touching the nerve in his soul, the pain and guilt of memories that floated on his life's stagnant pool. That's why he couldn't bring himself to play that old Mack Strum tune. After Kenny finished, it was on to Freddy Fender.

After Wally took over that morning, Waite went to the production room and found Possum's interview with Strum. He'd tracked him down at his farm in Alabama. Mack's voice was tired and Waite imagined him looking like gristle and bone after all the years of traveling and scraping to make a life in music. He'd never hit it big, but there was something in his voice that told Waite he was at peace with that.

"Every song, just like every person, has a story," Mack said through his tinny phone line. "All good songs leak from a broken heart. And the good ones don't give you something, as much as they take what's already inside and blow on the embers."

Possum broke in and gave the time and temperature and Waite fast-forwarded the tape.

"In the evenings, my mama would gather us kids in the kitchen and sing old hymns. She taught us the different parts and a switch turned on for me. I can still hear 'Church in the Wildwood.' 'Oh, come, come, come, come.'

"The pastor's wife of our little church looked a lot like Maybelle Carter. She showed me G, C, and D on her old guitar and it was like lighting a stick of dynamite. I give her credit."

"Mack, tell us the story about 'A Piece of the Moon,'" Possum said.

"That's hard because I don't feel like I had a lot to do with it. Some songs you labor over for months or years. 'Moon' dropped into my lap. It was like walking along the street and seeing a hundred-dollar bill. All I did was pick it up. You don't take credit for something like that."

"What does the song mean?" Possum said.

Mack chuckled. "Now don't ask me that because a song might touch one person a certain way and do something different for somebody else.

"At first, I thought 'Moon' was about giving somebody what they didn't have. The first line, 'If I were a rich man, I'd buy some hope for you.' Right there is somebody who's a giver instead of a taker."

Possum quoted the next line. "'If I were a carpenter, I'd build a dream come true.'"

"Right. The singer will do anything to help. But the further you go, the more you realize both people in the song need something. And the truth is, they need each other more than anything."

"But why a piece of the moon?" Possum said.

"I like the way it rolls off the tongue. And everybody's been stopped by the moon. You can't look directly at the sun, but you can stare at the moon all night. And the reason you can see it is because it reflects the sun. So there you go—both need each other."

"Also, you can see the moon but you can't touch it, right?"

"Well, a few people have, but most of us won't. I think it's a symbol for something you want so bad but feels just out of reach, like a carrot on a stick. We get so focused on it that we miss what we have right in front of us. What the moon illuminates down here."

Waite rewound the recording and put it in a box and back onto Possum's shelf.

TD stood at the end of the walk and stared at the house of his youth. The yard had seemed a lot bigger when he had to mow every inch of it. Now it looked small.

Flashes of memory.

Playing with cars in the shade of the front porch. Putting baseball cards in the spokes of his bike wheels to make it sound like a motorcycle. Playing cops and robbers and cowboys and Indians and trying to tame the Wild West with a cap gun and a stick horse. Watching *Wagon Train* and *The Wild, Wild West*.

What am I doing here?

He stared at his bedroom window at the end of the house. He'd lain inside reading about the Swiss Family Robinson and the Hardy Boys. He was reading *Combat* when his mother came to tell him Timothy had died. He read the same page all night, just stared at the words. Later, he dreamed of a time when he could leave, just pick up and go and seek his own fortune, live his own life. Now, here he stood, only a stone's throw away from the past. He'd have to try harder to get out of Emmaus. Or he'd have to settle his heart.

That was why he was here. He was ready to settle his heart instead of running. And he knew the path led straight to this house and the people inside.

The curtain fluttered at the window and the door opened and there was his mother smiling. She had cradled his head and caught his tears and it almost seemed like she hadn't been able to grieve herself. His mother's grief was always more communal and lived through others. And for the first time he wondered if being married to his father had caused her to distance herself from her own heart so that her life became something outside of her, like putting on someone else's clothes every day instead of her own. Whatever it was, she had comforted him and for that he was grateful.

He hugged her and she grabbed on and squeezed, her head on

his chest. She was a short woman but stocky, with braided hair down her back. "I'm so glad to see you, Titus."

"Glad to see you, too. Is he at home?"

"In his study. You can go on in. He'll be real happy you came."

"I'm not so sure about that. Would you mind telling him I'm out here?"

She pulled back and looked up. "Well, I suppose."

He put the toe of a boot in the clover covered in dew that grew in the yard and had second thoughts. Every decision had some ramification. He'd auditioned for the voice job and failed miserably. That sent him into the darkness, believing the laughter. But the risk was worth it, he told himself. How would he ever know what he could do, what he could become, if he didn't try? Something Pidge had said haunted him.

"Something's holding you back. . . . I see it, buried deep."

He had left home thinking all the pain and loss was behind him. But running away hadn't solved it and he figured he could run to the end of the earth and he'd still carry the same weight inside. So instead of getting back in his truck and driving away, he gritted his teeth and waited until his father appeared at the front door. He stared down from his perch. His mother, perhaps sensing the need for them to be alone, remained inside. Or maybe she was protecting herself from what she knew was brewing.

His father opened the screen and stepped onto the porch. He wore penny loafers and slacks and a buttoned shirt with a collar. When he approached, TD could smell the Brylcreem.

A little dab'll do ya.

"Hello, Titus. What brings you here?"

That voice. It was the whisper TD heard when he felt like a failure. The same voice that had said, *"He's been healed."* The same voice that had spoken confidently each Sunday morning and Sunday night and Wednesday night about things TD wasn't confident of at all.

"I've been doing some thinking."

"Well, that's good news. I'm glad you're using the brain God gave you. You haven't come because of all the treasure uproar, have you?"

"This is not about Quidley. This is about us."

"Us? I didn't know there was an *us*. You left. Turned your back on *us*."

"I've been trying to get what happened with Tim out of my mind. I've always thought if I could get away from here, I'd put it behind me. But it seems I'll carry it wherever I go."

"'The Lord gives and the Lord takes away. Blessed be the name of the Lord.'"

TD rubbed his neck and looked at his father's hands, more veiny and wrinkled than he remembered. "And that right there is what I've been trying to get away from."

"You can't outrun the love of God, Son."

"It's not the love of God I'm running from. It's you. It's the decision you made. God didn't take Tim, you did."

"Bringing this up won't do any good. 'Forgetting those things which are behind . . . I press toward the mark—'"

"You never let us talk about it. When he died, he was just gone. It was like he never lived."

"How dare you accuse me like this."

TD looked him full in the face. "All this time, I've been mad at God for taking him. I couldn't make sense of it."

"So you blame me!"

"It came to me the other day. I'm friends with a fellow who believes. Strong Christian man. He's been more than kind to me. When he talks about the Bible, it doesn't bother me. But when I hear you—"

"I don't have to listen to this." The man turned to leave.

"No, you don't. But do you think you could try for once?"

His father stopped but didn't turn.

"I'm not mad at God anymore. And I don't blame you for Tim's death. At least, I don't want to. I'm trying to get to the place where I can let it go. What I'm mad at is you using God."

His father turned. "Using him? You think that's what I did?"

"When this Quidley thing came up, I called it fake. I thought the guy was out of his head. Then I thought about you. If you really believed Tim was going to be healed, it made all the sense in the world to take him out of that iron lung. You were showing God you really believed. Except I don't think that was faith. That wasn't God telling you what to do. It was you telling God what *he* had to do. You put your faith in what you wanted, not in who God really is."

Through gritted teeth his father said, "'Though he slay me, yet will I trust in him.'"

"Book of Job. I remember. But with all due deference to Job, you were wrong. Tim didn't have to die. At least not when he did. And you have to live with that. We all do."

"Get out," his father said with a growl. "And don't ever come back. You're not my son."

"Yes, I am. You can't run from that any more than I can from you being my father."

"After all we've done for you. After all the sacrifices we made."

"You did make sacrifices. And I thank you. Deep down I don't think you wanted to hurt Tim. But you did. And that's got to be hard to live with. Instead of being mad at you, I feel sorry for you. I really do."

"The last thing I need is your pity."

The man turned and walked inside and slammed the door so

hard TD thought it would fall off the hinges. He stood looking at the house of his youth, remembering Tim sitting on the porch with a blanket over him, watching TD catch fireflies.

He watched the window to see if his mother would look out so he could wave. There was no movement inside.

"I've met somebody," TD whispered as if continuing the conversation. "I'm going to ask her to marry me, Daddy. And you're going to want to know if she's a believer. Well, she believes in me. And she's told me she can't marry somebody who doesn't believe in God. She has a past, though. Probably things you won't approve of. But I reckon we all have a past, don't we?"

CHAPTER 29

MILTON QUIDLEY SAT NEXT TO HIS WIFE in the conference room at his office. His father's estate lawyer, Wilfred Knox, took his place at the head of the boat-shaped table. Two men who said they were investigators from NASA sat across from Milton and his wife. He'd never heard that NASA had investigators, but they were interested in an item that his father might have hidden. Milton figured their presence might be more helpful in finding the treasure. They insisted on being present.

"Gideon left it to my discretion whether to read this to the public immediately or not," Knox said, glancing at Milton and the others. "Given the nature of what our friends from NASA have shared, I believe it prudent to keep this small." He glanced at the clock. "So I will now unseal Gideon's final communiqué."

He used a silver letter opener and pulled two pages from the envelope and spread them on the solid cherry table. He cleared his throat, adjusted his glasses, and began to read.

"Dear Milton and anybody else who has been chosen to hear these words,

If you are reading this, it means I've gone to my reward. Don't cry for me because I'm kicking up my heels on streets of gold right now. Opal says hey from glory.

My main reason for writing this letter, which is the same reason I hid the treasure, is to make sure people know about the love and forgiveness offered by God through his one and only Son.

I want to say a personal word to Milton. Son, we have had our differences, but I never stopped loving you and I've always wanted the best for you. In fact, one of the reasons I hid the treasure was to emphasize the fact that we're not to trust in riches. The Bible says that the love of money is the root of all evil. (This is not a clue, by the way, in case you were wondering.) What I'm saying is, don't trust in wealth or gold or any man-made thing, trust in the Lord. And, Milton, I hope you will open your heart to him if you haven't already.

With that said, I will close this letter with the prayer that the Lord will bless each of you and keep you and make his face shine upon you and give you peace.

Sincerely,
Gideon Quidley"

Knox turned the paper over and picked up the next. His eyes went across the page and he looked up at the others as if he wanted to apologize. He cleared his throat again and began to read.

"This is the final clue about the treasure. Proverbs 12:10. 'A righteous man regardeth the life of his beast: but the tender mercies of the wicked are cruel.'"

The lawyer looked up, pursed his lips, and folded the page in front of him.

"That it?" Milton said. "That's all it says?"

"I'm afraid so," the lawyer said.

"That makes no sense. Why wouldn't he just tell us where he put it?"

One of the government men leaned forward. "We noticed at his home there was a dish for food and water for a dog in the backyard. Where is the animal now?"

Milton couldn't breathe. "No."

"What?" Milton's wife said.

Milton stood. "I have to leave. You won't release this to the media, correct?"

"Gideon's wishes were that everyone would have the same access to this information, but I can wait an hour or so."

"I don't want you releasing this at all," Milton said.

"I'm sorry. I have to abide by the wishes of my client."

Milton barreled out of the room with his wife not far behind. The two men from the government were right behind her.

Pidge sensed something going on with Clay but she couldn't put her finger on what it was. He had snuck off on his bicycle and she wondered if he might be visiting a girl at Waite's church. Maybe he rode down to the gas station to buy her a pop. Wouldn't that be something, to see him come out of his shell like that? Or maybe he just rode his bike to get away from the salvage yard. She wondered if this was something a mother might feel about her own child, this sense she had that he was dealing with something he wouldn't talk about. Maybe he'd talk with Waite about whatever it was. Or maybe it was nothing at all.

She'd driven him to school earlier today to register and then walked the halls that held more memories for her than she wanted. A lot of hard recollections returned. She'd spent those years in junior high and high school feeling on the outside. Some kids had band. Some were athletes. Some had brains and poured themselves into their studies. Pidge looked at the black-and-white pictures in her yearbook and wondered if Clay would be like her, a misfit tossed about in a sea of kids who all seemed to know where they were going.

On the drive home they listened to Country 16. Wally played a song by Bobby Bare about a barroom fight. Clay reached over and hit the Off button before the guy with a hairy hand started talking.

"You nervous about school?" Pidge said.

Clay shrugged and stared out the window.

"Why'd you turn the radio off?"

Without looking at her, he said, "T-t-tell me about him."

She was about to say, *Tell you about who?* when she figured it out. He wanted to know about his father. Pidge took a deep breath.

"I called him Sammy and it bugged him. He didn't talk a lot, but he didn't have to. He let his actions talk for him."

"Like wh-what?"

"He sat with me on the bus. Made sure nobody picked on me. That kind of thing. He wore his hair kind of like yours. He was tall and lanky. Sometimes I see you walking down the hill and I think it's him. I guess it is, sort of."

"What d-did he like to do?"

"He caught the car bug like our daddy. Everybody in school

was talking about college or the military or trade school. Sammy just wanted to work on cars and trucks. Anything with an engine fascinated him. I think he'd be real proud of you learning to work on the radio. He listened to baseball some. Liked to fish and hunt."

"D-did he know about m-me?"

"He knew you were on the way. Your mother was sweet on Sammy. I'll leave it at that. When she found out she was pregnant, there was a commotion. Her daddy came over and spoke with Sammy and my daddy in the office. Yelled is more like it. From what I know, Sammy was planning to find work and then they were going to get married."

"B-but he got killed."

"Yeah. I've always thought if I'd been there or if Daddy had been there, he'd be alive today. He couldn't yell because he couldn't get a breath."

"Wasn't your fault."

"I know that in my head. It's hard not to carry it around, though. I've always felt I could have done something. Should have."

She checked her speed as she drove through town in the 35-mile-per-hour section. "We didn't touch his room. It was just too hard. I used to dream about him and wake up and check his bedroom and think maybe he'd be there. That it was all a bad dream. But now here you are."

"Y-you didn't have to take me in."

"I wanted to. For Sammy. And for you. And to be honest, for myself. You've brightened up the place."

Clay didn't smile, but she saw something on his face she hadn't seen before.

"I c-come with a lot of b-bills, though."

"Don't worry about that. We're going to be fine, Clayton." She glanced at him to see if he believed what she said. She wasn't sure she had said it as confidently as she wanted. "He would have been a good dad to you, I think. I wish he'd gotten the chance."

"H-he would s-say you're a good mom."

The words hit her heart and she looked out the window. When she'd composed herself, she said, "He might think that, but I guarantee you he wouldn't have said it, knowing him. But I'm glad you feel that way. And I thank you for saying it."

Pidge felt a flutter in her heart. Something was breaking between them. And it took the silence and the hum of the engine to let her notice. "I think your stutter is getting better, don't you?"

Clay shrugged and she immediately thought she'd wandered into forbidden territory. That was always the problem with relationships—when you opened your mouth, you might take a step forward or a step back. Then came the question that surprised her.

"Are y-you and TD getting married?"

"What gave you that idea?"

Clay shrugged. "He loves you."

"How do you know that?"

He glanced over at her. "Some things you c-can just tell."

She wanted to turn the radio back on. She took her foot off the accelerator and turned on her blinker. They were close to the station.

"And I think y-you love him, too."

Pidge put her foot on the brake too hard and they both lurched forward. How in the world did he come to that conclusion? There was a lot more going on in his head than she realized.

"Am I right?" Clay said.

"The jury's still out on that, Clayton."

"Wh-what does that mean?"

"It means you need to keep your nose out of . . ." Pidge stopped when she saw the cars parked by the fence at the salvage yard. "Who in the world is that?"

She wound down to the valley and pulled up behind Milton Quidley's shiny car. There were two other men in a car that had a government license plate. Jubal stood on the other side of the locked gate, sniffing the ground. The men were reaching through the gate, trying to grab Jubal.

"It looks about the right size," one of the government men said.

Pidge couldn't figure out what the man was talking about.

"I need you to open this fence," Milton Quidley said as Pidge stepped out of her truck.

"Hold your horses. What's this about?"

"We need access to that animal," he said.

"Jubal?" Pidge said. "What for?"

"Open the gate, ma'am," one of the government men said, like it was a court order instead of a request.

"You hang on," Pidge said. "Tell me why."

"Open the gate," Milton said.

Clay had gotten out of the truck and was petting Jubal through the fence.

"Leave the dog alone," a government man barked.

"He can do whatever he wants. It's his dog," Pidge said. "And this is my property. You people get off of it. I got rights."

"Wrong. This is a national priority." The man held up a piece of paper with a fancy seal on it. "Open the gate."

"National priority? At Emmaus Salvage?"

"Open it now!"

"Hold up," Clay said. "Wh-what do you w-want w-w-with him?"

The man studied the dog. "Get his collar. That's what we need."

"What do you want with his collar?" Pidge said.

They didn't answer but Clay stroked Jubal's head and his back until the raised hair settled.

"That piece of paper don't mean you can come down here and order me around. Now I'm going to go in the house and call the sheriff and get him down here. But you're not coming onto my—"

"Hey, what are you doing?" one of the men shouted.

Pidge turned and saw Clay climbing the fence at the corner of the lot.

Clay climbed up and over the fence and ran toward the house. He didn't have to call Jubal, the dog ran to him. There was a commotion at the gate, men yelling and Pidge firing back at them, giving them what for about her rights.

For some reason, those men thought there was something in Jubal's collar and Clay remembered the key. It was in his nightstand. And if Milton Quidley was with them, maybe it had something to do with the treasure. He couldn't let them get that key, but he also couldn't let them find the collar empty.

He raced into his room and Jubal followed. He unhooked the collar, his hands trembling. He pried open the compartment underneath and looked for something to put inside. Anything.

Pidge reluctantly unlocked the gate and before she could pull it back, the two men were inside with Milton not far behind. They ran toward the house.

"You go in there without a warrant of some kind and I'll sue you from here to Sunday," Pidge yelled.

The men pulled up at the front door.

"Get in there and grab the dog!" Milton yelled.

"She's right, sir. We can't legally enter the house."

Pidge made it to the front door and turned her back to it. "You people get back in your fancy cars and get out of here. Clay paid you a hundred dollars for that dog. It's his, not yours."

The door opened behind her and Clay stepped out with a worn leash in his hand. The dog, usually docile and friendly, became growly, showing his teeth. He barked when one of the men reached a hand toward him.

Clay motioned for them to get back as he led Jubal out to the porch and had him sit. "This is m-my dog. Like she said, I p-paid for him. So I n-need to know what you're going to do with him."

"We won't hurt him, son," one of the black-suited men said. "Not in any way. We just need to examine him."

"You don't need to explain anything to that kid," Milton Quidley said. "Grab the dog!"

"No, no, no," Pidge said. "This is America. You don't just take somebody's property—"

"It's okay," Clay said.

Pidge threw her arms up and stormed inside.

CHAPTER 30

WAITE SAT ON THE COUCH in Pidge's trailer and listened to her tell the story of what happened with Jubal. The Kid sat next to her, his arms crossed, hair hanging down.

"I checked the wire a few minutes ago," Waite said. "The story came over about Gideon's last envelope. He didn't say where the treasure was but left one clue for everybody. It was a verse from Proverbs that says a righteous man cares for his animal."

"So that's why they were in a huff about Jubal," Pidge said. She glanced at Clay. "Why did you give him up like that?"

The Kid didn't speak.

"Maybe it was for the best, Pidge," Waite said. "Less trauma for everybody. They'll give him back."

"What are they going to do with him? They think he's going to lead them to the treasure like a drug-sniffing dog?"

"I don't have any idea," Waite said. "What do you think, Kid?"

The Kid shrugged.

"What business does the government have with all this?" Pidge said. "Why were those fellows here?"

Waite shook his head.

"M-maybe the treasure is h-hidden on government land," Clay said. "And they kn-know that."

"Or it might be that something in Gideon's ark belongs to the government," Waite said. "Something they're trying to get back. Maybe Milton knows and he's not telling."

Clay walked Waite to the gate. The man put a hand on his shoulder. "We're going to get your dog back, you hear?"

Clay nodded and went back inside, where Pidge was making hot dogs and macaroni and cheese. Her face stayed tight through the meal and she didn't speak. After he ate and put his dish in the sink, he excused himself and told Pidge he was going for a bike ride. She opened her mouth to say something, then shut it.

He rode toward town and took the shortcut to Merrill's Ridge, which gave a scenic view of Emmaus. As he rounded a curve where the trees were cleared, he could see Main Street with the traffic light that led to the interstate. A little farther and he spotted Mel's Donuts.

The road dead-ended but there was a path he'd discovered that cut through to Chicken Farm Road and led him to a knoll that overlooked the back edge of town.

He pedaled uphill, getting off and pushing over tree roots, and at dusk he found the break in the trees he was looking for. Directly below, the aroma of Italian food wafting through the trees, he saw the Pizza Barn. Milton Quidley's car was there, along with the car with the two men from the government.

A couple walked out of the restaurant and headed for the parking lot. Clay's self-conscious ways were trumped by his curiosity now, so he walked quickly up to them.

"What's g-going on in th-there, mister?"

"Beats me," the man said.

"They're looking for something," the woman said.

Clay nodded and turned back to the bike. Then he heard muffled barking. It was Jubal, no doubt. They wouldn't have left him in a hot car with the windows rolled up, would they?

The back door of the restaurant opened, and Milton Quidley and another man Clay didn't recognize came out and walked to the edge of the nearby woods as if surveying the area. Clay didn't want to be seen, but he couldn't leave Jubal locked up like that.

Clay squatted and duckwalked to the car with the government license plate. Jubal went wild, barking and licking at the window, his tongue lolling. Clay knew a dog sweated through his tongue. He'd read it somewhere. And the more Jubal barked, the more determined Clay became to release him.

"Please let it be unlocked," Clay whispered. He tried the door. Locked.

He tried the front door. Locked.

"Hey, what are you doing?"

Clay jumped and turned to see Deputy Art Palermo.

"They took my d-dog. He's hot in there. I n-need to get him out."

"I ought to arrest you."

"C-can you get them to open the d-door? Or roll down the w-window?"

"You need to get out of here, Kid."

"He's going to d-die."

"He won't die. I'll take care of it."

"I ain't leaving till he's out of there."

The deputy shook his head and walked toward the restaurant.

"Hold on, boy," Clay whispered, patting the window. The dog licked at it and whined.

The deputy returned with a black-suited man who unlocked the car, and Clay opened the back door. Jubal jumped out and was all over him.

"Where's his c-collar?"

Black Suit was already headed back to the restaurant.

"Take him and go home," the deputy said.

Clay ran and took Jubal to a stream, and the dog took a long drink and splashed in the water. When he was satisfied, Clay called for him and the dog followed. They wound through the back roads and made it to the river as shadows fell on the hillside. They were nearly home when Clay turned and realized Jubal wasn't there.

He called and waited but the dog didn't come. Then he heard movement in the brush above and saw Jubal had climbed up to a clearing and stood looking down at him, his tail wagging. Clay called him but the dog turned and ran in the other direction.

Frustrated, Clay got off his bike and let it fall and climbed up the incline. The clearing was a cemetery and Jubal ran through the gravestones like it was an obstacle course.

Clay had heard it was disrespectful to step on a grave. His mother had gone further and said that every grave you stepped on, a ghost would haunt you. That had made him scared of even going to a cemetery. But now here he was with rows of ghosts between him and his dog.

He walked gingerly toward the first row, reading the names and dates and trying to get Jubal's attention. In the third row he saw something that stopped him in his tracks.

Samuel Lane Bledsoe. Beloved Son.

Clay reached out and touched the stone. His father was down there under the grass and dirt. Maybe if he stepped on the grave, his father would come and haunt him, like his mother had said. Clay shook the thought away and stared at the words.

Beside Samuel's stone was a bigger one that listed Samuel's parents, Clay's grandfather and grandmother, and he thought it was a shame he'd never know them except in pictures and stories Pidge shared. But maybe that would be enough.

He felt something wet on his hand and looked down. There was Jubal with his nose pushing up.

"Jubal, this is my d-daddy. And my grandma and grandpa."

He petted the dog and knelt between the graves. As darkness fell, he turned and saw the red light flashing above the metal building on the hillside on the other side of the river.

"The best country in the country, Country 16," he said. He smiled at Jubal. "Did you hear that, boy? I did it."

Two days later, the owner of the Pizza Barn, Clyde Benson, came to the station with his hat in hand and canceled all his advertising. Waite let him out of his contract but asked why.

"Milton Quidley bought me out, lock, stock, and barrel, Waite."

"Milton's getting into the pizza business?"

"No, he doesn't want to make pizza. He thinks his daddy's treasure is somewhere on the property."

"He told you that?"

"He didn't have to. He's been tearing out walls and digging in the woods behind the place to beat forty."

"I don't remember any Bible clue that mentions pizza."

Clyde shrugged. "You'll have to ask him about that. I'm real sorry to let you down like this."

Waite scratched his chin. "Did he pay you enough for it?"

"Paid me twice what it was worth. I just don't know what I'm going to do now that it's out of my hands."

"Word to the wise, Clyde: Something tells me after Milton's through looking, you might be able to buy it back."

"But he's torn it all up."

"It's been there a long time. You've always wanted to remodel, haven't you? Put in new ovens?"

"That's true."

"Maybe Milton's offering an opportunity. Be patient."

CHAPTER 31

The drizzle had begun on Thursday morning and felt more like a nuisance to Waite than something serious. Droplets had turned to showers on Friday, and by Saturday morning creeks and streams had swelled against their banks. The town of Emmaus, being as close to the river as it was, flooded to some extent every year. By Sunday, he felt it in his bones. This was going to be bad.

Sunday afternoon there was such an intense thunderstorm that it threatened the evening service at Waite's church, but the faithful gathered and the pastor turned the pianist loose and allowed people to call out any hymn number. They sang the first and last verses—except when someone called out "And Can It Be," which Pastor Gentry said had to be sung all the way through.

"It all hangs together and can't be chopped up," the man said.

There was talk in the narthex about the treasure, but most people were concerned about the impound dams, which were perched above the town. Shorty Lawson said he'd been up the hollow visiting his sister-in-law, who had just been discharged from the hospital, and the ground at the lower dam was like walking on a sponge.

"This could be another Buffalo Creek," Shorty said.

"I'll have a talk with the sheriff," Waite said.

He called from the church office and talked with the dispatcher and was told they were keeping an eye on things. He asked how people would know of a problem and the dispatcher repeated what he'd just said like he was reading from a script. Somebody sitting in a station all warm and dry was a lot different from someone in the middle of the storm. That made Waite uneasy.

He drove up himself after the service, and what he saw scared him half to death. The dams weren't engineered with concrete and steel—they were constructed of coal slurry and offal that the coal company had created in a rush. There was an upper dam that held the most water and the lower dam was an add-on the coal company had constructed as an afterthought. The Kid had asked if they could fish up there and Waite told him no fish could survive in that awful, oily mess.

He parked in the middle of the road, which was the only place he could stop and not have his truck slide because it was just muck and mud. He got out and tried to walk toward the top of the lower dam, but it was more like quicksand than mud and his shoes sank so deep he almost lost them. The black water hadn't breached the top but was lapping up against it. That wasn't the problem, as he saw it. The problem was the amount of water that seemed to seep through the face and create a steady stream running into the valley.

Waite got back in his truck, tried to wipe off his shoes—a

losing proposition—and drove to the first house he found. He knocked on the door and asked to use the phone. He didn't know the occupants, but like all hill people they welcomed him and offered the phone and a piece of pie and something to drink. He heard something familiar coming from another room. They had their radio tuned to Country 16.

"Don't take those shoes off. You can't get things any dirtier than they already are," the woman at the house said.

Waite called the sheriff again and reported what he had seen. Incredibly, the response was that things were under control.

"No, they aren't," Waite protested. "I'm up here at the dam and it's ready to give way. You've got to give an alert. This is serious. People are going to die."

"Deputy Palermo is on his way up there, sir. I caution you not to alarm people."

It took all he had not to say what was on his mind, which was *And I caution you to get some sense in your head and listen to me or there's going to be blood on your hands.*

Waite calmly reiterated his concern about an evacuation and the dispatcher promised to relay it. When Waite hung up, the homeowners said they had friends in the hollow they needed to call. Waite let them and noticed swirling lights outside and saw a sheriff's cruiser. He stepped outside and waved his flashlight and the cruiser pulled toward the driveway.

Deputy Palermo's face was white as a sheet. "Waite, that thing's ready to go. I can go down and reach a few families, but we don't have time. Your station could do it in thirty seconds. Tell people to call their neighbors. Get whoever's at the station to tell people to move to higher ground."

"All right, I'll do it. But there's no guarantee people are listening."

"It can't hurt anything."

"Don't get in front of this, Art. You'll get washed away."

"Do what you can. I'll do the same."

Waite ran inside, trying to recall who was on the board. And then it hit him and he closed his eyes and shook his head. He told the homeowner he needed the phone and dialed the station and the line rang and rang. It felt like the sands in the hourglass were gone. Wally had been scheduled for Sunday evening, but for some reason had switched with The Kid. At a time like this. If only Possum were there. Or Cody. He hung up and dialed again, the rotary taking its time to go round and round.

"Come on, Kid, pick up the phone."

On the third try, The Kid picked up.

"C-c-country s-sixteen."

"Kid, it's Waite. Listen careful. Grab something to write with. This is important."

"Okay."

"You ready?"

"Y-y-yes, sir."

"I need you to go on the air right now with an emergency message."

The Kid didn't say anything.

"I know this isn't easy, but you've got to do this."

"T-tell me what to s-say."

"Say this word for word. 'The Harper Creek dams are failing. The sheriff says you need to evacuate. Anyone living along Harper Creek below the dams needs to get to higher ground immediately. Don't get in your car and try to outrun this. Get to higher ground now. And call your neighbors and tell them to do the same.' Now say that three or four times just like I told you. 'Anyone living below the Harper Creek dams, get to higher ground now.' You got it?"

Waite heard wild scribbling and then The Kid said, "I g-got it. I'll go to the production room and r-r-record it now."

"No! There's no time. Just turn on the microphone. You've got to do it, Kid. Stop the song. Jump in and say what I just said."

The Kid didn't respond.

"Listen, Kid, if the dam fails, the phone lines and power lines will cut out. And people will get washed away in their houses. We need to get this on the air."

The Kid didn't speak.

"Did you hear me?"

"I c-c-can't do it."

"You have to. This is about people's lives." Waite was frantic now, his hands shaking. "I'm sorry to ask this of you. I know you can do this, Kid."

"I c-c-can't."

The Kid began to cry. Ugly crying. Begging not to go on the air. A thought crossed Waite's mind. Why hadn't he thought of it earlier?

"Okay, is the phone line patched into the board?"

"No."

"You know how to do it?"

"Yeah."

"All right. Plug the cords in and pot me up."

Waite heard scuffling and movement on the other end of the line.

"O-okay."

Waite heard a click. Then the sounds of "Kentucky Rain" faded quickly. He took it by faith he was on the air.

"Folks, this is Waite Evers with an emergency message. Listen close. If you are in the area of the Harper Creek—"

Lightning struck and thunder crashed simultaneously and

shook the house. Lights went off. The radio went dead. The phone line went dead. And Waite's heart sank.

"God, help him."

Clay looked at the phone line. He turned up the pot but there was nothing but a ground loop hum. The meter needle lay all the way to the left. Thunder rumbled furiously and shook the metal building. He turned off the pot and picked up the phone.

"W-W-Waite? C-c-can you hear me?"

Waite had said something about the power and phones going out if the dam broke. Clay realized it was too late. And if that was true, people were dying at that very moment. Those who had no idea what was coming were being washed away.

The thought horrified him, but he also felt relieved. That meant he didn't have to say anything. He could just play music. But that made him feel guilty for only thinking of himself.

"The radio ought to be a continuous river." That's what Cody had said. And you had to keep it flowing, no matter what. Clay glanced at the meters. There was no music, no commercials, no voice of Waite warning people. Just the awful, terrible silence. And Clay knew he had to do something.

His heart racing, he cued up a record on the turntable.

But what if there was still a chance?

What if the dams hadn't failed yet? What if the phone cut out because of the lightning?

In those seconds, listeners to Country 16 had no idea of this internal struggle. They only heard the screaming silence between Waite's last words and the first few bars of Johnny Paycheck's "Take This Job and Shove It."

Some listening might have thought Waite was playing a joke on them. Truckers who passed on the interstate were just looking for music to keep them awake. No one who tuned in at that moment expected to hear what they heard a mere twenty-two seconds into the song about a man fed up with his boss and his job. At the twenty-two-second mark, the music stopped.

Those on the other end of Country 16 could not comprehend the feeling of failure those twenty-two seconds brought. And as Paycheck sang, failure washed like a flood. And the flood became too deep for Clay to take, and like a swimmer going under, he reacted.

Johnny Paycheck's voice stopped. Then it returned for a moment. Stopped. Returned. And quickly there came a scratching noise.

What happened was this. Clay saw it in his mind. Water rushing down the mountainside. People swept away while they were watching TV. Children screaming. Dogs and cats clawing for air. But the image that stood above all of that was something different.

He saw Waite.

He saw him smile.

And he heard him say, *"I know you can do this, Kid."*

And when Clay realized he was letting Waite down, he screamed so loudly that his voice nearly broke. Out of his life's frustration, the words that stuck like a logjam, the secrets he carried that no one knew, he brought his fists down on the console and the force vibrated the turntable. The needle went flying and bounced twice and came to rest in the middle of the 45 and scratched on the middle of the record.

That's when Clay realized the source of his real frustration. Some higher power. And if Waite was right, God knew all and saw all. He had allowed this. He had put him here on a Sunday evening. It felt cruel and unusual, but he closed his eyes tightly and shook his head.

"Just do it," he said to himself. "God, help me do it!"

He turned down the record pot and flicked on the microphone and heard his own breathing. Everyone would hear it. But for the first time in his life there was something greater than the fear of his stutter. Greater than his fear that people would make fun.

Those listening did not hear a polished announcer. They heard The Kid, unedited for the first time, his voice shaking.

"I-I-I j-j-just got off . . . the phone . . . W-W-Waite said . . . if you're . . . b-b-below the H-H-H-Harp . . ." He took another run at it. "If you're b-b-b-below the Harper Creek dams, get . . . out now. G-g-g-go to h-higher ground. Don't wait. The d-d-dams are failing. The phone l-l-l-line c-cut out, so I d-d-don't know. But if you are in the path . . ."

He stopped. Something had happened. Something had clicked. He was still halting in his speech, but the words were seeping out.

"Don't wait. Go now. If you are b-b-below the Harper Creek dams, move to higher ground. Call a neighbor. Evacuate. That's s-s-straight from Waite. And you can trust Waite. He's up there. Again, the H-H-Harper Creek dams are failing. Get to higher ground. If you know somebody up there, call and tell them to get out."

Clay took a breath. He'd done it. The rest was up to them and God.

He glanced at the turntables. He reached back and took the needle from the middle of the record and placed it at the beginning. *Why not?* he thought.

"That's a news bulletin from C-Country 16. The best country in the country. We now return to Johnny Paycheck."

The Kid took off his headphones. There was no applause. No one to pat him on the back. But he had a feeling inside, a quiet confidence that comes from doing something good. He had believed what Waite had said. And that was enough.

Waite heard from officials who knew such things that the upper dam broke exactly seven minutes after The Kid opened his microphone and spoke his first words live, without the aid of a razor blade. The second dam only took a minute to fail completely. At the time all of that was happening, Waite did not know any of it because he was trying to get to his truck and then trying to get it unstuck. Once he finally rocked it free, he sped downhill to warn people. When he reached the dip in the road that led to the front of the lower dam, his headlights hit rushing water and he jammed on the brakes and slid perilously close to the deluge.

"Lord, have mercy," he whispered.

He put the truck in reverse and spun the four-wheel drive backward until he was a safe distance. He'd never seen anything like that and hoped he never would again. He abandoned his truck and with the aid of his flashlight walked along the ridge above the tumult. A quarter mile down the slope, he came upon a family standing slack-jawed and shivering in wet clothes, kids in pajamas, staring into the inky blackness as rushing water took everything but their lives.

"Waite, is that you?" the father said.

Waite recognized Kelvin Purdy, the newspaper deliveryman. "It is. You made it out?"

"We heard you on the radio and then you cut out."

"Lightning struck. Must have taken out a transformer and a phone pole. But I said enough to warn you?"

"No, we stayed put. Until The Kid came on."

"Say that again."

"The Kid. We turned on a battery-operated radio when the power went out. He said the dam was failing and for everybody to get to higher ground."

"He did?" Waite said, his knees almost buckling.

"Daddy, is that the sheriff?" a young boy said. He pointed downstream at swirling lights that looked like they were underwater. The lights moved with the force of the mud and sludge, then disappeared.

"We ought to pray for that man," Kelvin said.

"This is awful," Mrs. Purdy said.

"More than awful," Waite said.

"The Kid did a real good job, Waite. He was scared. His voice was shaking. But that's what got us out. How scared he sounded was what we needed."

"Look, Daddy." Lightning had struck and lit the world for a second. The kid pointed at their house, which had lifted off its foundation and begun to float downstream like a child's toy.

"Everything we own in the world is in that house," Kelvin said. "But the only thing that really matters is right here." He put his arms around his wife and children. "The Kid did good, Waite."

"Yes, he did," Waite said.

CHAPTER 32

PIDGE HEARD THE TERROR in Clay's voice on the radio, and since Harper Creek ran into Lick Creek, then into the Mud River, she knew what was coming. She grabbed some food and a change of clothes for both of them and drove her truck to the upper parking lot of Country 16, where she watched the banks overflow.

At midnight, Cody arrived, unaware of the happenings in town, but he got on the air and surprised Pidge with the concern in his voice. TD drove up and parked in the upper lot, spent from trying to help people who were stranded because of the flooding.

"It's real bad, Pidge."

She put a hand on TD's arm and wanted to say something but couldn't find the words. She pointed to the bottomland where the swollen creek had become an ocean. Because of the clouds there was no moonlight to speak of, but the red blinking light on the tower and the flashes of lightning showed the rising table that engulfed the landscape like a dark sheet.

When Clay walked out of the building, Pidge couldn't hold back and for the first time she ran and hugged him with all that was in her. He stayed stiff as a board. She told him what a good thing he had done by warning people and asked if it was scary and he shrugged. And that was okay.

TD drove away after getting a call on the CB. Pidge and Clay sat in the truck and ate the food she had brought, while Jubal sat between Clay's feet snagging crumbs. They even drove down the hill—slid was more like it—and she turned her headlights toward the brackish water. Some of the cars at the back of the Emmaus Salvage lot were totally submerged, but the house and office attached to it hadn't been claimed. She wondered how deep it would get.

And then she thought of Flap and her heart sank. How could she forget him? If the water got in the office, he'd be scared to death. If it rose to the roof, Flap didn't stand a chance. But she couldn't get across the raging stream in front of her, so she decided to wait and hope for the best, and she drove back up the hill.

Clay fell asleep first, his head propped against the side door. Sweet sleep for the weary, she thought. She almost cried as she watched him in the glow of the dashboard, not because of his pain but because of hers watching him. And she thought that pain would make you miss some good things in life. Fear would do the same.

She made God a promise as she listened to the rhythm of the falling rain. "Lord, if you'll show me a way through this flood, I'll go with you. I'll do whatever you want."

When Waite turned in to the driveway and his headlights flashed up the hill, she got out and hugged him, too. She was becoming a regular hug factory that couldn't stop production. Somehow it felt okay to move toward people now and she wasn't sure why. But she didn't need to understand.

"I got coffee and donuts," Waite said. "Bring The Kid in—he can sleep on my couch."

She woke Clay and when he saw Waite, his face lit.

"I th-thought you d-d-didn't make it."

"I made it, all right. And so did you."

Clay ate a long john and fell asleep as soon as he hit the couch, rolled up on his side and facing the wall.

It was almost like a family gathering in the station that morning. And as the sun lit the day through the deep cloud cover, Pidge looked out Waite's window and saw cars scattered haphazardly on the edges of the junkyard. There were places where the chain-link fence had been torn away because of the force of the water and the debris, but the house and the office had been spared. She breathed a prayer of thanks.

All morning people called in reports of property damage and loss of homes. The Farm Report was devoted mainly to which roads were now open and how long the ones closed would remain that way. Nobody knew for sure, but Waite did a good job of guessing. TD sat in with Waite and it seemed like old times again.

There were stern words from callers toward those responsible for building the dams and threats of lawsuits that everybody knew would never happen and wouldn't do a bit of good if they were filed. And there was gratitude expressed for Deputy Palermo and Country 16.

Waite became emotional when talking about the deputy and had to play a song. Then, a little after eight, the group learned of the man's fate. The news came in the form of Art Palermo walking into the control room and Waite standing and giving him a bear hug that people heard live—though Waite said bear hugs went a lot better on TV than they did on the radio.

"I have to be honest," Waite said after he calmed down. "When I saw your cruiser's lights go under the water, I never thought I'd see you again."

"Well, if I'd been inside that cruiser, you wouldn't. But I was knocking on Ida Snodgrass's door when that happened. The wall of water hit when she opened it and she pulled me in like she was roping a steer. We had us a prayer meeting in the kitchen."

"Her house didn't get washed away?"

"The front was damaged but the foundation held, Waite. I suppose there's something there you could use on your Sunday morning program."

"My anchor holds. There's an old hymn we used to sing with that title. And you made it through the tempest, didn't you?"

"I did, and I want to thank you for doing what you did last night. You didn't have to drive up there. And that young man at the controls—he did a fantastic job of alerting people."

"He sure did," Waite said.

Pidge couldn't hold back the emotion as she listened, looking down the hall from Waite's office. Ardelle had come to the station in hip waders, such was her devotion, and she walked toward Pidge.

"You must be proud of that kid of yours," Ardelle said.

Pidge smiled. He was hers.

When the waters receded, Pidge and Clay drove as close to the house as they could without getting stuck in the muck. An awful stench came from the sludge and slurry left piled along the riverbank. A hundred yards downstream she found the bloated body of a heifer that she learned belonged to a farmer named Sowards three miles upriver.

Pidge accounted for all the vehicles on the property. None had been swept away but all had been touched by the water. A few were on their sides by the fence at the back of the lot. She thought of her father and how he would handle the situation. With all of his imperfections and crazy ways, he'd always had a plan, always known what was next, even if that plan seemed ludicrous to everybody but himself. And in that sense, Pidge reminded herself of her daddy.

TD worked overtime pulling cars and trucks out of the muck. Mostly he helped people and he seemed to be in his element doing so. She couldn't help but think that something had changed with him, but she couldn't tell what it was. Maybe it was just that he was so busy he didn't have time to think about his radio career, but it seemed like something else, something she saw in his eyes and demeanor.

All week, he moved up and down the river rescuing vehicles from the force of the flood. Some of the newer models were salvageable and he took those to the shop or returned them to their owners. Most he found were junkers that had been left by barns or abandoned in hills and hollers. Those he brought to Emmaus Salvage in various states of rust and decay. The wall of coal slurry had turned every one of those cars the same color and Pidge had Clay hose down each new addition to the back of the lot.

TD dropped off three cars in one day, a Buick, a Honda, and a Toyota, along with a mangled *Harper Creek Road* sign still attached to the metal pole. Except over time some of the letters had worn off and it now read, *Harp   C   k Ro *. As night approached, he stopped at the office and turned off his engine, the CB radio squawking.

Pidge walked outside in her rubber boots, the ground still wet and spongy. The water had touched the steps of the house and she gave thanks for her father's foresight to build it on a higher foundation. The office had flooded to the doorknob, but she had fans going, drying everything out. She'd found Flap on the top of the air conditioner, sitting there like he owned the place, which, in a sense, he did.

"You've been busy today," Pidge said to TD.

"Worn-out." He stepped out of the truck and leaned against it. "I think we're close to the end."

"Of the world or the flood?"

He smiled. "We're going to make it, Pidge."

"Clay's been busy washing the sludge off of everything."

"I was listening the night he spoke on the radio. I know how hard that must have been for him."

"Just shows the power of words, doesn't it? Even if they come out slow."

TD nodded. "Speaking of which, you were right with what you said."

"What are you talking about?"

"About me. About something holding me back. Remember that?"

"Yeah."

"There's things I ain't never told anybody. Things I haven't talked about for years. Or at all. And I finally got up the courage or the gumption. It was because of what you said. So I want to thank you."

Pidge shook her head. "I don't know what all you're talking about, but you're welcome."

"My brother died when I was a kid. Timothy. It left a scar. My father . . . I've never been able to let him off the hook for it. You don't need to know all of it now, and I'll tell you more later if you want to hear it. But I went and talked with him."

"Did it help?"

"Depends on how you define *help*. I don't think he would say it helped. Didn't solve things. But it kindly broke the dam for me, so to speak."

"When the dam breaks, there's usually a flood and a fair amount of mud."

"Yeah." TD rubbed his nose with the back of a hand. "I made another decision too."

Pidge stared at his face, which was illumined only by moonlight and the blinking red light on the Country 16 tower. She could see it clear enough to get butterflies.

"I think I understand you better. Why you've been cautious about us. Part of it's your own past and part of it's me and whether or not I'm ready. Whether I'm done running from myself. I wanted you to know that I don't think I have to get out of here in order to find what I'm looking for."

"And what are you looking for, TD?"

He looked up. "I think it's best described as a piece of the moon. Isn't that what you said you wanted?"

"I did," she said, and her voice shook.

"I think I found my piece of the moon right here. And I'm willing to wait as long as it takes for you to agree with me."

She cleared her throat. "I knew it the day we pulled up to the station and you got your back up about Jubal. Fire in your eyes at the injustice of Milton Quidley taking that dog away."

"You knew what?"

"That I loved you."

TD's mouth dropped open. "Are you saying what I think you're saying?"

She looked him in the eyes and stood her ground. She wasn't going to reach out for him and do what she wanted him to do.

Instead she waited and soon he took her by the shoulders and she moved toward him. TD moistened his lips once and she closed her eyes. When their lips met, it felt as if something like moonbeams were shooting out of her heart. And at that moment she was glad for the broken parts that let the feelings leak out like a sieve.

PART 4

One month later

CHAPTER 33

EARLY OCTOBER 1981

Sharon Gardner walked into the business office of Clarkston Medical Center clutching her purse. She tried taking several deep breaths to still her racing heart, but it was no use. Robby had always taken care of the finances, but since he'd returned home, they'd found it difficult to get him out of the house because of his wheelchair. She hoped at some point they would be able to attach a ramp to the parsonage. The church had been more than generous, but even with all the help, she and Robby would be paying the hospital bill until they were old and gray.

The head of the finance department met her and showed her to the inner sanctum, an office with nice furniture she couldn't help but think was paid for by sickness. It was hard for Sharon to think of anything positive at that moment. Her thoughts went to how much money it would take to keep the collections agency at bay.

"How is Pastor Robby doing?" the woman said.

"He's better. Learning how to get around in his wheelchair."

"It's a big adjustment, isn't it?" The woman smiled as if she knew how much their lives had changed.

"We're glad he's alive. And grateful for the care he received here."

"Yes, and we're so glad about his progress. He's had such a great attitude about all of this."

Sharon tried to return the smile, but she just wanted to see the number. How much would she need to pay them from Robby's small stipend each month? She might need to get a job, but what would that mean for the children?

"Well, I have good news," the woman said. She opened a file on her desk and pushed a piece of paper across the polished surface. "This is the amount owed for Robby's stay with us here."

Sharon's mouth dropped open at the figure. It was twice as much as she'd expected. If you divided that by fifty years and then by twelve . . . She couldn't compute how much that meant each month.

"I'm sorry but I don't think that's very good news."

"Oh, but you haven't seen the next page. This is how much you owe now."

She pushed another page across the table and pointed to a line at the bottom. The amount read *0*. Over top of the ledger someone had stamped *PAID IN FULL* in red.

Sharon couldn't breathe. Her brain couldn't grasp the zero. She glanced at the woman, who had tears in her eyes. She nodded at Sharon as if trying to convince her it was real. Somebody had paid the bill in full.

"I don't understand."

"I had an anonymous call last week. A female. She asked how much the final bill would be. I told her that information was confidential but she asked if I could give her a ballpark. She said she wanted to help. So I told her anything she wanted to give would certainly help. And she pressed me, so I threw out a number close to the amount."

She pulled a large envelope from a drawer and pushed it across the desk. Sharon took it, opened it, and saw several stacks of hundred-dollar bills.

"This note was included with the money."

Sharon's hands shook when she picked it up and read the pencil-scrawled words on the paper.

Dear Hospital Lady,

This money is for Robby Gardner's bill. From what you said on the phone, this should cover it. I've added some that I want you to give to Sharon to help her and her family. Tell her to buy a van Robby can drive. Plus, they need a ramp at their house and at their church. Instead of putting it in the offering, I'm trusting you.

Sincerely,
A Friend

Sharon stared at the money. She looked up again at the woman.

"Isn't it wonderful?"

Sharon put her head on the polished desk and wept. And the Hospital Lady joined her.

There were six families with no insurance who'd lost houses in the Harper Creek flood. Kelvin Purdy's family was one of them. All six families received notice from a company that built double-wide trailers that new homes were arriving and would be installed free of charge. When pressed, all the company would say was that an anonymous donor had paid the tab in full. No further information was available.

Early one morning, as Vivian filled up Waite's thermos with coffee, Mel himself came to the front with a worried look. "Waite, have you heard of anything strange going on?"

"I hear it every day from Sally over on Lick Creek."

"No, I mean people telling stories. About being given things."

"What are you talking about?"

Vivian handed Waite the thermos, then dragged him inside and closed the door behind him and pulled the shade. She went behind the cash register and picked up a pillowcase. "This was at the back door when we got here this morning."

Vivian opened it up so Waite could see. Inside were several stacks of hundred-dollar bills secured by rubber bands.

Waite looked up at Mel. "Are you sure you're just selling donuts?"

"I swear, Waite, I don't know where this came from."

"How much is it?"

"We haven't counted it yet, but we think there's about ten thousand in each stack," Vivian said. She glanced at Mel. "If that's right, it's about what we owe on the place."

Waite shook his head and laughed. "If I were you, I'd get to the bank as soon as it opens."

Vivian said words Waite would hear repeated from others who confided in him over the coming days: "Don't say anything about this on the radio."

Waite promised he wouldn't.

Later that morning, Ardelle took a call from a woman named Cindy who asked to talk to Waite. "She don't want to go on the air."

He picked up the phone while Wally was taking his first call on the *Swap Shop*.

"I just wanted you to know about the miracle that happened today."

"I'm all ears."

"I called you some weeks back about what I'd do with a million dollars."

"I'm sorry, I don't recall that."

"Well, I do. I told you that if I had a million dollars, I would build a resort for Vietnam veterans to thank them for their service."

"Okay, I remember you now, Cindy. You said your little brother came back and hasn't been the same. What was his name?"

"Jimmy. Well, I got a call today from the local VFW and they said they got an anonymous gift that was to be used to refurbish the Vietnam Veterans Lodge. They're going to add some pool tables and set up a memorial marker for those soldiers from West Virginia who lost their lives. And whoever gave the money said it was in honor of Jimmy and his service. I can't believe it, Waite."

Other strange news came to Waite from churches in the area. Pastor Gentry had privately told Waite that he thought they would need to abandon their church building fund. The new gymnasium would have helped the after-school program they wanted to start, but the flood had strapped people in the area.

However, before the service the following Sunday, Pastor Gentry couldn't hold back his excitement. "You're not going to believe what I found in the office this morning, Waite."

"From that smile on your face, it looks like it was more than a dozen donuts from Mel's."

"It was, and I'm going to announce to the congregation today that the building fund for the gymnasium hasn't been canceled—it's been met."

"How in the world did you make up the deficit?"

"It showed up in a shoebox with the words *Building Fund* written on it. Right outside my door when I came in this morning."

"How would somebody have gotten in?"

"We got so many keys floating around, there's no telling. Or it could have been somebody after the potluck last night. I went home early. That's not the point. The point is the Lord has provided."

"Yes, he has, Pastor."

Milton Quidley hurried to his office in Clarkston, his mouth dry, heart racing. He'd received a frantic phone call from his building's security guard. When he pulled into the parking lot, he spotted a group gathered in the alley beside the building.

He ran toward the gaggle, pushing them out of the way and straining to see.

"I tried to keep everybody away, Mr. Quidley," the security guard said. "Folks, move back."

The man had draped a plastic tablecloth over something on the ground but it didn't cover the bottom of the ornate box beneath it. And when Milton pulled the cloth away, people gasped. There on the sidewalk sat the dream of his father. The ark. With gold seraphim above.

He'd put out a hand to open it when something flickered in his memory, a story about someone touching the ark when it was being moved. As a boy he'd wondered, What kind of God would kill someone for trying to steady a falling ark? He shook the memory and opened the top.

Velvet lined the inside of the entire box, but it was dirty and wet and had pulled away in several sections. He felt others pressing in behind him to look but when he turned, they all stepped back. There was only one thing inside, an envelope wrapped in plastic.

Milton picked it up and turned to the guard. "Move this thing inside," he said.

"I tried to lift it, sir. It's pretty heavy."

Milton asked several men to help. Four of them lifted the ark and brought it through the side door. Because the men labored, Milton waved them away from the elevator and asked the guard to open the storage room and lock it inside. He watched them shuffle down the hall as he waited for the elevator.

When he reached the top floor, Milton walked through the empty office and closed his door behind him and sat at his desk. He took off the plastic and placed the envelope in front of him, wiping his forehead with the back of his hand.

Finding the empty ark meant many things. His inheritance was gone, for one. Other than his father's house, he had been left nothing. His father had given the remaining money he'd had in the bank to his church and two other religious institutions.

Someone had found the treasure, presumably recently, while he was following the rabbit trail of the Pizza Barn. He had lost. If only he'd acted more quickly. Convinced his father to tell him the location. If the deer hadn't jumped out, the man he'd hired to follow his father would have pinpointed the location. Maybe if he'd gone ahead with plans to have the old man committed, all of this could have been avoided.

Milton tore open the envelope and unfolded the sheet of paper inside and read the scrawled handwriting.

Dear Mr. Quidley,

Obviously your father's treasure has been found. After pondering what to do with his ark, I figured it might be worth more to you than anybody, seeing as how your daddy had it made. Maybe you want it as a keepsake. Or you might melt the gold. Or it could be a tourist attraction. You could sell tickets. Whatever you decide, the ark is yours.

One more thing. I think your father wanted you to find the treasure. I'm sure of it, from reading all the things he said through the years. I also believe you can still find it if you'll look with all your heart. I'm not talking about gold or silver now. I'm talking about eternal treasure. That's what he would want you to find. And I sincerely hope you do.

The letter left him hollow and out of breath. He folded it and put it in a drawer and went to the lobby.

"Did you see anything on the surveillance cameras last night?"

"I went through the recording, sir," the guard said. "Whoever was here put the box across the alley out of view of the cameras. Must have known about them."

"Did you fall asleep last night?"

"No, sir."

His answer wasn't convincing.

"Did you hear anything out of the ordinary?"

The guard scratched his head. "About three o'clock I thought I heard a diesel engine rumbling. I checked the cameras but didn't see anything."

When he returned to his office, Milton pulled out a business card the men from NASA had given him. He picked up the phone and dialed the number.

Waite was in his office looking at the muddy river when Ardelle buzzed his phone. Before he could pick up, Boyd Cluff walked in and shook his hand and sat in a chair. He was a cinder block of a man, older than dirt, with deep creases in his face from years of making bad business decisions. To his credit, he had begun Country 16 and tried to staff it with salespeople and on-air talent, but he never made a profit until Waite came along. And profit was a loose term for what he received after all the bills were paid.

"I don't like that look on your face," Waite said.

"There's no way around this, Waite. No easy way to say it. I've sold the station."

"You what? You can't do that."

"I can and I have."

"You forget your promise?"

"What promise is that?"

"You said a long time ago that before you ever sold, you'd let me know so I could make a counteroffer."

Boyd laughed. "There's no chance in Charleston you'd ever come up with the amount of money this outfit offered, Waite."

"How much?"

Boyd told him.

Waite's jaw dropped. Then he took a deep breath. "Well, congratulations. You're the first millionaire I've ever worked for. And probably the last."

"I'm sorry, Waite. If I wanted to start another station, I'd hire you again, but I'm too old for this now."

"Who's the outfit that bought you out?"

"That I don't know. It was all handled through a lawyer down in Lexington. The FCC has to approve it, so you have a couple of months to get your people prepared."

"You don't think they'll want to keep us?"

"I'm just saying with the amount of money they're paying, I wouldn't be surprised if they cleaned house and did their own thing."

"You think they'll stay country?"

"I got no idea. Maybe they'll go all disco. I don't give a hoot."

"Well, I appreciate the advance notice. I'll let the staff know." When Boyd stood, Waite added, "You don't think Milton Quidley had anything to do with the purchase, do you?"

"He lost his shirt over the Pizza Barn deal. Took it down to the studs. For the life of me, I can't figure out why he thought his daddy's treasure was there."

Waite stifled a smile and shook his head. "Can I ask one favor?"

"Let me guess. You want to bring TD back?"

"Rich men sure are smart."

The two men sent from NASA had stayed at a hotel in Clarkston, observing the dismantling of the Pizza Barn and the excavation of the surrounding area with great interest. They had communicated with their offices in Washington, DC, and were also reporting to superiors in different locales, including the Johnson Space Center in Houston.

Their interest in the treasure of Gideon Quidley had nothing to do with gold, silver, or cash. Their sole mission was to retrieve an artifact of "national interest," meaning Gideon was in possession of something he wasn't supposed to have and they were tasked with getting it back.

It had come to the attention of the agency that an astronaut (who will not be named) had been in a Bible study with Gideon long before anyone set foot on the lunar surface. The man had brought back a souvenir in recognition for his faithful service to the Apollo team, surreptitiously presenting Gideon with a rock that had been taken from the Sea of Tranquility. While the astronaut knew it was forbidden to sell or trade such a priceless artifact, he didn't think there was a problem in giving it to someone who had supported their efforts and preserved their lives with his intellect and expertise. It was the ultimate thank-you.

The Nixon administration had given gifts of moon rocks to more than 100 countries and each governor of the fifty states. Already, some of those "gifts" had gone missing and there was a drive to locate the missing lunar treasure. After discovering the existence of Gideon's "gift" from a conversation the astronaut had with an elected official (who will also remain nameless), authorities questioned the astronaut. They determined that they should, at all costs, find the artifact and return it to NASA. In a phone call from the tearful astronaut, who explained his predicament to a surprised Gideon, that was recorded by NASA, Gideon did not give up the location of the hidden artifact but promised he would do all he could to "set things square." This all happened shortly before Gideon's accident.

When the search of Gideon's house and his safe-deposit boxes came up empty, it was determined that the moon rock could only be in one place. A plan was set in motion to be present when the treasure was uncovered.

The men from NASA had studied the clues Gideon left and were just as flummoxed as others who spent time trying to follow the scriptural bread crumbs. That was, until Gideon was found on a back road in Emmaus. The men descended on the site and followed the old man's son, who, they believed, had an inside track on the treasure's location because of his DNA.

The final clue given by Gideon led them to his dog and the dog's collar, which, when opened, revealed a key chain with the emblem of the Pizza Barn. It seemed outlandish to both men, but Milton Quidley insisted on extreme measures. He had bought the restaurant and torn it apart to no avail.

Then the two men heard rumblings from townspeople of financial anomalies. Hospital bills paid in full. A story in the local newspaper about how a single gift to a church put them over their goal for construction of a gymnasium. All of these had one thing in common—the anonymous nature of the giver.

They began inquiring of individuals who had received gifts and immediately met a wall of silence. Whether it was distrust of the government or protecting the anonymous giver, the effect was a total shutdown in communication. In other words, their mission was toast.

On the morning they were to leave for a meeting in Washington, DC, one of the agents went to the lobby for breakfast. While he was pouring his coffee, the front desk worker waved him over.

"This morning someone dropped off a message for you," the desk worker said. She pushed an envelope toward him.

"A message for who?"

"You. He said it was for 'those two government boys.' I assume he meant you."

The agent grabbed the envelope without thanking her and retreated to the hall and opened it. Inside was a single sheet of paper with words written in pencil: *Left something for you on your front bumper.*

The man hurried outside and saw a box duct-taped to the bumper of the car. Thinking it might be evidence, he used a hand-kerchief to pry it loose, then hurried to the room, where he put on surgical gloves and opened it in the presence of the second "government boy."

In the box was a plastic bag. He held it up and studied the contents. A single rock.

"Bingo."

Later, after analysis, it was determined that the paper used for the note was common stock available at stores around the country. The only clue to the identity of the sender was a faint design along the bottom of the page that was visible when exposing it to UV light. To the agents, it looked like a bird of unknown species had walked across the paper and left tracks. With the investigation at a dead end, it was closed and the rock was returned to NASA to be cataloged and stored for safekeeping.

PART 5

One month earlier

CHAPTER 34

FRIDAY, SEPTEMBER 4, 1981

The day after TD had kissed her, Pidge knew she needed to talk to Clay. He deserved to know what was happening and what was ahead, though she wasn't clear about it herself. She just knew things had changed. And there was something else on her mind. Something had come in the mail that disturbed her.

She and Clay had gotten into an easy rhythm to their days without a lot of expectation from either of them, and she didn't want to upset that balance. Clay was trusting her more and opening up, but she wasn't sure how he'd respond to what was ahead.

She'd heard someone say once that the easiest way to communicate something important to a child was in the middle of doing something else. In the process of doing that other thing, whether it was working on a car or fishing, you could talk while you both concentrated on the duty at hand. That made sense to Pidge, and when she saw him with three garden hoses attached to each other, stretched to the end of the lot, she approached him and grabbed it, acting like she was upset with his work. Instead of snapping at him, she turned the hose toward him and sprayed him in the face. Clay squalled and ran, laughing and turning around with a bewildered look.

"Why d-d-did you do that?"

Jubal barked and she turned the hose on the dog for a second. "I thought you'd like it. It's hot out here."

"Well, I don't like it," Clay said, smiling.

Sure enough, when he got the hose back, he sprayed her and she put her head down and got it wet, then turned around and put her hands up in surrender.

"I thought y-y-you'd like it," Clay yelled, laughing.

Jubal shook himself and returned to the car he'd been sniffing and barking at. Pidge walked to the end of the lot, examining the cars TD had delivered. The one that Jubal barked at was covered in mud and sludge. Somehow the windows were intact after the deluge. Another car next to it was tipped on its side and from the looks of it, she thought she could sell the exhaust. She called Clay over and they tried tipping it onto its wheels, but it only took one push to see it was sunk too far in the mud to move. She'd need the tractor.

While Clay went about his business spraying, she fired up the Massey Ferguson her father had pieced together from about four tractors. She drove it to the car and used the front loader to gently nudge it onto its wheels, except the gentle nudge pierced the front windshield and black water gurgled out.

"W-won't have to s-spray that windshield," Clay said, laughing at her.

She parked the tractor and returned. "I've got something to tell you."

Clay's shoulders slumped. His face fell.

"What's that look for?" she said.

He didn't look up. He mumbled, "Y-you don't w-w-want me anymore, do you?"

That look and those words about tore out her heart. But they told her something about him she wouldn't have known otherwise. He wanted to be here. And he was crestfallen at any other prospect. That gave her hope.

"You're talking crazy. Of course I want you here. Why would you say that?"

"You s-s-sure?"

"Sure as I know the dams broke. Look at all of this muck and mire. I can tell they broke because of what they left behind. And I know you belong here because of what I feel inside for you."

She could tell her words were like a low-hanging fog to him. He was looking through it to see something he hoped was there. And then she said words he'd probably never heard before.

"Clay, you coming here is the best thing that's ever happened to me. You know that?"

He opened his mouth but nothing came out.

"I'm not saying it's a cakewalk, you living here. You eat like a horse. And you're growing like milkweed. You're going to need new clothes, and I swear I've never seen bigger feet. And they're getting bigger."

Something crept up on her as she spoke. Something on the inside she had a hard time pushing down.

"And that singing in the shower. How long have you done that?"

"You can hear me?"

She nodded.

"Waite said M-Mel Tillis doesn't st-stutter when he sings. I was trying it out."

She looked away from him at the mud-covered car. It was hard looking into his face when he was being so honest. "Did it work?"

"You tell me," he said.

She cleared her throat. "I don't think Mel is sweating yet. But you sound pretty good. I didn't know you knew any gospel tunes."

"It was s-something they s-sing at Waite's church."

"Something the pretty girls in front of you sing?"

Clay laughed and that made her laugh, and she thought, *Laughter is like water to a dry pump. A little will prime it and pretty soon you have all you need and then some.* When her eyes cleared, she pointed at the car in front of them, a Honda, and motioned for him to spray it. It was mangled from the flood but all the windows were intact. Kind of like her life. Dented and bruised but not shattered.

She decided to skirt the discussion of TD since it would be harder and jump to the other topic on her mind. "I want to ask you something important. Who do you know in Florida?"

He kept spraying the car and looked at her with a frown. "Nobody."

"Well, a letter came today addressed to you from somebody in Florida. A radio station. That ring a bell?"

He dropped the hose and wiped his hand off. "Really?"

"Clay, one of my rules is we don't keep secrets. If you're in some kind of trouble or if you're writing somebody I ought to know about, I want you to tell me."

"It's n-nothing like that."

"Then what is it?"

"I'd rather not s-say until I read the l-letter. Where is it?"

"Back at the house. Kitchen table." She squinted at him. *Who in Florida would have written him?*

"Can I go get it?"

"Okay. If you promise you're going to let me in on it."

"If it's from who I th-think it's from, you'll know."

"Then why did you say you didn't know anybody in Florida?"

"Because I d-don't know the person."

"I give up. You don't make any more sense than Gideon Quidley did."

He smiled for some reason and ran toward the house. Jubal sniffed at the back of the Honda and barked again, and she yelled at him to stop. When he didn't, she sprayed him and laughed when he tried to drink from the hose.

Down the hill from the station came TD in his wrecker. He slipped and slid through the gate and got out and ran toward her, a weird look on his face. He yelled at Clay to follow him just as Clay got to the house. Obediently he turned and joined TD.

"It wasn't an ax," TD yelled.

"What are you talking about?" Pidge said.

Jubal barked again.

Out of breath, TD bent over, hands on his knees. "I talked to a fellow who knew Gideon. He told me Gideon said the location of the treasure had to do with something in Luke and that there were two axes."

Pidge stared at him, trying to make sense of his words.

"Luke 24. That's where he got the road to Emmaus. Gideon knew he was going to hide the treasure here. That's clear to me now. What's not clear is the two axes. But today it came to me." He stood straight. "I was reading Acts chapter 2."

"Go on," she said.

"Tongues and fire and Peter preaching and souls being added

to the church. I couldn't put it together. And then today I saw it. At the beginning of the chapter and at the end of it, he says the same thing in the King James."

"Wh-what's it say?"

TD pulled out his pocket New Testament. "Right here. 'And when the day of Pentecost was fully come, they were all with one accord in one place.' Then at the end it says, 'And they, continuing daily with one accord in the temple . . .' Did you hear it?"

"I'm not following you at all," Pidge said.

"Accord?" Clay said.

"Bingo."

"I still don't get it," Pidge said.

Clay's face lit up. "I do. S-stay right here!" He ran toward the house and Pidge thought he was going for the letter, but he returned holding something in his hand. Out of breath, he held out a car key.

"Where did you get that?" TD said.

"Jubal's collar," Clay said.

The three of them turned and looked at Jubal, still sniffing at the Honda and barking. Pidge turned the hose on the car and sprayed the back until a word appeared in silver.

Accord.

Clay was the first to the car, cupping his hand to the back window. He looked up at them. "That's the thing I saw at Waite's church. Pastor Gentry put it up on the overhead."

Pidge couldn't speak. All the air went out of her lungs. TD's eyes were bigger than saucers as he rubbed the side window and looked around the junkyard as if somebody might be watching.

"This is one of the cars you brought here, right?" Pidge said.

"Yeah," TD said. "Found it near where Lick Creek runs into the Mud River. And above that is . . . holy cow."

"What?" Pidge said.

"The road sign. Harper Creek Road. I'll bet you a million dollars there were willow trees in there before they flooded it."

Clay put the key in the lock. He turned it and the door unlocked.

CHAPTER 35

Waite's phone rang at 9:30 p.m., past his bedtime.

TD was on the phone telling him to get over to Pidge's place pronto. "We need your help."

"Is somebody hurt?"

"No, just get over here. I need you to see something."

"Can't it wait till morning, TD? I got to get up early."

"You think I don't know that?"

Waite sighed. "All right. I'll be there in twenty minutes."

Waite shook his head as he drove. In the distance he saw the blinking red light and wound down to the floodplain. When he pulled up, TD stood on the porch smiling.

"You're not going to believe it."

"A station offered you a job?"

"You're funny. But you're not going to believe it, Waite. Get inside, quick."

TD looked around the salvage yard like he was scouting for a war party. Waite walked past him into the double-wide and took off his hat. The kitchen light was on and he rounded the corner and saw The Kid at the table smirking. Pidge stood in front of the table with her hands in her back pockets. He'd never seen her smiling so big.

"What's with all the happy faces? This is not a surprise birthday par—"

He took one look at the kitchen table and couldn't finish his sentence. The top was covered by several black trash bags and spread over them were gold and silver coins and soggy $100 bills wrapped in rubber bands.

"Where in the world did you find this?" Waite said after he caught his breath. He had read *Treasure Island* as a boy, but nothing could have prepared him for this sight. Water and sludge had tainted the booty, but it hadn't taken away the value.

"Come on, I'll show you," TD said, flicking on a flashlight. He talked as he walked Waite outside. "I knew the harps on the willow trees was important, but I didn't know why until I read what Gideon wrote down. It was on a sheet of paper sealed in plastic. He explains every bit of it. He chose Emmaus from Luke 24. That's what he meant by 'where it all began.'"

"Tell him about Acts," Pidge said, trailing them. The Kid wasn't far behind.

"That's the funny part. Acts chapter 2. Two spots refer to people being in one accord."

"Why is that funny?"

TD stopped in front of a dented Honda. "He put the treasure inside this. Then he drove it down here from Gallipolis."

"The treasure was in a car?"

"He tells it in the note. He drove to Emmaus and asked the

Lord to show him where to hide it. That's where the harps in the willow trees come in."

Waite shook his head. "I'm not following you."

"That's why nobody found it, Waite," TD said. "Remember when the coal company bought the Harper family's land? They got held up from digging for a while. That's when Gideon drove down here to hide the treasure."

"Then they put in the dams and flooded that area," Waite said.

"Exactly. There was a willow grove right where they put the lower dam. I called my dad and asked him. He confirmed it because he's lived—"

"Wait a minute—you called your father?" Waite said, almost as surprised by that as he was by the ark sitting on Pidge's kitchen table.

"It's a long story. I went over there and had a talk the other day. Anyway, what I figure is, when the upper dam broke, all that water and slurry crashed down and old Gideon's car was pushed out of there and down that channel and it wound up by the river. That's where I found it."

"But you didn't know that when you towed it?"

"I didn't have any idea. I put it together when I was reading Acts 2. And The Kid found the key to the car."

"How in the world did you do that?" Waite said.

"It was in Jubal's c-collar."

Waite closed his eyes. "Was it in there when Milton came here to get him?"

"He'd taken it out," Pidge said. "When Milton showed up, he put a Pizza Barn key chain in there."

Waite slapped his legs with both hands and hooted as he laughed. "That's the funniest thing I've ever heard in my life. I can't wait to tell that on the air."

"You're not saying a word, Waite," TD said.

"Why not?"

"This has got to stay between the four of us. Now we're letting you in on this, but we can't tell anybody from here on out. Think about it. People will come with their hands out. Or believing we're something special because we have a load of treasure. All we did was find it. And you know Milton Quidley will take us to court. But the biggest reason we can't is because of the government."

"The government?" Waite said.

"The Kid will show you back at the house." TD moved to the back of the car to open it. "Get ready. It's a sight."

"Go on," Waite said.

TD opened the door and pointed the flashlight inside. Waite's mouth dropped. There it was in all its ornate beauty, sullied by the slurry. Seraphim and cherubim in gold.

"He was telling the truth, wasn't he?" Waite said.

"And then some," TD said. "I think the four of us can lift it now that it's empty inside."

It took them half an hour, but they managed to carry the ark back to the front porch. Pidge draped a scorched sheet over it and put rocks on the edges to make sure it didn't blow away.

Inside, Waite washed his hands in the sink and dried them. "I don't understand about the government. Why are they after this? The gold double eagles?"

The Kid retrieved an object from his room and placed it on the table. It looked like a baseball display case. It was six inches square with a clear top and a wooden base. Inside, on a platform, sat a black piece of jagged rock. It didn't look like a gemstone, didn't glimmer in the kitchen light.

"Remember the clue about Psalm 121?"

Waite thought a moment. "'I lift my eyes to the hills.' That showed he hid it in West Virginia, right?"

"That was part of it. But it goes on to say, 'The sun shall not smite thee by day, nor the moon by night.'"

"I remember."

"Do you remember where Gideon worked?"

Waite stared at the case and the inscription below it. *To Gideon, with gratitude for helping us on the journey to the stars.* "Well, I'll be. A piece of the moon."

"This is why those government boys have been hanging around here. I saw them up at Gideon's house, too. So I say we find a way to return it without them knowing who had it."

"What are you going to do with the rest of it?" Waite said.

"It's what *we're* g-going to do," The Kid said.

Pidge leaned forward. "We're in this together, Waite. The four of us. We've done decided."

"I don't understand."

"For some reason the Lord brought the treasure here," Pidge said. "It's kind of like being given a gift to steward, like the Bible parable. So the four of us get to decide what to do with it. And when."

"B-but we have to k-k-keep it a secret. We can't tell nobody."

Waite nodded. "All right. Let's get a plan together."

TD reached for the case in Waite's hands. "I know one thing I'm going to do."

PART 6

CHAPTER 36

At Emmaus High School, the talk of the fall semester had been Gideon Quidley's treasure and who might have found it. Clay listened to the conjecture in classrooms and hallways and at lunch. Many thought somebody from out of town had found it. Others said Milton Quidley had located it in the Pizza Barn and put the ark outside his office to make people think he hadn't found it. Clay's English teacher, a heavyset woman with a droll mouth, asked them to write an essay regarding the treasure and said the best writer would be asked to read it aloud in front of the class. Clay made sure his was not the best.

However, he had put his heart and soul into one other piece of writing. As he lay in bed on the night they had found the ark, excited and incredulous, he remembered the letter that had arrived. He opened it and glanced at the signature at the bottom by Emily Evers, then read it line by line, word by word.

> *Dear Clay,*
>
> *I received your letter and yes, you have the right person. Congratulations on finding me.*
>
> *I understand about the stutter and why it's hard to call. When you wrote about Hamm's, my mouth watered. They make the best sandwich I've ever tasted. Did you have the root beer in the chilled mug?*
>
> *Your letter gave me time to think through how I feel. I have to admit, the first thing I thought was if a kid at the station can find me, why hasn't my father done the same? If he loves me so much, why am I hearing from you instead of him? We did have a "falling-out," as you say. And I regret some of the things I said and did. If he were writing a letter to me, I don't think he would be as kind as you. After what I've said and done, I don't really think he would want me back. I know I wouldn't want me back.*
>
> *Take care of my fishing pole. I'm glad you're putting it to good use. Maybe one day when I get my life together and save some money, I'll make my way back and I'll take you to Hamm's myself.*
>
> *Thank you for writing. It was kind of you.*
>
> *Sincerely,*
> *Emily Evers*

Clay read the letter at least fifty times before he began composing his response. One night, after finishing his evening shift at Country 16, which had been cut to two hours because of his schoolwork, he sat down in the production room and in a flurry the words finally came.

Dear Emily,

I'm glad you got my letter and thank you for writing me back. I will take you up on the offer of Hamm's. I have had the root beer. Yum.

After reading your letter, I realized I'm reaching out to you for selfish reasons. I want to see the look on your daddy's face when you come home. And I know you think there's no way he could welcome you back, but you're flat out wrong. (I'm not trying to argue.)

There's a song on the radio and in the chorus it says, "All my life I've waited for you. All my dreams are yours." Your daddy has a hard time with that song because I think it's what he wants to say to you.

I've heard him say that the closest we ever get to loving others like God loved us is when we give somebody a second chance to hurt us. Give him another chance, Emily. Or if you're staying away because you feel guilty, give yourself a second chance. Or maybe both of you need another one.

Like I said, I don't want to stick my nose in where it doesn't belong. But I'm asking you to trust me that good things will happen if you make a trip back. I'm enclosing some money I found to help you pay for gasoline or a plane ride. If you decide not to come, keep it and use it for something you need.

I haven't told your daddy anything about this. At some point I probably will, if you don't come. But I got to thinking that if I were you and I had a daddy and we had gone through something bad, I'd want somebody to give me a chance to come back on my own terms.

I thank you for reading this.

Clay

Waite saw The Kid pass his window, then amble into his office and peck on the open door. "You w-wanted to s-see me?"

"Sit down," Waite said. "Got some good news."

The Kid sat and put his hands beneath his armpits and stared through his silky hair. The curtain seemed to comfort him, as if he could be by himself wherever he was.

"At the next city council meeting, the mayor is going to award two people for heroism in the Harper Creek flood. Any idea who that might be?"

"You and Deputy P-Palermo?"

"You're half-right. It's Palermo and you. What do you think of that?"

"I d-didn't do anything."

Waite shook his head and laughed. "Well, you're not going to convince the mayor. Or anybody on Harper Creek who heard you or got a call from a neighbor because of what you did. He's already had the plaque made."

The Kid shifted in his chair.

"You don't have to talk, if that's what's bothering you. Just stand up there and smile big for the newspaper. They'll be taking a picture."

"Why d-don't you get an award? You went up there."

"Yeah, but you did the talking." He pointed to the wall. "Plus, they gave me one three years ago. I don't want to be a plaque hog. I told the mayor that the two of you were enough and he agreed."

"What h-happened three y-years ago?"

"It was just something that happened on the radio one day. Not a big deal."

The Kid stared at him and Waite leaned forward in his squeaky chair. "There was an old boy who used to call us. He was a little scatterbrained but harmless. People saw him walking the road and gave him a ride. Well, he got in some trouble over at the Feed and Seed and he called from the store. I talked with him and it was clear something was wrong.

"I had the midday gal who was here at the time take the board and I drove over there. There were two sheriff's cruisers outside and deputies with guns drawn. I explained I was a friend and they let me go inside and talk with him. That's all it was."

"He had a g-gun, d-didn't he?"

"Yeah, he did." Waite glanced at the picture on his desk. "Sometimes people get themselves in situations they can't see a way out of. And you hope they'll find a friend. Somebody to reach out and tell them it'll be okay. Maybe that's what I do on the radio. I just tell people, 'It's gonna be okay. We'll get through this.'"

"Is that man st-st-still around?"

"They had to put him in a home. He's not a danger to himself or others now. His family's in town, though. They wave when they see me."

The Kid nodded. "Okay. I'll go to the mayor thing."

"Good. I'll let you know what evening they're having it and you'll want to get spiffed up. I imagine Pidge will get you a shirt and tie. It'll be good publicity for the station."

"Yes, sir."

Waite pushed back, ready to stand, but The Kid stayed seated. He stared at the back of the picture on Waite's desk.

"Is there something else you want to talk about?"

The Kid looked at the floor, then back up at Waite. For some reason he had water in his eyes. "Waiting's h-hard, isn't it?"

"Yes, it is."

CHAPTER 37

PIDGE LISTENED TO THE MORNING PROGRAM with TD and Waite and smiled every time they played The Kid's weather forecast. His voice was getting deeper and more relaxed when he talked, and Pidge guessed he wasn't using up as much splicing tape as when he started.

"TD's got some big news he wants to share with everybody," Waite said.

"Now don't go making a big deal about it," TD said.

"It is a big deal. I hear every eligible woman from here to Morgantown will be wailing because of this news."

"You go ahead and have your fun," TD said. Pidge could tell he was smiling.

"All right, give us the bad news for the single ladies and the good news for the rest of us."

"You remember how long people looked for that Quidley treasure?"

"It was a long time and still a mystery who found it."

"Well, there's no mystery to me about the real treasure in these hills. I found her and today I'm giving her an engagement ring."

"You haven't asked her to marry you yet?"

"I asked her and she said yes, but I didn't have a ring. I had it special made."

"Let me see it."

Dead air. A chair squeaked.

"Whooo, boy, TD. You went whole hog. How many Cracker Jack boxes did you have to open to find that?"

"That's funny, Waite. You ought to go on the road with those jokes of yours."

"Well, all kidding aside, this is a gorgeous ring, TD. Tell us who the unfortunate woman is."

"Her name is Pamela. That's all I'm going to say. Some people know her by another name. But we're getting married this weekend."

"Well, you have my blessing, friend. The only question is, do you have The Kid's blessing? He has to approve all the weddings at the station."

TD chuckled. "Since he's watching from the production room, I have a little announcement about that, too."

"Do I need to get the sound effect of a drumroll out?"

"No." TD must have turned his head because his voice went off-mic. "Me and Pamela have talked about it, and after we get married, we'd like to make you official."

"From the look I see on The Kid's face, you're going to have to explain what you mean, TD. And turn around so you can be on the microphone. There you go."

There was a pause. TD cleared his throat. "What I'm saying is, Pidge—I mean, me and Pamela . . ." TD's voice cracked. Pidge had a hard time holding herself together as she listened. "We want you to be our son. If you'll have us as parents."

"Lock, stock, and barrel?" Waite said.

"The whole shooting match," TD said.

Pidge heard sniffles and Waite gave an emotional laugh. "Folks, I wish you could see what I'm seeing right now. The Kid just opened the door, here he comes . . ."

Pidge heard the control room door open and there was a muffled sound of somebody crying and the patting of denim. She covered her face with her hands and shook her head.

Waite gathered himself. "I've witnessed a lot in my days, but that's the best thing I've ever heard on radio. Looks like TD has him a wife and son. But I still claim fishing rights with The Kid. And we still get to go to Hamm's on weekends, you hear?"

"Okay," Clay said, laughing and choking back his tears. It was a beautiful, ugly cry.

Waite sniffed into the microphone. "All right, to top that, I need to play a dedication for TD. This song is for you, requested by your sweetheart, Pamela. This is the song she's going to be singing to you a few years down the road. It's a beautiful sentiment. Straight from the heart. You ready?"

"I can hardly wait," TD said.

The music started and Pidge threw her head back and laughed as soon as she heard the guitar riff.

"It's twenty after seven on a sunny day in Emmaus, and here's Loretta and Conway, 'You're the Reason Our Kids Are Ugly—'"

"Oh, Waite!" TD yelled.

"Ha-ha-ha, on Country 16!"

Pidge heard the truck pull up to the office and saw through the space over the air conditioner that it was TD. She opened the door and smiled at him as he walked toward her with a little box in his hand.

"Did you hear that on the morning show?"

"The whole thing," Pidge said.

"You should have seen The Kid. He just about cut the oxygen off to my brain with his hug. He's getting strong."

She looked at the box. "Is this it?"

TD smiled. "Come out here in the sunlight where you can see it sparkle."

She followed him into the sun. "You shouldn't have done this."

"You're going to think different when you see it."

"A fancy ring on a hand like mine is like putting a . . ."

He opened the box and she stopped talking. He was right. She took one look at the stone and all the colors the sun brought out in it and it took her breath away.

"TD, that's way too fancy."

"Look here," he said, pulling the ring out with his callused fingers. "Right below the stone. You see that?"

She took the ring and held it up to the light. Beside the diamond was a small setting with a black stone that didn't sparkle or shine when she turned the ring.

"I had the jeweler set that in there for you."

"What is it?"

"That right there makes this the most expensive ring in the world. There's not another one like it on the planet."

She looked up him and then back at the ring.

"When I was taking the case over to those government fellows, I noticed there was a fragment at the bottom of it. A little piece had fallen off and was rattling around. The jeweler had no idea what it was and nobody else will know but you and me."

"You gave me a piece of the moon."

TD took her hand and she pulled away. "That's the wrong hand. This one."

He put it on her finger and she held it up and stared at it. She would have looked at it all day if he hadn't leaned in to kiss her. And they would have kissed all day if she hadn't heard the noise behind her.

Through the open door she heard flapping and a gray blur shot from the darkness into the light. Pidge yelled and ran after the bird, calling for him. She stopped by the fence and grabbed hold of it and hung on, watching him gain altitude.

"Flap, no!" she yelled.

TD caught up. "Get in the truck. We'll follow him. He won't get far."

"Yes, he will," she said. "He's gone, TD."

"He'll come back. You've been good to him, Pidge. He'll come home. That's what pigeons do."

"I don't think so," she said. "Look at him fly."

He put a hand up to shade his eyes. "He made it past the guy wires okay. It's been a long time since he's flown like that."

"Sure looks like he knows where he's going, doesn't it?" she said.

"But why don't you think he'll be back?"

"Because he knows," she said.

"Knows what?"

"That I don't need him to stay. It's okay for him to go. It's time."

TD hugged her and she buried her head in his chest.

CHAPTER 38

WAITE WALKED PIDGE DOWN THE AISLE and handed her off to TD in front of Robby Gardner. Robby conducted the service from his wheelchair, which sat on a special platform that had been built with anonymous funds. The Gardner family had also received money that Waite heard had made Sharon cry when they opened the envelope.

Waite was heartened to see TD's mother and father on the right side of the church. Both looked a little uncomfortable, like fish swimming in a different pool, but there was a sense of calm that the wedding put on the family.

Waite thought about the songs he played each day and realized that in country music there was a fair amount of revenge and bitterness and regret, but not a lot of forgiveness. Perhaps that was the difference between gospel and country.

TD and Pidge went to Pipestem Resort State Park for their honeymoon. They stayed in the biggest suite in the lodge. Waite offered to have The Kid stay with him in the back bedroom, but he said he wanted to sleep in his own bed. Waite told Pidge he would make sure he was well-fed and would check in on him each day.

"Don't worry about him."

It was a Thursday morning when Clay showed up early to do the weather before catching the bus to the high school. For the hundredth time, he walked from the production room to the front door and looked at the lower parking lot. The sun was over the hill now and he checked the clock. The bus would be there soon.

"You're going to wear a hole in the carpet if you don't stop," Ardelle said. "What are you looking for?"

"Somebody's supposed t-to be here today," Clay said.

"You got you a girlfriend to take you to school?" Ardelle gave a smoky laugh and coughed. "Come on, who is it?"

Clay looked at the closed control room door. "Can you keep a secret?"

"Kid, you have no idea how many secrets I've kept. Whup it on me."

He told her in one long sentence and Ardelle's mouth dropped.

"I wanted to b-be here, but I got to go to school."

Ardelle pulled a Pall Mall from a pack in her top drawer. "Pidge would call you out for something like this, don't you think?"

Clay nodded.

"Give me the number of the school. I'll say you'll be late. I'll drive you."

Clay could have hugged Ardelle. Instead he just said, "Thank you."

Waite sat in his office listening to Wally's *Swap Shop*, still cringing every time he heard the clunk of the phone line on the air.

"That was Jim on the line who has a portable chicken coop he's selling for twenty-five dollars," Wally said, recapping the call. "But the wheels need a little work. He also has three laying hens he's selling for five dollars each. And if you take the coop and hens, the cost is thirty." Wally mumbled Jim's number and there was another loud click. "Hello, you're on the Country 16 *Swap Shop*."

Waite had told Wally and DeeJay that the station was changing ownership. But he told them not to worry or look for a different job. He said he was trying to work something out with the new management. When Possum had finally been released from the hospital and was cleared for active duty, Waite called Cody in and let him know the situation. Cody said he was going to give his two-weeks' notice that day because he'd heard from a station in Dothan, Alabama. They needed an afternoon announcer who had experience.

Waite wished him well and added something to his paycheck for his overnight service.

"Wally, this is Imogene Coker, on Third Street. I have a vintage copy of Mack Strum's 45 'A Piece of the Moon' I'm willing to part with."

"And how did you come by it, Imogene?"

"I grew up near him and listened to him play at picnics and family gatherings. He'd play just about anywhere. When he came out with his record, I bought five copies and had him autograph the sleeves."

"So this is a signed copy of the original record?"

"Yessiree. By Mack himself. Way back before he ever got a record deal."

"And how much do you want for it?"

"Well, it's gonna be worth a lot more in a few years, but I'm willing to part with it for twenty. Or I'll trade it for a mixer in good condition. I bake a lot of cakes and my spatula got chewed up the other day and the mixer started smoking, so I need to replace it."

Imogene described a rum-sauce pound cake and offered to bring one to Wally, and Waite wondered if that would be considered payola by the FCC. The cake sounded like it might be worth more than the 45 and he would have said as much if he were in front of the microphone.

A quick swish down the hall and Ardelle peeked around the doorjamb and looked at Waite with wide eyes. He'd never seen that look on her face before and couldn't judge whether the news was good or bad.

"I think you need to come to the lobby."

"What's wrong, Ardelle?"

"Just come on."

Ardelle disappeared and Waite turned his chair. It squeaked so loudly he made a mental note not to return to the office without getting the WD-40 from the transmitter room. He lumbered out and turned the corner and the first thing he noticed was The Kid. He should have been at school. Waite was going to ask why he was still there, but he saw a little girl and a boy standing by Ardelle's desk. The boy looked to be five or six and had freckles, and when he smiled, Waite saw a missing front tooth. The girl was about three, maybe, and her hair was cut like Buster Brown's. And the sight took his breath away because he could swear he'd been transported in time. Back to the days he didn't dare try to remember.

He stared at the two, trying to make sense of it, and then he looked up, past Ardelle, to the woman who stood in front of the coatrack. Small frame. Long brown hair. When she gave a hint of a smile, it all came together, but he couldn't believe it. It felt like a dream and he put a hand on his barrel chest to make sure his heart was beating.

The woman brushed a hand across her cheek.

"Is he our grandpa?" the boy said, looking up.

Waite couldn't contain his smile. He got on his knees and opened his arms wide and the boy came in first. The girl wasn't so sure. She hung back, hugging her mother's leg. Waite patted the boy's back and studied the girl who looked so much like her mother it hurt.

He made the mistake of looking at The Kid, and the boy who rarely showed any emotion had big tears running down and was patting his hands together like this was something he expected, something he had engineered himself and it was happening like he had it planned.

Waite stood, holding the boy in his arms, and their mother drew close.

"Hi, Daddy."

He stared at her, shaking his head, feeling like his heart was ready to burst open and shoot out moonbeams.

"I'm so glad to see you," he whispered.

She laughed. "You and me both."

Then she hugged him, and her children too, and it felt to Waite as if a circle that had been broken came together in a knot so tight it would never come undone.

EPILOGUE

THERE'S TWO KINDS of people in this world. There's the kind that will hold on to something they love till it dies and the kind that will love it enough to let it go and even watch it leave. Pidge cried like a baby when Flap flew. She watched him rise above the station and it almost seemed like he looked back and waved. I like to think that he did. I would say there's two kinds of birds in the world—the kind that flies on and the kind that looks back—but I don't know pigeons as well as I do people.

We had us a celebration for the opening of the New Country 16. The sale, approved by the FCC, was made by Boyd Cluff to an entity identified as Moon Pieces Incorporated. Four people in the crowd that day knew the identity of the owners, but only two of them knew the true reason for the company name.

All kinds of people showed up for an all-you-can-eat affair.

There was a lot to celebrate. Possum made his first public appearance that day and nobody knew it was him because he had lost a ton of weight, and that's pretty close to the truth and not an exaggeration. I don't know if they did one of those surgeries that Ardelle told us about, but I believe he was well below three hundred, which was the target weight where he would be able to go back to church and not worry about pew insurance. When Possum arrived, Waite brought out a shiny wooden chair with his name engraved on the back and he smiled. He walked on the uneven ground with a cane in one hand and on the other arm was Sally from Lick Creek. There was a bit of talk about that.

Speaking of which, there was also talk about Wally and Ardelle, who had been seen at a steak house together and riding around town in Wally's car, which if you don't remember, he found on the *Swap Shop*. (Waite won't let me forget how important that program is.)

DeeJay wasn't there and that's a sad story that will have to be saved for another time. But she still works at the station and probably always will.

Clayton, The Kid, my son, mowed the grass at the side of the station down to the dirt and Waite hired an outfit to put up a tent and cater the thing with a big spread from Hamm's. Cold root beer and onion rings and sweet potato fries and mounds of sweet ham on toasted buns. Pidge ordered a cake from a bakery in town that said *The New Country 16* in big letters on top. And above it there was an antenna made out of about a thousand pieces of licorice. It was a shame to cut that work of art but you better believe we did.

The mayor was there and said a few words. Deputy Art Palermo came and so did a bunch of the firefighters who had carted Possum out the night he almost died. The big surprise was that Milton Quidley showed up. It seemed to me Milton was still trying to ferret out what happened to the treasure. I shook his hand and thanked him for coming. The harsh words he'd said to me had kindly faded to an echo.

I wish you could have seen Pidge walking down the aisle on our wedding day. I've never seen anything so beautiful and I doubt I ever will except for every day when I wake up and turn my head and look at her face. It made me cry when Waite put her arm in mine, and I don't cry over much of anything. We asked Clayton how he would feel about reading 1 Corinthians 13 and he said, "You mean, out loud?" We didn't put pressure on him, but he'd made such strides we wanted to include him. That boy charged up those steps like Teddy Roosevelt going up San Juan Hill and read those verses with all the confidence in the world. And get this, he'd had a haircut, so you could see his face. It was like somebody had taken the veil off old Moses. He stuttered a couple of times, sure. Life is not perfect. It never will be. But I was proud. And Pidge had to borrow my handkerchief while she listened. I told her just to keep it.

On that day, Pamela Bledsoe became Pamela Bledsoe Lovett. And I became the happiest man in the world. A few weeks later, after the lawyer got the papers signed, which was not the easiest thing in the world given that Clayton's mother was a pain about it, Clayton made it official and he took my name. But to tell you the truth, those two will always be Pidge and The Kid to me.

The Kid asked a girl out to homecoming. Pidge and I couldn't believe it. He bought her ticket and everything. It was one of the Hamm girls who goes to Waite's church. Real pretty little thing.

Jubal is the best watchdog you ever saw. He follows The Kid around everywhere and whines when he goes to school. Pidge keeps an eye out for Flap, of course. Sometimes she'll go down to the park and toss feed to the pigeons just in case he's there.

Every time I look up and see the moon moving across the night sky, I think of those days and all the struggle to them, the longing and the hope and despair, and my heart burns within me. Which is probably why I don't ever want to leave Emmaus.

So that's it. That's the story of the treasure of Gideon Quidley. If you ever get to Emmaus, make sure you get some donuts and coffee at Mel's and some of Hamm's ham. Elaine probably has a sale going on at her dress shop. The Pizza Barn is back up and running. And make sure you tune your radio all the way to the right side of the dial to hear Waite and me every morning. Wally and DeeJay and Possum and The Kid are there, too. You'll hear *New Country 16*, still the best country in the country.

A charming and engrossing novel for fans of Southern fiction
Turn the page for an excerpt from

UNDER A CLOUDLESS SKY

1

Ruby and Bean met in the summer of 1933 in a town called Beulah Mountain, in the southwestern coalfields of West Virginia, shortly before the massacre that has become a footnote in some history books. When people speak of that time, they talk of red and black. Blood was the price paid and coal was the prize. Miners' families were collateral damage in a war against the earth itself, a battle fought with pick and TNT.

There are a thousand places to begin the story. Ruby and Bean's first meeting . . . Bean's big regret . . . where her name came from . . . the shock when they discovered what was happening on the third floor of the company store. But there is another memory that floats to the surface and sits on the water like a katydid on a lily pad. The memory is wrapped in music and preaching and two friends tripping through the underbrush, hand in hand, giggling, and for a moment without a care in the world, the hurt and pain of life dismissed.

Ruby held on to Bean like a tight-eyed, newborn kitten, more afraid to let go than to hang on. She didn't know the hills like her friend, and the speed Bean gathered frightened Ruby. It is a grace to be able to hold on to someone who runs at life when you can only imagine walking.

"Slow down," Ruby said without a drawl, with a hint of northern refinement. To those in Beulah Mountain, Ruby sounded uppity, like she was putting on airs, and there were some in the congregation who questioned whether this daughter of a mine owner belonged in their church. Some thought she might be spying and trying to get information about the union rumors.

Ruby wore the dress her mother had picked from a catalog, a dress she only wore on Sundays and late at night when she couldn't sleep. This dress, other than the pictures and jewelry and sweet-smelling memorabilia she kept in a box on her dresser, was the last connection with her mother. The woman's voice was fading from memory, which troubled Ruby, though the fine contours of her mother's face and the rich brown hair and long eyelashes were still there when she closed her eyes.

Ruby's fingernails were finely trimmed and her hair shone in the sunlight as it bounced and wiggled in curls down her back. She wore pink ribbons that Mrs. Grigsby had positioned for her. Mrs. Grigsby, the wife of the company store proprietor, had been hired to watch Ruby and keep her from children who lived on the other side of the tracks, a task Mrs. Grigsby had failed at miserably.

Like water and coal slurry, children will find their own worthy level and pool.

It is a fine thing to see two hearts beat as one. And the hearts of Ruby and Bean did that. Their friendship raised eyebrows at the beginning, of course, but in the summer of 1933, as the church bell rang, Bean pulled Ruby a little harder and their shoes slid down the bank through the ferns and rhododendrons and saplings and onto the path that led toward the white church with the people streaming in from all sides of the mountain.

"I swear," Bean said, "this church is the most excitement I have all week. It's the only reason to stay in this town."

"You'll be here until the day you die, Bean, and you know it," Ruby said.

"Will not," Bean said. "I'm going to see the world. And take my mama with me. These hills can't hold me."

"Slow down!"

Bean's shoes were held together with sea-grass string and prayer. Her fingernails were bit to the quick and dirty from gathering coal for the cookstove and plucking chickens and digging worms for fishing. Bean—given name Beatrice—was lean and tall for a twelve-year-old, and she had seen more than her share of pain. She had helped bury two brothers and a sister who had never given so much as a single cry. She had held her mother's hand and comforted her when her father wasn't around.

"Don't never run for the doctor again," her mother had said after the last stillborn child. "You've got to promise me."

"Why, Mama?"

"That man don't care a whit for people like us," she said. "He just makes it harder. Next time I'm sick, don't you get him. You hear?"

Bean had promised but didn't understand the ramifications of such a thing and the turmoil it might bring.

Ruby was older than Bean, but not much. Bean was a lot stronger and tougher and her exterior was as rough as a cob (she ran barefoot most days). There could not be two girls on the planet who were from more different families, and yet, here they were.

"Hold up," Bean said when they reached the edge of the woods.

Ruby was out of breath and welcomed the pause. "What is it?"

"Look there."

Ruby saw movement and peered through the underbrush at an animal. Elegant. Stately. When its head passed a wide tree, she saw it was a deer.

"Ain't it beautiful?" Bean said.

"Will he hurt us?" Ruby whispered.

"It's a she and she probably has young ones. I'm glad my daddy isn't here or he'd shoot her quick as look at her. We'd have venison for dinner but the view here wouldn't be half as pretty."

The deer stopped and looked straight at Ruby and Bean.

"Stay real still," Bean whispered. "Deer know things people don't."

"What do you mean?" Ruby said. When she turned her head, the deer jumped and ran quickly into the brush.

Bean sighed. "They see things you and I can't. If I could have been born as anything else, I'd have chosen a deer."

Music from the old piano in the church lifted over the valley and Bean picked up her pace again. The heat and humidity of summer made the piano keys stick, but she recognized the introduction to her favorite hymn.

"Come on, we're going to miss 'Beulah,'" she said.

Though the church tried to keep the piano in tune, summer was hard on the instrument and winter was worse. Those occupying the pews sang louder each week to overcome the weathering effects on the Franklin upright. The piano's story was rich—Bean's father said it had been rescued and redeemed from a saloon in Matewan a few years prior, and before that it was used in a Chicago brothel that Al Capone had frequented and the bullet holes in the right side had been made by Bugs Moran. All of these stories seemed too wild for anyone but Ruby and Bean to believe, though neither knew what a "brothel" was. That a piano could be rescued and redeemed in a church felt like something God would do.

Benches creaked and snapped as the congregation stood, and nasal voices rose in unison as the girls neared the wooden steps. Bean let go of her friend's hand, grabbed the iron railing, and catapulted to the top and through the door where an older man with only a few teeth looked down. Sopranos strained to overcome the off-key male voices.

"Far away the noise of strife upon my ear is falling;
Then I know the sins of earth beset on every hand;
Doubt and fear and things of earth in vain to me are calling;
None of these shall move me from Beulah Land."

Bean rushed past women waving fans and men who had freshly shaved and washed away as much coal dust as they could. She found her mother in her usual spot and the woman drew her in with one arm as Ruby joined them, out of breath but smiling.

"I'm living on the mountain, underneath a cloudless sky,
I'm drinking at the fountain that never shall run dry;
Oh, yes! I'm feasting on the manna from a bountiful supply,
For I am dwelling in Beulah Land."

Not every church service began with this hymn, but at some point on either Sunday morning or Sunday evening, the congregation raised its voice in praise to the God who allowed them to live in Beulah Mountain and long for their heavenly home.

Ruby had never heard such singing before moving to Beulah Mountain. She had taken piano lessons early and could read music on the page, a feat that amazed Bean. But what happened when these people sang was more than just humans hitting notes. The music seemed to come from somewhere deep inside and when their voices united, it felt like goose bumps on the soul. Something like joy bubbled up from inside her and leaked through her eyes.

When they had sung the requisite number of choruses and verses, the pews creaked again from the weight of slight men and women and their children. There were soft coughs that would be termed *silicosis* in the years ahead, but for now it was simply a "coughing spell." Ruby burrowed herself under Bean's mother's arm and Bean did the same on the other side. Though it was hot and muggy, and the pregnant woman between them would have been more comfortable being left alone, she spread her wings like a mother hen.

The pastor was a thick man with thin hair slicked back. He looked like a miner who had moved toward ministry, but he talked with a wheeze and Ruby sat enraptured by his words and the readings from the King James Bible that lay open on the pulpit in front of him. His name was printed on the bulletin at the bottom, H. G. Brace, and Ruby thought it humble of him that his name was so low on the page.

The text this day was from the book of Exodus, about the plight of the Israelites enslaved by cruel Pharaoh and the Egyptians who used the Israelites for their own devices, having forgotten all that Joseph had done. Joseph had interpreted the dream of Pharaoh and had saved the Egyptians, but a new leader had arisen who either didn't know the story or didn't care. Pastor Brace reminded them that Joseph's brothers had meant to do him evil, but God brought good from it and could do the same in their lives.

There was a smattering of *amen*s in the room, followed by more crusty coughing. As the pastor continued, Ruby leaned forward and noticed a commotion coming through the open windows. There was noise down the railroad tracks. The pastor continued until they heard the audible voices of miners shouting for help.

The commotion outside the church that Sunday morning in 1933 was not a mine cave-in or explosion, though there had been plenty of those in the town's memory. No, what sent the congregants to the windows and the children spilling out the front door were shouts of warning that trouble was coming. And then there was the gunfire.

"What's going on?" Ruby said to Bean as she tried to see what was happening up the road.

"It's my daddy," Bean said. "I can tell by his voice. And he's got him a gun."

Bean's father, Judson Dingess, had survived so many accidents in the mine that many wondered if he hadn't caused them himself or pretended to be part of them after the fact. Injured miners received help from the company. When her daddy was hurt, he couldn't crawl into the mine but he found the energy to crawl up the hills where they made the good whiskey, not the stuff closer to town that was watered down. The most recent accident concerning her father was a collapse of timbers that rolled off a wagon and knocked him unconscious, and no one had accused him of manufacturing that event because there was too much blood. Plus, he had been disoriented when he finally woke up. He thrashed around like a freshly caught channel bass, thinking he was back in the trenches of France, until Bean and her mother calmed him.

While life in the mines had sent Bean's father running toward drink, Bean's mother ran toward the church and the stability that a tight hold on God would bring. This was the push-pull of their marriage and Bean was caught between. She adored her mother and the rock-ribbed belief she had that God was there and cared about hard-living people. But she also loved her father in ways she couldn't explain. She had seen him being kind and gentle, and he loved to laugh and played the fiddle like nobody's business. There was music inside him that came spilling out and echoed off the hills. Except he had lost that fiddle in a card game when he was trying to win money for another drink, so the house had gone silent.

"Bean, you get back inside," her mother said from the church door.

Bean looked back but didn't obey. She loved her mother more than life itself but she knew only she could coax her father away from what the devil was trying to do. She had awakened early each day with the first light coming over the ridge and walked with her father to the train, carrying his dinner bucket. She'd squeeze his hand tight before he left and then watch him join the miners climbing onto the cars as those returning home spilled out so black and dirty you couldn't tell they were human.

Ruby stopped at the bottom of the steps and watched Bean run toward the road.

"Ruby, come back here and stay with me," Bean's mother said. Ruby wanted to go with her friend, but she was gone, running toward her father, toward the shouts and name-calling. Bean flew like the wind, her feet barely touching the ground, it seemed. Just dust flying up from the shoes that were falling apart at the seams and her hair trailing behind her until she disappeared around the dense foliage that was taking over the road.

A shot rang out and Ruby ran up the stairs as Pastor Brace herded the women inside. Several men followed Bean. One went the opposite direction, saying he would get the sheriff. The pastor closed the doors behind him and said, "It's time to pray."

Ruby retreated with the other women as they knelt at the altar and the pastor raised his voice in supplication. Ruby closed her eyes and listened to the words prayed aloud and the groaning and moaning of the women. They rocked in pews, the wood creaking beneath them, as if their movement might tip the hand of God in their favor.

"What's wrong with him?" Ruby said. "Bean's daddy."

"Judd's got problems on the inside."

"What kind of problems?" Ruby said, lowering her voice to match the woman's whisper.

"The kind that don't have answers outside of the Lord's work in his heart. That's what I've been praying about."

"Has he always been like this?"

Bean's mother shook her head and her eyes pooled. "Stay here where it's safe, okay?" She stood, with some effort, and walked toward the door, reaching for a pew to steady herself. She closed the door behind her and Ruby turned back to the kneeling women.

"Please, God," Ruby whispered, "don't let Bean get hurt. Don't let anything bad happen to her mother. Do something for her daddy. Don't let him hurt anybody. Please, God."

It was a sincere prayer and the words tasted sweet to Ruby. Ruby's father was not religious and the death of her own mother had hardened him further to the thought of a deity who allowed such things. If Bean's daddy had run toward drink to soothe and salve his life, or at least allow him to numb it enough to be tolerable, her own father had run toward building his empire, as if the things of earth could fill such a hole of hurt. It didn't make him yell in the roadway and fire a pistol, but the effects were the same. There was distance in his eyes and a hunger no one could assuage.

Another shot rang out and there was more shouting. Ruby finally had enough and hurried outside. Praying was fine when there wasn't anything left to do, but it seemed like spectating would be better than sitting and just *thinking*. Was that all praying was?

The putt-putt of a motorcar came from down the ridge and Ruby figured it was the sheriff. He and her father owned two of the only cars in town and most of the time they had trouble navigating the muddy, washed-out roads. She caught up with Bean's mother and grabbed her hand. The woman was having a hard time catching her breath in the heavy mountain air.

They came around the corner and saw several men standing cross-armed a stone's throw away from Bean and her father. Bean was close enough to spit on him and she was pleading, holding out both hands. "Daddy, just give me the gun. Please. Nobody needs to get hurt."

The man swayed in the sunlight and tried to focus on her face, but he kept glancing at the men and holding the pistol out toward them at an odd angle.

"Bean, come away from him," her mother shouted.

Bean's father looked down the road at his wife and opened his mouth but nothing came out. Bean took another step closer and reached out to him.

"I swear, that girl has more sand than any man in this town," someone said behind Ruby.

Pastor Brace joined them and spoke to Bean's mother. "Cora

Jean, the sheriff is almost here and he's not going to like being drug out of bed at this time on a Sunday morning."

"I was on my way to church, Pastor," Judd shouted, his words barely intelligible. "You got room for sinners in that church of yours?"

"Put the gun down, Judd," Pastor Brace yelled.

"Play 'Beulah Land'! Can you sing that one?"

The sheriff's car chugged up the hill behind them, laboring.

"We'll sing anything you want. Just put down the gun."

Everything seemed to move in slow motion and Ruby wondered if, in years to come, she would be able to recall this scene. Bean reached to grab the gun. Bean's father was staring at his wife and saying something about being sorry. He made a pitiful sound like some animal caught in a trap.

Bean had the gun now, and she dropped it behind her. One of the men came up quickly and retrieved it as she led her father toward the church.

The car stopped behind them and Ruby relaxed. But Sheriff Kirby Banning set the brake and got out, clearly unhappy.

"I ain't got no beef with you, Banning," Judd called. He was leaning all his weight on Bean as he stumbled over rocks and tree limbs by the road. "I'm just on my way to church."

The sheriff cursed under his breath, then glanced at Bean's mother. He spit something black into the dirt and cinched up his pants.

Bean's father began singing alternate words to their beloved hymn. "'I'm working in the mountain; I can't see the cloudy sky. I'm drinking from a fountain I hope never does run dry.'" He laughed and stumbled and fell, Bean tumbling after him.

"All right, that's enough," Sheriff Banning said, glancing at the men from church. "Get him into the car."

"Where we going, Sheriff? A little religion won't hurt you."

Pastor Brace stepped forward. "We can take care of him. We'll get him sobered up."

Sheriff Banning shook his head.

"Oh, come on, Kirby," Judd said, struggling to make it to his knees. "I ain't got no problem with you. It's Coleman and Handley I want to use for target practice."

Sheriff Banning waved a hand at the men and they put Judd in the car. Bean's mother pleaded with the sheriff, "He's had a hard time since the accident. Please, let us take him."

"He can sleep it off in jail. Plus, he just made a threat. That'll have to be dealt with."

"Who's making threats?" Judd said as they closed the door. "I didn't make no threats."

Bean dusted off her clothes and stood by Ruby. As the car turned around in a wide place in the road and drove past them, Ruby heard someone singing "Beulah Land" and laughing.

ACKNOWLEDGMENTS

FIRST, TO MY WIFE, Andrea, and our children, thank you for your love, encouragement, and support through many dangers, toils, and snares.

The two biggest cheerleaders of this story were Karen Watson and Sarah Rische from Tyndale. They challenged me to make this the best book I could write, to have the courage to believe and keep digging until I found the nugget in the cavern. Thank you.

I also thank my friend, Robert Sutherland, who mentioned one day that in all his years of radio he had never met a man who had a good relationship with his father. His words challenged and helped me on several levels.

The moon rock idea for this story came from a man named Larry Burkett. His friend, Steve Moore, was the first to enlighten me. Steve introduced me to Terry Parker, who told more about the twists and turns of the story through the years. An astronaut gave the moon rock to Larry as a present. Of course, I've embellished things, but that is all I'll say about that.

Like the town of Dogwood in some of my earlier stories, Emmaus is fictional. The Mud River runs through both of them, but though the towns are only in my heart, the river is real.

Country 16 is based loosely on WNST, which was perched on a hill above the Mud River near Milton, West Virginia. My high school Distributive Education teacher, Mrs. Kesler-Errington, asked if I would like to gain some experience working at a local radio station. The prospect of going to school half the day and then to a radio station sounded good at the time and I said yes. I had no idea where her suggestion would lead me, but it has become a lifelong pursuit. Thank you, Mrs. K., for your vision when I had nothing of the sort.

I met a rich crew of broadcasters at the station, including the owner/manager, Naseeb S. Tweel (NST). Seeb told me that if I was hired, radio would always be in my blood. He was a kind man, though quirky, and he was right. Those call letters belong to another station now, but I'll always associate them with West Virginia and that tower near the interstate and the rolling green hills. Thanks to all who worked there who taught and encouraged me. I especially want to thank Gaines Johnson, Jack Varney, and Tom McKinney.

Finally, a big thank-you to Mack Strum for allowing me to use his lyrics in this book without charging me a royalty. Retired and done with traveling, Mack still plays his Silvertone on the back porch in the evening, mostly for crickets and fireflies.

If I were a rich man, I'd buy some hope for you
If I were a carpenter, I'd build a dream come true
If I were an astronaut, this is what I'd do
I'd bring you a piece of the moon

DISCUSSION QUESTIONS

1. Most of us have daydreamed about finding a fortune in the backyard. Waite asks Country 16 listeners what they'd do with a million dollars and receives a wide variety of answers. What would you do if you suddenly received a million dollars?

2. Early in the story, TD says, *Whether [Gideon Quidley] actually heard from the Lord, I'll let you decide.* What conclusion did you reach?

3. Waite seems willing to take a chance on almost anyone God sends his way. As a result, Country 16 is "a revolving door of misfits and castoffs, a radio Goodwill." How does Waite's philosophy work out for him? Has anyone extended a helping hand to you when you needed a second chance? Is there anyone in your life who needs a second chance?

4. Pidge reflects that "pain would make you miss some good things in life. Fear would do the same." What do characters in this story risk missing out on because of fear or past pain? Where have pain or fear threatened to hold you back in your own life? What was the result?

5. How old were you in 1981? If you remember the 70s and 80s, what memories did this story stir for you? Or if you're too young to remember, what "retro" details were fun or surprising?

6. As Wally laments the state of his life, Waite uses the image of a crumpled and stained twenty-dollar bill to challenge him, concluding, "We've all been baptized in something we didn't want to be baptized in. Doesn't mean you've lost your value." Have you ever been tempted to believe you've lost your value because of past hurts or mistakes? How does Waite's message speak to you? Who else in your life might need to hear it?

7. Listening to "The Class of '57," Waite muses that "the line that always got him was about Janet who taught grade school '. . . and probably always will.' He thought about his life and his own 'probably always will.'" Is there a "probably always will" in your life? Is it something you're at peace with or is it a source of discontentment? Is there something you thought was a "probably always will" that changed?

8. When TD asks Pidge what it would take for her to give him a chance, she replies, "How about you bring me a piece of the moon?" What do you think a piece of the moon symbolizes for Pidge? What might it mean to TD?

9. Listeners sometimes criticize Waite for playing songs that seem contradictory to his faith. Did you agree with his response to the comments? How can Christians be a light in places that seem to promote negative behavior?

10. TD finally confronts someone in his life for his past actions, saying that by his decisions, "You were showing God what you really believed. . . . I don't think that was faith. That wasn't God telling you what to do. It was you telling God what he had to do." Do you think he's right that this person tried to force God's hand? How would you describe the difference between trying to manipulate God and genuine faith?

11. Clay says, "I've heard [Waite] say that the closest we ever get to loving others like God loved us is when we give somebody a second chance to hurt us." Do you agree?

12. Mack Strum says, "All good songs leak from a broken heart. And the good ones don't give you something, as much as they take what's already inside and blow on the embers." What songs would you include on the playlist of your life?

ABOUT THE AUTHOR

CHRIS FABRY is an award-winning author and radio personality who hosts the daily program *Chris Fabry Live* on Moody Radio. He is also heard on *Love Worth Finding, Building Relationships with Dr. Gary Chapman*, and other radio programs. In 2020, he was inducted into the Marshall University School of Journalism and Mass Communications Hall of Fame. A native of West Virginia, Chris and his wife, Andrea, now live in Arizona and are the parents of nine children.

Chris's novels, which include *Dogwood, June Bug, Almost Heaven*, and *The Promise of Jesse Woods*, have won five Christy Awards, an ECPA Christian Book Award, and two Awards of Merit from *Christianity Today*. He was inducted into the Christy Award Hall of Fame in 2018. His books include movie novelizations, such as *War Room* and *Overcomer*, and novels for children and young adults. He coauthored the Left Behind: The Kids series with Jerry B. Jenkins and Tim LaHaye, as well as the Red Rock Mysteries and the Wormling series with Jerry B. Jenkins. He encourages those who dream of writing with his website heyyoucanwrite.com. Find out more about his books at chrisfabry.com.

also by
CHRIS FABRY

DOGWOOD

Small towns have long memories, and the people of Dogwood will never forgive Will Hatfield for what happened. So why is he coming back?

JUNE BUG

June Bug believed everything her daddy told her until she saw her picture on a missing children poster.

Christy Award finalist

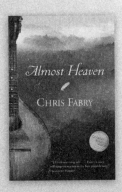

ALMOST HEAVEN

Some say Billy Allman has a heart of gold; others say he's odd. Sometimes the most surprising people change the world.

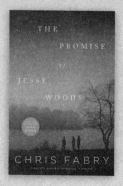

THE PROMISE OF JESSE WOODS

Years after the most pivotal summer of his adolescence, Matt Plumley returns to Dogwood, determined to learn the truth behind the only promise his first love, Jesse Woods, ever broke.

UNDER A CLOUDLESS SKY

Ruby takes a journey back to the mining town of Beulah Mountain, West Virginia, to face a decades-old secret.

NOT IN THE HEART

When time is running out, how far will a father go to save the life of his son?

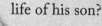

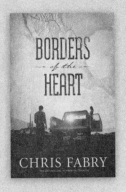

BORDERS OF THE HEART

When J. D. Jessup rescues a wounded woman, he unleashes a chain of events he never imagined.

Christy Award finalist

EVERY WAKING MOMENT

A struggling documentary filmmaker stumbles onto the story of a lifetime while interviewing subjects at an Arizona retirement home.

LOOKING INTO YOU

As Treha Langsam sets aside the search for her birth mother, Paige summons the courage to reach out to her daughter, never dreaming her actions will transform them both as she faces a past she thought she'd laid to rest.

Reading group guides available in each book or at
tyndale.com/bookclubhub

CP1092